THE
BARROS
PAWNS

Peter J. Earle

Copyright © 2011 Peter J. Earle

First published by PJE Publishing

The moral right of the author has been asserted.

Matador
5 Weir Road
Kibworth Beauchamp
Leicester LE8 0LQ, UK
Tel: 0116 279 2277
Email: books@troubador.co.uk
Web: www.troubador.co.uk/matador

ISBN 978 184876 552 8

British Library Cataloguing in Publication Data.
A catalogue record for this book is available from the British Library.

Printed in Great Britain by the MPG Books Group, Bodmin and King's Lynn

THE
BARROS
PAWNS

To Sheila
Beloved wife, check & balance.

Acknowledgements

My grateful thanks for their help, knowledge and encouragement to the following:

Sheila Maling, Robin Stuart-Clark, Brian Nicholson, Dirk Versfeld and Harry Bingham. And to Bernie Marriott for the cover photograph.

Any oversights are my own, where imagination overtook reality and questions remained unasked.

Author's Note

To the best of my knowledge there was no such plan as "Operation Insurance", nor were any South Africans or Rhodesians directly involved in the struggle against the *Frente de Liberteçao de Moçambique* (Frelimo). I once heard a rumour that a wealthy Portuguese businessman was recruiting troops for his own army to fight Frelimo but I never found any proof to substantiate this. Thus the characters of this story are purely from my own imagination and bear no relation to any real person, living or dead. However, the background and setting are authentic and one or two real heads of state etc., have been mentioned.

Peter J Earle
December 2008

ONE

The sign read: INHAMINGA – VILA FONTES. It gave the distances to these tiny villages in kilometres in blistered white paint on a split plank. It did not, however, say that, short of leaving the country altogether, this was the only road that linked Lourenço Marques and Beira with the substantial towns of Quelimane and Porto Amelia, not to mention a mass of smaller towns and villages. Possibly, the reason was that there are times of the year when one was lucky to even reach Inhaminga without four-wheel drive. When the rains have begun, the Zambezi is in flood. The floodplains of the lower Rift Valley are a quagmire and every depression in the sandy road a small lake. Then it would be of no consequence what the sign read because anyone who had reason to move in the area would go by train. Or fly.

The names on the sign meant nothing to the two men in the grey Landrover truck. They could not have pronounced them even had they tried. The sign itself, however, and the road it indicated were of vital importance. The driver slowed and pulled up on the verge just beyond the turn off. A six-berth caravan swayed and rocked behind it.

"It's in that quarter behind us, Stan. Let's stroll casually over it and see where we can get the Landy in." The passenger spoke over the cigarette that he was lighting.

The driver muttered, "'Kay, Sir," as he flipped open his door and got out, stiffly. The passenger watched Stan, six-foot-six and broad with it, as he passed the sign and walked with even paces back down the main road, muttering the count under his breath. At "three hundred" he stopped and did a few knee-bends. He would be noting a marker to use as a bearing to right-angle off the road. Sighing loudly, the passenger watched, flinging his arms back and back as if to remove some stiffness from them. The sun was setting straight down the road, purpling the tarmac. It glinted off a distant bicycle but otherwise there was nobody about. The grass on the quarter that they were interested in was burned in patches but a lot remained, taller than Stan's head as he left the road and disappeared.

Now the passenger stepped over the storm water contour, moving quickly away from the road. By good fortune he found a track that seemed to be heading in the right direction. He marked it with a knot of grass. He winced as the spears of grass seeds wriggled through his clothes and some of them pierced the tender skin of his crotch and belly as he followed the overgrown track. He could hear Stan whistling loudly in the semi-dark to guide him, but he nearly fell into an excavation that suddenly appeared. He skirted it. Soon he reached Stan and stood hunched, pulling grass seeds from his calf-length socks.

"There's an old quarry back there that we'll have to skirt," he jerked his thumb back over his shoulder. "But the track leading to it will be quite a help. I've marked it for you. It ends in a clearing where the loading lorries must have waited at the edge of the quarry. Sand for the road, about two years ago, I'd say."

"Funny they didn't mention it," Stan said. He snorted, "Still, they were right about the sand. They had to be, only giving us a hand auger, Sir." The other man smiled tightly. Orders were always given by 'they', all grumbles directed at 'them', always 'their' fault.

"It's not Sir, it's Bill, for Christ's sake. Now unhitch the Rover," he said, "after you've pulled the caravan up the track to the clearing.

Don't be too sneaky, just as if you're camping here for a few hours' kip on our way to Beira. Then bring the Rover here."

"Oh, we are going on to Beira, then? Nice to know," Stan said, sardonically, as he set off.

Bill watched him in the twilight: the broad-set shoulders too square, the pace too measured, the fists with the thumbs set tight on the forefinger. He knew that his own posture would be similar unless he concentrated on relaxing, even slouching. He smiled. Their short hair, too, was a giveaway in this age of shaggy styles, even in Africa.

Though both wore shorts and coloured shirts, any keen observer would guess that they were military: Rhodesian or South African. They were in fact Rhodesian Special Air Services men; a lieutenant and a sergeant, both with A-grade security ratings. Both had been recalled from Border duty, on the very Border they had crossed less than three hours ago as tourists, for a quick, thorough briefing in Salisbury. They were still trying to get used to calling each other Bill and Stan.

Bill waited, still plucking spear grass from his socks. The trees around him were now mere silhouettes. He saw that they were mostly *M'sasa* like ones near his home in Salisbury. He knew they covered quite a lot of Rhodesia but had not realised one found them so far east. He had only been to Mozambique twice before, as a child with his parents; each time a week in Beira, travelling in on this same road. But that had been more than ten years ago, back in sixty-one. He couldn't remember having enjoyed it much; they'd camped near the shipwreck on the beach. The mosquitoes had been bad both times, and the sea dirty.

He heard the Landrover start up, back, come up the sand road and turn into the track. He heard it stop at the clearing and he assumed the sergeant was unhitching the caravan. He had wondered if they should have the caravan at the auger site but then decided it would look less suspicious in the clearing than it would in the bush. Not that they were likely to be seen; there was not much traffic after dark, they had been told, as this was a road where terrorists machine-gunned passing vehicles from time to time. Here, at this spot, only six kilometres from the town of Dondo, it was safe enough.

After unhitching, Stan ploughed the Landrover through the bush, back to the place where Bill stood.

"Turn it around," Bill instructed as he got in. "It's just to mark the spot. We'll have some *skof* and come back with the auger later." Bill decided a beer would do no harm even though their job had hardly begun. He reached behind the Landrover seat for a couple of cans that they had bought in Vila Machado on their way down. There were a dozen, each individually wrapped in newspaper to keep them cold. The store owner had done it without their asking; it was a country that respected cold beer.

3

After a supper of tinned sausages and fried eggs, Bill said, "Well, Stan let's go build a bog."

"Oh, yes," said the sergeant, "the long drop. We wouldn't want to foul this lovely country."

Amongst the caravan tent poles were four lengths that had never supported any tent. Under the single bunk, wrapped in blankets, was a thirty centimetre bare auger head: a cylinder open at both ends except for the shaft-supports on one end and the two teeth on the other. These parts, a spade and *panga* knife were the items they shared out and carried back to the spot they had marked. They also carried a Coleman pressure lamp and a toilet roll. Stan cleared the place of grass tussocks with the spade, while Bill fitted the first shaft to the auger head. It had a ring at the top into which he put a one metre steel rod. He put the teeth to the ground then turned the rod experimentally. They had drilled a three metre hole in heavier textured material in Salisbury, three days ago, with a similar auger. It had taken them forty minutes. Without mentioning it, they were both listening for the sound of traffic. Some fifteen vehicles had passed on the main road since they had stopped: two on the side road. But it had decreased with the fall of dark.

The auger bit into the topsoil: organic dark for the upper ten centimetres, becoming paler with depth. The auger head filled before it had half disappeared. They shook it out at the edge of the hole and put it back. Each man had an end of the crossbar; they walked around with it, leaning on it to penetrate. They were nearing the limit of the first section when they heard a particularly loud diesel truck stopping. It had been coming down the road towards Dondo. The engine beat hesitated, roaring as the driver changed down and then down again, followed by the squeal of brakes. It had gone past, now it was being backed up. The two S. A. S. men hauled up the auger, hurriedly pushing the parts into the bush.

"Drop your rods and squat," hissed the lieutenant. Stan loosened his shorts, whipped them down and hunkered over the auger hole. Bill tried to level the sand taken from it. There came a muttering of voices from the road but no sound of anyone pushing into the bush. Someone shouted.

"D'you think it's troops?" whispered Stan, getting gooseflesh on his bottom, along with several mosquito bites.

"I hope they are, rather than police," the lieutenant replied, then he shouted back. "Who the hell is that? Why don't you all piss off?"

There was a muttering of *"Inglês, Inglês."* Then one shouted. "Are you English tourists?" in Portuguese, but since this sounds much the same in English, the two were able to understand.

"No, we are Rhodesian tourists," yelled Bill indignantly. "Not bloody English. Rhodesia."

"Ah," came the shouted reply, "Ian Smith." There was laughter and a brief consultation. "Good night, Ian Smith, good sleep." More laughter at someone's limited English. It faded. Later the diesel started up and moved off. Stan pulled his pants up.

"Silly bastards were too scared to come and see for themselves."

Bill shrugged. "Most of them come from Portugal and have no interest in this country; conscripts who can't wait to get back home."

"Do you think Portugal will lose Mozambique, Sir? I mean, Bill." Stan reached after the auger pieces, then stood scratching the mosquito bites through his shorts.

"At the rate they're fighting this war, yes. But I feel sorry for the Mozambicans when it goes." He meant the white Portuguese in Mozambique, some of them third or fourth generation settlers, and anybody else that had resisted Frelimo.

"And to them it is a war, isn't it?" Stan assembled the auger. "We use names like 'Border duty' or 'Insurgents' or 'terrorist infiltration defence'. We haven't got around to calling it 'the war'. Yet."

"We will. Let's get on with it. The mozzies are dragging me away," Bill said. They bent to the auger. In twenty minutes it was done. Three metres deep. They hefted the equipment, returning to the caravan. Under one of the bunks they uncovered a cardboard box. In the box was a steel reinforcing sheet. The box measured a metre by sixty centimetres. It was open at the end and seemed to contain plates, pots, pans, vegetables and meals in cans, and cutlery. Stan kept watch on the caravan step with a beer in his hand while Bill unpacked the food, exposing two cylinders that looked like cooking gas bottles. They even had a popular brand name on their sides.

"Okay, give me a hand will you?" The box weighed nearly seventy kilograms with its contents, which would have fallen out of the bottom had it not been especially strengthened. They staggered over the stumps and sticks, up the track they had made with the Landrover, to the auger hole.

"Bloody peculiar toilet roll we have this time," muttered Stan. They kept looking about for signs of anyone else about, knowing that they would have a lot of explaining to do if they were seen. They put the box down at the hole, then listened. Nothing but the buzz of mosquitoes.

Bill fitted a three-quarter inch steel plate to the bottom of the smaller cylinder, which seemed to be of two sections screwed together under a collar. To fit into the top of the cylinder was another steel plate, saucer shaped, which cupped underneath the larger cylinder. Assembled, the unit was nearly two metres long. Bill attached a cord to the nose, then they lowered it gently into the auger hole which it fitted neatly. Bill dropped the cord in after it. Then they pushed the sand into the hole on top of the cylinders, lastly a layer of the dark topsoil and a tussock of grass. Bill and Stan went off to finish the beers.

Less than eight months later the Portuguese built an army barracks over the spot. No foundation went that deep but it was fortunate that the latrine pits were not dug precisely there.

Bill and Stan had a pleasant weekend in Beira. The sea was clean and there seemed to be no mosquitoes. On Sunday evening they were returning home when the Landrover broke down between Beira and Dondo. Fortunately there was an army barracks nearby. They got permission, when they could find someone who spoke English, to camp in the bush near the outer fence of the barracks. They rigged the tent to the caravan. They augered in the tent, at a slight angle, pointing to the barracks and assembled a second set of cylinders. Sliding this into the hole, they buried it. The following day they were back in Salisbury.

During that fortnight thirty caravans were employed by South African and Rhodesian personnel for similar operations from

Lourenço Marques to Porto Amelia. Each team had been briefed separately and was unaware of the others. Also some fifty-five offices, warehouses, store-rooms, houses, flats and shops were rented in the major towns and cities throughout the country. This was done over the following year, very discreetly, by individuals and small companies. Each of these buildings was situated near a barrack, military headquarters, government workshop or military supply dump. In each, one or more sets of cylinders were concealed; either in the ground or in the new cement work, in places that would be unlikely to be disturbed.

Six South Africans and four Rhodesians, all of high rank, were fully aware of all the details of "Operation Insurance." All had the highest security ratings. One officer amongst them was to prove that his rating was undeserved.

TWO

From where he sat hunched against the near bulkhead of the Pilatus Porter's cabin, Geoffrey Nourse could see the Cherokee edge in closer until the wingtips of the two planes were a mere four metres apart. His altimeter needle sat steadily at a fraction under four thousand metres above ground, which made it five and a half thousand above sea level, here near Pretoria. The rarefied air made him feel fuzzy but they would not be here much longer. He tried to ease his cramped feet under him but Piet Visagie's backpack was holding down the reserve 'chute on Nourse's chest. Next to him, John Blair breathed with his mouth open, squirming to get a better view of the ground. Adrenalin pumped.

"Run-in." It came as a faint airborne whisper from the front of the aircraft above the roar of the jet-turbine engine and rush of wind past the now open door. Shortly after that, Nourse could see figures climbing into the doorway of the Cherokee. "Throttle back!" The engine note changed from a roar to a hum. Nourse had been watching to see what signal was exchanged between the two planes but he missed it. Jumpers from both planes left simultaneously; others cramming forward to cut down the time and distance to get the sixteen jumpers together as soon as possible. Nourse felt his stomach tighten into a ball, his mouth was dry. He caught a last sniff of the sweaty leather inside his helmet, mingled with aero fuel, before the wind whipped it away as he left. He was the last to go, so close behind Blair that the Englishman's boots brushed his goggles.

From the corner of his eye he saw a last figure leave the Cherokee just ahead of him. Below, a four-man had just linked, a fifth and sixth coming in soon afterwards. Nourse was in a delta now, head down, shooting after Blair. Something nagged for his attention. Something wrong. Ignore. He watched a seventh man overshoot the star, then turn and, spreading to catch air, he broke in as the star came down to him. An eighth came in neatly. The rest spread in two lines upward. There were too few. Something wrong. One missing. Nourse knew he had to keep on down, knew he would make the star. A record; it would be more than thirteen. Keep on down, his mind screamed; don't spread. Now the star was a nine-man. Could no longer ignore, something wrong!

Damn, damn, damn. Nourse spread, his speed dropped off – he couldn't make it now. Where was the bastard, the last from the Cherokee? Off to the right, just below. Thirty metres, a bit more; out of control. Falling, not flying; a spinning bundle, unconscious. There was no time to think of fear. Altitude one and a half thousand. Nourse went into a full track; back humped, hands at sides, curved. He was a human aerofoil. His altimeter was strapped to his sleeve; he couldn't see it without coming out of the track but it didn't matter; he could judge near enough. I'll make it, he thought, if I take him cleanly, first time. The gap narrowed by degrees. Nourse, in the track, was falling a fraction faster than the other man. With ten metres to go, he was level. Oh, Christ! The shout of agony echoed through his mind. Horror, like spilt molasses, began to spread blackly over his hope. He would go under the other man and being under he would have to come out of the track to see where the tumbling bundle was; to get his head up. Then he might not have tracked far enough, or too far, to catch the unconscious jumper.

Nourse tracked on, lifting his head back and sideways, keeping the figure in view. Five metres. Nourse strained his head back, conscious of the ground rushing up to meet him, not daring to look down. Slowly the brightly banded, flapping overall slipped up out of his sight, his track speed dropping as his head-back spoiled the aerofoil. His altimeter needle neared the red line but Nourse didn't see it. Abruptly he humped, picking up speed again, the figure out of sight. His mind raced, judging, praying that he would be level with the body as he came out of the track.

No, no … now!

Nourse flared; his body's delta streak slowed to match the speed of his target and he collided with the other man perfectly, simultaneously wrapping his arms around him. Feverishly fumbling hands found the other's reserve ripcord handle. He tore it out, pushed him away and did a hundred and eighty degree turn. He felt the ground rush; a split second from suicide. Hitting his own reserve, he flipped onto his back. There was a terrific jerk as the reserve blossomed. His altimeter read two hundred metres. Not too bloody bad, he thought, sagging with relief, feeling nauseous. Where was McNeil? He seized his steering lines.

Somewhere in the desperate minute just past – incredibly only just over sixty seconds had passed since he had exited from the plane – he had recognised the jumper as Dan McNeil. He thought he saw something above his canopy. Thankful that his reserve was steerable, he turned until McNeil came into view. He seemed to be moving now but making no attempt to steer his Navy Conical. He was rubbing his eyes and holding his head. The ground rushed up.

"Dan! You okay?" Nourse yelled. "Hey, Dan!" His voice must have carried over the gap because McNeil looked down at him. He seemed to stare for quite a few seconds before he showed any sign of recognition. He waved briefly as he reached for his steering lines.

Nourse turned towards the cluster of buildings that were the hangars and tower as the adrenalin dried up and his heartbeat began to slow. The wind was light but they had moved over the airfield in freefall and would have a little walk when they'd landed. Slightly above them, nearer to the hangars were the mass of brightly coloured canopies: the other fourteen jumpers. Nourse wondered how many had made the star. Had they broken the record? "Bloody Dan," he muttered without real rancour. Looking back he could see Dan following him in. Nourse braced himself with legs slightly bent, took the shock as his feet struck, and rolled. It had been a long time since he'd had to do the parachutist's roll that he had learned five years ago when starting this game. The Para-Commander canopy in his backpack invariably let him down gently enough for a stand-up landing. He stood up; six-two, wiry.

Behind him, McNeil's Conical put him down softly enough so that he only sagged to one knee, then he swung around, gathering lines to collapse the canopy. He stood a while, as if he were dizzy. Nourse unbuckled his own rig. He pulled off his helmet as he walked over to McNeil, exposing lank, pale hair.

"You okay, Dan?" As McNeil looked up, Nourse could see that one side of his face was covered in blood that had already dried in the wind of the fall, except where it still oozed from a gash at one temple, just at the edge of his helmet. "What happened?" Nourse asked.

"Hit myself on the step, I think. This bitching strap," he searched behind him where part of the harness hung loose. The end of the webbing was curled over and sewn to prevent fraying –"got hooked under the pilot's seat. Took a helluva while to get it loose, then my foot slipped as it came free. Fuck, I must have been knocked out for a while. I don't even remember dumping my reserve, although I seem to have, thank Christ. Got a smoke somewhere?"

Nourse's features split into a grin. He found cigarettes under his overalls. They lit up. McNeil's hands were shaking. He was a big man, powerful and fit, though carrying a little fat at present. He was a construction site-agent, but he had fought in the Congo, years back, Nourse knew. The fact that Nourse had also come down on a reserve parachute did not seem strange to McNeil, as yet; he was still too concerned with his own narrow escape. He loosened his helmet. The curls of his dark hair stuck to his forehead with sweat. Gingerly he fingered his temple. There was a blue mark across his cheekbone, already swelling to half-close his eye.

"Wonder how many got in?" McNeil gazed at the empty, blue, African sky. A blazing February sun looked back. He turned away. "Did you see?"

"No." Nourse moved to help him gather his 'chute, careful to keep the cigarette away from the fabric. They trudged over to Nourse's rig.

"You had a total mal!" Only a total malfunction would have explained it. "Christ." McNeil saw the backpack was intact, the reserve used.

"Popped too low to use my main." Nourse was grinning in that lame, embarrassed fashion some people have when lying. He shot a glance at McNeil. The latter was a picture of puzzlement.

By now the other jumpers were at the clubhouse, near the hangars. Nourse could see the ripple of excitement in the gestures of the group as the word spread. In the air they would have been unaware of McNeil's mishap. It would have baffled them to see the two reserves open below them. Now several jumpers strolled towards them with apparent nonchalance as they approached the edge of the aeroparking bay.

"These low openings have got to stop! You're both grounded."

"What the hell happened?"

"Hey, man that's what skydiving is all about!" Someone enthused, punching Nourse's shoulder. Praise of a sort, but if that's what skydiving is all about, thought Nourse, I'm selling my rag to-day.

It seemed that on the ground a girl skydiver briefed to report on the action using the telemeter, a type of telescope, had been watching the star forming, had seen McNeil out of control, and had seen Nourse trying to get to him. Her words, tumbling out in horror and excitement, as she tried to keep focus on the two falling men, gave those about her a very garbled account. It is very difficult to follow falling skydivers with the naked eye. Most people centre on the star itself and are unaware of what any dots in the area are doing, unless they are joining the star. But the girl's report spread, clouding the fact that the country's record had been equalled: a thirteen-man.

"Don't ask me," McNeil said, half angry because he really did not know and was slowly becoming aware that there was more to the story than he knew. "I wasn't bloody there." They pressed Nourse to tell them.

"Dan seemed to be having a kip," he said lamely, his ears crimson with embarrassment at the limelight, "so I dumped his rag for him."

The muttering and exclaiming that followed passed over him. Dan McNeil was only now beginning to understand what miracle had saved his life. His throat became so dry that he could hardly speak.

"Thanks, Geoff Nourse; you can get pissed on me tonight." His shaky tone and shattered expression belied the casualness of the words.

"Should hope so, Dan."

As Nourse dropped his kit, someone came at him. He heard a delighted squeal as a girl slung her arms around his neck. He recognised her only when she was kissing him.

"Hey, Manuela! Hello, what are you doing here?"

"Jumping, of course, my dear Geoffrey. What else?" She looked up into his face, her smile wide and white, her olive skin blemishless; black hair gleaming, fell to her tee-shirted breasts. Her charm was an embrace, tangible, like a warm, sweet vapour. "It's so good to see you," she changed to Portuguese, "I have just arrived. Will you organise a jump for me, soon? Oh, I am glad you are here. You said you would join this club near Pretoria. It's big; plenty people. Only in Portugal have I seen big clubs like this – bigger than this, of course. Geoffrey, leave your packing for five minutes. I am hot, I must have a Coke." Breathless, she tugged at his arm. She had obviously been there long enough to have found the restaurant herself, but he took her around to the red-bricked building and seated her on the veranda. Leaving her there, he went to the counter, returning with two Cokes.

"Was that you in that C. R. registered One-Eighty-Two that landed just before we went up on this last load, Manuela?" Nourse asked. His mind had taken in the Mozambique registration on the white and blue Cessna but only now did the memory strike him as unusual. He remembered that she was a pilot.

"Must have been. I missed your exit, my dear, but I heard terrible things about you. Everyone is talking." Her eyes shone as she reached out to squeeze Nourse's hand. Then abruptly she shouted, "Hey, Rosa! José! Here." She waved her hand above her head, gaily. Her firm little breasts shivered under the lettering *Aero Clube da Beira* on her tee-shirt.

Nourse turned. A beautiful girl was coming towards them on the arm of a swarthy-skinned man. She was very like Manuela to look at but a little older and a little taller, though still not much over a metre fifty, dressed in blue bellbottoms and matching striped top. They had appeared to be a trifle lost until Manuela called. Nourse stood up, reached for two more chairs. He smiled at the two as they approached.

The girl smiled back, a broad open smile. The man nodded, his face made blank by the dark glasses that he wore, his mouth unmoving. The chemistry clashed; they instantly disliked each other.

"My sister, Rosa. She also used to be a skydiver. And her husband, José da Silva. Meet my good friend, Geoffrey Nourse. We met at the club at Beira about three years ago. Geoffrey has just saved his friend's life. His friend was unconscious and luckily Geoffrey pulled his ripcord for him. My hero!"

Nourse muttered how-do-you-do in Portuguese and escaped to buy two more Cokes. There was a short queue so he had to wait a few minutes to be served. He was reflecting that it was fun seeing Manuela again, wondering if the chance might not arise to repeat a very pleasant link-up they had had not too long ago in her apartment in the luxury hotel her father owned in Beira. Then a girl was asking him if he could help her.

"What's up?" he smiled at her abruptly, encouragingly.

"I want to join the club, you see. I would like to jump." The voice was low, interesting.

"Ah, you want to see Steve van Deventer. He's the Chief Instructor. He'll give you the forms and your ground training." Nice-looking girl, he thought. She was blonde, round-faced with a sprinkling of freckles. A little plump? No, perhaps just well-rounded. Bell-bottomed denims. Broad leather belt, tee-shirt with Fly United written under two ducks, in flight, doing just that. "Just ask anyone, they'll point him out. He's probably manifesting in the clubhouse." He half turned away.

"What's manifesting?"

"Two Cokes, please, pal." Nourse paid. "All jumps have to be manifested. We fill in a column for each jump and sign it before we go up." She was still at his elbow.

"Wouldn't you ... Point him out to me ... Please?"

Nourse hesitated. Well, he had to go and get Manuela onto a load. Maybe put himself down for one, too. It wouldn't take long to pack his reserve. He could get this bird to help him. He put the Cokes down in front of Rosa and José da Silva. "I'll get you onto a load, Manuela. Are you packed?"

"Of course, Geoffrey, my love." That lovely smile again. "Don't be long."

Someone stopped him to comment on the incident with McNeil. Nourse laughed it off with a flippant remark. The girl watched him curiously.

"I heard about that. That's super! I hope it never happens to me. I told my friends skydiving is really safe, if you obey the rules. Now this happens. I'm sure it happened to put me off. But it won't, though. You'll see; I'll be jumping soon." A rule had been broken, alright. Dan had not checked his rig well enough to make sure his webbing strap-ends were properly tucked away. And he should have taken his time releasing it when it hooked – too much eagerness to be part of a record-breaking star. But Nourse knew perfectly well it all could just as easily have happened to himself.

"What's your name?" he asked the girl.

"Cecile Cradock." They went into the clubhouse. Steve van Deventer was chalking a new load on a blackboard. He was a tall, lean, brown-haired man with friendly blue eyes. Two girls were looking after two little children in nappies, three men played darts, and one read a paperback at the bar, which had no-one behind it. An army T10 parachute, with the rigging-lines cut off, regaled the ceiling. Several satirical cartoons on skydiving decorated the wall, alongside poster-sized pictures of massive stars, usually flown over the USA. Broken but serviceable chairs lined the walls. A stiffened bra with miniature rigging lines suspending a doll hung in the corner. A large board held a hundred-odd photos of events at the club.

"Hello, Steve. Meet Cecile Cradock. She wants to join the club. How soon can you train her, Steve?"

"Hi, Cecile. Welcome! Man, I haven't a moment to spare right now. How about tomorrow? We've a new chap, too. I can get you started together. Then you can have your first jump next week-end if you check out okay. Alright? I'll get you some forms. Ask Geoff to help you with them. You know you need a medical certificate?" Steve rummaged in a drawer and passed her a couple of forms. She nodded briefly, not looking at them.

"What loads have you got waiting, Steve?" Nourse asked.

"The Pilatus is full. The Cherokee's up now but there's no-one for her next load except two static lines. Oh, and a chap wants to do a tracking test, so I can't despatch them and watch the tracking from here with the telemeter." Steve scratched his chin. "Can you despatch them, then take the other bloke so that I can watch him? How many do you want?'

"Myself and one. Maybe two. That'll fill the load. Okay? I'll check back."

John Blair, a sharp-faced, slightly built Englishman, appeared in the doorway.

"De-briefing, Steve, Geoff. Where's Dan?" Blair looked around.

"He's probably sticking a plaster on his head in the loo. I lent him my first-aid kit," one of the dart players said.

"You help me pack my reserve just now, as soon as I'm finished with the de-briefing, Cecile, and I'll help you with those forms. Okay?" Geoff Nourse said.

"Fine." Her smile was warm. Nourse hurried out, briefly explaining the jump situation to Manuela, who pouted.

"When do we go?" she called after him.

"Soon as the Cherokee's down."

The de-briefing was short. Besides McNeil and Nourse, Clement White, a chunky, blond man with a slightly buck-toothed grin, was the only one not to get into the star. Piet Visagie had something to say about sticking to the slots they had agreed on.

Clement muttered, "Yes, Helmut."

A big solid, sandy-haired man with a German accent shrugged and said, "Sorry, Clem."

Piet, equally big but with curly brown hair and brown eyes, said, "And wasn't our star good enough for you two buggers?"

"We just didn't want to hold your hands, Ducky." Dan replied, glaring at Piet with his remaining open eye. The meeting broke up. The Cherokee returned but had to refuel which gave Nourse time to pack his reserve. Both Cecile and Manuela helped him, the latter snapping little orders at the South African girl with a superior air.

"We have phoned for a taxi," Manuela chattered to Nourse in

Portuguese. "We are spending the weekend at the Culemborg Hotel. D'you know it? We booked from Beira. What a business with the telephone! When the taxi arrives, Rosa and da Silva will go. You will take me later, eh? You have a car? Good, where shall we eat? I hear you have a barbecue here at the clubhouse to-night. A good idea. We stay and drink beer, eh, my love. I want to meet your friends."

Nourse had never known her to be quite so overwhelming. He thought it odd that she should be so possessive on strange ground. It might have been understandable in Beira but not here. Nervous, perhaps? Perhaps that was it, but he felt a slight annoyance at Manuela's attitude to the other girl. He said in English to Manuela: "We call a barbecue a '*braai*' here; a good old South African word." He looked up at Cecile who stood holding the folded canopy and was slowly bringing it towards the pack as Nourse folded the lines into their rubber bungees. "There are meat packs on sale in the clubhouse. Drinks at the bar. Stay and meet the lads. And the few lasses we have."

Manuela took the reproach with only a slight tightening of her mouth. A taxi arrived, the driver got out, standing, looking lost. Manuela dashed off towards him, calling to her sister and brother-in-law who had stood watching the packing of various multi-coloured parachutes spread over the ground behind the clubhouse.

"I think I'll do that, Geoff. I've got my own transport so I can go when I've had enough. Do you live in Pretoria?" Cecile asked.

"Yes. I've a flat in Sunnyside; had it only two months now. I don't spend much time there."

With a few carefully chosen words she got him to talk a bit, before the Portuguese girl returned. It appeared to Nourse that Cecile already disliked her intensely.

Well, no, he wasn't working at the moment. On leave, sort of; a botanist, actually. Spent the last three years in Mozambique. The northern part. Yes, there was terrorist activity up there but they hadn't bothered him. He used names of towns and villages she had never heard of before. He said he hadn't been near Cabora Bassa Dam, where most of the trouble was, at the construction site there.

The memories captured him for a while, vividly. That dry, crisp smell of sun-baked grass, a tang of one's own sweat, the sharper smell of his African assistants. The dust cloud behind his Landrover. The grinning face of Francisco, his boss man. Buffalo by the thousand, lumbering across the floodplain – a sight that would before long cease to be. He sighed. Such a myriad of scenes and incidents. Given up now – but why? He had had good reasons for dropping a highly paid, interesting, varied job. Reasons like personal safety, lack of social life, getting bush-happy too quickly, too often; too little skydiving. The latter had been a very important factor, as jumping had been an extremely special part of his life. It was too awkward: a hundred and fifty kilometres or more of abominable road to get to Beira, praying all the way that the weather would behave and the Landrover would hold together. There was the alternative of a train from Inhaminga or Sena which he loathed equally; the awkward times of arrival or departure and being without transport in Beira. This brought him around to thinking about Manuela again. She had made Beira more than bearable on two occasions but she hadn't always been there or had been with someone else. An apologetic smile from her would suggest he should have warned her he was coming down. But that wasn't possible, as he seldom knew whether he was going or not, more than a day or two in advance.

Now, he was not at all sure that he'd made the right decision. He missed the solitude in place of the social life he'd missed three months ago. The grunt of a bushbuck, the rattle of porcupine quills, the bush evenings at a waterhole. The crash of elephant ripping trees down to feed. Drinking *cerveja* in a dingy trading store that smelled of dried fish and rolled tobacco, but the glass would be icy in his grimy hand. The thought of it all made him feel hollow inside with longing. He'd traded it for a flashy car, an apartment with new furniture, regular dates. And noisy engines and exhaust fumes and traffic cops. He still had a lot of money in the bank; he wouldn't have to work for a while if he didn't feel like it.

"Well, Geoffrey, we're sorry you're leaving us. Wish you had given us a bit more warning. Going to have trouble replacing you. Still, your work's given us enough to start serious reaping in some of the areas you've demarcated, and we'll get on with that till we get someone to carry on the survey work." His boss had been really sorry to lose him. "Remember, you're always welcome back, anytime. I mean that, lad. And I'm sure we can organise more time off for you. Too much bush isn't good for a young fella, eh?"

He had almost changed his mind, then. Being sought after, he could have made his own conditions. It wasn't in him, though, to chop and change. His firm was a chemical company that specialised in herbal remedies found in various plants. Briefly, it had been his duty to map areas, searching for these in sufficient quantity to warrant setting up a gathering centre and processing plant. Nourse tucked in the last flaps on his reserve and rose. The taxi left and Manuela came back, hips rolling subtly, making him catch his breath and quickening his pulse. But a shadow at the back of his mind made him wonder a little. Granted, South Africa was a strange country to her, making it natural that she should seek out someone she knew, but never had she been so blatantly affectionate. And that she should come to jump on her own? So many of the Beira club members would have leapt at the chance to jump at a new club with her. Instead she had brought her sister and surly brother-in-law, both of whom, instead of appearing to enjoy their trip, were looking thoroughly bored. Something did not gel. Nourse frowned, but was unable to say why he felt uneasy.

"The Cherokee must be refuelled by now. I must kit up." Manuela squeezed his arm. Her kit was in the clubhouse. Nourse walked with her, leaving Cecile Cradock standing with her papers still blank in her hand.

"Like a bitch in heat, poor bastard," Nourse thought he heard the girl mutter.

THREE

"Yahoo!!" came a bellow, followed by something that sounded like an Indian war cry. Through the centre of the twenty or thirty people sitting on the lawn with beer and braaied meat in their hands, dashed two naked men, the firelight dancing on their legs. They leaped over the fire and disappeared into the dark on the far side. The party burst into catcalls, shouted remarks and laughter.

"Streakers!"

"Mind, you'll singe your curlies."

"You'll trip over it, Sharpe."

"Where are their clothes? We must hide them."

There were stars and a half moon. A slight breeze took the edge off what heat there might have been. The trees and hangar showed very dark on the skyline. Geoff saw, in the shadow of the hangar, an African watchman stand, interrupting his round to recover from the sight of the streakers. It must be incomprehensible to him, Geoff thought; clothes, which were what the African people had come to wear as a symbol of their civilised advancement, were something the whites seemed to be trying to shed. Geoff saw him shake his head slowly, in confusion, and then continue on his rounds.

"One cannot get away with that in Mozambique, eh, my Geoffrey?" Manuela giggled, finishing her last pork chop. They had had a good jump, a quick link-up during which Nourse had spent several seconds attempting to kiss her but their helmets were not conducive to such manoeuvres.

Once, at the fire, Cecile had reminded him of her papers. He'd cursed inwardly but apologised and offered to do them now, but she had told him that if he was coming to the club the next day he could help her then. Later he'd seen her chatting to Dan McNeil. The latter was keeping his promise and continually plying Nourse with beer.

"Let's get away from the fire a bit, my Geoffrey. It is too hot." They walked away into the dark.

"Come back to Mozambique, Geoffrey." It was not said wistfully, as on a personal level, although it implied that, too, but more as an introduction to a proposition. Nourse looked at her but it was too dark to read her expression. She squeezed his arm as if to take it back into a personal, intimate sphere but it was too late. She had to continue.

"My father is the richest man in Mozambique. But we have lived there too long and broken our ties with Portugal. There's nowhere else to go if Mozambique should fall to Frelimo. We would lose everything."

Nourse let the silence spread a little then said, uneasily, wondering where this would lead, "You could move somewhere. Brazil, maybe ..."

"No, Mozambican money is almost worthless anywhere else. Do you know that while the official exchange rate is about thirty-eight Escudos to the Rhodesia dollar, they are selling a dollar on the black market for between sixty and seventy escudos. No Rhodesian changes his money at the border anymore. The same with the South African rand. Everybody is grabbing whatever they can, ready to run." Her voice had risen in anger and disgust. Nourse knew all this. He knew that Mozambique could go at any moment, whether taken by the freedom fighters, Frelimo, or given away by Portugal. In over four hundred years of colonisation the Portuguese had not managed to get the province to be economically independent. Most of those with the industriousness to get rich off the country had salted their money away in Portugal, ploughing nothing back into the land that had provided their wealth. There were a few exceptions, like Manuel D'Oliviera Barros, who had put down all their roots and were now regretting it. They had built their castles but now the serfs were stealing the drawbridges.

"We Mozambicans want to stay," Nourse heard Manuela saying. Thinking that she was using him as a sounding board rather than discussing it with him, he refrained from interrupting her. "The

Portuguese army is not trying to fight. What for, anyway? It's not their country, what do they care? They should get out, so we can manage our own affairs." Managing their own affairs meant squashing any black that murmured "freedom" under his breath, Nourse thought. He said nothing. He knew also that violence was the only way in which the settlers could save their hides, temporarily. Nourse sighed, thinking that there were never any good moral answers that would save the whites of Mozambique, or South Africa for that matter. But there were a few practical approaches, if the latter day, moral-minded world would give them time to develop, which he doubted. Nourse himself favoured a multiple, qualified vote, but nobody seemed to be seriously exploring that avenue.

"Some of us feel we can do something about this, Geoffrey. We think that if we can do something about Frelimo in the North, Portugal can be approached for independence." He was caressing her back, working his way down under her belt, his mind not on politics. She twitched in annoyance; what she had to tell him was more important, for the time being.

"What do you mean, do something about Frelimo?" Nourse stopped to light a cigarette. He felt her hesitation. This was it. Somehow, he knew.

"Well, Geoffrey, I hope I can trust you to keep quiet about this. Can I?"

"Of course," Nourse said, putting his arm around her shoulders re-assuringly, knowing he would tell anyone and everyone; if he really felt they should know.

"We are forming a force to hit at Frelimo. Not to patrol aimlessly but to hit at their camps, get at their leaders. My ... we have a good intelligence system." He knew she had nearly said "my father". "We know a lot about Frelimo's movements both in the bush and their underground. What we need are men. Brave men with nerve, who have had military training. Like the mercenaries that fought in the Congo." She went on eagerly, now that it was out. "They would be very well paid, of course. Have quarters in Beira in between missions, every comfort."

"Well paid in Mozambique escudos?" asked Nourse sardonically. He felt Manuela stiffen.

"Only partly," she said coldly. "The remainder: any currency in any foreign bank."

"Okay, I'm sorry." Nourse said, wondering where this other money was to come from if escudos could not buy it.

"Don't make fun of this, Geoffrey." She was facing him now, her voice low and surprisingly dangerous. He remembered someone at the Beira club telling him that she had spent some time training Portuguese parachutists, that she was a karate or something expert. Nourse smiled politely. She certainly flew an aeroplane and was an accomplished skydiver.

"Don't be cross, Manuela. I am beginning to understand that it means a lot to you. What do you want me to do? Find some men who might be interested in going to Mozambique as mercenaries?" She glared at him a while longer as if to make sure he was now serious.

At last she said, "Yes, but I would like you to be amongst them."

There was silence while she let this sink in.

"It's been years since I did my training," he said after a long pull at his beer can. He could not believe this was real. He had to put an effort into keeping his face straight, afraid she might see some trace of amusement there, even though it was dark.

"You're fit. You're a skydiver. You can use an automatic rifle. You'll be re-trained before going into action. Most of all, you know the area." As she spoke, the doubt left her voice. "How many men do you think you can find?"

With an effort, Nourse allowed himself to pretend he was serious about this thing. Committed, for an idiotic moment, he put his mind to it.

"Dan McNeil is an ex-Congo man. Let me talk to him about it. I should think he could judge who would suit, better than I can."

"The chap who had the accident today? Can you do it now?" She took his hand and turned back towards the clubhouse.

"Just how much are you offering ... er ... us?"

"The equivalent of five hundred rand outside Mozambique, three hundred inside. And an indemnity to be discussed."

"Mm … how many men have you so far?"

"Ah, that you will see, my love." Her warmth was back. "It is best only to tell you what you need to know. Later, you will be part of us and it will not matter. Let us find this McNeil."

Dan McNeil was jolly but not drunk, chatting gaily to the Cradock girl. Nourse took Manuela into the clubhouse, through into the kit room. He went outside, called to McNeil.

"Dan, just come have a look here a moment."

"What? Oh, it's you, Geoff. Are you dry, bugger? Here, Steve, give us a couple o' Lions, will you? And one for yourself. What is it, Geoff?" He paid for the beers at the bar.

"What do you know about this kit, Dan?" Nourse led the way into the kit room. He turned to McNeil. "No, Dan, nothing about kit. What I want to ask you needs some privacy. You've met Manuela Barros?"

"Briefly," McNeil said, frowning, cracking his can, "Hello, again." He got the full treatment of her smile. "What's up?"

McNeil was in his early thirties, unmarried. His broad, deep chested body was carrying a little excess weight but he was still a powerful man who moved lightly. He seldom spoke of his Congo experiences; when questioned he made light of them in such a way that, unwittingly, he still gave one the idea he had seen a lot of things he'd rather forget.

"Would you be interested in making some money the way you used to, with a gun?"

McNeil's eyes widened first, then narrowed shrewdly. "Mozambique? For whom? Against whom?"

He hadn't asked about pay; that was a bad sign. Manuela took over.

"For Mozambique. We want to get rid of Frelimo and become independent of Portugal."

McNeil didn't laugh but Nourse read the flickering that crossed his face. Manuela took it for excitement. She gave him the bit about being looked after in Beira; told him what the pay would be and how. Also that she wanted more men: did he know of any?

Scratching his head, McNeil stood thinking about it. Geoff thought he could read his face from its twitches and blinks. He was finding it difficult to take the girl seriously but if she was, then he had better tell her here and now that the answer was no. It didn't wash. It was illegal. It was an impractical idea, a gesture. Or was it? And if it was impractical, did it matter? He glanced at Geoff over Manuela's shoulder and as quickly away so that he didn't laugh. Geoff had flicked his eyes to the ceiling and his mouth was pulled down at the corners. If he strung along it might be fun; might get some dough out of it. And it would be good to get into the bush again – if it got that far.

Deadpan, Dan asked, "Supposing for the time being that I'm interested, what men do you have already? Who'll command?"

"You don't need to know that. The less ..."

"I do nothing; go nowhere, before I know that," McNeil snapped. "I take it that I would be an officer of some description – I must know what sort of men I will have; mercenaries, patriots, black or mulatto, what tribes, how armed. I have to decide that what you offer is a feasible trade on my services. The higher the risk, the higher the money. Poorly armed, ill-trained patriots up the risk. Well-armed, untrustworthy mercenaries who may change sides when it suits them – it ups the risk, d' you see? I'm not going to –"

"Okay, okay." Manuela interrupted, abruptly smiling. "I can see you'll be a good man to have." She lowered her voice, glanced at the open door of the rig room to see if anyone was near. Apparently, nobody. "Our tactics are such that we shall not fight a war so much as a series of raids, guided by our intelligence branch. You will be well armed, small groups of eight or ten, half being mercenaries like yourselves. The other half will be Mozambican volunteers, trustworthy whites or mulattos with military training. Does that satisfy you?"

"Almost. Who's in charge?" Dan emptied his beer down his throat.

"There is a man at the head of military operations but usually he will not be in the field. Unless of course the operation is large enough. He is answerable to a group of men that head the movement."

"Who is he?" McNeil insisted. "I know, or know of, most of the military men outside of the army in Southern Africa. A good commander I'll fight for, a bad one, I won't …"

"No. I draw the line there, no names. Take it or leave it." Manuela's voice rose. Her mouth formed a thin line, her jaw jutted. For nearly a minute McNeil stared at her before he shrugged. Nourse relaxed. He reckoned that either McNeil was hooked or was pretending to be.

"How many men do you need?" Nourse asked. Manuela said ten to fifteen now. More in a couple of months. "What do you mean, now? If we find anyone, they've got jobs to give notice to …" He stopped. He saw a derisive look in Manuela's eye. "Well, wouldn't questions be asked if several people just left their jobs and disappeared? Bosses would have the police investigating. I mean, if this got out it could mean adverse publicity for South Africa – interfering in other countries' internal affairs. The Portuguese authorities would complain to South Africa. Anything could …"

"He's right." McNeil cut in. "You wouldn't last a day openly in Mozambique if the Portuguese government found out …"

"Alright." The girl gave them both a black look. "Then they must come as soon as possible. And they must start training here and now. If you are with us, you must get them fit before they come. They must be men you can trust, d'you see? This must remain a secret; it will be bad for you if you open your mouths." Before either man could take exception to this threat, she smiled, taking their arms. "Tomorrow night, we meet here to discuss progress. You must have some names by then, eh?" As she reached the door of the rig room, slightly ahead of them, she was saying, "… so much equipment. I wish our club in Beira had so much. Only army equipment we have plenty of – all static-line rigs."

As Nourse came into the clubhouse, he saw Cecile Cradock waiting for them. Not that she would be interested, but she might have been close enough to overhear. She turned from a poster of a jumper under a canopy in a search-lighted sky. She smiled. Nourse saw Manuela glare at her coldly a moment. They all had another beer at the bar. The Englishman, John Blair, had taken duty there to relieve

Steve van Deventer, the chief instructor. Nourse looked around as people began to drift in from outside as the night air chilled a little and the fire died. Possible candidates, Nourse thought. Blair, promising. Steve, out, married. Sharpe, the New Zealander, possible. Helmut Muller, the German, possible. Clem White, Piet Visagie, Rafe Schulman, maybe. Jan de Groot, doubtful. Nourse introduced Manuela to some of them. She seemed to relax, then: smiling, talking skydiving, various meets she had been to, the good fortune of being able to use military aircraft in Mozambique thus bringing down the cost of an otherwise expensive sport.

Later, Nourse took Manuela back to his flat in his newly acquired elderly Jaguar XK150. He had the top down under the starlit sky; the wind was cool and fresh. Manuela snuggled up to him, so like a child that Nourse found it difficult to see her as a revolutionary, a trainer of parachutists or a karate expert.

His was a fifth floor corner flat in a block in Troye Street. For two months he had come back to it most evenings but it still felt foreign, just a temporary dosshouse. They took the lift; he carried her small case, tense with anticipation. There was a bedroom and a lounge, a kitchenette, bathroom, toilet and a tiny balcony. Wondering what she was thinking as she looked about her, Nourse made himself look at it as a stranger might. He found it easy to do; he almost felt himself a stranger. The only personal part of the apartment was stacked along one wall of the bedroom: a mess of camping kit, tin trunks, a cased rifle, some plant sample-presses and curios from Mozambique including a figure of a man in wood with enormous buttocks and tiny feet which had a bullet hole just above its flat nose. Manuela noticed the hole. She asked about it.

"That's Fred," explained Nourse, a little embarrassed. Fred looked sorrowfully out of place in these surroundings but he had looked much more at home in Nourse's reed hut in the Zambezi Valley, even with the bullet hole. "My boss man, Francisco, tied a string to Fred one night when I was out drinking. I'd had a skinful by the time I got home. Anyway when he thought I was nearly asleep he started pulling Fred towards my bed. I got a helluva fright and grabbed my revolver. It was pretty wild shooting but I got poor Fred by pure chance. Also gave my boss man a fright. He never tried anything like that again, especially when he'd seen where I'd shot."

His work team had spread the word and the local blacks had given him a nickname, meaning *don't prod the mamba*, because of the incident, but he didn't mention that to Manuela. The Portuguese girl looked at Fred in distaste. She obviously felt no empathy for the tale and only contempt for his sense of humour. Shortly afterwards, when she had undressed him and he was fumbling at her pants, his breathing ragged, and though the table lamp was shrouded with a dark shade, he noticed with a smile that she had covered Fred with a blanket.

—⁂—

"Damn it, but she sticks to me like a burr to a sock," Nourse said disgustedly, drawing rainbows on the urinal with a jet of last night's beer. "Scared we'll discuss this thing without her hearing."

"Bloody right, too. We must discuss it, Geoff." McNeil leaned against the convenience wall, smoking. "Our risks are too great, man. Not the bush risks, but the Portuguese, as opposed to the Mozambicans, are our problem. If their army sees us in the bush, or their security finds out what we're at, they'll stop us – their offensive has cooled right off. There is talk of negotiations with Frelimo, ceasefires and so on. They won't let a bunch of mercs fuck things up."

"I know. I wondered how to bring it up. She can't give us a guarantee, I suppose, that the Ports will leave us alone. I reckon we tell her it's off." Nourse shook the dew from the lily and zipped up. McNeil surprised him by laughing.

"Man, I don't expect we'll even go into the bush, let alone see a terrorist. I'm game just to see what happens and see what we can get out of it. This guy, Barros, Manuela's old man, needs his head read. What a joke, his private army." Nourse saw a tremor of excitement run through Dan as he thought of what it could lead to, belying his words. Action again. A void sucked at his own stomach, similar to the feeling he got just before a plane throttled back to his order, and he jumped.

McNeil seemed to be thinking the same thing. "It's still a good feeling, no commitments. Anything could happen. In six months time, I could be in the Argentine. Or Australia. I could be fighting, scuba diving, working or skydiving. Or dead." He grinned at Geoff. "I'm getting a bit bored with this construction lark; I've been pretty inactive of late, drifting. No action for a couple of years now – not since I strong-armed for that merchant in Asuncion, old Perez, up and down the Rio Paraguay. When was that, now, sixty-seven?" Geoff hero-worshipped the older man, envying him his adventurous life.

McNeil looked at Nourse, seeming to be summing him up. "I'm thinking that you'd shape up alright in a scrap, if yesterday was anything to go by! I'm in debt to you, Geoff, but I don't like being obliged to anyone. If this razzle comes off, then I'll probably get the chance to pay off soon enough, though."

Nourse didn't reply, embarrassed.

McNeil told Geoff that he had decided to broach Manuela on the fact that they could not see themselves being left alone by the Portuguese authorities. If she could convince them, the recruiting could start; otherwise it would be laughed off.

Later, Nourse felt an odd pang of regret when he found that the girl who wanted ground training, Cecile Cradock, had attached herself to McNeil. Having cake and eating it, he thought, smiling wryly. McNeil sent her on an errand, then they were able to get Manuela alone. Nobody else was near.

The Portuguese girl heard them out, her look darting from one to the other, eyes narrowed and shrewd. She perched on a high stool at the club bar counter, the golden skin of her bare midriff rippling below her very brief top as she swung a smooth brown leg in controlled impatience.

"We have that sorted out. The police chief is a Mozambican, an old friend of my father. Provided you all keep your mouths shut – and you will for your own sakes – you'll be alright. Now, is there anything else? When can you start getting men?"

McNeil sighed. He had phoned three old colleagues of his earlier that morning. Two were interested. He and Nourse had each compiled a list of jumpers. These they now swapped. They discussed the names they disagreed on.

That day, after two loads of student jumpers, the cloud that had been sitting at one thousand metres with a few gaps closed up completely, and darkened the sky with intermittent drizzle that put paid to further jumping. McNeil and Nourse drifted amongst the jumpers there in the clubhouse, approaching ten privately. Seven were pretty sure they would go, which Geoff thought was amazing, considering the short notice. That they were mostly thinking it would come to nothing beyond a trip to Beira and back, hopefully leaving them a little richer, was partly his fault. It was what he and Dan believed themselves.

Geoff heard McNeil arrange for Steve van Deventer to give Cecile her ground training. Her papers were in order. She told him her doctor had said that she was mad.

"Said I should see a psychiatrist, not a G. P."

McNeil smiled at the old, old parachuting joke. Geoff thought that Dan was getting fond of the girl and the irritation he'd first felt at the girl hanging about him was fading. Some jumpers left, now that there seemed little chance of jumping that day, while the rest sat in the clubhouse drinking beer.

Cecile Cradock said that she had tried to start her Volkswagen but it wasn't having any. She had fiddled about with the engine and had a smear of oil over her nose when she arrived back in the clubhouse; dishevelled, hands dirty.

"Dan," she said pathetically, "I wonder if you wouldn't…"

McNeil cut her short with a look, threw back the last of the beer in his can and followed her out into the drizzle and the dark. He told Geoff later that she had a torch and it had taken him five minutes to find that the stem of the rotor was cracked. In the light of the torch, with her hair stringy, the oil smear on her nose, chewing her lip in chagrin, he had been lost. He casually put an arm around her shoulders, careful not to soil her tee-shirt.

"Never mind, we'll think of something. Come have a beer so long."

They went back. He questioned her. She was a saleswoman for a Pretoria sports shop, she said. Specialised in lady's sportswear. McNeil said he thought sporting ladies didn't wear anything. Chuckling, she seemed to relax.

Later someone suggested they all move *en masse* to a steakhouse in town. McNeil took Cecile with him in his panel van, promising to bring her back later and fix her stranded Beetle. Manuela had other plans and persuaded a slightly drunk Nourse to take her home. They went to her hotel, had a dozen escargots in garlic sauce with brown bread and a chilled Stein wine before bedding together. Manuela kept off the subject they'd both concentrated on all day. She had arranged for McNeil, Nourse, Da Silva and herself to meet the following evening to tie up the ends and make a rendezvous date. Despite himself, Geoff began to feel excited about the thought of returning to Mozambique, and the prospect of adventure.

FOUR

"This is no bloody good!" The fat man hardly gave Morné Brand a glance as he sat down quietly on the other side of his desk. The large secretary gave Morné a conspiratorial smile as she patiently replied to their stout superior's fit of pique.

"Full dossiers would take too long, Sir. Except for mercenaries, there are virtually no records except military and educational. If you would prefer, I shall tell Records to keep digging but you specified basics, Sir, military records, police records, activities, languages, political outlook. As you see, Sir, we also have photographs…"

"I know!" A huge fist pounded the desk. "But I have to use a slide-rule to get anything out of these. I have to … how much is six feet and two hundred pounds?"

"Work on 180 centimetres and 90 kilograms, Sir." A sniff. "Will that be all?"

There was a faint hum from the air conditioning and heavy breathing from the man at the large, solid desk; nothing else. Although the traffic moved five metres away, its rumble was effectively blanketed. The large office was windowless, the blank walls broken only by the door and three paintings of nondescript South African bush scenes. All six chairs in chrome and black plastic faced the desk.

"No," the fat man told the enormous woman holding the files. He flicked a glance at Brand. "Have you seen these?" Brand nodded without a word, slumped in his chair, looking like a vagrant applying for a job. He had over-long untidy black hair, shaggy eyebrows, a lean, lined face and dark brown eyes.

"Very well." With grace, the personal assistant lightly turned. Her boss did not hear the door close. The fat hands pulled the pile of slim dossiers towards his vast stomach. His chair groaned. He began to skim through them, muttering.

"Blair, John Raymond, 22, British. Blah, Blah ... too young to have been up to anything, just arrived in the country, anyway ... Electrician ... description, blah languages, French ... sports, sky diving ... so much for our young Pom.

"De Groot, Johannes Marthinus, 24, South African....who'd have guessed. Mm ... educated, blah ... charged with theft of refreshments at ... Ho, a dyed in the wool criminal ... fined a whole ten Rand. University, only two years of a BA. Ah, Citizen Force training, Army Signal Corps, 1971. I wonder if he knew van Rooyen? Must have ... blah, blah ... good army record, good radio op. Sports: skydiving, rally driving, squash. Usual languages ... ah, here's one of the mercenaries.

"McNeil, Arthur Daniel, 33, blah ... mm, Army Gymnasium 1961, light heavyweight boxing title ... University of Witwatersrand, Engineering, three years and chucked it up, silly fool ... recruited for Congo October 1964 ... training ... made sergeant after a month. They must have been desperate or he's good ... wounded at Stanleyville, both legs, returned to Johannesburg. Back in three months ... mm, good grief, personally sank rebel boats with mortars ... made second lieut. at Faraje, under Captain O' Donnell of 510 Group. Remained 'til end ... mm, travelled about South America with O'Donnell, returned to SA. married Susannah Holt, July, '68, divorced January '70 ... emigrated ... travelled ... so on ... returned last year. Description ... mm, no political involvement. Languages: Swahili and French as well, eh? Picked them up in the Congo, I suppose ... efficient, determined officer. Intelligent, resourceful ... mm, seems like it ... sports: sky-diving, as usual, hunting, fishing.

"Muller, Helmut, 28, German, born Torgau, near Leipzig ... father unknown ... so on ... mm, worked passage to South West Africa, late '62, apprenticed as motor mechanic to ... qualified ... often in court for minor offences, details follow ... no jail sentences... dismissed '67 for assaulting foreman, no official case ... returned West Germany, called up for national service, in army two years ... made sergeant but returned to ranks for insubordination ... travelled Europe ... emigrated to Australia, 1970 ... no record so far of court appearances ... so far, eh? ... arrived South Africa December '73. Employed ... languages: English, Afrikaans, German, French. Sports: you'd never guess, skydiving ... aggressive temperament, criminal tendencies. Known to have been friendly with Josef Andries van Tonder at present in prison in Cape Town for larceny. Further investigation being conducted in Australia ..."

The fat man sighed and reached for a cigar. He cut it, licked it and lit it. He sighed again and reached for another file. He glared at the silent Brand as the shabby professor-type pulled out a pipe.

To find his matches, Brand stood up and patted his pockets, a tall, stooping man in an old-fashioned lightweight suit with an equally ancient, broad, food-bespattered tie, yellowing white shirt and black-rimmed spectacles. He had indeed been a professor; there was a wide spectrum of letters behind his name including a doctorate in physics but he no longer moved in the circles that knew him as such. Even his present boss and the obese secretary were inclined to forget his academic past. As a team, they had now worked together for more than ten years. Brand lit the pipe, before sinking into the chair again. Puffing vigorously, he got it going. A foul cloud permeated the room.

The fat man sucked furiously on his cigar to overcome it. The air-conditioner sucked the competing clouds of smoke towards itself.

"Nourse, Geoffrey John, 26 etc ... citizen force training with Pretoria Highlanders, 1966 ... leadership course, Sergeant ... University of Witwatersrand 'til '70, BSc Hons. in Botany ... joined Africhem Ltd, ah, doing field work in lower Zambezi valley, Mozambique. Interesting. Resigned three months ago. At present unemployed ... description ... blah, blah ... English, Afrikaans, German, Portuguese, Sena, good grief, a linguist. Sports: the inevitable and scuba diving... Good army record, no offences known ... very interesting. Now then ... ah.

"O'Donnell, Ryan Dougall, 34, naturalised South African, born Kilkenny, Eire. Educated ... immigrated to SA June '56. Joined Cape Town Highlanders 1958. Resigned commission as lieutenant, March

'63. Went to Congo as a mercenary, September '64. Made lieutenant ... made captain commanding 510 group, defending the north east boundary from Lake Albert to Aba for a time, involved in the northwest sweep to Bondo ... blah, blah ... left at the end of the Congo campaign ... went with his ex-lieutenant, Arthur Daniel McNeil, to the Argentine, Paraguay and Uruguay, as bodyguards for often shady, businessmen ... involved in smuggling activities but no record of anything more serious ...Ha, that's a national sport down there, smuggling ... returned May '68, after ... mm. Bought salvage tug *Spartan*, Cape Town. Worked as a diver from *Spartan* until April '72 then dismissed his skipper and commanded the tug himself ... blah, blah ... good grief, not a skydiver. Excellent military record, aggressive, respected leader ... looks like a useful bloke ...

"Schulman, Rafael David, 29, South African ... blah, blah ... ah, citizen Force training in air force ... pilot, conversion to jets. University of Cape Town ... qualified as chartered accountant, 1968, went to Israel, applied for citizenship ... became a paratrooper, involved in some of the raids constituting the 'War of Attrition' ... returned December '70, joined firm of ... blah, blah... returned to Israel, rejoined old unit. Made sergeant. Fought in October War ... crossed Suez Canal with General Sharon ... returned South Africa January '74, last month, eh? Trying to start his own accounting business ... description ... languages ... sports, yes, obviously ... now, let's see ...

"Sharpe, Arnold Peter, 28, New Zealander ... blah, blah ... service in Vietnam, no details, foreigner, anyway ... political liberal, quite outspoken in these views – under observation ... mm, another of those madmen who jump out of perfectly serviceable ...

"Theunissen, Theodorus Johannes, 51. Born ... good grief, joined Middelandse Regiment, '41, sent to North Africa ... mm, to Italy ... wounded in ... hell, he could have been only eighteen ... returned to front ... end of Italian Campaign ... home 1947, worked passage to France ... yes, the Legion, no less. Fought in Indo-China ... mm, that's eight years ... naturalised Frenchman 1952, did not relinquish his South African passport. Served in Algeria another four years ... returned to South Africa, coincided with father's death, took over family farm.

Sold it. Joined Hoare in time for first attack on Albertville, Congo ... fought throughout Congo campaign as commander of 511 Group, rank of lieutenant then captain, until wounded on return from Buta to Stanleyville. Flown to Johannesburg. By the time he recovered the Congo campaign over ... June 1967 flew to Paris, then Biafra ... returning when French mercenaries withdrew from Biafra ... back in July '68 with fellow ex-Congo officer, Ryan O'Donnell ... left finally December, same year ... present occupation: karate instructor, gymnasium owner, since 1971 ... blah, blah... politically Nationalist ... Arabic, Malay, French, Italian, Swahili, Afrikaans, English ... good God. I could use a man like that ...

"Visagie, Pieter Johannes Jacobus, 24, guess what nationality, mm ... citizen force training, started artillery, volunteered for paratroopers ... '69-'72. University of Pretoria, BSc in Civil Engineering ... December '72, found guilty of assault ... bashed up the local constabulary, no less ... three months' imprisonment, two months suspended ... joined Katz Construction ... mm, good army record, no political involvement ... the inevitable sport and skin-diving ...

"White, Clement, 26, South African, citizen force training in S.A. navy, 1967; T. A. S. Weapons rating ... B.Sc Agric. at the University of Natal, '68 – '71. Joined National Sugar Research in January '72. Politically liberal, active. Involved in demonstrations at university, thought to be connected with Herman Bosch who fled the country before Security could investigate his involvement in the Zulu Riots of 1971 ... Under observation but no further subversive activity, apparently. Typical 'varsity loudmouth, nothing else to occupy his time ... mm, speaks Zulu, too. Sports: gliding, skin-diving, and surprise – skydiving, too. Why can't they play tennis or rugby or something." The huge rounded figure sighed, stubbed his cigar carefully, then sat staring blankly at the opposite wall, thinking deeply.

"*Ja-nee,*" the fat man spoke in Afrikaans, using that marvellous contradiction that is usually said with a sigh and indicates that a debatable point has arisen. "Officially, no mercenaries are permitted into Portuguese territories from the Republic. Needless to say the Wild Geese Club is getting somewhat restless, but they have been warned off. We can't afford to have even a rumour of South African blessing to meddling by the ex-Congo people. I believe the French are not being too fussy with regard to Angola. Word has it that the *Affreux* of Katanga have been approached."

"Three of the Wild Geese are on this list." Brand said. "The rest are amateurs but some could be competent with a bit of training and experience. Not that there is time for either."

"Now, Brand, do you think that we should stop them going to Mozambique?"

Looking uncomfortable, Brand shook his head slowly. "Not if we can get at van Rooyen through them. Carstens didn't come back. Someone got to him. Somehow, I don't think van Rooyen can handle that sort of protection himself. His client, then. Or a prospective client. Who have we got? Three Portuguese-speakers, mostly messengers. Only one for our purpose, but they all know only the South: LM and so on. No-one knows the North. That's where van Rooyen is."

"Damn it!" the fat man exploded. Again the inevitable fist crashed to the desk. Brand wondered how long the top would last. "The most stupid thing they ever thought up was 'Operation Insurance'. Now that the cracks appear they want us to patch them up."

"The Rhodesians have two men onto it, I believe." Brand had not reacted to the other's outburst. "They must know the northern parts."

"On it, since van Rooyen deserted the cause. Can't find him. Rumours are that he's in Lourenço Marques, then Vilancoulos, then Beira, then gone, then back, then even as far north as Nampula. And what do the Rhodesians think of us? Van Rooyen is a South African. We are the ones that must deal with him."

"Barros is in Beira. The Rhodesians tell us that van Rooyen went to see Barros. Then disappeared again, I know. But Barros is looking for mercenaries. Is there a connection? What van Rooyen knows can only be used against the Portuguese at the moment. What use is that to Barros? He is only anti-Frelimo. At the moment it is of more use to Frelimo. Or Peking, maybe?"

The fat man squirmed in his groaning seat, searching for another cigar.

"Perhaps we've misread van Rooyen. Maybe he has scruples about who he sells his information to. He is, or was, a soldier; perhaps it's only his military experience that is for sale to Barros. A mercenary. Simply that."

"Simply what? Simply the communications genius of the Southern Hemisphere? And for that reason you won't call the axe because he may only side with Barros as a radio operator? *Kak*! What a laugh! Remember: the keys he holds can turn Africa, from the Zambezi down, into a holocaust. The 'Operation' itself assumed that the Portuguese cannot hold their colonies so that we would then be in a position to blow their successors to Hades after they take over. Van Rooyen is surely not waiting that long. Eliminate him. No motives he could possibly have can be pro us at this moment." The words came from around the pipe stem.

Once again Brand had proved his worth. The fat man glared at him. The dilemma was exposed but not solved. Brand went on. "Okay, we have the commodity. Where is the market? Frelimo cannot pay for what he knows in the going market. Peking can, certainly. And Barros presumably could, but it would be no use to him unless Frelimo was in possession of the territory. Scruples might decide which, if he has any left. The question is what the … what has he decided?" Brand sounded fiercer than his superior had ever heard him. "Don't forget, Sir, we are also prospective customers."

"We would have heard from him by now."

"I don't know. It's only two months since he resigned his commission. Perhaps he's still comparing markets."

"From his behaviour thus far, we are assuming that he is in the market. We dare not assume otherwise. He's seen Barros. We decided that he should be kept under observation. Now the man we sent is dead. The question is, does that warrant allowing these …" the fat man gestured at the files, "… budding soldiers of fortune to enter Mozambique? It seems that Barros is a man of great influence, the only man in the territory with the power to introduce a private army discreetly, without being stepped on by the Portuguese government. The ultimate blind eye. And whom do we choose from this shower to keep tabs on Barros and a lookout for van Rooyen? One of the professionals, I think."

"Mercenaries! If they thought they could get more money from the other side for info on van Rooyen, would they hesitate to sell out on us? Is patriotism dead, Sir? I would say one of the other South Africans."

"The Wild Geese are men tried under pressure. Look at this O'Donnell chappie. He was a regular officer. I think we should get onto him. Have another look at the files, Brand."

"But he doesn't have to be anything but an intelligent observer. Just to report. Actually, I prefer McNeil. We'll have a man there to deal with whatever the situation warrants." Brand relit his pipe and puffed furiously in agitation. He knew that the fat man was using him as a sounding board, looking for flaws, making his own decisions only after he had Brand's complete input. Over the years of their association this had proved unerringly sound. "Okay, maybe O'Donnell, if you insist. Who else?" It was Brand's job to direct operations, brief men, designate equipment. In this he was the expert, his eye for detail and fantastic memory made him a human computer. Human only in a vast talent for dealing with men for he was certainly almost inhuman in his ability to cope with a crisis, so smooth and unruffled was he under the agitated, pipe-puffing exterior. There was certainly no need for him to refer to the files again; he could have quoted them all, nearly word-perfect after a single reading. "With his knowledge of the area, I like the sound of this Nourse fellow." In fact, Cradock had recommended both McNeil and Nourse.

They tossed six names back and forth. They argued whether there should be more than one man, eventually deciding that there should. Then the question arose as to whether these should be ignorant of each other or work in teams. Eventually they agreed to wait until the six had been investigated more fully in the aspects that the files had left out – temperament, decisiveness, constructive imagination and a lot more.

"You've got a man to move in when you give the word? Someone who will eliminate van Rooyen if you can't get him out of Mozambique any other way, someone who will not be too conspicuous up in Beira?"

The fat man leaned back, looking tired. The chair groaned in sympathy.

"Yes, Sir. de Souza. D'you want his files? He's just back from Portugal. I wanted him to return there but he is better suited to this. But we need another man there to do the skull work."

"No, I remember him alright. Yes, I am afraid he is not bright enough to operate on his own. Get a good man to head the operation. Maybe Summers; he's free isn't he? This thing is vital. You don't have to be a genius to guess that if this gets into the open, at the best we'll look such a bunch of 'nanas that it will put our pursuance of détente back fifty years. At worst it will set fire to the whole of the sub-continent."

"Can't we de-activate these bombs, mines, whatever they are?" Brand had asked when he had first heard of the debacle.

"Oh, yes, we thought we could. Chemical switches built in, acids, that sort of thing. Why don't they? They ran tests before van Rooyen left. 90% failure. So, even if they do try to de-activate those in position they won't know which few won't blow," the fat man had told him.

"So now we have to pull their chestnuts out of the fire. These are the orders for the present. Bring van Rooyen home, if possible, or squash him if not. It's so important that it may be better if you go up yourself." He waved a stubby hand, dismissing Brand and dispersing a smoke cloud simultaneously. "*Ja-nee*. Get some more detail on those six. Eliminate the duds."

FIVE

The rain drummed on the windows incessantly. The balcony was awash, keeping Nourse and the rest of the team to their hotel rooms. Four days now. The square below was a blur through the torrent. The harbour beyond it was quite invisible. They had been in Beira for four days and it had rained every day; buckets. Rare patches of sunshine that broke up the dark mass overhead never lasted for more than an hour or two, but during these times it was possible to appreciate the magnificent view.

They were perched on the top storey of the new Hotel Zambeze. Anywhere else in the world it would have been nothing to shout about but eight storeys in Mozambique was impressive, in the Seventies. One could see several kilometres up the Rio Pungwe to the west, across the vast flood plain that formed part of the Great Rift Valley to the north, the mangrove swamps to the south-west. The whole of the city lay at one's feet, spreading from the white sand of the eastern beaches to the ribbon of road winding through swampy ground to the airport to the north. How many times had he landed thigh deep in the swampy grassland whilst skydiving from the Chota? One-jump-a-day days because 'chutes got wet unless one managed to land on the road amongst the coconut palms. They used Manga airport to take off from, at this time of the year because the jump-club airstrip on the Chota was thirty centimetres under water until it dried out in April.

Nourse glared at the rain, sighing. He thought of the Government man called Brand. The untidy man who looked like the quintessential forgetful professor had arrived at his flat, unannounced, early one morning a week after Manuela had got their agreement to go to

Mozambique. Well, it had seemed early to Geoff, who had a bit of a hangover. The man had shown some identity that might have been bogus, for all Geoff knew. Brand said yes to the offer of coffee and inspected the wooden statue of Fred with interest.

"My department needs your help," Brand had said as soon as Geoff sat down with his eyebrows raised in query. "We cannot, in fact, let you, McNeil and the rest, go to Mozambique without your agreement to help us to look for a certain person."

Geoff had frozen in shock. He knew what they were doing was illegal, but how had Brand come by the information so quickly? He had swallowed. There was no choice, and besides, it might not make it legal, but at least acknowledged.

"Of course. Anything I can do to help..."

He had been shown several photographs of a sandy-haired, round-faced man in his late thirties. He was short, slightly plump and wore spectacles and a small moustache. His name was van Rooyen. Then Brand told him that he would be working with Dan McNeil, but that nobody else was to be informed.

Here they were in Beira with no chance of going out of the hotel without getting soaked, never mind looking for anybody. There seemed to be a choice: get drunk or play poker with the bunch next door and still get drunk. They were free to move around Beira, as had been promised, under the pretext of all being on holiday from Rhodesia, except himself, who was to appear to be engaged in the botanical work he'd been doing in the area during the preceding three years. However, besides a couple of movies and one abortive attempt to go swimming, they'd been cornered by the rain. Every year at this time, the rains were a part of the natural course of events; floods. People were left homeless, or drowned, or starved as their crops submerged. And every year, when the water receded, they would go back to rebuild their huts and plant their crops again in exactly the same places. What choice did they have?

Sighing, Nourse dropped back onto the rumpled bed. It had not been slept in, for Nourse slept with Manuela in her apartment in the far wing. Lovely, bouncy Manuela. He'd thought she might go cold on him, now that they were back on her home ground. But no, she had only made him promise to remain casual towards her during the day – she did not wish her father to know of their relationship as she said it might interfere with the professional aspect of his being there. But she was so demanding at night that he was beginning to feel exhausted during the day. They had not yet met their commander, but Barros had welcomed them on the day of their arrival. He was a sallow-skinned, handsome, slightly-built man with jerky nervous movements and gold-trimmed teeth that showed up to their roots in rare quick flashes. There was a gymnasium, small but well-equipped, on the same floor – obviously all part of the Barros family's section of the hotel. This was put at their disposal. Some of them put in a couple of hours exercise a day, in between shaking off their hangovers and starting to get down to serious drinking again. The Barros family constituted, as far as Nourse could make out, three sisters – only Rosa was married – and the father. All except one daughter, studying in Portugal, lived in their own apartments in this hotel on this floor; their playground. There were some ten luxurious apartments, each consisting of two spacious bedrooms, a large lounge panelled in local wood, a bathroom, toilet and balcony. The men from South Africa were spread over three apartments, roughly four in each.

Staring at the ceiling, Nourse wondered if Francisco had got his telegram. Francisco wouldn't be expecting him this year as he'd explained that he wouldn't be back in the district. The poor fellow had been stunned: shaken his head as if he'd taken a hook to the jaw.

"Sorry, Francisco, but that's the way it is."

"You have a woman, Boss? Is that why you don't come back next year? You go make a family?" All he wanted was a reason. But there wasn't one a man could put a tag to, that Francisco could understand. Having accepted that Nourse wasn't likely either to take a black wife or to want a Portuguese wife, this might be the reason he'd not return. For most of the important things, surely he lacked little. Meat, beer and companionship. The quiet of the bush, the excitement of the hunt. Francisco had, after several days' consideration and profuse apologies for daring to broach the matter, discussed this momentous decision with his *Patrao*. And drawn a blank – his *Patrao* had waffled on about enough being enough and can't have too much of the good thing and don't meet anybody out there and the jump scene is no good.

Only the latter point was Francisco prepared to concede. He'd watched this mad thing his boss liked to do. He had told and retold tales of it to the people of the hinterland and earned many a free meal and much beer around the campfires and villages they had visited. So, anything could be bigger in the fabulous *Africa do Sul*, of which Francisco, although he'd never been there, had heard so much about from those who had worked on the mines. Francisco himself, Geoff knew, had lived in Rhodesia as a child and planned to return someday, for he had no liking for most of the Portuguese. But he never would, for he hadn't the drive to uproot his family and go through the long involved rigmarole of getting the permits necessary to travel to and across the Rhodesian border. Permits which were almost impossible to obtain in these troubled times of *Guerra*. But it made a nice dream: the security of a good boss on a Rhodesian farm with substantial rations and a house and garden. It became more and more of a heaven compared with the pitifully low wages in Mozambique. Also, Geoff thought, there were the *Aldeamentos* – or 'the line' as some called villages where the indigenes were forced to live for security reasons; the floods year after year; the disease and poor medical facilities; the troops and their weapons both of the reproductive and the destructive kind so that neither a man nor his sister was safe. To Francisco the word freedom meant free to work for a good boss. And thus he could think of many reasons why he himself should leave Mozambique but none why Nourse should desert his *Secundo*.

"Mr. Nourse," Jose Da Silva stood in the doorway, surveying with distaste the untidy apartment. Dressed in a lightweight grey suit of modern cut with floral shirt and tie, he looked out of place in the muddle of discarded tee-shirts and strewn bedclothes, especially with his dark glasses. Nourse didn't get up; he didn't like Da Silva and wasn't going to pretend to, either.

"Yeah?"

Da Silva's lip curled. "I'd like a word with you."

"Go ahead." Nourse waved at a chair. He sat up. Da Silva ignored the chair but he came to stand in front of him.

"Two things," he stood stiffly, his forefingers tapping a nervous rhythm on his thigh. "Firstly you must not again try to contact the indigenous population behind our backs. We were forced to intercept your telegram and although it is easy for us to do, it can attract unwelcome attention as to why it was done. Do you understand?"

"You what? No. Francisco Mwaga was my bossman, my *Secundo*, for three years. He's an excellent tracker and he is antiterrorist."

"Maybe so. And such men are valuable, but why didn't you come to us with the proposal that we recruit him? Just remember that you are a soldier under orders. Don't make decisions on your own: you are a danger to the security of our own mission."

"Whose orders?" retorted Nourse. "When are we to meet this commander of ours?" The whole issue is a big joke, he thought. We will sit on our bums here till the Portuguese arrest us along with Barros, then they will deport us and we will all live happily ever after.

"All in good time, Nourse. In the meantime," Da Silva said with a touch of grandeur, "you'll take orders from me. The other thing is you are to keep your prick in your pants, understand? Don't you so much as speak to Manuela again!"

Nourse shot out a foot that caught Da Silva on the middle button of his immaculate jacket, driving him back so that the chair he'd been offered caught him behind his knees. As he went over backwards, flailing, his head met the beautiful *m'bila* wood panelling with a sharp crack. Nourse followed him, coming off the bed with fists clenched and chin tucked away but Da Silva slid down the wall. He lay with his head on the floor, his legs over the chair; his dark glasses were down over his nose revealing that he squinted. Semi-conscious, he swam with leaden arms, moaning, ineffectively trying to get up. A dart of pity punctured Nourse's anger. The foot he'd drawn back to kick him with hesitated, then relaxed. Grasping a fistful of shirt front, Nourse hauled the smaller man to his feet, ramming him against the wall to keep him upright. With a stiff finger he pushed the dark glasses back into place. Then he slapped Da Silva's face lightly a few times, almost playfully.

"Don't go telling me what to do, you *merde*. And don't interfere between Manuela and me. If this is Barros' idea, you just turn a very blind squint eye. Understand me?" Da Silva pushed ineffectually at Nourse's hand twice before the South African let him go. Without looking at him, Da Silva pushed past the door, breathing with a raspy noise. Nourse stared at the empty doorway, suddenly feeling that shaky, rubbery feeling a schoolboy feels after he has been bullying the headmaster's son. He thought: What the hell did I go and do that for? It's hardly the time to get hard-arsed with my employers.

A mixture of apprehension and regret made him stand hesitantly in the middle of the room. He decided to confide in McNeil, if he could find him. His mind whirled, trying to plan his reaction, should he be sent for. With a bit of luck, Da Silva would be too ashamed to say anything. But he'd have to watch the man; Nourse wouldn't put it past him to find a way of getting revenge, somehow. McNeil was in the gymnasium, rowing, sweat flooding down his forehead and naked chest. Schulman and O'Donnell, one of Dan's associates, circled one another, warily. A lean, powerful man did double somersaults on a trampoline, his grey hair flopping on his forehead as he landed. He was Theunissen, another of McNeil's finds. Nourse had heard that he'd been a soldier since the Second World War.

It was a shock. Nourse hadn't noticed before, but here they were, just four men in the gym and all four had fired shots in anger. Schulman had fought in Israel, the others in the Congo and elsewhere. All seemed to be taking this thing seriously; but the others, who, if anything, needed the fitness more, were playing. These four drank as much if not more than the others but they kept active while they did it. Nourse resolved to follow their example. He beckoned McNeil. When he got him alone, he told him about Da Silva. McNeil shook his head in derision, his silence more eloquent than words.

"What was I supposed to do? Take it?" Nourse demanded, his ears burning.

"Say yes, Sir, no, Sir, three bags full, Sir. But do not bite the hand that feeds you and don't queer our pitch. And what about our friend, Mr Brand?" McNeil spoke in a low voice, his face and body wet and running with sweat. They were backed into a corner of the gym. Geoff had hardly taken the man from Security seriously. He was a bit surprised that Dan appeared to do so.

"You know the crap about ten men behind the lines to keep one man in the field? Well, it is not that many in guerrilla warfare, but all it needs is a fit of pique from some son of a bitch in the supply line and we could get caught short of grub. Or ammo. And not just the guy who started it. The rest of us too. You know the pork-and-cheese in high positions get offended easily. If I was your commander and it came out that you'd done this, I'd smack you publicly, inside our own group, of course, as a lesson to the rest. The other guys are getting cocky, too. I've seen them on the street shouldering any bloke who gets in their way. Okay, it's boredom, but we're a group and we all carry the comeback. We are illegal here, not like Katanga where we were supporting a legitimate government. Us here," he indicated the others with a thumb jerk over his shoulder, "reckon we should change our minds and pull out but we're staying because we are hoping it will fizzle out. Maybe we can still get some cash out of it. We'll see which way the cat jumps. Obviously, for you and me, there's this other matter..."

"You seem to be keeping prepared, anyhow," Nourse said, chastened. He'd felt a surge of anger when McNeil said he'd smack him, but it passed when the latter had not ridden the point. Inevitably, Nourse wondered if he could take on McNeil; they were both over a metre eighty, but McNeil was heavier, broader of shoulder. Also the difference was not just physical: the ex-mercenary had self-confidence, a power of command, which Nourse had never proved in himself. Before McNeil could reply, the gym door was flung open. John Blair, barefoot in dirty tee-shirt and jeans, unshaven, hair uncombed, panted at them, his eyes shiny with excitement:

"Fight! Piet and Muller knocking shit out of each other," Blair disappeared. Nourse saw McNeil and O'Donnell look at each other. O'Donnell raised his eyes heavenward in despair. Evidently Theunissen had read their meaning, for without any hesitation in his somersaults, he said cuttingly: "Leave them to it. It's no concern of ours."

"Attracts attention, Theo. We don't need that." O'Donnell was already at the door. Inevitably the fight was taking place in the gambling den, which was the lounge of the apartment shared by Muller, Visagie, de Groot and White. The coffee table was tipped over and cards were scattered on the beer-wetted carpet. Two glasses were smashed; their shards lying scattered amongst the bare feet of the battling men. The onlookers were quiet, except for Sharpe, who was very drunk, whining, "Come off it, Helmut. Cut it out, now, Helmut."

Both were big men and nearly evenly matched in weight; neither was getting the better of the other. Both were smeared in blood. Visagie's nose was showering his lower face and shirt front while Miller had a cut over an all but closed eye. Theunissen was the last in. A glance told him that all the room's occupants were of the group, so he shut and locked the door, standing with his back to it. Washing one's own dirty linen, Geoff thought.

"Cut it out." O'Donnell was not as tall as the fighters but much broader and, fit as he was, he would still break a scale that couldn't carry more than a hundred kilos.

They backed off. "Yes, cut it out Helmut!" Sharpe whined, not aware of what had happened. With a small movement, McNeil backhanded him over an unmade bed. There was quiet but for Visagie's and Muller's ragged breathing.

"From here on out we behave, d'you all understand? When we fight, we fight for our money with whoever our employers pay us to fight. Otherwise, we behave; we don't need attention or publicity. Our purpose is illegal in this country; we would be clever –"

"Who do you think –" Muller started to say. O'Donnell merely looked at him coldly. Muller turned away, chewing his lip.

"– be clever to pull out right now, because, if this mob lose whatever immunity they've bribed for themselves, they get the chop and us along with them. However, we are in, for the time being. But we've still got to be damned careful. Be polite to everyone, especially here in Beira, for your buddies' sakes, if not for the sake of your own necks." He turned for the door then paused to say: "I'm not your commander but if I were I would have you in the gym all day. If you haven't done a full day's route march with complete kit and no grub and your socks full of blood, you may do so, soon. It helps to be fit while you're doing it."

He wasn't their commander then, but at a meeting with Barros that evening he was made a full lieutenant. Theo Theunissen was made his second officer. For their meagre numbers, Geoff thought, it was ludicrous: they should have been a sergeant and corporal, unless their numbers were to swell significantly. The group's uniforms arrived – Portuguese army camouflage. Their insignia had the beaver of a unit known to be in the area and with whom it was planned they would be confused if seen. At 10 o'clock that night, in a covered army truck, they moved out without a clue as to their destination.

Seven spine-jolting hours later the truck stopped for what seemed to be more reason than to void their bladders. When they raised the rear canvas, they found themselves in a forest clearing, the site of a defunct sawmill. No effort had been made to re-clear it. Once their kit was offloaded, the lorry swung down another track into a parking bay covered with cross poles that supported a canopy of forest. Neither the track nor the bay could be seen from the air, Nourse guessed; nor could the several tents that squatted amongst the trees, twenty metres in from the clearing's edge. The parking bay also held another truck, two Mercedes Unimogs, three jeeps, and a small tanker, all in army khaki-green.

Very little was left of the sawmill. All its buildings had been of wood and had long since burned. There were three severely rusted tin water tanks, some derelict machinery and the gaily printed shells of timber truck cabs, well battered from weaving up the narrow tracks of the forest. Besides several concrete slabs where buildings had stood, there was a long heap of sawdust, thousands of rotting planks and logs and a trench below the mill itself where sawn timber fell and was moved away on railed trolleys. Threaded through these remnants, the forest re-growth was thick, but a lot of grass had established itself, whereas in the forest proper, there was none.

"God. I could do with a shower," Sharpe muttered as they gazed around. They were covered in a film of dust because only the first twenty-five kilometres of road had been tarred. Their noses were lined with it; it crackled between their teeth when they chewed.

"There is no water here," Nourse said.

O'Donnell rounded on him. "How do you know?" he demanded.

"Camped here for a week, two years ago." Nourse told him. "Right over there in that corner," he indicated. "It was not in use, even then, but a fire has been through here since then."

Where the others saw only a blank forest wall, he saw a sub-humid, mixed deciduous and evergreen high forest with botanical individuals joggling for his attention. Nourse realised this and laughed. Life wouldn't be too boring here – he could walk through the forest and greet old friends by name.

Their driver, a soldier with sergeant's stripes, told them in Portuguese to follow him. He led them past the vehicles to two cottage tents. Dappled shadows and sunlight danced on the canvas as the upper canopies of vegetation swayed gently. The undergrowth had only been cleared in the immediate vicinity of the tents. A sallow man of obviously mixed blood with major's rank stepped out of one of the tents. He was wiry of build, of medium height with a lean hawk-like face but a broad flat nose. His uniform was clean and pressed. He eyed them wordlessly for a moment, then in good English told them to sit down, spread out, so that he could see them. Standing, their heads and shoulders had been invisible in the foliage. Sitting cross legged in front of them, he pulled a list from his breast pocket and read out their names. Then, as each man answered, he paused long enough to give the individual an appraising scrutiny.

"I'm Major Texeira. I hope you gentlemen will be happy with us. Conditions are a little primitive here but at least it is private. We could be shot for what we are doing, impersonation being amongst the lesser of our crimes, so privacy is essential. No one comes here as there is no water within fifteen kilometres. The nearest water is in a hunting concession whose owner is sympathetic to our cause but there we cannot prevent the local inhabitants from living and moving about. As it is, we fetch water from there by tanker at night. Now you'll be here a little over a week to familiarise yourselves with your weapons and get in some training so that you can work together as a unit. Unfortunately there is a commonly used road within eight kilometres so we cannot even fire any weapon at all. In the unlikely event that anyone may attempt to approach us, we have all three tracks that reach here well guarded. Between them, the forest is virtually impenetrable." He paused long enough to light a cigarette, then continued.

"We also have aircraft spotters in place, and no one is allowed to move in the clearing when aircraft are in sight. Fortunately, these occasions are rare. The forest is green at the moment but special care must be taken about fires, although I shall not ask you to refrain from smoking altogether. Lieutenant O'Donnell, remind me to give to you your badges of rank when we adjourn. You will for the moment remain together as a unit, answerable only to me, regardless of the rank of any other man here. Understood?" Again Texeira glanced from man to man. Then, to Nourse in rapid Portuguese, he said; "Do I understand that you are sufficiently conversant with my language to act as main translator for this group?"

"My Portuguese is rather colloquial, Sir, but I shall manage," Nourse replied in the same tongue, after a brief hesitation.

The Major beamed at him. "*Bom!*" Then in English again, "but I wish to attach another man to you who speaks good English. You will use him as messenger and interrogator – he also speaks the local dialect. Now I shall leave you in peace to settle in, have breakfast and a sleep. I expect the trip up was rough. Then I shall ask Lieutenants O'Donnell and Theunissen to report to me to discuss how you spend your time. Shall we say twelve hundred hours?" He stood up and stooped back into his tent. O'Donnell went after him for their badges.

They turned to find a cheerful, round-faced, young Portuguese behind them, who said, "Hello, I am José Lopes, your translator. Shall I show you your quarters?"

"Lead on, Mac Lopes," said Arnie Sharpe, the New Zealander, as he shouldered his kit. The rest followed, bending under the low branches and lianas, to two bell-tents set up together. From here it was impossible to assess the size of the camp as each tent occupied a minimal clearing of its own.

"What's your total strength here?" Rafe Schulman asked.

"Sixty-two men, including officers, before you arrived. Of course,

as soon as we have had some success, many more will rally to the flag."
They heard a trace of bitterness in with the humour.

"Have there been any sorties?" asked Theunissen, "Any action?"

"Once," Lopes said. "We heard that a chief near the Rio
Nhambaua, in the mountains, was hiding a group of twelve Frelimo
men. We went there by lorry, twenty of us, to within twenty kilos of
his village. There were two guards, both asleep. We shot them, then
stormed the village. We killed eight Frelimo, but we killed two old men,
a woman and two children too, then we set the huts alight." Lopes had
grown quite pale at the recollection.

"How did you find the place?" queried Theunissen. "Have you a
good guide that you can trust? Why didn't the Portuguese move in on
them?"

"We have a very good man with us, Santos, who was a white
hunter with *Safrique*, the Safari people, who knows his way around
these parts. Too few roads. The army won't go anywhere on foot, so if
a Unimog can't get there, they won't go. They stick to the towns and
only go out on road patrols. If it were the Commandos, a different
thing altogether, the Commandos are very tough bastards, real
professionals, but they are spread pretty thin on the ground. They are
needed in the North where there is more fighting. Nearly all of *Cabo
del Gado* Province is in the hands of the Frelimo."

"But the roads are mined," McNeil chipped in. "Surely the bush
is safer?"

"They get by with an it-will-never-happen-to-me attitude," Lopes
said, "or they stay in camp."

The newcomers rolled out their sleeping bags, dividing themselves
between the two tents. There were no special quarters or facilities for
the officers. Their breakfast consisted of ham and cheese rolls and
coffee, this not being a meal that the Portuguese take seriously. The
cooking fires were wood fed, but were undercover, the smoke dispersed
by fans run by vehicle batteries so that it was impossible to see it above
the forest.

At noon the two officers reported to the Major. They later said
that for the first time they were able to see, on a map, where they were

situated; also where the army was based, and where the enemy was thought to be.

Mozambique, in this area just south of the Zambezi, and north of the Beira-Umtali road, grades from mangrove swamps and the flood plains of the rivers near the sea, over a sandy plateau and its remnants, where they were camped at present, across the Rift Valley grasslands and thorn country which includes the Gorongosa Game Reserve, into the hilly and mountainous area that stretches to the Rhodesian border. The camp was chosen for its seclusion: waterless, no people would live there and as most of the valuable timber had already been extracted, there were no timber mills anymore. Geoff knew that it had been suspected that there might be possibilities of finding oil here, as this was the southern-most part of the Rift Valley complex in which oil had been found further north. However, an oil survey had drawn a blank some four years before. Thus, the area was free of prospectors, too. The bush was mostly too thick to support grass needed by game, so, beside the tiny suni antelope and thousands of crested guineafowl, there was nothing to attract hunters to the forest, especially as the surrounding plains were so abundant with buffalo, elephant and most of the larger antelope and big cats.

That afternoon O'Donnell took his crew for a run, wearing only shorts and boots. They jogged almost to the edge of the forest near the hunting camp, where the outer guard sat in a tree. The sun had set by the time they got back and the water tanker was starting out. Despite the fact that the ex-Congo men had reminded them to bring worn-in, comfortable boots, Blair and de Groot were hobbling badly. Nourse, too, found that he had blisters but they were bearable. He rubbed methylated spirit, which Lopes found for him, into the skin to deaden and thicken the epidermis.

The following morning at four o'clock, they rolled, protesting, from their warm bags to face the chill air and a hard day. Theunissen handed out FN 7.62mm NATO "FAL" rifles. "Carrying, for the purpose of," he said. They crawled into the forest on a campus bearing. They wore long battledress trousers and shirts of camouflage pattern, but within a hundred metres their arms and legs were bleeding inside the material from the thorny smilax creepers. They were back in camp by noon, exhausted, having covered less than three kilometres. Even Nourse could not identify all the thorns that had torn at him.

After a lunch of goulash and potatoes, followed by tinned guavas and interspersed with beer, they stripped and cleaned their rifles, then took turns behind the two NATO MGI machine guns that were allotted to their group. Loading, sighting, traversing, stripping but, to their frustration, not firing. Likewise the mortars, grenades and radios were handled. Most of these were familiar to the majority of them but some had forgotten the finer points. Blair, it was discovered, had no military training at all but he learned fast.

That set the pattern for the following days: they were restricted to the forest around the camp so that variety was limited. McNeil was made a second lieutenant at O'Donnell's insistence for, as he said, it may have been odd to have three officers in so small a group, but not so odd as having a competent officer, as Dan was, in the ranks. It was McNeil who borrowed the diversity of arms that there were in the camp so as to familiarise the men with each of them. These included some captured enemy weapons. It was essential, he told them, to know how to use any weapon they might encounter, even in the dark, so there would be no valuable time wasted in an emergency.

"So there you are, used your last mag on the mother's son then as you pick up his rifle, his mate appears and you can't find the frigging safety." McNeil shook his head sadly.

Portugal had a rather large choice of weaponry, an ammunition quartermaster's headache, but of late, more and more NATO arms had been introduced as an attempt at standardisation. However, the camp yielded several G3s – the German G rifles, and several Dreysa MG38s – the MG13 machineguns that Germany had sold to Portugal in 1938. Two 9mm Model 48 FBP sub-machine guns, used by officers, were lent for scrutiny. Made in Portugal at the *Fabrico de Braco de Prata*, they were one of the few arms manufactured in that country.

Of the various small arms used by Frelimo and other freedom groups, usually from the same sources, the S. R. S. Simonov 7.62mm carbine with the folding bayonet and the 7.62mm Avtomat Kalashnikov carbine were represented – collected on their first and only raid – and two Tokarev TT pistols came to light. All were duly stripped and handled.

For that week, time became a meld of pain, and gratitude when it ceased. Night manoeuvres were impractical as there was absolute dark in the forest. No moon could penetrate the dense tangle. Thus the days were made full use of and when one could crawl lamely into one's sleeping bag, it was indeed something to be grateful for. The only night activity undertaken was simulated guard duty and guard stalking. A 'guard' that was taken unaware received a beating. All were trained how to 'put a guard to sleep', trained to the best ability of Theunissen, the unarmed combat expert, who also taught counter moves. Nourse found himself knocked unconscious by Visagie, a bitter pill to swallow until Blair, the novice, successfully stalked Visagie and laid him low with a single blow.

The other men in the camps spent their day doing PT, camp chores, water detail, guard duty or playing football. Some belligerent talk could be overheard from time to time about how they were risking their lives for the cause close to their hearts, receiving only a pittance, whilst these other foreign bastards were getting a fortune and had done nothing to earn it, so far. It was said in Portuguese in loud tones and Geoff passed it along, but they ignored it and nothing came of it until later. It was not a generally-held feeling – those intelligent enough to realise it, knew that they would need every bit of help they could get, regardless of the source. And some of these, if they didn't know it then, certainly were beginning to suspect that their attempt was but a piece of flotsam bobbing on the tides of change.

Thus, Lopes was left in the forest as a marker in a manoeuvre of O'Donnell's. When the group had moved off a distance, they sat down and discussed it all. O'Donnell once more stressed their position; their activities in Mozambique were illegal. As soon as Barros put a foot wrong, their own security was worthless. The war could drag on indefinitely or it could end tomorrow with a Portuguese withdrawal. Both alternatives might allow Barros to continue his activities as long as the authorities were either powerless to stop him or prepared to turn a blind eye. But they could certainly try to clamp down if a ceasefire was arranged prior to talks. It was O'Donnell who also said that they would have a good chance of survival, even if things turned against them, if they stuck together and headed for the safety of Rhodesia.

It was the challenge that held them now, more than the money. For Theunissen it was a way of life that he could never force himself to leave. For McNeil and O'Donnell, just once more, then chuck it. For Schulman and one or two of the others, if they survived, it wouldn't be the last time. The rest held it as a one-time adventure, a doorway in the corridor of life that they feared but felt compelled to enter, hoping to leave it behind them unscathed. "I won't blame anyone if you want to pull freight, lads," O'Donnell said. "Who wants to go home?" Most were to wish that they had gone, then, but for the moment there was only the far off calling of the crested guineafowl and the faint rustle of the forest.

SIX

One thing nobody seemed to be able to deprive themselves of was cold beer. There were six enormous refrigerators busily taking the chill off the answer to seventy-odd thirsts. Men came to take a case at a time back to their tents. O'Donnell and his men got a more-than fair share of this luxury but it wasn't every night that they gave themselves leave to enjoy it. He, McNeil and Theunissen made the rules, and adhered to them themselves.

They had been there a week. It was dark in the forest. And dark in the clearing. Lights were only allowed on inside the tents; the power was provided by the heavily silenced generator and engine unit. They sat in a circle around the crack of light that escaped from the tent's closed flap. Theo Theunissen was telling them about Indo-China when they heard a vehicle come in. It stopped on the track to the parking bay. The water tanker had already returned so they knew it wasn't that. Doors slammed but, through the foliage, they could see little except the dim shapes of men getting out and being met by other men. The murmur of voices reached them.

"Somebody from Beira," Visagie hazarded a guess.

"Barros?"

White came up with a case of beer a little while after the voices had faded and the figures were out of sight. He carefully put the case down then handed the beer around. He found a space on one of the logs that they were using for seats before he remarked: "Unfriendly bastard, that Colonel." He cracked back the ring on his can and threw half the contents down his throat.

"What Colonel, Clem?" asked O'Donnell. He only used first names in camp.

"Bloke that came in that Land Cruiser, just now. South African by his accent." Another slug of his beer. He had all their attention now. "Major Texeira said welcome and all that – the guy was in civvies of course, 'Colonel, I'm sure you would like to say hello to your fellow countrymen before we get down to business? Perhaps you would like the officers in on our discussions?' Well, this bloke said no, what they discussed now, the Major could discuss with the relevant people when he'd gone. He'd prefer to get on with it and get back to Beira.

"'As you wish, Colonel Sanderson, Sir,' Texeira said, and then they pissed off into the Major's tent." Clem finished.

"Sanderson, yeah? What did he look like?" O'Donnell frowned. "Any of you know a Sanderson in this game?" he asked the others.

"Several Sandersons, on and off," Theo murmured in concentration, "but none that fit, I don't think."

"Short, broad. Got a bit of a moustache. Wears glasses. Hair blondish brown, I think, the light wasn't good. A civilian, that Portuguese, Da Silva was with him." Clem White supplied.

"No one know him?" O'Donnell was looking worried. "I assumed that the man at the top couldn't be Barros or Texeira. I asked Texeira who he took his orders from and he said; '*Senhor* Barros, for the time being', whatever that may have meant."

"This guy a colonel, you said?" Theo asked

"We had a Lieutenant Sanderson that looked a bit like you say, Clem," Jan de Groot said, hunched over his beer, as he stared blankly into the past with dark, brooding eyes. "He was a paymaster in the signals when I was there in the '71, a right bastard. Took us on a route march and he drove in a car all the way. He was standing in for another officer that was supposed to take us. We marched nearly 30 kilos in five hours to get to the lorries that were supposed to take us back to camp. Some of us had passes to go and watch the rugby at Loftus Versfeld and we would have made it back in time but this son of a bitch sent the lorries home without us and made us march back again."

"A paymaster doesn't fit in here, Jan," McNeil told him, but they kept the possibility in mind.

"Bring your beers, lads. Let's go and take a look at this joker."

O'Donnell swung to his feet. Theo made a protest about leaving him alone and not stirring trouble but O'Donnell snorted and led the way. It was only half an hour after that that the two men came out of the Major's tent with the Major, himself. The driver in the Landcruiser, with *Zambeze Safari Lda* on the door in white lettering, straightened in his seat and hastily hid his beer can. Nourse had been chatting to him. He'd brought the two men from Barros' hunting lodge near the Rio Mungari where they'd landed by Cessna earlier that day. Barros had come with them but stayed at the lodge. They would all return to Beira on the morrow. Unfortunately, he could tell little about the Colonel, except that he had stayed there before, but had kept himself to himself.

"What do these men want?" snapped the plump man in a grey safari suit. Beside him, Da Silva, in his inevitable dark glasses, made to speak, but the Major beat him to it.

"Ah, Lieutenant," he addressed O'Donnell, ignoring Sanderson's question, "meet Colonel Sanderson. Colonel, these are Lieutenants O'Donnell, Theunissen, McNeil … and their men. The Colonel is *Senhor* Barros' military adviser. He has been discussing the present situation in this sector. Well, goodbye, Colonel. Have a pleasant trip."

Grinning broadly, the lights of the Landcruiser flashing off his teeth, he swung back to his tent, leaving Sanderson to his countrymen. It was obvious to McNeil that Texeira was pleased to be rid of the Colonel.

"How do you do, gentlemen? Please excuse me, I must be getting along." He brushed past them and slid into the vehicle. Da Silva followed without a word, twisting his mouth sourly as he shot a glance at Nourse. The Landcruiser backed away, then accelerated down the clearing. They could still hear the hum of its engine when they were back at their tents.

"Well, Jan?" McNeil demanded tersely

"No," de Groot said slowly, "it's not the Sanderson I knew," he took several swallows of beer, then said, "in fact, it's not the Sanderson at all. It's the van Rooyen."

McNeil exchanged a significant glance with Nourse.

Confirmation, but there was absolutely nothing either of them could do about it.

"What do you mean, van Rooyen?" O'Donnell queried, hardeyed.

"He is, or was a Colonel, though," Jan said, "Colonel P. A. van Rooyen of the South African Signal Corps. My ex-C.O., way back when."

SEVEN

The convoy moved out at dusk two days later. O'Donnell and Schulman, now a sergeant, rode in the second jeep with Nourse driving. Theunissen and McNeil rode in the canvas cab of the second Unimog with Lopes at the wheel. The remaining mercenaries and four Portuguese rode on the back of the 'Mog with their kit, food and fuel. Thus the two vehicles were a self-contained unit. The first jeep and 'mog formed another unit under the command of Major Texeira. Two five tonne trucks and a small tanker constituted a base of supplies manned by Captain Suares, a lieutenant, and all the remaining men. They crossed the Rift Valley by the way of hunting tracks and timber trails, guided by the ex-white hunter, Santos. Santos knew these parts better even than did Nourse who knew most of the tracks hereabouts. The little Portuguese, only a fraction over 150 centimetres tall, was from Coimbra and retained that special love of his people for the *fado*, Portuguese folk singing. He was a cheerful soul, spoke English with an American accent picked up from safari clients, and played the guitar with a natural flair singing the *fado* in a deep baritone. He and Nourse had met several times in past years, the latter being his guest at the *Safrique* hunting camps to which Santos had been attached.

Some of them managed to sleep, despite the roar of the diesels, the dust and the frightfully rough road surface. Most merely clung to their weapons and lost themselves in their own worlds. Nourse, concentrating on driving and refusing to get mesmerised by the forest rushing by on either hand, thought of his fellow skydivers who were now to be judged as fellow soldiers on whom he must rely, and trust with his life.

"There must be some way of making a fortune here, Muller had announced to Geoff and a couple of others during a smoke break in the training period. "Hit a jewellery store in Beira, or maybe that museum, there, that's got some valuable stuff in the precious stone exhibits. The Ports are a pretty stupid lot when you think about it. *Gott*! and so gutless. I couldn't see much opposition if we decided to pull off something, a hard, fast hit. Well organised, with a plane waiting. May be the Jew will be interested?" He had called Rafe Schulman over. "You're a pilot. Would you fly me out of the country if I rob a bank, hey? Get a big share. We'd need some of the others, too, though. Those Congo guys, they robbed banks in the war there, didn't they? Surely they'd be happy to have a go. They're pretty ruthless bastards. I don't like that O'Donnell, though. Too big for his boots by half! Maybe I'll teach him something, yet!" Muller had laughed and the others had looked both startled and uncomfortable.

"You fuckin' mad Kraut!" Visagie had said, "You are out of your tree. O'Donnell would flatten you without even noticing."

Muller had ignored that. "Now, you, I like. You fight pretty good, but I would a fucked you up if that piece of shit hadn't interfered." He had laughed loudly and patted Pieter on the shoulder. "What do you think, old Geoff? I wandered around Beira looking at the jewellery stores and I thought that they didn't seem to have much in their windows, but the museum, now, that took my fancy. Gold, ivory and things. Not well guarded either." Banks were out, he went on, you couldn't do anything with Mozambique currency outside the country, anyhow, and the value of the escudo was dropping every day as the future of the colony got more and more uncertain. But that museum ...

Another time, Geoff had been sitting with Arnie Sharpe, Jan de Groot, John Blair and Clement White. Sharpe had brought up the subject of racism. He hoped to be a journalist, one day. He had hardly been aware that Mozambique existed when he had started out from Hamilton, New Zealand, and now he was here. He'd had three articles accepted at home since his arrival, but none provided great insights into the country's problems. He had grinned, admitting that two covered Kiwi sportsmen visiting South Africa and Rhodesia, and why they had ignored the pressure put on them by the anti-apartheid league not to participate in sports with the racists. The world-class track athlete had laughed and said; "You ask me about racism? My racism is the one that I run in. The other, I leave to the politicians." The third had been about the skydiving scene in southern Africa for his club magazine in Hamilton.

"History in the making, my God," he had said, quickly whisking his notebook from his pocket to show them. *The changing face of Africa*, by Arnold Sharpe, our man on the spot..." This was his account of being a part of history as well as an observer. Southern Africa; he'd heard so much of the place; last bastion of colonialism, police states, Nazi leftovers, racial injustice. As the pressures built up in South Africa, Sharpe was sure that some violent change must take place. It would be the scene of history-in-the-making of immense proportions, a vastly more intense Mau-Mau blood bath, and a struggle as bitter as Vietnam and as complex. Jan and Geoff had exchanged amused glances behind his back. Sharpe believed in racial harmony, equal rights; one man, one vote. His convictions received blow after blow when he reached the country of his curiosity. He chose to ignore the neatly painted, clean houses with the well-dressed people and educated children and the successful black businessmen in other parts of the Golden City; it would have stolen some of the glory from the cause. What if someone delivered the grail to Galahad's door? He went looking for dirt and he found it. The shanty towns of the same city were to him grist to his mill. For him the poverty and filth could never be anything but White Injustice. He brushed aside the reasons for universal poverty and put it down to suppression by the whites. He saw and noted the injustices with relish. However, even as he sought to pin them down, the injustices and examples of petty *apartheid* were dying away, one by one, like lights in the city by midnight. But, he demanded, would it stop the bang?

Actual Apartheid, or separate development as it was meant to be, where each tribe, including the white tribe, were meant to have their own patch, is a pipe dream, Jan had returned. The patches will never be equal or fair. Then, with the forces of Communism ever nudging, tension keeps mounting. If there is an explosion, it will be ignited by provocateurs.

"So, what are you doing here, Arnie?" Clem White had asked, sardonically, echoing the thoughts of the others, "with a gun in your hand?"

That was something their correspondent refused to take seriously. He was an observer, with the weapon as a sort of passport to being there. The offer to go to Mozambique, a country increasingly in the news of late, but to Sharpe's mind inadequately covered, couldn't be passed up. He had done national service at home, so he was no stranger to soldiering. However, the stint that he had done in Vietnam was as a clerk; he had fired no shot in anger. Although he had objected to fighting someone else's cause, he'd realised that, in New Zealand, they theoretically shared the same threat in that part of the world as they did in this – Communism. But, here he was, an out and out intruder, who, if he used the FN he snuggled to his body, would be supporting another evil he professed to oppose; Apartheid. Geoff smiled. Arnie was sure there would be a way out of using it, when the time came.

"Actually, I don't know what the hell I'm doing here, either," Clem White spoke up. "I keep wondering if the bubble won't burst and I'll be back in Tongaat, Natal, with sugar cane around me as far as the eye can see." He told them he might be cutting selected samples of each crop to take back to the lab for testing. He might be checking slopes, laying out streets and contours on the new cane lands, testing run-off after each rain, with a little gadget he'd rigged in the contours all over the area under his control. He would be chatting to the labourers in their own language. Of all the Africans with whom he had had contact, he maintained – be they Xhosa, Sotho, Shangaan, or Tswana – he preferred the Zulus. He reckoned that they had lost little pride over the years that had passed since the days of their mighty chiefs, Chaka and Dingaan. At university he had belonged to a group of students involved in trying to reach the intellectual Zulu, to discuss their lot as voteless South Africans, to keep tabs on the injustices, real and imagined, perpetrated by the authorities, and demonstrate against them.

Clem had looked at his audience, assessing whether it was safe to admit what happened next. He must have thought that he was in safe hands, Geoff thought. Slowly the group had become extreme, Clem went on. The most militant among them were looking for martyrdom by blatant incitement of strikes and riots, mostly to bloat their own egos rather than from a true sense of injustice. He had smiled into the dark. He had been so near to being one of them, he had said, not seeing at work the gently pushing Bosch, the true Communist, who'd later fled the country. Bosch, never holding the billboard in the city square, just painting a little Marxism here and there; the backroom soapbox man, the manipulator – organising meetings in the house near Grey Street at the dead of night with Rashid, Ishmael and Suleiman. There had been more to it than that, but no one knew just what part had been played by Bosch for he had disappeared. Rashid too. The other two had been detained by State Security and it was certain that they were languishing in Robben Island Prison, even then. White said that he had got out of Durban just before it happened because he knew he had become too involved, but he had read about it in the papers.

"Riots in Durban – twelve Zulus, three police dead." White had been questioned soon afterwards; they'd found him too quickly for his peace of mind. Nothing came of it, but he'd steered clear of such doings after that.

"Now, here I am, rifle in hand, off to do battle against the freedom fighters that I once championed!" He had shaken his head, admitting a kinship to Sharpe, who was fascinated by the tale. "I hope to shit that I don't have to kill anybody. I can't rationalise it: *It is them or us.* It doesn't wash too well. It's not even my own country that I am going to fight for. So why? It's personal, I suppose. I have to know how I will shape up in a scrap." The opportunity had arisen to answer the question that lies in hearts of most young men; *How will I shape under gun fire? Can I take it?* There was no ulterior motive of a flag, a quest, an ideal or even a dark hate. The same energy, the same antagonism and rebellion that turns young men with time on their hands, anywhere in the world, to take drugs or to demonstrate and challenge the authority of the country, or to streak naked in a public place or show the brown eye and challenge the morality of the community, had driven him to take the opportunity to discover the quality and endurance of himself as a soldier in battle.

For man, thought Geoff, is a fighting animal and the luxury of most civilised countries breeds boredom, especially in the young. Not having to fight for a meal or an education or a few pennies to make ends meet, we cast about for other avenues of escape for this excess energy. Our fathers and our grandfathers had the World Wars to accommodate that need. Here, on the brink of the Third War, there is the fear that the manner of fighting is reduced to mere button-pushing. Annihilation is hardly a cure for a need to let off steam. The need is channelled into small freedom wars, and tribal rebellions. Arms manufacturers probably aren't fussy, either, he thought. He, himself, had seen action in the army. He had been scared shitless but eventually overcome the fear so that the question of whether he was a coward or not no longer had no answer. However, that didn't mean he would not be scared all over again. He felt his scrotum tighten at the thought.

The Unimog rumbled on into the night. By now they were on a slightly better road and the convoy had picked up speed enough to raise a thick fog of dust around each vehicle except the first, the Major's jeep in the lead. Along this part of the way they only met one other vehicle, a Landrover, coming towards them. It pulled aside and they crept past.

"What's the matter?" called the driver of the Landrover above the growl of the engines. Convoys seldom moved at night because their lights could be seen too far off and an ambush prepared.

"*Nada.*" Nothing, Lopes shouted assurance, "No problem." The Landrover's tail lights soon disappeared in the dust. Geoff was wondering who it was out there – a storekeeper, a farmer? He knew that there were still plenty of them scattered about. Timber millers, missionaries, cotton transporters.

"What about you, Jan," he had asked de Groot. "Did you see action on the border?" Jan de Groot had stared back at him and Geoff knew that he was remembering his border service with some passion.

"*Ja,* I was mortared, a few times. Ambushed once. But I wonder if it will ever be like this in the Republic, where farmers will sleep with their guns, knowing that an attack could come at any time, wondering if they should leave their farms and move to town?" Jan had pondered. He told them that he had been brought up on a farm in the Waterberg, that chain of hills that curves, sickle-shaped up the western half of the Transvaal. His family still farmed there, west of Vaalwater, pretty isolated, not far from the Botswana border, he had told them. When Botswana decided to harbour terrorists, they would be the first to take the crunch. Not that he cared, much, he had reflected. Geoff was a bit shocked when he had said that he wouldn't miss them. It would be a pity about Suzy, though; he said he liked his little sister. It kicked him hard, the bitter memories of what had been home. Of the eight children, he had been the only one who had matriculated and gone to university.

"Not a *verligte* varsity like yours, Clem!" Jan had said. Any university at all had been due to Oom Jan, after whom he had been named. Oom Jan had been his mother's brother, an insurance salesman from Johannesburg, a bright, breezy person who had visited his sister just once after her marriage to de Groot. Klein Jan had been seven then, a barefooted, ragged wraith of a child with the marks of his last flogging still on his back. Oom Jan gave all the kids presents and suckers when he came, but the three eldest let his tyres down, a bit later in the day. The eldest girl put a pile of dog turds in his bed. Then, on the second day, when he tried to calm the drunken de Groot as the latter harassed his sister, Jan's mother, his brother-in-law gave him a black eye. Soon after, when his sister came to advise him to go, he was already packing. Klein Jan had sneaked in with the pair of boots that he'd been looking for, neatly polished.

"Please take me with you, Oom Jan."

Stricken with compassion, the kindly man could only shake his head. He left with only his haunted-looking sister to say goodbye to him. After twenty minutes of driving over the rough and twisting track, he saw a little figure standing in the way. Klein Jan had taken a path over the hills to reach this place ahead of him. He left blood in his footprints as he walked towards the car.

"Please, take me with you, Oom Jan!"

"Would you like to go to school, Jan?" Oom Jan had said in despair. "And maybe to university, afterwards?" He winced at the disappointment on the boy's face, but the boy steadied.

"Yes," he had said in a whisper, "I want to go to school. I want to go away from here." Oom Jan dared not look in his rear-view mirror as he pulled away. But a month later Jan was at boarding school in Nylstroom, a town about eighty kilometres away from the hardscrabble farm.

"I never discovered how my uncle had got around my father. Perhaps he'd threatened to report him to the Child Welfare authorities or maybe my pa simply didn't care, reasoning that it was one less mouth to feed," Jan had told them. Sheer guts had got Jan through two years of University but he had failed the third. He had seen a lot of his uncle in those three years and they'd become pretty close, but when he failed he'd been too ashamed to face him. Then, soon afterwards, Oom Jan was killed in a motor accident and Jan never got the chance to apologise. After the army finished with him he, too, went into insurance, like his uncle and he was good at his job. He took up rally driving, which took all his spare time and money, then skydiving took over, to which he applied the same dedication.

"It seems to me that fighting here will also be a way to serve my country. Indirectly, perhaps, because, if Mozambique falls, South Africa will be naked all up her eastern border. Although I hated my pa, I was brought up in the old Afrikaans tradition and everyone I knew, all the farmers around us, believed that the *kaffirs* must be kept in their place." He loved his country with the same fierce passion of his forebears, the *Voortrekkers*, but, he said, he lacked their hate of the British, which a dying section of Afrikaner, he knew, still felt for their English-speaking fellow countrymen. His own family had derided the *rooinekke*. He really only got to know that other section of his countrymen in the Army, as his school and university had both been Afrikaans-speaking. Now he thought of himself only as a white South African.

"As a child I played with the native children; I learned *Sepedi*, their language, but I couldn't get used to the idea that someday they might rule my country. We were properly indoctrinated and on the farms, our blacks were the least educated, so we were convinced that they were not very bright. Arnie, as a New Zealander, and you, Johnny, as a Pom, you will find it impossible to understand, we really believed that baboons could make better use of the vote!"

Geoff remembered John Blair's look of distaste and Arnold Sharpe's expression of incomprehension, but Clem's look of understanding. He knew they had all been subjected to at least a certain amount of indoctrination. But Jan went on to tell them about his first real suspicion that something about his convictions was faulty. He would always remember old Moatsi, the black school inspector he'd met in Nylstroom – a softly spoken, well-educated man. Jan had fallen on the street curb, grazing his knee. Someone had helped him to his feet. He'd looked up gratefully into the round, shining face of Mr. Moatsi and Jan's look had changed to puzzled resentment. He had pulled away from the old man, as if he might be contaminated.

Pointing to the red smear on Jan's knee, the old man had said. "That's the colour that matters, young sir. Yours and mine are no different." Jan ran away without a word of thanks.

"I still run away from the memory of those words. Maybe I am beginning to understand them." That had given them all pause to think, Geoff thought. He was grateful that he was overcoming his own prejudices with less reluctance. He smiled, thinking of Francisco Mwaga. He truly called him friend.

"What about you, Johnny? You've been in Africa a while now. Was it a shock when you came here, the Apartheid stuff?" Arnie Sharpe had asked the Englishman.

"Oh, the *Japies* are okay, once you accept that they're racist bastards," Blair had laughed, pronouncing it correctly as 'Yarpees', "But the world certainly has a down on them about Apartheid. I came to the country expecting to find the place a mass of riots and police with machine-guns. The 'Whites-only' and 'Non-Europeans only' signs were an eyesore, but I couldn't find many riots. Then I began to notice that many of the signs had been painted over, began to read in the papers about multiracial this and non-segregated that, began to realise that most South Africans were striving to make the change, despite enormous obstacles of tradition and the fear that they, the ones who could work out a practical solution to South Africa's problems, would not be allowed to. The world has of late developed a remarkable affinity for attempting to remove the splinters from other's eyes while ignoring the logs in their own."

He held up his FN rifle. "I've never even fired this bloody thing in my life and when the time comes, I hope I do it right. But if I have to shoot anybody, paradoxically, I'll be contributing to continued white supremacy. This is simply an adventure and I dare not think of it as anything else." He had never fired a rifle; now, the first time would be with a man in his sights. Maybe this morning, Geoff thought, shaking his head at the incongruity of it all.

They stopped at midnight to urinate, stretch their legs and to smoke. They were on the border of Gorongoza Game Reserve, south-east of Maringue, a village with a few stores, an administration post and a small Portuguese garrison. This they were avoiding, aiming for the hills beyond. A soldier went down the track, to return with a black man dressed in ragged shorts and a blanket. The latter gave the Major a sweeping salute, a brief word passed between them, then they went off into the dark together.

"One of our spies," Lopes said to Nourse. They were having a smoke together, leaning against the jeep. O'Donnell, Theunissen and McNeil were pouring over a map with the other officers.

"I seem to remember him from somewhere. I think he's a carpenter from Maringue," Nourse said, thinking back. When the Major returned, it was with four other Sena men. Three of them went to the officers who quizzed them, Santos interpreting. The fourth, carrying a bundle, come over to the men. He shuffled nervously, weaving this way and that, with his hand capped over his brow to aid his eyes in their search.

"Boss Geoff?" he called, unable to recognise anyone in the dark.

"Francisco!" Nourse yelled. He leaped around the jeep to grip his ex-*Secundo* by the hand. "What the hell are you doing here?"

"Heh-heh," Francisco giggled in pleasure, holding Nourse's hand in the manner of his own people, rather than shaking it. "All the while I thought my boss would come back; yes, I knew in my mind that you would come. Welcome, Boss Geoff."

"You should not be here for me, Francisco," Nourse said, gently pulling his hand away. This custom was something that still embarrassed him.

"*Aikona*, Boss. I am a guide and tracker for you. Maybe I even shoot a Frelimo, then I can go to *Africa do Sul* with you." His dream hadn't changed nor his naivety. Nourse opened his mouth to tell him he'd be better off to track and guide for Frelimo but he asked after the grinning man's family, instead.

"I am a father, Boss Geoff! A boy. I wished to name him Geoffrey but when I go to fill in the papers, the Portuguese say he must have a Portuguese name, so he is Alfonso. My woman is well, and my pigs and my chickens are well, but my corn is bad again this year." Nourse let him chatter on, making encouraging comments from time to time. It was twenty minutes before the officer's meeting broke up. The spies melted away into the dark, engines roared, men swung aboard. Francisco Mwaga joined the South Africans on their Unimog with his bundle of blankets and his food.

He'd told Nourse that a man, a Barros-group scout, had come to tell him that his boss was back in Mozambique, that he wanted him. With the others, Francisco had set out from Caia, on the banks of the Zambezi, where he lived, for the village the scout had named, near Maringue. As they went, it was explained how his boss was now employed and Francisco's political views were sounded out. Satisfied with his lack of enthusiasm for both the Portuguese and Frelimo, the scout had made him an offer for like employment. Francisco cared little for political causes, but the chance of working with his old boss again was incentive enough to go along. For three days he had stayed with the man at his village as his cousin, visiting. Then the word had come that the convoy was on its way.

EIGHT

"Where are we headed?" Nourse yelled to O'Donnell.

"Village of a chief called Dundo, 'bout twenty-five kilometres north of Macossa. Heard of him?"

"No. I know the way to Macossa, though."

"We turn off before we get to Macossa."

Nourse kept his attention on the twisting track. The forest flashed by in a mesmeric blur, now and then opening into sparser woodland. Most of the South Africans were able to fall into an uneasy sleep. They weren't expecting trouble on this stretch. Maringue was the last haven, except for isolated villages with garrisons of Portuguese troops. The territory between them was unsafe, even for the convoys. These were ambushed and mined as often as Frelimo could set them up.

The previous year the personal surgeon of General Franco of Spain had been killed as he arrived for a hunting safari in this area. Frelimo forces had waited some hours in ambush at the edge of the bush landing strip. The light plane had put down without incident, but as the passengers walked to the safari vehicles awaiting them, Frelimo opened fire. Two dead, one wounded, Frelimo slipped away. The white hunters, their hunting rifles discarded and replaced by previously concealed automatic weapons, returned the fire without much effect. Later, they tracked the Frelimo men and were able to point them out to a passing army convoy that was guarding trucks containing part of the local cotton crop. But the army men said they had no orders to leave the cotton convoy. They drove on, leaving Frelimo to melt into the bush. Nourse had heard the shots fired from where he had been collecting herbs, a kilometre away.

Texeira had said that he wasn't bothered about bumping into the army at night, so the small convoy kept going. O'Donnell was half asleep when Nourse slowed abruptly as he caught up with the major's jeep ahead that was stationary, indicating that they'd reached the turn-off. The jeep swung away into the bush. Nose to the windscreen, he sought the opening. Almost overshooting it, he swung hard, the jeep bumped violently, and then settled into the ruts of the track, followed in turn by the rest of the convoy. The grass reached above the lights and into the sky. One wheel track was pronounced – a footpath. These tracks were only cleared once a year for the maize collection. When the grain had ripened and been harvested, a storekeeper would send his truck to collect it, often paying with credit notes to be used at his own store.

From here it was just on ten kilometres to Dundo's village. The convoy pulled up well down the track, concealed from the Macossa road, and doused their lights. The night broke into a hubbub of nocturnal sounds after the engines stopped. All the officers, Santos and Nourse gathered at Texeira's jeep. He spoke first in Portuguese and then repeated his words in English.

"I shall remain with the vehicles. Captain Suares will take his men up to that path I showed you on the map, then cross that ravine and get into position behind Dundo's village. Lieutenant O'Donnell, you will head, as I told you, around the southern end of Serra Mipwa. That's it there." With a finger he pointed out the dome-like silhouette that showed against the moonlit sky. "You'll strike a path at the foot of the hill. Follow it until you reach the continuation of this road we're on, go right, through the pass in Serra Chicossa. A few hundred metres from there is the village, on the left. Wait until you hear the engines then move in. Don't let any Frelimo escape. We shall be there at six-thirty, two hours from now." They looked at their watches. "Questions?"

"How steep is the Chicossa? Can they escape over it?" Theunissen directed this at Santos. The little hunter shrugged.

"When you climb it, you carry your rifle in your teeth. I have been there only once, three years ago. Maybe there is an easy way over, but I doubt it."

O'Donnell nodded. Calling his men to him, he told them to kit up. They moved down the track, leaving a pair of Portuguese drivers to take over their vehicles. He called Nourse.

"We've some bush to cover to reach the path from Macossa to the village. The map says there is one small river to cross. You know the bush. Would it be better to travel on the crests or down the ravines?" Nourse had already summed up the vegetation. It had been disturbed at one time and the re-growth was thick. The path would be on the main crest after the stream.

"Ravines, if they're dry. Should be, this time of the year in this part of the country," Geoff said.

"Alright. You lead the way with the guide," O'Donnell said. "You can interpret what the guide has to say and also choose the route through the bush that will be the quickest." They set off in single file.

At a dip in the track, Nourse turned off, finding the top end of the ravine without difficulty. Each man carried a hooded penlight. Nourse led down the steep, rocky ravine, the guide at his elbow, followed by O'Donnell then the rest, with McNeil bringing up the rear. The column moved with surprising quiet, despite the broken terrain and the dark.

At the foot of the ravine they turned upstream towards the black hill, still walking on rock but with it showing patches of damp. Two men slipped on the same stretch but did not fall. Nourse led them up another ravine. This was slower going as there were more boulders and less sheet rock. Up and out of the eye of the ravine, they went, and onto the ridge. The grass reached high over their heads, whipping their faces as they pushed through. Geoff almost missed the path. He tramped a small clearing flat for those behind to see and turned towards the hill.

"Careful." O'Donnell cautioned in a low growl. "We can only be a click or two, now."

Slowly the troop moved up the lower slopes of Serra Mipwa, which rose sharply from the scree slopes on their right. They hugged its edge, twisting among the silent trees. Nobody used their torches. The moon clothed the land in silver, dappled by the ebony of the shadows across the path. Now the larger mass of Serra Chicossa could be discerned behind Mipwa, an almost vertical sheet of rock. It seemed that Mipwa was really just a branch of the larger mountain; it was simply a low ridge that disappeared into the side of the other. It was at this point, as Chicossa loomed over them like a forbidding battlement, that they abruptly came out on to the track. Being so rocky here,the ground was not overgrown. To the right, it seemed to lead straight into the black bulk of a mountain. To the left, it apparently went along its base. O'Donnell halted the troop. He spoke to McNeil, his lips against his ear. Dan nodded, patting the heavy Dreysa machine gun he carried. He beckoned to Visagie who carried two belts for it; they moved silently together down the track to the left.

"There is a gap in the rock, *Senhor*, through which the road comes," the guide whispered. Nourse translated. O'Donnell said that he had already guessed as much. He conferred with Theunissen. The latter nodded, whispered a reply and led those who remained off the track into the bush. Schulman, with the second Dreysa, White with its ammunition, Nourse and O'Donnell walked towards the towering walls. The track twisted abruptly and a cleft of starlit sky appeared through a vertical crack. O'Donnell signalled. Rafe and Clem melted into the inky shadows. Geoff followed the Irishman's barely discernable shape into the gloom, treading on the edge of his boots gently before committing his whole weight to either foot. They made not a sound but it seemed to Nourse that the pounding of his heart was a Sunday beer-drink tom-tom. Then it nearly seized in fright.

Someone hawked and spat a mere five metres from them. He sensed rather than heard a movement, then came a dull thud, a slithering noise and a sigh. Still he froze, guessing, but not sure what had happened. A figure moved.

"Pssk." He edged forward. O'Donnell was holding a man under the armpits. Nourse could smell sweat and woodsmoke. He felt for the feet and lifted him. Back down the track they went, telling Schulman to wait. Nourse shuddered, his breath rattling in his chest with reaction. O'Donnell must have hit the guard with his rifle butt. It had been close. Nourse was sure that his leader had not been expecting a guard there, for this track petered out in the mountains at this side. This was Frelimo domain – the earlier Portuguese offensive had died out, their role was now purely defensive. Had there been a warning? Were they expected? But O'Donnell was a professional; he would always be prepared for the unexpected. Until the unexpected killed him.

Nourse heard him cluck a few times but he didn't recognise the Morse for "OK." Theunissen glided ghost-like out of the grass. O'Donnell breathed something into his ear as they gave the unconscious black man to him, then they returned up the track. There was an almost imperceptible lightening of the sky, the silhouette becoming fractionally starker. Again they joined Schulman and White.

This time the four of them moved forward together. The crack widened, and then opened. O'Donnell signalled to Schulman, whispered in his ear, waved him away. Schulman moved up the base of the slope with White at his heels. O'Donnell reconnoitred the left. At the base of the bare rock walls was a boulder-strewn slope with frequent bushes, thickening further down the clearing abruptly to show the dark vague shapes of the huts of Dundo's village. They could see the dull glow of coals under a cooking lean-to. O'Donnell took up position under the twisted trunk of a wild fig behind a boulder. Concealed, they could watch the huts and guard the track. He motioned Nourse to call Theunissen.

Turning back into the black vault of the pass, Nourse glanced up the further spur to see if he could spot Clem or Rafe. Nothing. He walked back down the track, once stumbling with a clatter that echoed back hollowly from the walls. He cursed, hoping that it didn't matter anymore. He was flattening his lips to say "pssk" when Theunissen appeared at his elbow with a whispered, "Let's go."

He led them back, feeling better for knowing that it was safe as far as O'Donnell. Dawn was almost on them as they approached O'Donnell's position. At the mouth of the pass Nourse stopped abruptly. Those behind all but bumped into him. A man was walking from the huts towards them, rifle over his shoulder, one hand in his pocket. He seemed to be alert, his capped head swivelling to glance about him. For some seconds he was out of view behind some bushes. Theunissen and his men froze in the shadows. When the man came in sight again they saw that he was not alone. Two figures approached them, then they merged. The combined silhouette froze. Then O'Donnell was dragging the Frelimo off the track. He beckoned them over to the boulders at his fig tree. Crouched there, they got their orders.

"Take Sharpe, Muller and de Groot along this slope to where you can cover the flank," he told Theo, "lay back a bit until things start popping, then climb in. I don't have to tell you to watch out for crossfire from Suares' men – they should be in the trees directly opposite. I'll cover this end with Nourse. Okay? Move, then!"

Nourse followed his leader on his belly, out of the last bushes into a patch of cassava near the first huts. It was light now. A rooster crowed at the far side of the village. A dog, prowling near the fire, knocked over a tin and leaped away from the noise. Nourse could pick out the details of the village. Some unfinished huts along the incoming track showed that the Portuguese had attempted to make it into an *aldeamento*, a village where all the stray inhabitants of the area were forced to live together so that it could be controlled, protected or a curfew imposed to combat insurgents. The huts had not been worked on for some time so it was evident that authority had waned. He lay in the cassava feeling vulnerable, even though the nearest hut was thirty metres away and O'Donnell was nearer to them than he was. He wished he had never come. He could still be in bed, maybe shacked up with a bird in Pretoria. Anywhere but here in a cassava patch. Despite the dawn chill, sweat broke out on his forehead.

Later Geoff had read Sharpe's notebook. *It is dawn. The grass huts of the African village are yet quiet. Soon the freedom fighters will rise and go forth*, he had scratched out the last word, *out into the villages to spread their message of hope to the oppressed people of Mozambique*. He had been scribbling in his pocket notebook, his rifle across his knees, forgotten. *Messages of hope to some, of terror to others. They don't know that they themselves are but seconds from a holocaust of flying lead and steel wrought by a handful of men, equally desperate to hold on to the land they feel is as much theirs as anyone else's.* Arnie had almost completed a little map of all he could see of the village and surrounds when he died. Two shots hit him in the middle of his back. He pitched onto his face, his notebook and his rifle under him.

Immediately afterwards a machine gun fired a short burst up on Serra da Chicossa. Dan McNeil told Geoff later that he had just come over a ridge behind the guard above the Frelimo camp. He was too late to stop the shots that killed the New Zealander. The Frelimo man fell down the cliff and his body crashed into the bushes below his look-out position. A glance told Theo that Sharpe was beyond help. No use waiting for the vehicles, now. He waved his men into the attack. McNeil would watch their backs. O'Donnell and Nourse were on their feet. A grenade sailed over the nearest hut. The blast; the ground still trembling as they parted, one each way around the mud and pole structure. Nourse was more afraid of being shot by his own people than he was of the enemy – the Portuguese should come pouring through the village from the further side at any moment.

Four Frelimo in ragged camouflage were crouching beyond the grenade crater, armed. A woman lay at the side of the hut, a bloody stump showed where a leg had been. One of the Frelimo turned, lifting his AK47. Nourse's first bullet hit him in the stomach. O'Donnell knocked over two others, the fourth fled.

Standing dazed, Nourse stared at his victim as he crawled about on his knees, groaning, his weapon dropped and forgotten. O'Donnell downed him with a blow on the neck with his rifle butt. "C'mon, damn it!"

Nourse followed him around another hut. Two Frelimo ran down a row of huts. The FN in O'Donnell's hands bucked twice, one of the blacks staggered, and then Muller charged out into his line of fire and the men got away. The morning air was torn by the sound of shots and the roar of grenades.

"Muller, Nourse, search these huts, then torch them!" O'Donnell disappeared into the smoke that was now hanging over the village. The German fired at doors and windows, covering Geoff as he lit the thatch of hut after hut. The noise was deafening: screams, wailing, shouts, shots and grenades. Flaring fire and acrid smoke. Only a few women – Frelimo whores? – running, wailing; let them go. Two men. Fire, again. Fall, you sod!

Theunissen, de Groot and Blair had hit the village further up; same system – grenades, mopping up, firing the thatch. Those inhabitants that were not cut down, fled, still dazed with sleep and grenade blasts. McNeil was able to drop some of these from his position on Chicossa; Rafe Schulman got two others who made for the track, down which Texeira's convoy was coming. The attack had started too early for the men under Suares to get into position and a few Frelimo got away on that side of the village. Now they couldn't fire on the huts for fear of hitting O'Donnell's men.

Several women and a few children were rounded up in a central square. Schulman said he had seen eight bodies from where he had sat over his machine gun. He'd seen at least a dozen men and a few women get away. He admitted that he hated this sort of fighting. He told Geoff that he preferred the conventional fighting in the open of the Sinai. Even the rocky Golan was preferable, to this slinking around in the bush. The roar of tanks, the crack of artillery filled his mind with reflections. It hadn't taken him long to realise that he loved fighting for the sake of the scrap itself. He'd mentioned to Geoff that his engagement to a South African girl was on its last threads before breaking and he'd been considering abandoning his ideas of an accounting partnership, so that he could go back to Israel. He loved the country of his forebears and there would be hardly a moment, as a paratrooper, before he would see action again. Trust the Arabs to see to that. He preferred physical combat to transport flying, for which, as a pilot, he was qualified. He said that he had seen a shadow move in the further cassava lands. He had nudged White gently, nodding in the direction of the gently swaying plant tops.

"Have a bash, Clem."

White crouched behind the machine gun, mounted on a boulder that also served to cover them. Sweating, he gripped the weapon tightly. He thought he saw a movement beside a stump in the land, sighted and squeezed a burst across it. A figure lurched up, staggered towards the track. White walked the bullets after him but he put on a spurt and disappeared into the trees. He sat back and rubbed his shoulder and wiped the sweat from his eyes. His hands shook. He cursed. They watched the convoy. It was only a hundred metres off but still not in sight of the village.

Then there was a loud BOOM! and the Unimog behind the leading jeep bucked, slewed off the track and over, into the ravine, tossing the men off it like rag dolls.

"Christ." Clem stood up. Rafe pulled him back.

Fortunately, on the final count, their only other casualty, besides Arnie Sharpe, was the Unimog driver who was now a cinder in the burning vehicle. The only injured man had a broken arm from landing awkwardly after being flung off the back of the Unimog. A medical orderly with the group set his arm. The rest of the convoy skirted the crater and reached the village. When they switched off, all was quiet again. Texeira stepped out of the jeep. O'Donnell and Theunissen moved to meet him. De Groot and Suares' radio men were at the radio hut, hoping to intercept any transmissions that came through before Frelimo realised what had happened. Suares exited the radio hut, which had been spared damage. Nourse joined them.

"Poor bastards," Texeira sighed to O'Donnell, talking about the mined Unimog as they were all gathered for the debriefing, thoughtfully fingering his chin. "It seems they were pretty well set up, here. Roads mined, four sets of guards, radio. I wouldn't have thought that they would be so prepared. This is their area, not much army around. I wonder if they weren't warned about us. Of course, they couldn't have known exactly when we were coming or they would have ambushed us ... still, it seems they were a bit over-cautious for a mere camp in their own neck of the woods."

"True," said O'Donnell. "What about these so-called guides we're using?"

Texeira's mouth tightened under his moustache, acknowledging the possibility. He turned to Suares. "What happened?" he asked grimly. O'Donnell and Suares looked at each other. Suares spoke first, in Portuguese.

"I had my men in the ravine," he gestured behind him, "ready to move up just before the attack, so they wouldn't be seen. I had two men at the edge of the trees to keep watch. One came to report that four Frelimo had left a hut and gone in different directions, changing the guard at six o'clock. One was on the Lieutenant's track, one on this path that goes along the mountain, one in the pass, one on the mountain itself. This last saw and shot one of O'Donnell's men…" he paused to insinuate that it was O'Donnell that had loused up the attack by being seen, "and so we were not in position when Frelimo were warned, or nobody would have got away."

Briefly Texeira translated. Ryan O'Donnell explained his moves and the results.

"We didn't expect this many guards, Major," he admitted.

"We didn't expect the track to be mined, Lieutenant." Texeira glanced back at the smoke rising from the ravine. "They must have known that we were in the area and I'm wondering how. However, I commend you for your actions. You did well, all things considered. I'm sorry that you lost a man. He must be buried here, I'm afraid. No such thing as sending his body home." He grimaced. "Now, we must obviously be extra careful about trusting our local guides, suspect all the information that they give us and, how do you say? – keep our own moves in the darkness? We will post our own guards. Now, we see to the wounded and have some food. Then we must see what the prisoners can tell us and decide our next actions."

The guards took over McNeil's and Schulman's machinegun positions, the track, the pass and the path. A burial detail dug a hole for the New Zealander's body. Nobody knew what religion he had had, if any, but O'Donnell said a brief prayer and his comrades stood quietly with their caps off, shocked, thinking about what little they had known of him. A good skydiver with a cheerful grin, who got cantankerous when he was pissed. An aspiring freelance journalist. Some epitaph, that.

O'Donnell placed the notebook on his chest, the men placed stones on the body to stop jackals digging it up, and then they filled the hole.

NINE

At ten o'clock, the officers, Schulman, Santos and Nourse met. Texeira spread his map. At some length he told them his plans and how they had to be carried out; first in Portuguese then in English.

"Somewhere in this area is a concentration of several hundred Frelimo, increasing daily with crossings from Malawi and Zambia. Several villages are suspect but no Portuguese Army troops have been into the area for nearly a year. Air reconnaissance has revealed little, because the enemy move frequently, usually in very small groups, and it is almost impossible to spot them. Also there is a block in the Portuguese Command, somewhere. No action and only superficial investigation is undertaken. It is felt that Portugal is selling us Mozambicans up the, er, stream."

He was still framing the area with a jabbing finger, some two and a half thousand square kilometres in the hands of Frelimo, plus all the western enclave of the country bounded by the borders of Rhodesia, Zambia and Malawi. The exceptions were the islands of Portuguese remaining at the town of Tete and the Cabora Bassa dam, which was still under construction.

"It was essential that we first had a combined operation to get an idea how we work. From now on we shall be divided into three units. Headquarters, consisting of the trucks under my command: One Commando, under Captain Suares, and Two Commando, under," he beamed, "Captain O'Donnell." He paused to let Ryan's promotion sink in then repeated it all in Portuguese. "Air cover is impossible. However, wounded may be taken out by helicopter and we may get some recce work done by crop-spray planes."

Ryan had realised that there would be no air cover – they were an illegal force, afforded no more assistance than a blind eye. It was not a very happy feeling, especially with even road travel fraught with the necessity for darkness and subterfuge. He'd have preferred mines and ambushes. He had answers for these. He knew that he had good men. He had less faith in his superiors, he admitted to his group, later, and was forming some alternatives to get them out of the country when the crunch came. By sticking together they could make the border alright.

No Air. God, he said, he remembered when Air had failed them in the Congo, through bad weather, misinterpretation of signals or when they were needed elsewhere; being numerically a vastly inferior force, they'd had a rough time of it. There were few roads, here, other than the ones they were to keep off, so they would have to do a lot of foot work. More and more he was regretting their involvement in this.

Before the officers had a chance to hear about the coming course of action, there was a call from the radio hut. They hurried over. A gabble issued from the set. Several of the men spoke Sena but none of them could understand a word of this. O'Donnell felt a sweat of frustration break out on him. Such a waste of information. Then Santos wandered in.

"That's Maconde," he said casually, "the language of the North."

"Don't just stand there, damn it. Do you speak it?" Texeira and O'Donnell leapt at him.

"Of course. I lived at Mozimboa da Praia for –" they rushed him to the set. He listened. "It's two units discussing some new men that have arrived ... they are at the one unit now ... a hundred and twenty new men ... some must be sent to other units ... a guide must go to fetch them ..."

The radio hut was tripwire tense, every eye on Santos. Jan de Groot scribbled as Santos spoke, sweat shiny on his forehead. Suares was getting restless as the translation came from the ex-white hunter in English. He droned on, the American accent incongruous in their primitive surroundings. "... they are moving so cannot wait for the guide ... other unit impatient because they are under strength ... what does Colonel Wanga think? ... he is back at Headquarters but will be returning in two days ... What do Headquarters say? ... couldn't get them on last night's transmission ... we shall now call up Unit Six at Chicossa ... calling Unit Six ... come in Unit Six ... " Unit Six was called several times but nobody replied.

"That's us." Theunissen hissed. "Go on, reply. Make it up as you go."

"Unit Six reading you," Santos said, in Maconde. There was no trace of American drawl now, and a slight Portuguese accent and phraseology would make his voice acceptable. Four hundred years of Portuguese rule had left its mark on the languages of Mozambique. Now it was intensely frustrating for the listening men in the hut, for Santos could not reply and translate. Only when it was over did they learn what it was about.

"This is Unit Two. The reinforcements have come. Send two men to the confluence of the Pompue and Matanga Rivers to meet them and guide them ... wait, some men have come, something has happened, there are some wounded ... I will call you again in five minutes..."

"The Frelimo that got away from here have reached them," said Santos and told them what had been said. O'Donnell looked at his watch: 10.31 hours.

"It took them about four and a half hours to reach that Unit Two camp. Could we look at your map again, Major?"

They gathered at the Major's jeep again and spread the map in its shade. One should dismiss anywhere east of the Chiramba-Meringue line and then take an arc of four and a half hours jog through hilly country, say maybe thirty-odd kilometres, to cut the region of the Pompue River, then one had to be pretty close to the position that Unit Two was occupying.

"If I may make a suggestion, Major?" O'Donnell's eyes narrowed as he studied the map. "It is this. We divide our forces as you said except that we divide the vehicles into two convoys as well – one lot on this southern road that heads west then north to Guro, the other on this northern road to a point nearest to this area on the Pompue River. One foot column should take a line to the southern side of the area and the other, moving parallel, to the northern side. Thus all four groups will be relatively close to each other in the end and we should have their position sandwiched. Of course, radio contact will be maintained to help us converge on any sighting of the enemy. The convoys must move off the roads once they have reached their objectives and get as far towards the convergence point as they can without damaging themselves. Naturally we shall get all possible information from the prisoners first. What do you think, Major?"

Texeira stared thoughtfully at the map. "It has a lot of merit to it." He turned to Captain Suares, aware of the resentment that had crossed the man's face at O'Donnell's promotion and wishing to placate him by asking his opinion. He repeated the Irishman's suggestion in Portuguese but Suares hardly listened, his face darkening in anger.

"I won't take orders from this mercenary trash." The South Africans understood the tone if not the words. Suares poured out a stream of abuse. "You can lick their boots, you mulatto bastard, but I won't." He looked around wildly for support from the other Portuguese, his face purple.

"Suares." The little Major was ramrod straight, his face tight with strain. "You are under arrest! De Groot, cover him!"

Jan, coming from the radio hut where he had dismantled the set, swung his FN into line. Suares saw him and the fight went out of him when nobody seemed like offering any support. His shoulders slumped.

Later, Geoff was able to ask Lopes about Suares. He had been a lieutenant in the conscript forces. Born in Lourenço Marques, the son of a doctor, he'd studied agronomy in Lisbon and qualified as a landscape gardener. He had returned to Mozambique, only to be called up. It was with extreme relief that he'd completed his four years' service. He'd looked forward to being again the big fish in the small pond of Lourenço Marques that he had once been. He loved Mozambique and it seemed to him that it was slipping out of his grasp.

He formed a little club that called itself the "Mozambique

Patriots." It collapsed in a few months due to the fact that its members' views differed too widely. He was for a white Mozambique, others for a white and coloured upper class; others simply wanted independence from Portugal. Barros' network inevitably became aware of the club and its members. Because of his military experience, Suares, amongst others, had been recruited into Barros' forces. Again, he was a large fish in a tiny pond – third in command of an army of seventy-odd. The inactivity had irked at first but then, just when things seemed to be livening up, the South Africans had arrived. Now this! Anger and frustration, confusion and disappointment, nearly choked him. He most regretted his outburst of disdain at the Major: there was a split second when he was sure that the latter was going to hit him and he felt a wild surge of welcome for the physical expression of his bitter turmoil. Then Geoff saw it fade and realised that he was ashamed and afraid.

Texeira waved de Groot away when he saw that Suares showed no tendency to violence. He signalled Suares' lieutenant, a thin young man with a prominent Adam's apple, to take him away. The lieutenant put his arm around Suares' shoulders and led him off to one of the trucks. There was an embarrassed silence. Santos spat but said nothing.

"Gentlemen, shall we continue?" Texeira moved to the maps. "I think your suggestion has validity, Captain. This way we cover the area without breaking up our force into too small groups. Because the vehicles must only move at night, except in an emergency, the scouts will guide me to Guro, and as near to the target as possible, on existing tracks. Fifteen men will come with me. Lieutenant McNeil, Lieutenant Borges and ten men with the remaining vehicles will proceed to Mteme on the northern road at the same time and work towards us through the bush. The remaining men will be divided between Captain O'Donnell and Lieutenant Theunissen." He paused to glance at each of them in turn. They couldn't help but admire his restraint with Suares and his diplomacy now. "I suggest that we iron out the details right now, then the two commandos can get off as soon as we have spoken to the prisoners."

The prisoners had a rough time but it was soon evident that there was little information to be had besides the fact that there were two villages in their proposed line of march that might or might not be occupied. One at the foot of the next mountain, Serra da Chimbala, to the northwest, was called Nyamesi, the other beyond Chimbala at the headwaters of the Muira River, was called M'Tessa. Obviously the two columns were to check these out.

Of the prisoners, there was only one wounded Frelimo soldier and a new recruit, who'd only been in this part of the country for a fortnight and knew nothing of importance. The rest were civilians. Two old men were enrolled as reluctant guides; it would mean their deaths if Frelimo caught them, despite the unwillingness of their assistance.

Before the men moved out, Texeira promised to do what he could about Air assistance, limited as it might be. He would be in radio contact with Barros every evening and would ask Barros to get his crop spraying fleet active for their benefit. They left just before noon. O'Donnell led twenty-two men through the pass, along the track through the hills to M'Tessa's village where the track ended. From there it depended on the enemy but, loosely, they were to strike west to link up with Texeira near Guro. The code name of this group was '*Palapala*,' the Sena word for that noble creature, the scimitar-horned sable antelope. The other commando, called '*Gondonga*," Sena for hartebeest, was tracking the fleeing Frelimo who seemed to be heading for Nyamesi's village.

The sky was an undecorated blue bowl; even in April, the Zambezi valley is a sizzling vault. In no time their armpit sweat circles had moved down halfway to their waists. The tsetse flies moved in the moment they left the open ground of the village. Their protective slapping became part of the noise of their progress but it didn't help. Some were hardly bitten, as if their blood was not to the liking of the flies but others were turned to a mass of unbearably itchy bumps. Nor was this the only torment of the bush. Grass seeds were not content only to brush off on their victims but actually appeared to leap from a distance at them and work their way through the clothing of the striding men, causing a hundred maddening pricks. A further torture were the mopane flies, little stingless bees that craved the moisture of the mucous of their noses and the wax of their ears, that settled in their eyes, so that each man had a moving cloud buzzing about his head. No talking was permitted so all cursing was expressed with clenched teeth and soundless snarls.

The vegetation varied from ravine thicket to open woodland, the latter infinitely preferable for a better field of vision and fire. The path and track were tailor-made for ambushes and it was with gut-tightening apprehension that they approached each dip that heralded thicket and the greater chance of attack. But speed was paramount and they could not afford to leave the paths.

It wasn't long before some of the Portuguese were muttering rebellion at the pace that the two South Africans were driving them; this added to their natural resentment of being under the command of *estrangeiros*.

It would be only the next night that Nourse would hear what had transpired with Theunissen's *Gondonga* group. Theunissen halted his column as soon as it became obvious that the continued bitterness of the Portuguese might endanger the mission. With his own men out on guard, he spoke to the Mozambicans in a whisper.

"In time I am sure we could find those among you who are more fit to lead than I, but we don't have that time. I am your leader for the present so please trust me, my friends. I am the boss." His leathery face cracked into a smile. Then he squared up to them as one of the men translated his French. He found the language to be more widely known than English. "If any of you cannot abide by this arrangement," his voice was a whiplash, now, "then speak your mind." His glance raked them. "This is your fight. You should be more eager to meet the enemy than I. You should be setting the pace, not I. Speak now or shut up."

A sergeant with them said, "I am prepared to follow this *estrangeiro* through hell and be glad the devil will see him first to stick his fork into, my friends. Who is with us?"

They laughed, the tension dissolved. The veteran warmonger briefly asked them their names – no man likes to be called "hey, you"

– and before they reached Nyamesi's village he'd committed a name and face for all seventeen of them to memory.

O'Donnell's problem was solved in a more dramatic fashion. He had a bad egg supported by an equally smelly cohort, the two of which were getting infectious. He, too, halted his column when the mutterings got too obvious.

"We cannot operate as a unit if we are divided." O'Donnell eyed them keenly." I have under me sergeants Oliveira and Ribeiro. Ribeiro has something against me, but he hasn't got the guts to say it out loud. Have you, Sergeant?" French again.

Ribeiro was a big man for a Portuguese, a head taller than the Irishman and as broad. He had been a sawmill operator near Inhaminga and in the early sixties he'd run one in the Congo. O'Donnell knew that he spoke French. Ribeiro flexed his great shoulders, bristling. It was a matter between the two of them.

"We Portuguese can settle our own problems, not so, Campos?" A thin individual behind him moved his FN casually into line with O'Donnell's knees. A flick of the wrist and finger would send a bullet into his body. He'd been prepared to root out the growth of malcontent on his own, so, except for Geoff Nourse to bear witness, the South Africans were on guard. Geoff couldn't believe his eyes as O'Donnell shrugged and turned away with a gesture of defeat. Even as Ribeiro registered his victory, a flash of pain exploded in his groin. O'Donnell moved in a blur before him. Ribeiro's rifle dropped, his hands trying to cover the pain between his legs, hardly aware of the blows to his belly, face and neck. He was unconscious before he hit the ground.

Campos nearly pulled the trigger in pure reflex but his target was long gone, concealed by Ribeiro's bulk. Then Sergeant Oliveira was on him. He'd picked the wrong side and he gave no resistance. Geoff stood rooted in shock and was ashamed that he had not moved to assist his leader.

"Choose, my friends, whether you want Ribeiro as your sergeant. Perhaps he means well but we are too few to afford this kind of quarrel. I will not tolerate mutiny so I give you the chance to air your grievances now. After that I shall have obedience; I'll have the next mutineer shot. Mozambique does not need them."

"Send the bastards back," someone shouted. Oliveira held up a hand.

"They are fighters and these we need. For my part, the choice is theirs. What do you say, Ribeiro?"

The latter was sitting up now, moaning through clenched teeth. He was not given the opportunity to answer.

"Get rid of the sons of bitches," a little Algarvean averred vehemently. "We don't need their kind of fighting." Nourse translated. There was a murmur of agreement from the men. One snatched up the Dreysa LMG that Ribeiro had been carrying, another took Campos' machine gun ammo belts and disarmed the two men.

The two of them went back down the track, followed by jeers, Ribeiro still weak and dazed. O'Donnell gave a brief word of praise to his men, knowing that there had been more dissenters than just the two, but the point had been made. He radioed Texeira about the incident and asked him to keep a watch for the two men. He told Geoff to call in the guard and the column snaked out. At five o'clock they moved into position to attack M'Tessa's village but the preparations were superfluous.

The eight huts were deserted. There were signs that people had moved through the village but it had not been lived in for at least two months. They filled their canteens at the spring below the clearing, picked several camouflage caps full of tiny sweet red tomatoes that grew wild amongst the overgrown huts, and then went into cold camp among the rocks of a nearby hill. Due to their night march and the activities of the day they were all but dead on their feet. The Portuguese who had been with the vehicles and had had the most sleep formed the first two watches.

One down, thought Nourse, with a sense of foreboding, thinking of Arnie Sharpe. How many more, before it was over? And the man, van Rooyen, who he had been told to find and watch? He had disappeared even as he and McNeil realised who he was and, anyway, what could they have done about it?

—✵—

For Theunissen the afternoon had been more eventful. As far as he could tell, the refugees were heading for the same village that he was and although this simplified their immediate objectives, it guaranteed a forewarned target.

They had run into an ambush as they rounded the last shoulder of Chicossa. Here several falls had gathered at the base of the almost sheer rock mass in a series of gigantic boulders through which the path wound. As always, there was a vanguard of two men, unencumbered by surplus equipment, buddy-buddying each other from cover to cover, searching for booby-traps and sign of the enemy.

The place was well chosen but the attack was poorly executed and premature. Rafe Schulman said that he actually saw the man who threw the first grenade before it left his hand. He dived behind a boulder and yelled a warning. Behind him, crouching in good cover, John Blair froze, watching the little RDG 5 grenade as it bounced on a rock and disappeared into a crack. Rock splinters lashed the air but both men were well down. An instant later they were off the path, climbing boulders on either side, adrenalin flooding. As the dust cleared from a second grenade, the rocks came alive with men. Blair and Schulman fired as fast as their fingers could cope, their counter attack unexpected and unplaced.

Thirty metres back, Theo deployed his force: half up the path in support of the vanguard, a handful flanking right, along the top of a ravine and two men to watch their backs.

Two more wild grenades shook the hillside in a spray of dust and flying splinters. The crack of rifles merged into a rarely broken, deafening roar, with a cacophony of barely heard orders, curses and cries of pain drowning the gasp of hungry lungs. The ambush and counter-attack became a series of individual confrontations.

The Frelimo men broke towards the ravine only to run into Muller and six men. The big German had the FN bucking in his hands, a humourless grin on his face. The men they ran into fired a single burst then were mostly killed in retreat, sprawling like dolls and rolling down the slope, until caught by rocks or lianas. Two scrambled away unscathed. Two wounded men, one with a punctured stomach, the

91

other a leg wound, were shot by Muller. The Portuguese with him didn't object although more than one thought that they should have been questioned. They certainly felt no compassion. They were a tough bunch – for the most part farmers and storekeepers, more than one of them had lost homes or family members to the marauding Frelimo.

Gathering his band, Theo set his guards and ordered Jan to get news of the attack to Texeira and O'Donnell; then he went to look over his casualties. Blair had had the ring finger of his left hand amputated at the base by a piece of flying rock. He was immensely proud of this, or rather his lack of it.

"Can't get wed, d'you see. No bloody finger to put the friggin' ring on." The Englishman had been through two battles on the first day he'd ever fired a rifle.

"Lucky you didn't lose the next one or your girl wouldn't want to marry you anyway, *Ja.*" Muller roared with laughter at his own wit and went on to explain his joke whether those in hearing had caught on or not. A combination of pain and excitement made it impossible for anything anyone said to penetrate Blair's absorption in his own wound. One of the Portuguese was trying to put a dressing on it but John's gesticulations made it difficult.

A fifty-year-old farmer from Mutarara, across the Zambezi, had a bullet hole through his forearm.

"Pires, isn't it?" asked Theo in French.

"Okay, Lieutenant, I spiks a little English."

"How d'you feel?"

"No too bad, okay, y'know. I no go back, eh? I don' farken want go back, eh? Okay, y'know."

"We've got three wounded Frelimo, Pires. I think that two can talk. Would you be able to ask them some questions?"

Antonio Pires' hair was grey-streaked curls, the stubble on his chin was salt and pepper. He was broad and squat. A year back he'd had a store a hundred kilometres up stream from Mutarara and, returning one day with a load of supplies, he'd found his buildings a heap of ashes and smoking, blackened timbers. He'd buried the remains of his wife with a charred shovel and driven bitterly away. Over a mine. It took him twenty-eight hours after he had crawled from the wreck with a broken leg to hobble to another store at the Zambezi's edge, owned by his brother-in-law. It took him six months to recover. He and Nourse had known each other quite well, on and off.

"Okay, Lieutenant. I start now, okay? What I ask the farken bastard?"

"How many groups in the area? Where are their headquarters? I want the names of the commanders, locations of the groups, strength of the units and their heavy weapons, reinforcements expected and so on. Remember, especially the headquarters." Pires repeated it in his own peculiar fashion, then summoned two of his compatriots and Theo took them to the three Frelimo. One had died in the interim. Theo left them to it to go and check the guards. The screams didn't really bother him; he'd heard many before...

He found two men asleep and kicked them awake with a harsh warning. It had been a long day. He doubled the guard and allowed fires and hot food. Frelimo knew where to find them, anyway. In the hills, there weren't enough mosquitoes to keep them awake. Pires had to shake him to tell him what the prisoners knew, which was precious little.

"Sorry, Lieutenant," Pires said. "One, he farken die."

TEN

J ust before midnight, the two convoys parted at the Maringue-
Macossa road. 'Convoy N'zo', the elephant, under the major,
headed for Guro; 'Convoy Nyati', the buffalo, turned left to Maringue
then north and west to M'teme. Nyati consisted of one Unimog and
one jeep, under Dan McNeil.

Dan had expected the young Borges to show some resentment at
being subordinate to him as they pulled away from Dondo's village.
But Borges had said, flashing a grin, "I am glad to have someone to
look after me. When I realise Captain Suares is not with me anymore,
I am much fright."

"Have you seen action before?" McNeil eyed him speculatively.

"Oh, no, I was only in the south, around LM. Never saw one
Frelimo there. You know Lourenço Marques? I like very much. Is more
nice than Beira. Plenty young people there."

There hadn't been time for any more; the engines drowned further
conversation. It was understood that if anyone but the enemy stopped
them, Borges would be the spokesman. For this reason, McNeil was
without his insignia of rank. Lopes followed them in the Unimog with
fuel, supplies and a handful of men. The two vehicles rumbled on into
the starlit night. McNeil huddled behind Borges in the back of the jeep,
his eyes glued to the dipping, bouncing headlight beams as they
bumped and twisted down the rough road. They roared into Maringue
and out down the street lined with brothel huts that were for the troops
quartered at the barracks there. The mango trees were a dark flickering
blur on either side.

Part of McNeil's mind stood guard, tensely seeking out suspicious shapes in the road, alert to ambush. The other part wondered what Cecile was doing. Asleep, probably, in that tasteless little flat in Arcadia, behind that horrible potted creeper.

He had seen a lot of her in the weeks preceding their departure. They'd remained lovers and something deep had developed between them but neither had spoken of it because they both had other secrets and the time for telling had not yet come. He knew that she must be connected to that man, Brand. Her hanging around Manuela and themselves, swapping attention from Nourse to himself and eavesdropping in the club house, were only significant in retrospect. The clincher was when she had quietly got out of bed, then taken the list of volunteers from his pocket to the bathroom, before returning it to his trousers. She didn't know that he had seen her – the Congo had taught him to sleep lightly. He'd been tempted to broach the subject, but then reasoned that further observation might reveal more.

That first morning he was up at six, wondering where she was; then he'd heard the eggs sizzle and she brought him coffee. He had been surprised, expecting her to be a late-sleeping city girl who snatched a sandwich at work. She had kissed him warmly as he came out of the shower.

"Pity we don't have a little time, Dan." Her eyes twinkled as she pretended to pull the towel from his waist. He rounded his eyes and mouth in a shocked "O", theatrically clutching at his covering. The urgency to know more about her curiosity in the Mozambique venture receded in the face of her obvious happiness at being with him. "D'you like Chinese food?" she had asked suddenly. "There's a natty little restaurant downtown that I've been dying to try out. Come tonight. I'll stand you."

"Sounds like a bit of alright," McNeil had smiled, "like you."

Later that afternoon, he'd been supervising the pouring of concrete into the second pierbeam at the new flyover complex, to the south of the Golden City, when he'd become aware of the man watching him. He was gangly and untidy looking, in a clean but rumpled grey suit, puffing a pipe, and was looking up from beneath the scaffolding. He removed the pipe from his mouth, nodded and smiled but didn't attempt to challenge the roar and clatter of the mixers, a crane, several compressors, jack hammers, a bulldozer and the chant of the black labourers.

Dan gave a last look at the works, shouted "Keep it going, Sam," and strode down the ramp. He and the man walked away from the noise. Also, McNeil noticed, away from the site offices which would have been an obvious place to talk. They stood alone between two deserted tip-trucks before the man spoke.

"Afternoon. My name is Brand. You are Mr McNeil?"

"*Ja.* How d'you do?"

"I am from security." He flashed identification and continued before McNeil could get a good look at the card in the wallet's window. "You are going to Mozambique soon, if we don't stop you, to fight as a private soldier for Mr Barros. You are aware that we have forbidden South Africans to carry arms for foreign countries or powers, especially, in the present circumstances, in Mozambique and Angola?" The voice was clipped and precise but the man himself moved from one foot to the other agitatedly and as soon as he finished speaking, the pipe seemed to leap into his mouth. He puffed furiously.

"Yes," McNeil said shortly. The man knew too much for there to be any point in denying it. He eyed Brand's creased maroon necktie and wondered what was coming.

"Then why are you going?"

"Because," McNeil said after some thought, "I feel that nothing will come of it, that it's all a farce, that I shall not, in fact, fire a gun in anger. Therefore I am going simply to see something of Mozambique at someone else's expense while I have the chance."

This hadn't occurred to Brand before and he puffed at his pipe for a minute, staring blindly at the precast concrete beams lying at the far end of the site.

"Are you proud to be a South African?" he asked abruptly.

"Hey?" McNeil hadn't expected such a naïve-sounding question.

"You've been a mercenary, Mr McNeil. Would you fight for your own country for purely patriotic reasons, not for money, if you had the choice?"

"For South Africans against outside aggressors, like the forces of Communism, yes. But for White South Africans to stop Black South Africans attaining at least some measure in the running of their own country, no, I like to think that I wouldn't." His mouth twisted sardonically for a second. "If I had the choice."

"Interesting and involved, Mr McNeil. However, let's think about Mozambique. I'll come to the point. We wish your aid as a source of information when you reach the country, possibly more than just that, but we'll see later. Unless you agree to cooperate with us fully, we shall be forced to prohibit any of you entering Mozambique. Of course, there is no threat if you refuse, it's just that a bunch of South Africans, if caught there as mercenaries, would be an acute embarrassment to us. This we are only prepared to risk if we can achieve certain ends there. Needless to say, very important ends."

"You haven't told me much, have you? Okay, I see your point; and you have me over a barrel. Who else have you spoken to?" A picture of Cecile stealing the list came to mind.

"No-one, yet." Brand had eyed him speculatively. "If we decide on another, who do you trust?"

"Ryan O'Donnell," McNeil didn't hesitate, "Perhaps Theo Theunissen. I don't really know what the others would do under pressure. Oh," he remembered the jump the previous Saturday, "Geoff Nourse, I'm sure. They're mostly good blokes, though, but I can't say I've had reason to think about them from the trustworthy angle. Can you trust me?"

Brand smiled. "That's a chance we'll have to take, McNeil. We'll consider one other. Then, with his cooperation, you'll be allowed to go. Needless to say, you must discuss this with nobody but us. We shall arrange a meeting soon. Phone this number tomorrow night at seven." He had delved a hand into his jacket pocket and handed McNeil a pink slip of paper advertising a stock car meeting in a fortnight. At the bottom was *Entry Inquiries* and a number.

McNeil had been left gaping at it as Brand, puffing clouds of smoke, sauntered away.

At the end of a fortnight McNeil had resigned his job. The

evenings had already become regular PT classes with Theo Theunissen at his gym, the nights were usually spent with Cecile. There had been a meeting with Brand at which he had been not too surprised to find Geoff Nourse. It had not been long. They had been given a series of instructions about what to do, given various contingencies, and a simple code for messages. They were shown several photographs from which they had to memorise three people. Two were agents who would be in Beira, named Summers and de Souza, and the third was the object of the exercise, named van Rooyen. This man had to be found and the agents informed. It was suspected that van Rooyen was connected to Manuel Barros in some way.

In Beira it was with some difficulty that Summers made contact as the recruits were followed wherever they went and the rain had also made things difficult, but there was nothing to report. They saw very little of Barros, and Da Silva discouraged questions on grounds, he said, of security. When they moved out of Beira it had been at such short notice that it was all McNeil could do to leave a message at the 'post-box', the water closet system at *Johnny's Place*, a restaurant on Avenida Paiva Andrade. Now that they had actually seen their quarry, there had been no opportunity to use a radio in private to contact Summers and inform him. McNeil sighed. He regretted both joining Barros and being roped in to finding this van Rooyen character. He settled down as comfortably as he could with his kit under his knees, letting his mind slide back to Cecile.

Soon after three o'clock they roared into Canxixe, the Unimog hard on the heels of the jeep. The two vehicles swung left-handed towards another small village and the men, tense, gripped their weapons when they passed the army barracks. A guard moved in his box at the gates as they tore by but by the time he'd wiped the sleep from his eyes, he would have barely seen their tail lights in the dust. The men relaxed again but the drivers kept their accelerators down. They turned off at the little settlement and crossed the Pompue River. McNeil had actually nodded off, his big frame hulked over his kit, when his world erupted. He had a brief flash realisation that the jeep had hit a mine, and then he lost consciousness.

It took the jeep under the driver's seat and tossed it away, both up and over, momentum carrying it forward. It flew in a lazy parabola, the headlights miraculously still burning but only a dull glow in the dust of the blast.

Connected in series, there were five mines set off by the jeep. To their misfortune, one of them blew two metres behind the Unimog. The blast killed three of the five men in the back instantly. It lifted the back of the Unimog a metre into the air, throwing it forward and doubling its previous speed. The wheel was wrenched from Lopes' hands, the vehicle left the road and hit a sturdy tree with bone-crunching force. The steering wheel entered Lopes' chest, the soldier next to him had his neck broken and the third was hurled through the windscreen. The fuel cans on the back were strewn far and wide, some torn open. The vehicle and surrounding forest became a blazing inferno.

A soldier from the back, with his shoulder out of joint, picked himself up twenty metres down the track, only to be blown flat again by the blast of igniting fuel. The other survivor lay unconscious beside him, all but naked. Before the first mine and beyond the last, Frelimo released the sawn-through trees which now fell across the road, and at these points crews settled behind their machine guns to await the survivors of the ambush. The remainder converged on the sprung trap to see what they had caught.

The jeep lay upside down, supported by its windscreen and on the logs that remained from clearing the road. His knee jammed between the seats, McNeil was not thrown clear. The logs, the windscreen and the fact that the jeep did not catch fire saved his life. At first, as he regained consciousness, he couldn't move and panicked, the pain making him black out again. He heard a high-pitched screaming and couldn't understand why it was so light. The crackle of the flames could not be heard above the scream. It was only when the scream changed to a sobbing moan that he realised that the windscreen lay across a man's legs. In the light coming in streaks under the jeep, he could see a pair of canvas-sided boots, unmoving, next to his face. The moans came from beyond the windscreen where he could see a shadow moving. The movement and the moaning stopped abruptly but his ears were singing and the noise of the fire came through, muffled and unreal.

He moved again, but found that he had one hand pinned behind his back, one against his chest. His body was trapped between the front seats, one knee painfully held under the passenger seat. At first he could only move his other leg which seemed to be held behind what he presumed was his kit. This he kicked at and found he could straighten in the space beside the logs.

Eventually he got the arm at his chest forward past his face but could grip nothing with it except the boots of the trapped soldier. He rested then, staring at the frosted windscreen. Eventually he realised that the jeep was facing back the way they had come and the light came from the burning Unimog. The glass hung in the bent frames like sagging sheets of ice until he plunged the palm of his freed hand through it.

Gingerly, he cleared a hole, ignoring the splinters that entered his fingers. The road was clear between the two vehicles; he could see the two bodies on the sand but they seemed to be out of reach of the blaze. The forest on the far side of the road was alight, burning, but not spreading fast.

A soft moaning started near him from the forest, and then some muttered curses in Portuguese. Then, in English; "Hey, Lieutenant. You anywhere?"

Before McNeil could reply to Borges, there were several bursts of automatic fire, FN mixed with the sharper, faster AK47s. Several bullets struck the jeep, coming from behind McNeil. He couldn't turn, so froze, staring at the bodies in the road, sweating in fear. There was a babble of voices then, and a crashing of undergrowth. More shots, shouts and cursing.

Incredibly, one of the bodies started to crawl away, infinitely slowly. McNeil had to blink several times to make sure he wasn't imagining it. Beyond them, skirting the fire cautiously, came half a dozen men in camouflage, carbines at their hips. Then four things happened in quick succession. The other body sat up screaming; two

Frelimo shot him; a fuel can exploded in the fire; as the Frelimo men reeled back from the blast, the crawler leaped for the trees.

Behind McNeil, shouting continued. Twice an AK fired, like tearing fabric. The FN did not reply, but it seemed that Borges was getting away, if it was he, for the crashing and shouting faded a little as men went after him. McNeil saw those ahead of him take to the forest after the crawler. His trapped knee shot a lance of agony up his thigh as he struggled, desperate now. He tried pushing his pack away to give himself more room. Managing to do so, he was then able to move back a bit by pushing on the boots near his face. At last he could use his arm that was pinned backwards but he couldn't reach the automatic in its holster on his hip. He could feel nothing that might be his FN and suddenly the need to be armed became a priority. Frelimo could return at any moment. Frantically he groped ahead of him, with more reach, now, and his hand felt something warm, soft and sticky. Strangely, it was only then that he registered the smell: flesh, blood and guts. He jerked back. It was the remains of the driver. With reluctance he forced his hand to continue the search around the wet, sticky seat-frame. Nothing. Reaching upwards he could feel the jagged hole that had been the floor beneath the driver's feet. It might be big enough to crawl through if he could free his knee.

Then he remembered his pack. Wriggling and twisting to reach it caused the man under the windscreen to moan louder and louder as he regained consciousness. He was obviously the other soldier who had been sitting beside him in the back.

"For Christ's sake, shut up," gritted McNeil, afraid it would draw attention to the jeep. Eventually, with agonising cramp gripping his wrist, he got the buckle of the pouch in the pack open. The crushed man was screaming piercingly. A man stepped into the road near the body that lay there. He looked, apparently, straight into McNeil's eyes and raised his carbine, sighting at the windshield. McNeil humped desperately between the seats, his head hard up against the floor. There was a single shot. His heartbeat drummed in the ensuing silence. The screaming had stopped; the man was still, without pain, now.

The Frelimo man laughed and said something over his shoulder. Another man stepped out of the trees. Their boots crunched on the road and they began to walk towards the jeep. McNeil was pleased rather than frightened, for his knee was free. He took two grenades from the pouch and sneaked them as far forward as he could then dropped them. Moving quietly backwards, he was then able to pick them up in his forward hand. He could try to get one out of the jeep but if it were stopped by the sand, it would blow him up as well. The hole in the windscreen was large enough but he had no room for a forward throw except a weak shot-putting action. The hole on the floor was the only possibility, if he could get there.

With his knee free, it was easier than he thought but the jeep shook with his efforts, lurching, as the logs on which it rested slipped a little. The carbines swung into line as the Frelimo muttered in surprise and quickened their pace. McNeil pulled the pin with his teeth, chipping one, incongruously thinking that movie heroes must have steel canines or a new set of dentures after each battle. He was giving them a few seconds to get nearer when one of them fired a burst. Most of it was lost in the bonnet but it so unnerved him that he let go of the lever. It flicked onto the dash with a metallic clang. Hesitating for a count of three, he unleashed the throw, impaling his wrist on the jagged edge of the floor.

Wrenching his wrist free, he kicked and scrabbled around the seats, forcing his body forwards. The hole was too small, he saw at a glance, but the sand of the road surface gave readily as he forced his head and shoulder into the gap under the side of the jeep by the logs.

The jeep shuddered badly as the blast shook it, but the windscreen held. Someone started keening but it didn't last. McNeil wriggled through. He got slowly to his feet, his automatic in one hand, the second grenade in the other. His knees sagged under him, a flame of pain misting his vision for a few seconds.

Both men were down. The grenade had got one of them up close, the body was incomplete – an arm was recognizable three metres away. McNeil, tucking his horror away for future revulsion, hobbled across to them and scooped up their AKs, choosing the coolest, surmising that it might hold the most ammunition. These were, in fact, the Chinese version, called the Model P590. From the bodies he took seven full magazines. Pausing to scan the bush, he listened. He hoped that the grenade had passed off as another fuel drum in the fire. There was shouting but it was faint. He limped back to the jeep to search for equipment. The radio had been between him and the soldier with him in the back seat but he hadn't felt it after the explosion. He hooked his kit out from under the wreck and strapped it on. He'd have preferred an FN. It was slightly heavier but more accurate over distance, slower and more deliberate on the burp, but he couldn't find one. The AK was more suited to a wider range of ill-trained soldier

He wasted a few precious minutes searching for the radio without any luck then limped into the trees. And there it was, hanging on a sapling. Unbelievable! He muttered a pleased curse and shouldered it, thanking the Lord and praying that it was undamaged.

Dawn had broken an hour later, when he felt safe enough from pursuit to try using it. Borges had told him that the river they had just crossed was the Pompue so he had followed its southerly course, upstream, knowing it would lead him to the area on which the two foot columns were converging.

"Good God! Behold, she works!" He grinned to himself, straightening the folding aerial and slipping it into its socket. He set a frequency and raised Texeira. He reported and promised to keep in touch. He changed the frequency and got a message in code to an operator in Beira to pass on to Summers.

Then, what he thought might well be the only remains of Convoy *Nyati* crawled under the bush and, curling up, his pack under his head, he went to sleep.

ELEVEN

It was barely light; the shadows were still deep, the sky indigo. *Palapala* Commando breakfasted on stale bread, tomatoes, bullybeef and Bar One chocolates. O'Donnell gathered his men around his map.

"We're here." His stubby forefinger stabbed a point just southwest of Serra Chimbala. "We head this way, in the direction of this mountain, here, beyond the Rio Pompue but as soon as we cross the Pompue we follow it on that side until we cross the Rio Tangadze. The base that Lieutenant Theunissen speaks of should be on a flat-topped hill just across the Tangadze." He had someone call the old black man they had brought from Dundo's village. O'Donnell got Nourse to question him.

"Yes," replied the old one gravely. "I know of a hill beyond the Rio Pompue that is flat on top. It lies near where the Pompue joins the Tangadze, but it is many years since I was there. As a young man, I shot a big *nyati* there, at that place." He was rheumy-eyed and none too clean, his skin hung in wrinkles, his clothes in rags, but there was a simple dignity about the straight, thin figure.

"Tell him to warn us as we get near the place, Nourse. By my reckoning, it's a good thirty kilometres. We shall have to shake it up, if we want to make it by dusk." O'Donnell stowed his map, settled his pack and led the way. They followed an old trail, barely discernible in places, that led along the high ground at the foot of Serra Chimbala. At ten o'clock, the file was dipping down into the Pompue valley by way of a ravine, the path having swung away, due north. They reached the Pompue itself by noon. It was dry except for the occasional pool.

A brief scouting had shown that the country beyond the river was very rough and covered with thicket, so O'Donnell decided to travel down the rocky bed. Although this was further in distance, it would still be quicker.

Often they came across antelope, once five zebra drinking at a pool, several groups of warthog and, once, in a moment of nerve-shaking horror, they rounded a bend and came face to face with a pair of fully-grown lions. O'Donnell stopped dead, Nourse nearly bumped into him. They eyed the lions, a shaggy old male and a lithe young lioness, and were eyed in turn. But, as the numbers of the men were swelled by those coming up behind, the cats' nerve broke. In a few powerful bounds, they were up the bank and gone.

At three o'clock, O'Donnell spoke briefly with de Groot on the radio; the old man guiding them had just informed him that they were near the junction with the Tangadze. Theunissen was positioned on the Pompue, opposite the flat-topped hill; he reckoned that he could get into position to attack by sixteen hundred. O'Donnell said, no, he'd be ready only by seventeen hundred.

"Roger," Theo said, then: "They hunted the *Nyati*. They wiped out the entire herd, except the old bull. Maybe the young bull and one calf also survived."

O'Donnell swore, his face paling at the thought. However, all he said was, "Roger. Out." Telling Nourse, briefly what he knew, he led them out of the river. Geoff felt sick at the thought that Dan was alone and so vulnerable, out there. He had not realised how much he had come to like and depend on the man.

Now, the file was broken into pairs that covered each other, moving in a series of dashes, each man fully aware that the next bush might start shooting at them at any moment. There was no time to do a proper recce and Nourse was wondering how wise O'Donnell was not to delay the attack until dawn. He muttered a question to that effect when his leader stopped on a ridge top to scan the other side of the valley. Both men were sweating heavily. They were tense and alert as Doberman Pinschers. O'Donnell whispered his reply.

"Don't like it, either, but they mustn't be allowed time to get organised. They must know that we could have got the info from a prisoner to find them. Dawn tomorrow would be better for us but by that time, they could be gone." He handed his binoculars to Nourse. "Take a squint. I can see something at the base of the hill in the trees, something that may be a hut roof. If it is as big a camp as we think, then it would have to be well disguised so as not to be seen from the air. Possibly spread out all around the hill."

Nourse searched the lip of the steep, almost vertical hill. He eventually made out three large, tawny patches that could be thatch. He said as much to his leader. He heard the other men catching up to them, going belly down on the rocks. Involuntarily, he spoke a subconscious thought.

"They're expecting us!" He blinked in surprise at himself.

"Or they are gone." O'Donnell smiled, grimly, as he once again scoured the hill opposite. There was a broken ridge of rock that had, geologically speaking, once been part of the hill, running towards the point where they were now lying. Its end fell sharply to the Rio Tangadze at their feet. To the right of it lay a shallow ravine that divided the ridge from the boulder-covered ground where they thought they could see the huts. The distance between was about two hundred metres. If O'Donnell had been defending the hill ... His eyes swivelled to the large bulk of Serra Chiranga that loomed over them. A search with the binoculars revealed precisely nothing, but his stomach was tightening into a cold knot. The palms of his hands felt damp on the field glasses. Nourse, watching him wipe them dry on his clothes, guessed how he felt and his own fear increased. O'Donnell sank into a crouch, motioning his men to gather around him. If, indeed, there was a watcher on Serra Chiranga, they had lost any element of surprise they might have had. This they had to assume, regardless. Then, the ridge was the key to the whole position; it must be manned, thus, it must be taken, for it not only commanded the area of the huts if anyone was foolish enough to be there, it also commanded the flank of the flat-topped hill. What's more, it led into the hill itself; the ultimate position of defence. If they were in the area, that is where they would be. Ridge and hill, with the huts heavily mined and booby trapped. O'Donnell was hoping to Christ that Theunissen kept away from them and the paths in the area. Having decided on his course of action, he felt the grip of fear slacken a little. The eyes of all his men were on him, except one pair.

"Where is that old *munt*?" He snapped. The old man was indeed gone. O'Donnell cut short the tirade of Portuguese invective that started. It was too late now, and he doubted that the old villager was doing anything other than looking after his own skin. He would not have time to activate any action that a lookout on Chiranga had not already taken care of.

"Sergeant Oliveira, I want two cool men who can rig a grenade trap in that ravine over there to do it and stay to stop any enemy escaping down it." Nourse immediately translated without being prompted.

"Antunes! Ferreira!" Oliveira indicated a stocky man and a taller, slighter one, the latter very good-looking. Oliveira barely finished explaining what they had to do before O'Donnell continued.

"All of you keep off paths and away from the huts. They will certainly be booby-trapped. Keep out of sight of the ridge and the hill, whatever you do! They may know that we are here, but it will help if they cannot see us before we hit them. Three blasts on this whistle means that you must move up, but go carefully, all the time. Got that? Okay, off you go, you two! Now Sergeant, choose nine men – I want you to cordon off the area between the ravine and the Lieutenant's men, who should be over there." He indicated the lower end of the hill and swept his hand down the Pompue. "Get yourselves into groups of three, with yourself in the middle. Find yourselves some good defensive positions and stop anyone getting through until you hear the three blasts from my whistle. Don't get it mixed up with Lieutenant Theunissen's; his is much higher pitched. Like this." He blew softly to demonstrate. "Now, off you go. Good luck."

The remaining men watched them go, the tough sergeant leading them, keeping them low. They disappeared into the undergrowth. O'Donnell asked for a man who could speak English or French. The Portuguese looked at each other, then two stepped forward. The captain chose a wiry individual who spoke good French, called Martins.

"Now, Nourse. You speak their lingo; take these three and a Dreysa. Go up behind the ridge and make for the top of the hill. Find a good place for the MG, to cover the top of it. Hold it until you hear from me. Ignore the three blasts but when you hear short, long – twice, you come in at the double. You will know where to, by then. I am taking White, Visagie and Martins up the ridge, so watch out for me and for the machine gun nest there may well be on it. Also, expect a mortar up on Chiranga, this mountain, here. I would have put one there. Now, questions?"

"I take it Frelimo won't be in their huts, Captain. That means that they'll all be up there waiting for me. Aren't we a bit thin on the ground? You sent ten men down to the lower slopes, where the enemy are not ..." Geoff faltered in the face of the hard look in O'Donnell's eyes, and then the latter suddenly smiled.

"While the enemy is waiting to repel that massive force of ten men," his smile broadened, "I'm counting on schnucking in around their flank. Thus, when we go, we must go in the direction of the others, and then, when we are out of sight in the bottom of the Tangadze, we go our own way. Alright, then, let's go!"

—ᴍ—

Blair watched as Helmut Muller stretched his thick legs out, one at a time, and eyed his watch for the third time in ten minutes. Still only twenty past four; they'd been lying behind these boulders for the last hour, slowly stiffening up after the day's hard march, just because, as Muller muttered, "that bastard, O'Connell couldn't get here earlier." Blair later told Geoff, when they were discussing the events, that he wondered what the German was thinking when he sneered like that as he said O'Donnell's name. The German grinned so broadly at some thought that Blair forgot the pain of his throbbing finger for a moment to stare at him in amazement. With them were five Mozambicans; they lay in a bush-choked ravine on the northern side of the flat-topped hill, westernmost of the *Gondonga* Commando. Two hundred metres away, lay Theunissen, de Groot, Antonio Pires and another five men, awaiting zero hour. Beyond them again, on the lower slopes of the hill, were Rafe Schulman, a handsome, tough mulatto named Simoes, and another five men.

Muller's job was to get to the top of the hill and to overwhelm the enemy there long enough to establish a machine gun position that would cover the rest of the hill and at least a part of the slopes. Schulman and his men were to pretend to attack the huts, in fact dodging them to hit the boulders beyond, where they had detected a movement some while back. Theunissen's mob was to remain in position, flexible, so that they could strike as things developed.

"Peculiar, how a man just can't stand a man, sometimes," Muller mused, aloud. "Like I can't take that Irishman son-of-a-bitch. I couldn't stand him even before he'd opened his goddamn mouth. Well, never mind, he'll get it one day." Blair remembered that day in Beira when O'Donnell had faced him down. He supposed that was what was eating the big man up. The shock of realising that he couldn't take O'Donnell on, couldn't make him eat shit; that's what had hurt!

For Blair, the time dragged too, each minute tightening his stomach further until it became a knot that seemed to hover just above his rebellious bladder. He badly wanted to urinate, again, knowing full well that he was dry. For some of the time he would think of the throb up his arm and pray that the Portuguese medic had cleaned the wound properly. Rarely, he would glance at the German and spare the time to wonder what he was thinking of when he smiled to himself, like that. Some bird, most like. He wasn't at all sure that he liked the man. He was too sure of himself. Arrogant was the word. Wouldn't move over halfway, if he met you in a corridor or doorway, that sort of thing. Annoying, really; made a man feel that he always had something to prove. That fight with Visagie, now. He'd found himself wishing that Visagie would smash the German, but it had been stopped by O'Donnell. Now there, by God, was a tough swine! Piet Visagie hadn't cared, one way or the other, but it had been quite something to see Muller eat mud! He'd glared murder at the Irishman, that day. Even now, you could see him look at O'Donnell in a peculiar way. Blair wondered if Muller would use the opportunity of a dark alley and a broken bottle.

"Scared?" Muller asked, abruptly.

"Happen."

Muller couldn't work that one out, so he grinned. "Twenty minutes to go. Where do you think they are? Think they're gone? That would be a laugh. We would look *idioten!*" His accent was noticeable, but not very strong. It was, however, a peculiarity of his that he would use a German word now and then even though he knew the English, almost as if he simply wanted to remind people that he was German. In fact, his French, learned briefly at school, was still passable and his Afrikaans was good.

Blair had no time to reply to this for the battle abruptly began. Both men jerked with fright as a mortar crumped from somewhere ahead of the hill that they faced. With a shattering roar, it exploded on the dry bed of the Rio Pompue, hurling a storm of dust and pebbles into the air. It was the start of a barrage that stitched a ragged pattern along the river. It was by no means a very accurate attack, but, nevertheless, it had Sergeant Oliveira and his men flattened well into the river bank. The mortar fire was indeed coming from the crouching hulk of Serra Chiranga, as O'Donnell had feared, but wisely taken into account. From the same position, a second mortar was hurling bombs in the direction of Theunissen's positions, again with no great effect. There was, however, no point in waiting out the remaining twenty minutes to zero hour. The whistle between Theunissen's lips shrilled twice.

Muller, Blair, and the five men with them snaked out of the ravine, from rock to tree to grass tussock. Their trouser knees wore through, their elbows bled, grass seeds speared, ants bit. A heavy machine gun tuttered from the boulder-scattered lip of the hill ahead, scything the thick grass, fragmenting on the rocks. Nobody got hit; they reached the scree slope without mishap. The cover was good with plenty of boulders, but that advantage was reduced as the enemy above could look over them. The gun position was directly above them. They could see two heads crouched over it. They were too close, thank Christ, and the weapon was firing beyond them at something else. Other guns chattered, it seemed from everywhere. None of Muller's band could see any targets, but a couple of AKs kept them doubled up as Muller led them on up the slope.

There was a mind-numbing roar as a grenade went off just out of range ahead scattering splinters of stone like shrapnel. Their breath sawing, Muller signalled a halt and crawled to a large boulder behind which he could get to his feet. With his FN to his shoulder, he cleared cover for a moment, seeing only the tops of some heads with rifle barrels glued to them. Nothing came his way that time, so he tried again, in time to see a figure rise to a crouch for throwing. Muller fired. The man tumbled. Another fired back wildly. Abruptly several figures leapt to their feet, scrambling away in panic. The grenade went off next to the body of the man who had dropped it. With a shout of triumph, Helmut began to claw his way up the hillside, the others close on his heels. Near the top, Blair, with a sudden flash of intuition, threw three grenades in quick succession over the lip. Two happened only to be demoralising, but the third killed three men and wounded two more. They had survived the grenade dropped by their comrade and were trying to return to re-man the deserted machine gun.

The top of the hill was not in fact flat. It rose to a low crown of rocks not seen from below; the surface was a mass of boulders and stunted bushes. The grass cover had been burned to black stubble. Men in camouflage seemed to be everywhere; a number were manning the rim in a series of gun posts, glistening with sweat as they hunkered over their weapons. Many were part of the central group awaiting dispersal orders from the command post that squatted amongst the boulders of the crown. When Muller and his men achieved their lucky but precarious foothold on the lip, it was only minutes before Theunissen and his band joined them.

Schulman's group, keeping off the paths, skirting the well camouflaged huts, got to the base of the scree slope with only one small mishap: a wild shot took a Portuguese through the forearm. They overran the small force left to mop up when their minefield in and around the dwellings had been set off, then a sheet of fire from the top killed a man and sent them to cover.

The mortars on Chiranga still bumped and crashed bombs around the battle perimeter. The men on the Pompue lay doggo; they were lucky that nobody was hit. The attackers on the hill were too close to their own positions for the mortar men to risk trying for them.

—◊—

The spur hung over them like medieval battlements, foreboding and grim. Pieter Visagie later told Geoff that he had tried to still the trembling in his legs, tried to forget how tired he was as he crawled under the overhang with Clem White close behind him. The muscles of his calves were knotted, his ankles ached, and his knees were grazed. A dozen areas of his body itched abominably from an inadvertent brush with the hellish fur of a buffalo-bean. They were still out of sight of Chiranga's observers. Now, they had got to a bulky buttress which would continue to cover them, if only they could find a way up. They were in deep shadow, here; only the top of the hill was still bathed in the gold of the westering sun. O'Donnell led them up a crack in the face of the cliffs, one that proved deeper and of greater cover value than was at first apparent. They could see no sign of movement: thus they hoped that they were likewise unseen.

They were only metres from the lip when the first mortars went off. Pieter had been looking back at White and they had both nearly lost their holds as muscles had spasmed in fright. Even the battle-hardened O'Donnell ducked hard into the rock face. However, when it was evident that the barrage was not directed at them, he realised that zero hour had arrived, like it or not. He called to Martins below him to shake it up; they would attack as soon as they crested the ridge. Visagie caught on too, and passed the message to White. They scrabbled at the rock, grunting as their tired arms strained.

Firing broke out on the far side of the hill. O'Donnell hoped that their own target, whatever it might turn out to be, would have its attention drawn away from them. With a heave, he rolled over the lip

112

and found himself in a slight hollow, his way blocked by a chest-high boulder. He scrambled to it and rose to peer over.

The eyes, that gazed widely into his own, were mud-coloured with yellowed whites. The two pairs locked for what seemed like minutes, then broke off as both men tried to bring their weapons to bear simultaneously. But only the FN fired; the AKs safety catch had been forgotten in the owner's haste. O'Donnell's bullets briefly stitched the man's face, then hit the two men behind him who were fumbling with their machine gun. One crumpled immediately, the other continued to stagger about after the FN mag was empty. Feeling a trifle sick, O'Donnell vaulted the boulder and struck the man down with the butt. Visagie and Martins joined him, gasping for breath.

Someone opened fire on them from another MG position and O'Donnell yelled, "Fire grenades!" at White and Visagie while he and Martins re-positioned the machine gun and found a RPG2 rocket launcher. The former two attached their grenade launchers and fitted blank mags, firing their first ever grenades within seconds of each other. Both went wide. They re-cocked and as they fired, O'Donnell screamed, "Down!"

An RPG2 rocket roared over their heads and terminated in a ball of flame at the foot of Serra Chiranga. With a gut-wrench of terror, O'Donnell knew that they had to get out, keep moving, or the next rocket would blow their inadequate cover apart, turning it into a beehive of rock-sliver shrapnel. White's grenade killed a machine gunner and wounded his mate. Visagie's grenade fell short, but three men scrambled from cover and began to run back along the hill top, one limping badly. A second later, O'Donnell broke cover after them, his men on his heels, his FN in one hand and the rocket launcher in the other. They weaved desperately as they ran.

The second rocket blew the gun position into fragments. The blast knocked the rear three men down and made O'Donnell stumble. Visagie staggered to his feet, weaving with shock. Ahead of him, on the blackened stubble, Martins' body writhed, the left side of his head blown away, a carotid artery spewing angrily to cover the indecent exposure of his brain. Visagie's stomach balled, convulsed, as he lurched about, more to hide from the sight than look for White. The latter was down, too, hit and gabbling in shock. He was chest down with head up and arms spread, his eyes searching for comprehension. O'Donnell and Visagie got to him simultaneously. He knew them, for his face cleared. With stunned shock, they saw him smile.

"Help me up, will you, my legs have gone numb."

Over his shoulders they could see what remained of his pelvis, just beyond his webbing belt. O'Donnell, swallowing hard, forced the bile back down his throat. Keeping himself low, he took Clem under the armpits and hauled him behind a boulder. It wasn't much, but it was all there was.

"His rifle!" snapped O'Donnell. Pieter scooped it up from where it had fallen and put it beside White. "Hold the fort for us here, Clem, okay? Cover us as we go. We'll be back as soon as we've sorted out these bastards! Go with God, lad!"

It made no sense at all but Clem nodded eagerly and the pain didn't hit him until they were forty metres away, heading for the crown of the hill.

―※―

Any moment now, Geoff would wake up from his bad dream and he would be able to reach over and pull Manuela to him, hide himself in her body, wrap the blanket of her warmth around him so that it blocked out the dread that edged in on him. But the dream kept on, a haze of pain and exhaustion, fear and regret. Damn, damn, damn with each breath, each heartbeat. Shit, shit, shit! If there were no Manuela, he would not be here, doing this. *Damn Manuela, damn Manuela* became the chant and rhythm of his hacking breath until she became a more real thing to hate than the enemy on the hill.

The mortars brought them to a shocked standstill. Francisco Mwaga's eyes were saucer-large, his mouth a thick, rubbery "o". His enormously wide shoulders made the Dreysa that he clutched tightly across them look like a child's toy. He and the white man stared at each other. One of the Portuguese began to mutter a prayer.

"*Depressa, amigos! Vamos imbora!*" Nourse yelled, turning up the ravine again, the adrenalin driving his legs like pistons up the path of the summer rains. A wayward liana around his ankles nearly tripped him but he recovered at the price of a grazed palm, then they were clawing their way up a series of small waterfalls, tottering through a shallow pool, slithering over waist-high boulders.

All hell broke loose on the top of the hill as the waiting Frelimo first defended one front then a second. Nourse and his men clambered desperately on with a hundred metres to go. They had almost made it when, over the rattle of rifles, bump of mortars and roar of rockets came a distant but unearthly, penetrating shriek of pain. It came again and again, and then it faded. Then they heard the whistle; short, long; short, long. They didn't have the strength to go any faster, they simply climbed on up, almost vertically, now. Geoff finally hauled his battered body around a pillar of water-worn rock then turned to relieve Francisco of the machine gun. The squat black man pulled away, holding on grimly.

"Don't worry, Boss, I got it okay! Jus' show me where to put for the shooting?"

"You stay here with it, Francisco," gasped Nourse, with sudden remorse that this loyal man had been caught up in this terrible fight against his own people. He had fired Nourse's hunting rifle for the pot in years past but would have no idea how to use the big weapon with its belt and tripod. In thirty seconds, Nourse set the weapon up and cocked it. Fuck it, but he felt good about keeping Francisco out of it.

"If Frelimo comes this way, hit them!"

He led the other two men flat out at an exhausted jog towards a jumble of rocks that spat flame in pin-prick winks and the occasional broader flash. He caught a glimpse of O'Donnell scampering for new cover, heading for the same target. A scattering of shots kicked up gravel at his feet. He hit the ground, sideways, followed by his men. The shots were coming from a nest at the rim, maybe a hundred metres away. One of his men rose, rifle in hand, towards the menace, cursing foully. He shrieked, falling back into the depression. His comrade crawled to him. Nourse wound on his grenade launcher and slipped two blanks in on top of his mag, clipped on a grenade and cocked it.

His brain told his finger to pull, all but triggering it.

Bounding from boulder to rock was a squat figure heading for the same target, Francisco, the Dreysa at his hip, the belt bouncing over his forearm. The gunners in the nest saw him, tried to swivel, then the weapon began to buck and wriggle in the powerful grasp and cases danced past Francisco's head. A man threw his hands up, his AK firing at the darkening sky; another hurled himself over the lip. A third died in the nest beside the machine gun that he had been feeding.

A minute later, Francisco had covered the intervening ground to join Nourse, unscathed. He put his mouth to Geoff's ear.

"Excuse, Boss, but I afraid by my own self!" Oddly, there were times when he would use his own brand of English, despite the fact that Nourse was fluent in Sena.

For a second, Geoff stared at him in wonder, and then abruptly turned back to his objective. He yelled at the Portuguese to follow him, but a gabble of cursing was the only reply, so he hauled the man to his feet by his shirtfront. They stared at each other as the anger built up in Nourse, squashing the fear in him. Even as he opened his hand to slap the pale face before him, the man seemed to feel the power of that anger and he quietened.

They left the depression at a weaving run, into a confused curtain of darting figures, streaks of fire-flash, and a thickening pall of gun smoke. Nourse fired the grenade at the crown of boulders and ejected the second blank, ready with live rounds again.

The sun straddled the horizon, showering the western sky with a multicoloured fan that eased from fire-orange through lemon to indigo. No-one noticed it, that it heralded the coming dark. The battle ended just as it set.

The central group of Frelimo broke cover suddenly, not as a counter-attack, but as a mass of individuals simultaneously bent on self-preservation. They erupted on all sides, about twenty of them, all firing their weapons at anything that moved. It was later deduced that Frelimo killed five men and wounded eight in those brief minutes, which was more than they had achieved in the whole of their preceding

116

defence. It was during this brief, vicious exchange that Nourse saw Muller fire at O'Donnell. Nourse and his two companions were very near the central boulders when Frelimo burst out. A wild shot skimmed the ankle of his boot; he went down on one knee, firing at the dashing figures. Behind him Francisco took a bullet along the forearm and the young mulatto soldier was hit in the left shoulder. Nourse stayed down, firing burst after burst at the scrambling enemy. Two dropped, another staggered, then they were gone. He reached for a new magazine. In turning, he saw Muller beyond the boulders, sighting at – what? Nourse followed the line, past the Irishman, and saw no target. The shot sounded, lost in the clatter of several others. O'Donnell flinched in the dash he had started back to the edge of the hill. The bullet mushroomed on the rock that had been O'Donnell's cover and whined into the twilight. When Nourse looked again, Muller was gone.

TWELVE

McNeil's breath sawed in his throat, his chest ached, and several parts of his front were embedded with thorns, planted with the force of his passage. He plunged along a footpath that wound along the Rio Pompue, heading upstream towards the sound of battle. Somewhat behind him trotted Borges with his arm in a sling, and a slim mulatto named Brandao, all that remained of Convoy *Nyati*. The latter two had by good fortune found each other in the dark. In the morning they had come across McNeil's tracks and eventually caught up with him.

First the mortars stopped their crumping and the sound of automatic rifles increased, interspersed with grenades, then, with the sun just above the black hills, the first definite lulls became apparent and the shots were only sporadic.

"It's over," thought Dan, stopping for breath. "Just mopping up, now." But who had won?

The other two caught up with him. When their breathing slowed sufficiently to allow them to speak, Borges asked: "You think we finished them, Lieutenant?"

He was pale. He had taken a bullet through the bicep and lost some blood. He held his FN in the hand of his uninjured arm. Brandao was unarmed, but he had relieved Dan of the radio. The latter took it from him and switched it on.

"Sure, we did," he said, by no means sure. "We'll ask them and see."

Surprisingly, de Groot came through almost at once.

"*Gondonga* to *Nyati*, strength five. Glad to hear you are okay. Here's the old bull of the *Pala-palas* for a word. Over."

"Listen, *Nyati*, where are you? Over." O'Donnell spoke in French.

"Be with you in about twenty minutes coming in from the north. What happened? Over."

"Later. Be careful as you come. We're on the flat-topped hill, but watch out for hunters. They've scattered in all directions and some will be coming your way. Out."

Even as McNeil slid the folded aerial into the canvas pouch, Borges grabbed his arm and hissed, "Someone come!"

The three men had no time to do anything but slink a few metres off the path into the dense undergrowth when several men came noisily down it. They made no attempt at concealment and a continuous moan was heard from a wounded man at the rear. It was still too light and Dan knew that they must be seen.

"Run!" he whispered fiercely, pushing Borges down the bank, but it was covered in riparian thicket and there was no way through, even on their bellies. McNeil cursed as he turned the AK on the startled enemy.

It seemed to McNeil that no-one retaliated; they were completely rattled. The scything arc of fire cut two of them down and sent the rest, screaming, scrambling for cover. Their determination must have been greater, for they had better fortune forcing their way through the thicket. A steady crashing indicated that the survivors were managing to circumvent the threat of Dan's fire. The noise of their retreat gradually faded away and only when it was silent again, did he call to his companions.

They set off warily up the path. The flat-topped hill loomed over them, a black silhouette against the last glow of pink. The guard that challenged them nearly got himself shot, then showed them the path up. In fifteen minutes they were joining O'Donnell. He had a deep cut on one cheekbone; his eyes were lined with dark shadows and pouchy from lack of sleep. McNeil scraped up a grin.

"Hello, Beautiful!"

"You're rather fetching, yourself," O'Donnell said with a wry smile, then added, bitterly, "There's plenty here not to joke about, Dan. We've lost a lot of men. We can't go on like this! Either we get proper

Air, or I'm resigning. I thought we could make it work, but by Christ, was I wrong! We can't keep creeping about in the bush, like this, avoiding the Portuguese army and the local populace and still be expected to get at Frelimo in their bases without proper air cover!" He struck a fist into the other palm for emphasis.

Around where they stood in the last defended circle of rocks, men sorted out rations from what Frelimo had left behind; mostly cassava tubers, a bit of maize meal and some fly-blown meat that they threw away. Some cleaned wounds and bound them. They prepared for another night on the ground.

O'Donnell was elsewhere, staring off into the gloom, looking undecided for the first time since McNeil had known him. More than that, a little lost.

"Who of our bunch got whacked?" McNeil peered into the fading light for familiar faces.

"White." O'Donnell shrugged off the mood that gripped him with an effort. "Only White, thank Christ. Altogether, we lost, um, your nine, six of mine, six of Theo's, that's twenty-one! Not counting the two of mine that deserted, it still makes a nasty percentage."

"And just where is Theo?"

"There was a mortar nest on that hill over there. Chiranga, it's called. Theo took some men to make sure that they don't start shelling the shit out of us. They know exactly where we are! And I don't intend sleeping anywhere else. I'm pretty sure they didn't take anything heavy with them, but we had to make sure of the mortars. Theo should be back any moment – ah! Here he is."

Right on cue, Theunissen trudged out of the dark, followed by Muller, Visagie and Nourse, lugging two mortar tubes and their base plates. Theo unslung a rucksack of bombs.

"Hello, Dan. Glad to see that you made it, boy. Ryan, there were a few more bombs we couldn't manage. We tipped them down the *kranz*. Did you get onto old Texeira?"

"Ah, yes." O'Donnell rubbed a tired hand over his eyes. "He says he'll pull us out tomorrow night. Back to base. Next night, Beira. Couple of days to get pissed and liberate our spawn, then back to work. He says."

Theo threw his head back, as if to laugh, but he didn't.

O'Donnell went on: "So we move over to him at our leisure, in the morning. He says that he found a track out of Guro that led him quite a way back towards us. So much so that he could hear the mortars, so we won't have far to walk."

"Then why didn't the bastard come and give us a hand?" Muller asked in his booming voice, a question that everyone else would have kept to themselves to quietly speculate on, later.

"How do you know he wasn't on his way and that I stopped him?" O'Donnell's eyes turned hard.

"And was he?" demanded Muller, before he could stop himself, starting to tremble with anger.

"Take care, soldier, how you speak about an officer before another officer!" The Irishman was facing Muller squarely, now, hands empty, seemingly relaxed. "Now, is there a complaint that you'd like to take up with the Major?"

But Muller wasn't taken in by the quiet voice.

"*Nein, Herr Kapitan*! Sir!" He peeled off an exaggerated salute, did an about-turn and goose-stepped off into the dark.

—◆—

It was only the following day, as they did a recce amongst the booby-trapped huts to see the best way of detonating the whole devilish trap, that Nourse had a chance to talk to McNeil without being overheard. The night had passed uneventfully, but a sharp watch had been kept. They had heard only one burst of firing, away to the north, that was assumed to be accidental, or a brush with an animal by a Frelimo on the retreat.

McNeil found a tripwire concealed in the grass. He gingerly attached a length of cord to it, and then they took cover amongst the boulders at the foot of the cliff.

"And you're sure that Muller didn't see you? I mean, he doesn't know that you saw him pop a shot at Ryan?"

"Pretty sure," Nourse wiped the sweat from his forehead. It was not yet eight o'clock but already uncomfortably hot and Nourse said that he was prepared to put money on it that, although there was not a cloud in the sky at present, there would be a thunderstorm before the day was out. He added: "And I'm also sure that O'Donnell didn't see Muller shoot at him. Should we warn him? Muller may try it again."

McNeil shook his head. "I don't think that he'll get another opportunity. And if Ryan knew, he'd get rid of him. I feel it's better, somehow, if we have Muller where we can keep an eye on him. Anyway, just maybe you imagined it."

"Do you think he might be tied in with this van Rooyen business?" The thought had only just occurred to him. McNeil shook his head, this time with uncertainty.

"I haven't a clue. It does seem possible, I suppose. Shitting hell, I just wish that I hadn't got tangled up in this cloak and dagger business!"

"Me, too!" Nourse said with feeling. "I wish I wasn't even in Mozambique!"

"Never mind, Geoff. Ryan says he's proud of you. All of you. Especially your black friend, what's his name? Mwaga? I just feel sorry for him when we have to pull out and Frelimo hear what he's been up to. They'll stuff his balls in his mouth and cut out his liver, man!"

"*Ja*, I know!" Geoff paled at the thought.

"By the way, I got a message through to our contact in Beira. Told them we'd seen van Rooyen, calling himself Sanderson, definitely working with Barros." McNeil gave a vicious tug on the cord. With an ear-numbing roar, the hut and its immediate surrounds disintegrated. Debris rained down.

By nine in the morning, each man showed a half-moon of sweat under his armpit and the sun began to tighten its thermometric thumbscrew in the cloudless sky. Heat waves shimmered over the sheetrock outcrops. They laid the last stones over the bodies of their comrades; some without remorse, but most with at least a certain feeling of regret that they should be so devoid of ceremony or epitaph. O'Donnell carried a list of their names; Major Texeira would pass it to Barros to inform next of kin and to pay indemnity.

They moved out, slowly, but alert, their two badly wounded men on improvised stretchers, the Portuguese with the shattered shoulder and the mulatto with the broken femur. It took them only four hours to reach Texeira. Two of his guards guided them in.

"My God, is this all that's left of you?" Texeira gazed at their depleted ranks with pain in his eyes. Thirty-three men were left of fifty-four, of whom there were six walking wounded and two serious casualties. Texeira was camped at the foot of a low hill at the end of a long-disused track, the vehicles well covered with cut foliage. He claimed that there was no human being within ten kilometres of them. He gathered the officers, Nourse and Schulman around him. They gave him verbal reports: McNeil of the ambush, O'Donnell and Theunissen of the attack on the flat-topped hill.

"...and we were damned lucky to break them up, Major. We estimate twenty or so dead, the same amount wounded. Never again will I allow myself or my men to get caught up in a fiasco like this! No air; we sneak off to find the enemy, sneak back to base again. Major, we should be chasing those bastards to hell! A plane or a chopper should be over them right now with us hot on their heels. Does Barros really think he can make an iota of difference to the outcome of this war with this outfit as it is? And I bet you are going to tell me that Barros won't even send us a chopper for our wounded!" O'Donnell rounded on the little major, a vicious curl to his lip. Texeira eyed the Irishman with unexpected coolness.

"No helicopter, Captain, but we leave right now."

"What, no cover of darkness? No protection against the Portuguese army?" McNeil saw that O'Donnell's temper was starting to slip, but something in the little man's level gaze kept it in check.

"We leave now because we have two urgent hospital cases and because we have no helicopter. We have a good chance of not even bumping into the army, but we shall bluff them, if we do. We had better get going; I think there's a storm coming." He glanced at the grey smudges in the sky, gathering over the mountains.

O'Donnell slowly unballed his fists and saluted. "Yes, Sir!"

In half an hour, the vehicles were loaded and moving. The only other vehicles that they passed, beyond Guro, were two Unimogs, convoyed with three loaded cotton trucks. Without mishap, the band of men of Barros's army was back in base by midnight.

From there, the wounded, including Francisco Mwaga, were rushed to Barros's hunting camp on the Mungari River, where a doctor and two nurses, flown in from Beira, were awaiting them. The rest of the O'Donnell's men and some of the Mozambicans were trucked to Beira the following night. A skeleton staff was left at the base to maintain it in readiness for future operations.

THIRTEEN

It was raining again. Torrents of that kind that coined the label 'cloud burst'. Somewhat leaner, wiser and more battered than the last time they were there, the mercenaries were once again quartered in the sumptuous Hotel Zambeze. All, that was, except Arnold Sharpe, who had wanted to be a witness to history in the making, and Clement White, who had once risked prison for his fellow man, then died, trying to kill him. Nourse said as much to McNeil.

They were seated over beers at a corner table in a rather dirty Chinese restaurant off the Rua Correia de Brito. The pavement was awash and the assorted tables and chairs, left where they stood, were warped and cracked from the weather. Inside, the furniture was in no better state of repair: the concrete floor was cracked and littered with cigarette butts and the crumbs of hand-broken bread. An elderly black man asked them to lift their legs as he swept beneath their table, a white man got up to expectorate out of the open door into the rain then went back to his plate of *camerao piri-piri*. A sad *fado* crooned from a radio behind a crock of yellow-shelled hard-boiled eggs. Nourse peeled one such egg and commented to McNeil:

"They boil these in tea, you know, to get them this colour."

"They look bloody awful," Dan returned, tapping one of them on the edge of the table, "but they taste the same as any other egg. When's our bloody *skof* coming? And, more to the point, where is our bloody contact?"

The trucks had arrived the previous night. Still in combat rig, they had slipped up in the Barros's private elevator to their previous apartments. Da Silva had briefly met them as they arrived, impeccably dressed in a light suit, even though it was four in the morning. He had told O'Donnell that Barros was away, but would return in time to attend a meeting with O'Donnell that evening. O'Donnell had merely nodded and brushed by him, in no mood for mere underlings. He was not happy with the situation and his men were waiting for him to have it out with Barros, or the elusive Sanderson.

Nourse had seen no sign of Manuela; neither had he managed to find out where she was or when she might return. He had accompanied Dan to Johnny's Place at eleven o'clock, to find a coded note in the cistern, as Dan had arranged per radio, three days ago.

"Chin Won, noon," it boiled down to. As Nourse knew the Chin Won, they went there immediately they lost the ever-present tail, firstly by separating, then McNeil, whom the unfortunate youth had chosen to follow, had lost him in a maze of people at the market.

If the Chin Won was unsavoury in appearance, it still had a reputation for excellent food. McNeil's dozen and a half prawns arrived a minute before Nourse's sweet and sour pork, pork chop-suey and bamboo shoots. They were busy stuffing themselves on this and fried rice when Cecile Cradock came skipping in out of the bucketing rain. She shed a light raincoat and shook the water from her hair, grinned at their astonished faces, then turned to watch the man that came in behind her. He was some twenty years her senior; he was tall, stooping, dressed in a dark poloneck sweater and dark slacks. They had both met him very briefly: Morné Brand. It was with some shock that they recognised Cecile, her appearance being totally unexpected. However, as Geoff guessed from the look on his face, she had seldom been far from Dan's thoughts of late. She was in flared blue denim slacks and a windcheater. She was laughing at Brand about the rain.

He took her hand and led her to a table near to that shared by McNeil and Nourse, but the two pairs ignored each other completely after a first cursory glance. They dropped their voices, as people are wont to do in foreign places when suddenly confronted by people who might understand them. There were very few tourists in Beira at this time of year.

All went through with the charade.

"Excuse me, waiter!" That much was obvious to the waiter from the gestures that accompanied the words. Brand persisted in English. "Do you have a menu?" The waiter, a black youth with an ivory grin, frowned. Brand repeated his request with his hands held in front of him, like a book. The lad's face lit up. No, there was no menu, but they had prawns, crab or shrimp, grilled, fried, piri-piri, sweet and sour, chop-suey; or beef, pork, goat or chicken, grilled, fried, piri-piri, sweet and sour, chop-suey; or barracuda or crayfish or oysters or Brand held up both hands in surrender.

"Excuse me," he called across to McNeil and Nourse, "You appear to be Rhodesians. Do you have any idea what this fellow is saying?"

Nourse pushed back his chair with only a very slight show of annoyance, and came across. "We're South African," he said, "I speak a little Portuguese. Can I help you?"

"Thank goodness for that!" Brand smiled, half rising from his seat and extending his hand. "I'm Hanekom; this is my wife, Jean. We are also from down south. We are spending a couple of weeks on holiday here in Beira before I have to go to the Islands to do some research work on the fish there." Brand indicated his table. "As you see, we have a language problem. We would be grateful if you would join us, that is —"

"I think it would be better if you joined us, seeing that we are already established, Mr. Hanekom —"

"The Professor," said Cecile, pointedly, getting gracefully to her feet, "and I, would be delighted to, Mr. er..."

"Nourse. Geoff Nourse. Dan McNeil, meet Professor and Mrs. Hanekom." Nourse thought that he saw Dan wince. He grinned, rather enjoying it all.

When they were all settled and a plate of crabs lay between Brand and Cecile with a cold bottle of *vinho verde*, they slipped in detailed reports between the things to do in Beira when on holiday; bracketed instructions with the mysteries of the colour changes of parrot fishes.

They had flown up directly their man in Beira had picked up Dan's radio message saying that they had seen van Rooyen, alias Sanderson.

It seemed that van Rooyen was closely connected to Barros, if not selling out to him directly. Brand felt that their best chance of getting at him was here in Beira. He did not explain to Nourse and McNeil what exactly "getting at him" might mean; for they were little more than observers, but neither of them was under any illusion that van Rooyen was a threat to their country and as such might have to be removed. Nourse made up his mind that he would have nothing to do with the removal if it meant killing him. Empty-gutted fear filled him at the thought.

"What's so important about this guy?" Geoff asked. Brand's face gave him a clue as it seemed to blanch and then tried to keep his expression casual. His smile was a grimace.

"I've only said he's a traitor. But unless we get him back under control, he can and doesn't care if he does, detonate the whole of Mozambique, and as a result, the whole subcontinent. I beg you to believe me! We have got to get him!"

There wasn't much more to say except to arrange a contact at the slightest possibility of a meeting between van Rooyen and Barros, or, indeed, any sign of the man. McNeil was slipped a couple of objects they were told were miniature transmitters that were to be activated if van Rooyen was spotted and there was no time to pass on details. Left on, Brand would be able to follow them. Several flicks on and off would mean that they had not yet left the hotel but a message might be found under the washbasin, if there was time. It was the best that they could do in the circumstances, as even McNeil could not transmit Morse. Later, they found that the transmitters resembled pens.

The Chinese proprietor himself served them, seeing that his customers were tourists. Replacing the waiter, he had taken their orders through Nourse as he seemed to know him from previous visits to Beira and spoke Portuguese to him. Puzzled, Geoff thought that he remembered that the old man also spoke passable English. Yet he went so far as to ask what Brand had said when he asked for pepper, as if he had no knowledge of the language. Nourse frowned, but forgot to remark on it when the man was out of earshot.

They broke up when Brand and Cecile left, with loud, cheerful promises to meet again, sometime before the couple left Beira.

"What did he mean by 'getting at' van Rooyen?" Geoff asked as he and McNeil downed another quiet beer or two. "Surely not kill him? I couldn't do that! Not in cold blood."

Dan smiled. "You probably would if you had to." Geoff watched as a hard expression took over McNeil's face and thought that Dan could be somewhat more ruthless than he.

"As an officer in the Congo, I once executed a deserter from my own group whom we caught in the act of looting and rape. No choice. We couldn't lug him about as a prisoner. There was another guy …" He didn't finish, but Geoff shuddered to think of having to make that sort of decision. A change of subject seemed a good idea.

"Hey, you really do fancy that Cecile bird, don't you? I saw the way you looked daggers at Brand!" He saw also that he had touched a nerve and regretted his statement. But Dan smiled and shook his head.

"You observant shit. Yes, I like her. I was surprised to realise how galled I was to see Cecile in Brand's company. They are staying at the same hotel, and in the same room!" Geoff knew he would be thinking: The same bed? He supposed that Dan could not but suspect that their relationship might be more than just master spy and assistant. Dan's mouth twisted, sardonically. Geoff thought he was trying to tell himself not to be an idiot, even though the girl had really got under his skin.

"What about your piece of Portuguese fluff? Have you seen her yet?" Dan asked.

Geoff was worried. He shook his head. Where was Manuela? Why was there no message? Of course, that damned da Silva was behind it, somehow. He had expected retribution in one form or another, but not her disappearance. Barros wouldn't allow anything to happen to his daughter, he told himself.

FOURTEEN

It was only the next day that Geoff heard from Jan de Groot what he, Visagie and Muller had been up to when they heard the horrific news. Despite, or indeed, perhaps because of, their fight, Pieter Visagie found himself in the company of Helmut Muller. The German was going out of his way to be friendly and Pieter, Jan thought, was still feeling the aftermath of the shock of the ugly deaths of Clem White and the Portuguese, Martins, so he was not averse to a little friendliness. He, Muller and de Groot were walking somewhat unsteadily back from a dim back-street bar to their hotel, tailed by a mulatto youth that they'd invited back with them for a drink.

"What would you have done if we had split up, you silly bastard?" Pieter asked him in Afrikaans. Jan smiled.

"*Senhor?*" The lad grinned.

Muller led them up the steps of the Maritime Museum. The youth hung back at the steps. He wasn't worried; there was no other exit for his charges. But he himself would not be allowed inside, for he wore no shoes, he indicated by signs.

It was, in fact, a little museum of extreme interest to anyone delving into the early history of Manica and Sofala. Exhibits with yellowed, typed labels, proclaimed the glories of the Navigators, starting with Pero da Covilha, who, as early as about 1489, is reputed to have reached as far south as Sofala and started the myth of the fabulous riches that were supposed to have been the source of the gold for King Solomon's Temple. Then followed Vasco da Gama, Bartholomeu Dias, Pedro Alvares Cabral. The museum staff did have the grace to mention the Arab slave traders of up to a thousand years before that. The fly-smutted labels were in both Portuguese and English, but Jan and Pieter hardly read a word. Muller certainly did not bother.

"Look at the dates of antiquity," Muller said in a low voice and then went for value in his own scale of preference – diamonds, gold, silver, ivory, and other gems. "I once knew a fence in Sydney. He knew what to look for and he gave me a few tips on it. That knowledge will come in handy, here."

"What the fuck are you on about, Helmut?" Jan asked.

Scattered around were four armed security guards, lounging in doorways or slumped in chairs. They rarely glanced at the visitors. It was Visagie who voiced a thought before Muller could plant the seed by suggestion.

"What a dozy bunch!" Pieter watched a guard whose eyes were shutting for several seconds at a time. "We could stuff our pockets full of those coins over there and he wouldn't even notice!"

"So, what's stopping you, then?" Muller asked, casually. Jan began to suspect what Muller was on about. He thought he was joking, concocting a scenario.

"Because, even if there was only one chance in a hundred of getting shot at by these Porcos, I wouldn't chance it," Visagie grinned. "Be a different thing if I had my FN or a G3 to point at them!"

"You'd be too shit scared to use it on them if they tried anything," supplied Jan, starting to take interest as they stood over a case of gold inlaid flintlock pistols. "There's a lot of junk in here, but there is stuff that must be worth a bit, if one knew what to take. Look at this set of silverware, over here! Must be over two hundred pieces of the stuff they've pulled from wrecks and whatnot. And that ivory; there must be a couple of tons of the stuff …"

"Fit that in your getaway car, Jan!" Muller laughed. "What you want to go for are those ceremonial swords with the gold and jewels and crap, those ornate snuff-boxes and…"

"Why scrimp? Don't fuck about; just bring some commandeered Army Bedfords, ten tonners and load 'em up. Have the whole gang in on it. Ransack Beira; do all the banks, all the jewellers. Put the stuff on a Dak and Rafe Schulman can fly it home for us!" Jan did a little dance which inspired one of the guards to shift his weight from the door to his feet and actually take his hands out of his pockets.

"Watch it, we're surrounded." Pieter raised his hands in surrender. The others laughed.

Just then, there was a stir from the main hallway. A piping voice argued with the deeper tones of a guard. Another guard was called. A slightly excited chatter ensued for a minute then one of the guards came over.

"You must go hotel," he stuttered uncertainly in English, "Go to hotel, yes?"

"No. No go hotel, now," returned Visagie evenly.

"Oh, *filho de puta*!" Son of a whore! The man raised his eyes to Fatima in heaven to help protect him from stubborn, obstinate foreigners. He tried again. "Go hotel, now. You amigo falling hotel. Falling dead. Amigo, he falling dead, maybe. Now, you go hotel?"

FIFTEEN

He was dead, alright.

Running, they got there at the same time as a grubby, cream-coloured van with a red cross on the sides. Already, a crowd that must have constituted half of Beira had arrived. Most of the rest of their band had gathered at the side of the shattered body, having got there through the crowd by virtue of their generally larger stature.

Both arms and legs were broken, the body was curiously flattened and the head had burst.

Several people there were already violently sick, Nourse amongst them. McNeil seemed to drop into a boxer's crouch as if to ward off an attack. Ryan O'Donnell and he had been close friends. They owed each other their lives several times over, both from their Congo days and through several adventures in South America. Closer than most brothers. Now all that remained of the strong, shrewd Irishman was a flattened, shattered corpse. Slowly Dan raised his eyes up the face of the towering hotel, knowing that O'Donnell must have fallen from the top.

But men like O'Donnell never fall.

"Christ!" No prayer, the word exploded from his lips. "C'mon!"

His heavy hand nearly wrenched Nourse from his feet. Dumbly, he followed McNeil's headlong run for the entrance, wiping the puke from his mouth with the back of his hand as he ran. Dan hammered the buttons of the lift, cursing until it dropped the one floor from the dining room. When they leaped in, de Groot, Visagie, Muller and Blair were with them. The lit floor numbers flicked by, painfully slowly. At length, the cage halted at the top; the doors slid open.

They leaped out straight into the trap. Theunissen was down on his knees, hands to his face, blood seeping between his fingers. In front of him stood da Silva, covering him with an automatic pistol. It shook, slightly, but da Silva's voice carried conviction.

"Keep still or I will shoot him!"

They froze, stupidly, in the middle of the room. Two men with G3s at rapid fire edged in from either flank. It took them several seconds to recognize Ribeiro and Campos. How these two had found their way back from the hills beyond Maringue was more than their shocked brains could fathom.

Only the move from these two men saved da Silva's life, however, for Geoff saw that McNeil would have moved in on him, regardless of his weapon. The tableau stood, atrophied. Then Theo Theunissen staggered to his feet. When he took his hands from his face, they saw a flattened mash of a nose plastered over a split lip. The grey hair hung in rats tails around his ears. His voice came as a croak.

"This bastard…" Ribeiro got a thumb pointed in his direction, "jumped me as I came in …. Ryan … was sitting on the parapet, arguing … with da Silva … Ryan turned to me … da Silva jumped him, he … slipped … fell …"

Their imaginations laid it out for them. Da Silva's cry helped to deaden their doubts.

"He wanted more money for you, said you couldn't fight with no air support. He threatens me, understand? I get pretty mad, jump forward. I dunno what he think I gonna do, but he twist away and then he's a gone, over the edge. Then this son of a bitch, he tries to kill me and Ribeiro hit him with his gun."

"I am going to kill you, one day, you syphilitic whore!" Theo was clenching and unclenching his sinewy fingers in a strangling movement. Again McNeil all but leaped at the Portuguese, but the G3s waved him back.

"You are through, you bastards," Dan grated through clenched teeth, his face deathly pale. "We quit, as of now. You go fight your own goddamned battles and I hope Frelimo sticks a mortar right up your arse!" In his rage, he forgot the necessity to search for van Rooyen.

Geoff and the rest of them turned with him towards the elevator. It was not the threat of the automatic rifles that stopped them in their tracks, but the appearance of Manuel Barros and the man called Sanderson. The businessman was not looking well; he was leaden under his tan. His usual golden smile briefly appeared, but lacked conviction. Sanderson, too, looked tense. It was Barros who spoke first, rapidly in Portuguese to da Silva, asking what had happened. Da Silva answered somewhat harshly, which seemed to Nourse to be rather out of character compared to his usual subservient manner to his father-in-law. Barros nodded without replying.

"I am extremely sorry that this has happened. A monumental tragedy. A very good man if I am to believe a quarter of what Major Texeira has reported. That he should go in this tragic manner! I shall immediately have his body looked after." He reached for a telephone that stood in a niche in the wall. He murmured some instructions into it, then continued quietly, waving aside the weapons of Ribeiro and Campos. "Now, gentlemen, would you please come through to my rooms, we have some strategy to discuss. Are you badly hurt?" he asked Theo, who shook his head. "Then we shall expect you in five minutes when you have washed that cut. And José has found you a plaster." He was turning away and da Silva was reaching for Theunissen's arm, when a voice froze them all.

"Don't move, you Portuguese bastards!" Rafe Schulman crouched at the top of the stairwell, cradling a revolver over his elbow, sighting squarely on Barros's chest. There was a stunned silence, then Rafe's voice grated on.

"Rye and I were discussing this whole deal, an hour ago. He was quitting. He was determined not to lose any more men in this fiasco that you call a war. No Air, no efficient officers, dodging the army, no medi-vac. His mind was made up, he was quitting! And there's something funny about his death, too! When he left me, he was coming to tell you his decision, but now he's dead! I don't believe he fell off that balcony!"

That Schulman had all but worshipped O'Donnell was obvious, but his last statement lacked conviction. He could not be sure of what had happened, even if events did not make sense. He looked to Theunissen for support, but the latter swallowed hard and shook his head.

"If I hadn't seen it with my own eyes …" he croaked, at last, "I wouldn't have believed it, either."

Schulman seemed to slump in defeat for a moment, then he straightened.

"I'm still quitting. I'm still with what Ryan said. The reasons haven't gone away." He appealed to his mates; "Who's with me? Dan?"

Yes, Geoff thought, McNeil would be for quitting. Three times in the last five minutes, he had almost gone into open rebellion. Most of the others were only waiting on his cue, but the consequences regarding the obviously vital matter of losing contact with the man called Sanderson were too terrible to contemplate, if Brand were to be believed.

"We agreed to fight until we either won, or Mr. Barros agreed that it was useless to continue," McNeil heard himself saying, "so, I'm staying."

Several of the South Africans looked at him in disbelief. Blair, the Englishman did more that that.

"Fuck that! I'm with you, Rafe. The sooner we get out of this god-forsaken fuckin' country, the better."

Nourse tried to back McNeil with his mind while his heart was siding with Rafe; he couldn't speak at all.

The whole situation was like a coiled, angry mamba, right then. The rifles covered them; the burly Ribeiro was steady, but Campos shook, his tongue flickering nervously over his dry lips. Muller and Visagie were near breaking point and both made little movements of tightly held explosiveness. Shaking with anger, Blair continued to berate Barros, while the latter said nothing, although the muscles of his jaw worked under the tension. Only Jan de Groot appeared to be calm, his dark eyes summing everything up, calculating.

"Put that gun down, man, or I'll have you shot down!" Sanderson spoke for the first time. Stalemate, it seemed, as Rafe didn't take any notice. Da Silva, keeping well back against the wall, but with reasonable calm as he was not in line with Schulman's steady aim, told the two riflemen to hold their fire until he gave the order.

Then, with a blur of movement behind him, Rafe pitched forward out of the stairwell. The revolver in his hand remained unfired as he stretched out on the hall floor. Manuela stepped around him to take the weapon from his hand. She handed it to da Silva but retained the revolver with which she had hit Rafe.

"Is it too late, José?" She asked her brother-in law in rapid Portuguese. She had not even glanced at her father or Nourse. Da Silva swallowed.

"I think so. Some want to leave. We may persuade some to stay, but not all and we need the numbers. We must hold the sons of bitches."

"Okay." She swung around on the confused group of men, levelling her revolver at them. When she told them not to move and to keep their hands clasped behind their necks, none of them doubted that she would shoot if anyone made any suspicious gestures. Both McNeil and Nourse had forgotten to activate their transmitter pens that Brand had given them and it was only when they were being herded into the Barros private elevator that McNeil got the chance.

All, in their own ways, had demanded explanations, but Manuela had silenced them with a wave of her handgun. They all remembered her reputation as an army para instructor. Nourse was thrown into anguished confusion, not believing that he could not get through to the girl with whom he had been falling in love. Manuela had shut him up with a cold glance and a sneering twist of her lip. Barros was obviously not in control; his normally handsome face was twisted in anguish and pain as he looked at his ruthless daughter and turned away to leave the room. Sanderson watched events with a deadpan face, not involved, but seemingly more relaxed now that matters were under control.

Blair was told to drag the unconscious Schulman into the elevator. It was spacious enough so that the mercenaries at one side could still be covered by the riflemen from the other. The South Africans made ominous rumblings, but once again it was Blair, pale with fury, who stepped forward to demand what the hell they thought they were up to. This time it was da Silva who lashed out with his pistol. Blair stepped back smartly to avoid it, but it served to silence the mutterings. They now glared at their captors in bitter resentment, assuming that they were being herded away because of their proposed desertion. Because of his involvement with Manuela, Nourse was not taking all the facts into account and probably McNeil was closer to the mark when he muttered that Barros was no longer in charge, that somebody, somehow, had a hold over him. That made Geoff wonder. Van Rooyen? What forces did he have at his command? That da Silva and Manuela were a part of that force seemed obvious, but unfortunately Brand had not seen fit to tell them about other possible allies that the turncoat South African might have gained.

They waited in the corridor of the basement while some handcuffs were sought. These were applied in harsh fashion by da Silva, and then they were all escorted into a large windowless storeroom. It was air-conditioned, however. They were given mattresses and blankets and buckets by the grinning pair, Campos and Ribeiro. The door was shut and locked. Either of the two was a constant guard from then on, covering them when the door was opened to feed them or allow the removal of their toilet buckets. Never once were they given any chance to turn the tables, although they were tensed for it at every opportunity. They were there for nearly a week.

SIXTEEN

The day after Beira was rocked by the news of the tragic death of that unfortunate holiday maker, Mr. Ryan O'Donnell, another foreigner was found dead on the beach at Macuti, near the wreck of the coaster, *Willem Eggers*. He had been staying at the Motel Estoril. It appeared that he had drowned during his early morning swim. He was identified by motel staff, according to his South African passport, as one William Simpson. In fact, he had been born Charles Howard Summers.

If two other visitors had not been alerted by this mishap they, too, might have met an untimely end.

It had started out by being a lovely day. Brand was up early enough to catch the sun rising over the sea, while Cecile lay hovering between sleep and wakefulness, missing out on the splendour. Their single beds were pushed close together, for appearances, but there was nothing physical between them. Brand, however, could admit to himself to a fatherly fondness for the girl. It had been some time since he had personally been in the field in this capacity, but there was always unnecessary strain if field agents were incompatible.

Brand was worried. He had to assume that his two amateurs were still at the hotel but had seen their quarry. It was thirty-six hours since O'Donnell's death and the activation of the transmitters, but Brand was none the wiser as to what had happened, except that the transmitters were together in the basement. He paced the balcony. The phone rang at their bedside. Cecile sat up to answer it, becoming instantly alert.

De Souza's voice said: "Summer's gone and winter's coming on." He disconnected.

Cecile repeated the message to Brand. Summers had disappeared from his motel. This was a shock: covers were quite possibly being blown. They needed to meet with de Souza within the hour to hear if he had more news. Yesterday, de Souza had been in contact to report that someone answering van Rooyen's description had been seen by the Barros's personal servants in the upper suites. There was no way of getting at him except by direct assault on the Barros's apartments. The operation had to be clean and quiet, so he could not risk it. Yesterday, too, Summers had reported that he had followed Barros's son-in-law, José da Silva, to a rather scruffy restaurant off the Rua Correia de Brito and was in time to see him ushered into a back office by the old Chinese owner of the Chin Won. That had raised some confusing questions. It was Summers's opinion that the visit was not social and not on hotel business.

If the Chinese were in the game, they were on opposite sides to Barros but could well be bedfellows of van Rooyen. Then Barros and van Rooyen would not be co-operating! Everything pointed to Barros being no communist; he had spent millions trying to hold on to Mozambique as a white-dominated state where his own empire would retain its value. No Chinese lackey, this Barros.

Brand stood on the balcony, his mind buzzing with the permutations and trying to decide what they should do and what had happened to Summers. His adrenalin was already in circulation , when the room's door swung open without warning. A black man with an automatic shotgun stepped into the room and swung the weapon towards the beds where Cecile was still sitting. Perhaps it was the sight of the empty one that made him hesitate. Brand yelled Cecile's name and threw himself backwards. There was a shattering roar and the glass of the sliding doors fragmented over his head. He thought that he had had it then because all he had between himself and the next shot was a small table that he hugged against his chest as he came up against the balcony rails. The nightmare gun came through the gap, looking for him. He flung the table in a pathetically futile gesture of defiance and hardly heard the two muted coughs from the bedroom. The shotgun discharged again, but now into the morning sky, and the man collapsed onto the railings in an untidy heap.

Feeling nauseous, Brand got to his feet. He took a few deep breaths, his eyes on Cecile as she unscrewed the silencer from her .25 Beretta. He nodded, in approval and gratitude. He went to kneel at their attacker's side and felt his pulse. He wasn't dead, yet, but as far as Brand could tell – and he had experience in such things – it would be only a matter of minutes before the hesitant heart stopped. The man was mouthing something, but it was in his own tongue and Brand, who was adept at lip-reading the several languages that he could speak, could not understand. The man was in tatty grey jeans and a faded black tee-shirt. A deft feel through his pockets revealed a roll of notes and no identity. Also, he seemed to have been on some drug; his pupils were dilated. He shuddered and gave a long sigh that turned out to be his last.

Shouting from adjacent rooms and pounding footsteps indicated the imminent need of charades. Cecile cried hysterically into the phone that they'd been attacked by a madman. She kept the pistol in view; she had a permit for it for self-protection, but not for the silencer. Brand swiftly hid any items not in keeping with a professor of ichthyology. People surged into the room, shouting, demanding. Brand added his own shocked and quavering voice to the noise. He wanted the comfort of his pipe, feeling too much at the mercy of the fickle fates for the peace of his normally cool, commanding mind.

—⁂—

That same day in late April, 1974, it was announced on the radios and televisions of the world that there had been a change of government in Portugal. It appeared that the public hero, General Spinola, was to head the new government. For the first time in years, people throughout the Portuguese-speaking world were free to discuss their country's politics without thousands of informers passing the word along to the dreaded D.G.S. This, the Department of State Security, was almost immediately disbanded; hundreds of its officers were imprisoned and hundreds of others were beaten up by a populace that had for years lived in fear of an organisation whose tentacles had reached everywhere.

Some, however, thought it was all a farce behind which the forces of Communism were at work, slowly separating the ducklings from the safety of their mother, so that the big red fox could gobble them up in her own sweet time.

SEVENTEEN

John Alistair was a freelance journalist of international repute, but it was the first time that he had visited Mozambique. It took only two days before the D.G.S. found out who he was and apprehended him in Lourenço Marques. They were very polite. What was he doing in this country? No, they were afraid that they could not believe that he was here to cover the war. The war was not news any more and, besides, the only journalists still writing about it were being escorted by the army. Why had he not applied for permission to be taken to the war zone? For six hours they were sorry that they did not believe him. Then some soldiers arrived with a colonel and a few curt words were exchanged. The colonel apologised to him and told him that he was free to leave. By now he was reluctant to do so as he sensed that something extraordinary was afoot. Although he spoke a little Spanish, it was not enough to enable him to fathom the excited babble of Portuguese that washed around him. He dashed to the nearest large shop and demanded to be told what had happened. He learned of the coup, of Spinola, and how things would be different from now on.

"Will it be a change for the better?" asked Alistair as he mopped his balding head for the umpteenth time that day. The short squat woman who spoke English looked around, out of habit, to see who might be listening, then shrugged.

"Some say that the Communists in Portugal Continental are strong. If they get power there, then I think that here in Mozambique we are finish. Is possible, I don't know." She shrugged again, and, she being white, Alistair assumed that she meant that the whites in Mozambique would be *finish*.

Someone shouted something from outside and the woman and other customers poured out into the street to watch. Alistair joined them, keeping close to the woman, demanding in her ear above the noise; "What's happening?"

"The army are arresting the D.G.S. It is good, the sons of bitches! And my father-in-law will be arrested, too, for he is also a D.G.S. man. Ha-ha!" The last was said with much glee and her two chins shook as she laughed. They watched as the men who had so lately been questioning the journalist were edged into waiting cars and driven away. Excitement buzzed all around him.

He ground his teeth in frustration as he walked back to the Tivoli Hotel where he was staying, noting the happiness on some faces and the concern on others. He wanted to get journalistically involved; interview people around him, but he had another mission. As he turned towards the entrance, a voice at his elbow spoke.

"Take the taxi, please, *Senhor* Alistair."

He glanced around instantly, but could not make out, of the throng around him, who had spoken. However, he was not greatly surprised. He had only been told that he would be contacted; sometime, somewhere. A black Peugeot with a lime green roof waited at the kerb with the nearside rear door open. Alistair hesitated, then walked over to it, his stomach tight with anticipation. He slid in and shut the door. The taxi moved away smoothly. The driver was black, with heavy, rounded shoulders. The man in the rear seat with him was white, slightly built, with a sharp, intense face that remained unsmiling as Alistair looked at him enquiringly.

"My name is Smuts, Mr. Alistair," he said in a flat voice and the journalist was sure that his name was not Smuts. "I am sorry that your stay has not been too pleasant, so far. But interesting, surely? As you can see, things are changing in Mozambique. The people of this country will soon be free of the yoke of Portuguese tyranny. Sorry, does that sound trite? However, the zephyrs of dissatisfaction are becoming the winds of change. The rule of the last four hundred and seventy years is at last at an end. If there is no outside interference, that is. How much was explained to you in London?"

The man kept his gaze on the journalist. Alistair lit a cigarette without asking permission and was perversely pleased when he detected a twitch of annoyance in the man's almost expressionless face. Alistair needed a drink. The sweat beaded on his round face and he wound down the window, welcoming the slight breeze. He thought back.

A woman had come to see him at his Chelsea apartment, the day he got back from Zurich, where he had been to interview, and attack, an agency that was recruiting mercenaries for the FNLA freedom fighters in Angola. He was strongly against outside interference with the internal affairs of emergent African nations; he fought it in his articles in the major papers of the western world and his views were well known. So it was no surprise when the woman had asked him how he would react if he knew that South Africa was sending troops to Mozambique to fight Frelimo. He disliked her bombastic attitude, but had been prepared to listen.

He had asked her if she had any proof. It was the first time that he had heard of the allegation. No-one would believe it, she had said, unless someone of international repute, such as himself, saw it personally. Would he be prepared to go there? His fares and expenses would be paid, naturally. And there was a retainer of five hundred pounds. He would have gone, anyway, he reflected, but the retainer made him suspicious. He was going to be used, and the only people who might throw in such a persuader would have other motives besides the welfare of Mozambique. The new colonialists, maybe, who would like a foothold in Africa, from behind the Iron Curtain, or the Bamboo one? Still, it would be interesting to see if there were really South African troops there, although he didn't think that they were that stupid. And he was also keen to see for himself to what degree these other forces had a hand in the emerging embryo that was the new Mozambique. With a bit of luck, he could get back with the whole story. The money would be useful, too. As a freelancer, his income was irregular and things were very tight after his recent divorce. He had agreed to go.

"Just that there are supposed to be South African troops in

Mozambique and that it can be arranged to see them. Nobody else has, as yet." His shirt was sticking to his back and he leaned forward to allow the breeze to cool it.

The man, who sounded like a South African himself, allowed himself a slight smile.

"Except for the freedom fighters they are trying to kill. Yes, it will be arranged for you to see them. But let us get one thing perfectly clear. You have probably been warned, but I must stress this again: you must not in any circumstances divulge this meeting of ours, or any further meetings, or any details of the people that have arranged this for you. You have the intelligence to realise that you could endanger the lives of many people if you should contact anyone before you leave the country. So you can understand that your life is of less consequence than the security of this matter. Forgive me, but you will be closely watched and you will not try to 'shake your tail' as they say." The man called Smuts watched him closely. Alistair tried to ignore the cold slime that seemed to cling to his back.

"I am accustomed to being threatened, sometimes by the very causes that I champion," he said with almost no tremor in his voice, "but I haven't been noted for taking much notice of them, have I? Or have you not done your homework?"

Smuts's mouth tightened, but he nodded. "We are only hopeful that you will help bring the world's attention to bear on the interference of outside powers in the internal affairs of a struggling nation," he said, pedantically. He handed Alistair an envelope from his breast pocket. "Here is your ticket and letter of permission to visit the war zone. You will fly to Beira tomorrow. You will go to the Hotel Ambassador where you have a booking. You will be contacted there." He then said something to the driver and the taxi slid to a stop at the kerb, only ten metres from Alistair's hotel entrance. Alistair opened the door, stifling any reply, and heaved himself out. He headed for a pavement table and ordered himself a double whisky. He had heard that they made the whisky in Angola under some well-known brand names, but it tasted okay and he downed it in two swallows. He ordered another.

A taxi, identical to the one in which he had received his instructions in Lourenço Marques, took him from Manga Airport down a narrow road between two expanses of marshland, then past the Estoril complex along the coast to Beira central. The Hotel Ambassador was a squat-looking building, but it was air-conditioned and pleasant enough when you got off its windy, balcony-type corridors. He vaguely wondered if the driver of this taxi was also an employee of the man Smuts, for he had seen no car following them. He dumped his meagre luggage in his room and headed for the bar on the top floor, determined that, if he was needed in a hurry, he would be too drunk to take any action.

In the days that followed, he went through the motions of a journalist interested in the war. There was the added slant of how the attitudes to the war may have changed since the coup. He bothered army personnel until their Latin courtesy wore thin; he got a vague date to visit the battle zone subject to permission of the Army Command in the north. He suspected that he would never have to make use of this permission when Smuts met with him briefly to warn him that he could expect to be headed to the bush at any moment.

Beira was still agog with the news of the change of government, but Alistair soon heard of the deaths of the two *estrangeiros* and the attack by a hopped-up madman on a visiting ichthyology professor and his wife. These facts swam around in his brain until they settled, like a mass of tadpoles; individuals, but part of a pattern. Could they be part of the reason that he was here? They were all apparently South Africans. He was here to show that South Africans were meddling in Mozambique. Anywhere else, he would have had the contacts to get background on any of the people involved in these tragedies, but here his hands were tied. Still, he reflected, no harm in going to see this professor fellow, sort of accidentally, like.

He sauntered out of his hotel and along the Avenida Paiva de Andrade in the direction of the docks, and the Hotel Zambeze. The street thronged with a multiracial conglomeration of humanity. Some black boys, barefooted and ragged to invoke sympathy, but well-fed from a successful tourist season, each wielding polish, brushes and a small box, badgered the few customers at the pavement cafes into having their shoes polished. A man in sandals was getting annoyed with one persistent fourteen-year old, while other boys yelled encouragement to the lad. It was not yet ten o'clock, but the sun was hot in a cloudless sky.

Alistair whistled tunelessly. He crossed the street, dodging traffic of Landrovers and black-with-lime-green-roofed taxis. His tail that morning was a middle-aged, squatly-built mulatto man with a bored expression on his face. Alistair paused at the cinema on the banks of the winding Rio Chiveve to see what was showing. "Cabaret" with Liza Minelli and Michael York. He remembered that he had seen it in London three years before, remembered that he had had a fight with his wife and walked out halfway through. He thought that if nothing got in the way, he would go and see it tonight. He sauntered along towards the steel bridge that crossed the Chiveve, near the railway station, and stopped to watch the boats. Presently, he made his way to the Moulin Rouge windmill and eyed its gay but faded paintwork. The doors were closed and uninviting. He walked slowly down a back street lined with workshops and warehouses until he was past the Hotel Zambeze. Hesitating, he looked at his watch. He seemed to be in a quandary, then he shrugged and headed down an alley to the hotel. He went in. His tail hesitated then sat on a parapet outside. Alistair went back to try and entice him in for a drink.

He mimed. "Drink, you know, *cerveja*!" The man licked his lips and shook his head. He touched his own skin and then his frayed clothes and gestured at the plush hotel. Abruptly, Alistair's face lit up and he fished out a one hundred escudo note.

"Go have a drink somewhere else, then," he gestured. "Meet me back here at midday, okay?" He pointed at his watch.

The man's face brightened, his eyes on the money. He took it with profuse thanks and backed away. Alistair went back into the lobby. The air-conditioning hit him and he shivered with relief. He went to the lounge and sat in a soft chair where he could see who came and went, but could not, himself, be seen from the street.

A group of young Rhodesians were drinking beer on the veranda, laughing loudly at something someone had said.

"And make it quick, *Kaffir*," one of them said to the waiter that had just taken their order. The smartly dressed man with a green cummerbund gave no indication that he had understood, or even heard.

"Cut out that crap, Johnny, or you'll get us locked up!" another admonished. Then one of them whistled. They all turned to watch a blonde in her twenties come into the lounge, followed by a tall, middle-aged man sucking on a pipe.

"That's that prof that shot that munt a couple of days ago!" A loud whisper.

Alistair's luck was in; they took seats near his own. The girl was tanned but he could still see the freckles which made her look younger than she probably was. Her face was intelligent and strong, attractive and also compassionate, he thought. The man was showing grey, but he moved with no wasted action. The journalist sensed an athlete, despite the spectacles and the intellectual look. He got up and crossed to them.

"Excuse me, Sir, Ma'am? I'm a journalist." He spoke softly so that the youths on the nearby veranda could not hear him. My name's John Alistair, from London. Would it be presumptuous of me to ask to join you both for a while?"

Brand eyed him for a moment, speculatively, and then stood to take the proffered hand.

"Hanekom. This is my wife, Jean. Won't you take a seat?"

Alistair gestured for a waiter and insisted on buying the drinks. He and the Professor had whisky, Jean had a Coke.

"Won't you tell me what happened when this African attacked you? I'm sorry, you needn't, if you don't want to – you must have told it so many times."

"We have," Hanekom smiled, "to the police, several times, to the local journalists, to half the residents of the hotel and several people

149

on the street! So, once more won't matter." He gave Alistair the same version, briefly.

"I find it exceedingly strange that a professor and his wife should both be armed, Professor. Is Africa such a dangerous place, these days?"

"Indeed! The incident proves that we are correct in being a bit cautious. Most whites on this continent have a firearm somewhere near at hand. Our actions and decisions are mostly governed by caution. By fear, if you like. As an outsider, you may find it hard to understand our feeling of insecurity, but Communism, Black Power and world opinion, often ill-informed, are nibbling away at us, our stability. They would wrest our country from us. So, we live in fear."

"But South Africa is a rich and stable country. Surely there is enough there for all to share?"

"Equality is what it boils down to," Jean said. "Equal rights, equal opportunities? *Some animals are more equal than others.* What we do not have is equal numbers, Mr. Alistair. So, people of some responsibility, call them Europeans and Indians, if you like, would be swamped by people that, thus far, are proving to be less responsible. Zambia, Kenya and so on, have not yet proved to be a great economic success. The economy of our country will grind to a halt and it will take generations to recover, to stamp out the inevitable corruption. Britain and others would be dishing out assistance and loans that they won't get paid back and the tribes will fight each other for control. Chinese and Russians will quietly step in with arms and promises…"

"Come, now, Mrs. Hanekom! You over-dramatise the situation, surely? Nothing as drastic as that will happen."

The professor looked at his wife with interest, almost with amusement, as Jean replied.

"It's already happening, Mr. Alistair. None so blind …" she smiled to take the barb out of it. The conversation continued in the same vein for a while then turned to fish and the professor's work; then at five to twelve, Alistair excused himself. He was walking somewhat unsteadily through the entrance when he caught a glimpse of Smuts. His tail was waiting outside looking very upset. Perhaps Smuts had torn a strip off him? That had indeed been the case, as Smuts told him when they met with high drama that afternoon.

He received a note to meet at the Chin Won restaurant, urgently. He took a taxi to the Rua Correia de Brito where the driver pointed it out. The dumpy old proprietor beckoned him to a door behind the till counter. He found a furious Smuts waiting in the room beyond.

"What the hell do you think you are doing, Alistair?" Smuts nearly choked with rage, "What were you saying to that man at the Zambeze?" He whipped a small calibre automatic Beretta from his pocket and pointed it at Alistair's ample stomach.

The latter shrivelled, inside, but he stepped forward into the weapon and commanded angrily; "Put that thing away, Smuts! I am a journalist! Two days ago, those people were attacked in their hotel room by a dope-crazed madman. The whole of Beira is still talking about it! It would be highly suspicious if I did not interview them, for God's sake!"

Smuts was a picture of indecision, and then the muzzle pulled back. "Are you sure that's all you talked about?"

Alistair was sweating freely and it wasn't the heat.

"Oh, no! That, and why the South Africans think they have to go about armed, and the foothold that Communism has in Africa, and why parrot fishes change colour with age. Why the fuss? I certainly did not tell them the real reason why I am here. Who are they, that you are so paranoid?"

Smuts put the gun away, battling with his doubts.

"Okay," he said finally, "I'm sorry. Just don't go near them again. We think they may be South African security people. We don't know why they are here, but we don't like it and they must know nothing of your mission. As it is, they must know your reputation for championing the non-interference by other powers in the sovereignty of developing nations and will wonder what you are doing here. They still have no reason to connect –" He broke off, fearing that he had said too much. "Please confine yourself to your room from now on, and you are forbidden to telephone anyone, whatsoever."

Mozambique, a sovereign state? Alistair nearly laughed out loud.

"Won't that be more suspicious, a journalist that stays in his room for days?" He allowed himself the luxury of a little scorn.

"Not for days," Smuts said. "You will fly to Blantyre in Malawi, tomorrow. You will be taken south to the border where you will join a band of Frelimo who have been in contact with the South African forces recently. When you have seen enough to persuade you that what we say is true, you will fly from Blantyre back to London, via Johannesburg. I shall be with you."

The last was another warning, thought Alistair. He thought that there was probably more of a story behind the story. He would keep his senses tuned. Smuts opened the door for him and summoned the Chinese, who in turn called a mulatto who got the instruction to make sure that the journalist went straight to his hotel and stayed there.

EIGHTEEN

When Alistair left, Smuts drove back to his apartment and phoned da Silva at the Hotel Zambeze. He spoke in English. "All set up. He leaves tomorrow and should be in position by noon, Thursday. So, drop them at six on Friday morning, as we planned. I'll come over at eleven tonight, and we'll go over the details and finalise everything. Arrange a call to the camp for a quarter past so that I can talk to the Colonel. Got that?"

Da Silva curtly said that he had and rang off. The man calling himself Smuts narrowed his eyes and made a mental note that José needed a talking to. He showered, got a 2M beer from the fridge and lay down naked on the bed. He sipped and went over the plan again. Nothing could go wrong. Or everything. Perhaps this journalist would get suspicious. Of what? Nobody knew about the mercenaries. As tourists, they had left the country again. They would never be seen again, except where they were meant to be seen. Dead, in South African uniforms. Smuts would keep the journalist under control. The other side of things seemed simple enough, but that was up to da Silva. He didn't doubt his loyalty, only his competence. Still, the girl would be with him in the plane and she was a ruthless cookie, all right. Quite a woman, that! He thought that she would be a tiger in bed, too. At their first meeting, there had been some current between them, he had felt. She had made it plain that she was interested, if he was. Da Silva said that she'd been screwing one of the mercenaries to help lure them here. He had seemed quite annoyed about that.

Smuts smiled, but it was a pity that some of the South Africans had been knocked off. More would have been more convincing. One was Clement White, he had heard. He remembered a Clement White from his days at university in Durban, when he had still used his real name of Bosch. He had been employed to foment the riots there, and then when things got too hot, he had escaped to Swaziland, then London. There he had joined the Anti-Apartheid League, but soon found them too tame and stopped going to meetings after he met a Chinese lad who had promised a much more active opposition to the white regimes in southern Africa. He painfully read through the little Red Book that James Won lent him, then, when they met again, he threw it at him.

"What a load of crap, James!"

James roared with laughter. "Tonight, you will meet some friends of mine." It had developed from there and, three years later, here he was, still working for them in Mozambique. He was well paid for his work, into a Swiss bank account, but his heart and loyalty were in it, too. He operated a small import/export business from an apartment in Lourenço Marques and this one in Beira. The Chin Won restaurant was connected to his employers; in fact, the old man was some sort of uncle to James Won. In Lourenço Marques, there was a large textile factory owned and run by other members of their group. Both the Russians and the Chinese were sending arms into the country. Smuts felt that the enterprises were more commercial than political and were embedding themselves to both push for the inevitable change and be in position to take advantage of it when it happened.

He was a natural linguist, spoke fluent Portuguese, three indigenous languages and passable Mandarin. He knew several of the Frelimo leaders personally, and he had developed a network that spread the length of the country that fed Frelimo with information such as troop movements, shipments of supplies and arms and the like. One of his biggest headaches was the lack of co-operation between those leaders, and he was often called on to liaise. The Maconde, of the north, for instance, some of the fiercest fighters to be found, would tolerate no orders except from a Maconde leader.

But, in his chameleon-like way, Smuts had had contacts in the D.G.S. and he was thought by them to be a reliable businessman, keen on keeping the existing status quo. He allowed himself a smile and thought again of the imminent operation. In a week, the country would be in flames, free of the Portuguese yoke. It would have taken its freedom and not been given it. Fence-sitters would now also rise up when they saw which way it was going. Right across the subcontinent the people would rebel as they saw what was happening in Mozambique.

A week. There were still those weak links that might snap and jeopardise everything. One was the 'survivor' who would 'talk under pressure'. The mercenary was being given a very fat sum, indeed, but he might suspect that he would not live to spend it. He shrugged; these possibilities would be dealt with as they arose, and his thoughts passed on to the other man who expected not only to survive, but to become an extremely rich man: van Rooyen, or Sanderson, as he thought they knew him. The powerful radio set had been completed and installed. Van Rooyen had been stupid to go it alone, for, once he had activated the mines placed in "Operation Insurance" and the Portuguese military was pierced through its heart, he would have nothing else to give them. True, they would lose the half million dollars they had already given him that was salted away safely in Swiss banks, but van Rooyen expected a further half million. Unfortunately for him, he was a virtual prisoner as he didn't know that Smuts would not protect him.

And what of Barros? He had known him to be a ruthless businessman with interests in almost every activity in the country from hunting safaris, shipping, coconut and cashew nut plantations, cotton, and sugar, to timber mills and marble mines, but he had crumpled the day they threatened to knock off his daughter, Rosa da Silva. He was a puppet now. José da Silva and Manuela Barros had been part of the network for years, even before Smuts came on the scene, although, for a long time, they had not known about him. It was Manuela's idea that da Silva should marry Rosa, although José preferred little boys. It gave da Silva a lot of influence, being part of the powerful Barros family. It was Smuts' idea to get the mercenaries in for Barros's Army, and Manuela who had implemented it.

When things seemed to be coming apart, it was the ruthless

Manuela who suggested that they take control of the Barros resources by kidnapping Rosa and holding that axe over her father's head. It was something that worried Smuts, this total treachery of Manuela's regarding her father and family. He wondered what was behind it. The dossier he had read on her was no help. She had been born in Mozambique, educated in Portugal. She had her first parachute descent at the age of fifteen and her private pilot's licence by the time she was seventeen. By the time she was twenty-one, she was an army parachuting instructor. As a child in Lourenço Marques, she had been befriended by a Chinese business associate of her father's, Lee Chong, who was in textiles. Lee was Smuts's superior in Mozambique and it was said that he had been at the spying game for thirty years or more. Yes, of course it would have been Lee who had recruited the adventurous Manuela, but that did not explain the totally hard core she seemed to have. Or was Smuts missing something?

As he thought of Manuela and that beautiful body of hers, he began to fantasise. He watched his member begin to rise from his naked thighs and reached for the telephone. Little Rosetta would do in the meantime, he thought, and she was a lot closer.

NINETEEN

They had not been physically uncomfortable but their nerves were stretched to the limit. Escape was in all their minds, but nobody got near it. John Blair, the Englishman, made the most serious attempt. There was a short, globe-less, disconnected light fitting near the ceiling over the door. Blair got Muller and Visagie to give him a leg up until he was standing on the two-centimetre ledge above the door, and held onto the light fitting to keep himself there, with a galvanised iron ablution bucket in the other hand as a weapon. But Ribeiro's visit came much later than expected, by which time Blair was trembling with the strain. His hand slipped from the fitting just as Ribeiro opened the door and he fell in an ignominious heap at his feet.

Ribeiro read the situation at a glance and thereafter they had to stand against the far wall and be counted when they got a warning knock before the door was opened. They were told that if there were any missing at the count, then the guard would open fire on those he could see. They didn't believe this as, after asking repeatedly what was to become of them and receiving no answer, they thought that they were being kept for some other reason that required them to be alive, not just to be press-ganged into taking the field against Frelimo.

When Visagie and Muller had succeeded in cracking the door with repeated kicks in the first few hours of their incarceration, a steel plate had been bolted to the inside with an eye-level peephole and four stout pad bolts on the outside. Their lights were out of reach in the ceiling and the air-con ducts were too small to bother with. They lost hope, then.

There was more than enough space for them all to lay out their mattresses without being crowded. Their food was anything on the menu that they cared to order, but it was served on paper plates and they ate with plastic spoons. They had plenty of beer in cans, which were counted, full and empty, in case any sort of weapon could be made of them. They were given packs of cards and a chess set to play with. Their clothes were laundered every day.

McNeil left his transmitter off to conserve its miniature batteries for use in the event that they be moved or separated. Nourse lengthened his off time quickly until it was on for only three minutes in the hour. They hoped that Brand would guess what they were up to. McNeil suggested physical exercises to keep themselves fit for any possible escape opportunity that might present itself. All of them were willing. The days dragged and their spirits dropped. They learned every card game that any of them ever knew and invented others until they were sick of cards. They drank beer until they were sick of that. Theunissen's nose and lip healed, as did Schulman's head cut. They even started language classes, starting with *Fanagalo*, the *lingua-franca* of the mines, also known as *Chilapalapa* in Rhodesia, then Swahili. Muller even offered to teach them German. They reminisced about their parts and experiences in the two battles that they had been through.

It was during this time that Geoff, in quiet conversation with the Englishman, Blair, heard what Muller had had to say about his grudge against O'Donnell. There was no way that Muller could have been involved in the Irishman's ghastly death, but Muller had admitted to John that from the time of his fight with Visagie onwards, he was biding his time. No man sat on Helmut Muller and got away with it.

He had smiled, John told Geoff, repeating Muller's words.

"There have been a few that have tried it on. Ha. There was that foreman in Windhoek, Smit, I remember. Aways pushing a little, until he wound up in hospital with a broken jaw. He wanted to take me to court, but I had a little talk to him about what would happen to his wife and kids, if he got over-enthusiastic. Ha ha, he saw the light, then, but I lost my job, anyway, because I been seeing too much of the boss's daughter!" He had laughed again and Blair had wanted to tell him to shut up, but admitted to Geoff that he didn't have the nerve. The boss had even paid his fare to Germany to get rid of him. Everyone thought that he'd been fired for smacking Smit. The joke was still on the boss because, after Muller was gone, the boss had discovered that his daughter was pregnant and was trying to get on a boat in Walvis Bay. Helmut hadn't known about that until he had returned to the territory four months previously. What a laugh he had thought that was! John had asked him if he had seen his kid and Helmut had looked at the Englishman as if he'd taken leave of his senses.

In changing the subject, he set out to impress John with the high-rolling criminals he'd worked for. Helmut had never been involved in anything heavy, himself, he said, either here, Australia, where he had lived for a while, or in Germany, but he knew some big men in a lot of different businesses that were not straight. Occasionally, he had done a little work for them, a bit of leaning on reluctant dealers and such like. He kept out of trouble not for moral reasons, but for fear of being caught due to the stupidity of other people. He had the brains to pull off a job on his own, but not the resources, he had said. Blair thought it was because he had not quite enough nerve. However, he had given a John a vague notion that there was some idea tickling away at the back of his active mind.

"No comeback, that is the thing. If I knew exactly when we were leaving the country, then I could pull something, just before we left," Muller had said. It didn't tie in with anything, now that O'Donnell was dead, so Geoff did not mention it to Dan.

They were so caught-up in their routine that it came as a shock when they were told, after supper on their sixth day, by da Silva, that they were to dress warmly as they were going for a truck ride.

"How far," Schulman asked, not expecting an answer.

"To Mr. Barros's hunting camp on the Mungari River," he said without expression. "Nourse can tell you how far that is."

Issued with their camouflage bush gear again, they were herded into the back of an army-green Bedford five-tonner in an enclosed yard at the hotel. They were handcuffed there, well forward , and guarded by the inevitable Ribeiro and Campos from the back. The canvas flap was tied down and the engine fired. The truck did a three-point turn then they were on their way. What lay ahead of them, they could not begin to guess. Nourse tried questioning the guards, but they seemed to know as little about it as themselves, except that da Silva and Manuela would be coming by Dakota. Nourse was able to extract from them how they had got back to Beira from beyond Maringue. They had walked to a nearby village and persuaded a Sena man to take money to go and buy them two sets of civilian clothes from the only store. They also gave their camo overalls in payment. They had then hitch-hiked a ride on a cotton truck to Inhaminga, saying that their Landrover had broken a spring: that they were going to look for spares. The trains were still running from Inhaminga to Beira, although Frelimo blew them off the lines from time to time. By the next day they were in Beira, asking da Silva for a job, knowing that there was no love lost between him and the mercenaries.

The truck made the journey without mishap, except for the discomfort of the reluctant passengers, but it was nearly dawn when they could stretch their cramped limbs and climb down. The camp was a series of squat silhouettes against the starlit sky and they could make out little detail. Their new quarters were another storeroom, newly cleared out, judging from the marks of crates on the dusty floor. It, too, was windowless. The door had no hatch but it was built of solid partridge wood. The walls were whole borassus palm logs, covered with mesh and plastered. Whole logs pushed tightly together formed the ceiling. When McNeil and Schulman tried to lift them, they did not budge and there was an angry hiss from behind the netting.

The agony of Manuela's behaviour had died to a dull emotional ache; Nourse clutched his breast in theatrical fashion and abruptly grinned to himself, muttering.

"Fucking bitch!"

McNeil chuckled in sympathy, guessing who he was thinking about.

"Hey, Dan! You awake? What the fuck is going to happen to us?"

Dan had also been trying to piece it all together. "They are using us, somehow. A bloody Commie Plot!" he smiled, wryly, in the dark.

He whispered his thoughts. "Barros is out of it, no longer at the helm. Sanderson, too, is being used, I think. There's some sort of setup between your girl, Manuela, and da Silva? No, their orders are coming from somewhere else. The Russians? The Chinese? More likely the latter, as the Russians' influence is not established so far south, I don't think." He swore softly, "I feel so fuckin' frustrated at our helplessness. True, there've been no opportunities to make a break, but until now I've been reluctant to do so for fear of losing this tenuous link to van Rooyen. If we could somehow free ourselves, you and I could take van Rooyen back to Beira at gunpoint and hand him over to Brand. Then get the hell back home."

"Home? Where's home?" Geoff chuckled a little bitterly.

"Home for me, now, means some place with Cecile in it," Dan surprised himself by admitting. "I was married before, you know? Suzanna, her name was. That was a fuck-up. Beautiful, shallow Suzy. Our compatibility lasted as long as the honeymoon. The day after the divorce came through, I got on a boat to Aussie. But Cecile, now if she will have me, we can live together for a year or two and, if that works out, get married. Well, I can only dream, can't I?"

"We've got to get out of here first!" Nourse muttered, but he smiled, anyway. At least one of them had optimistic thoughts.

TWENTY

Alistair and Smuts were on the same plane, but ignored each other until they were through Immigration and Customs at Chileka Airport. Then a well-dressed Chinese touched Alistair on the elbow.

"Excuse me, but if you are looking for a taxi into Blantyre, they are rather expensive. I have transport and it would be a pleasure to give you a lift." His English was precise, his accent sing-song. Alistair smiled, thanked him, and followed him out of the building into the blinding sunlight. The Chinese said no more until they reached a canopied Landrover truck in the car park. He took Alistair's suitcase and put it in the back. A cloud of dust arose as he slammed the door.

"I believe you have met Mr. Smuts?" Smuts was already seated in the middle seat. They nodded at each other.

"In the restaurant business?" Alistair asked, laconically. The Chinese smiled.

"Sorry, I didn't introduce myself. I'm Lee Kwan. I have several trading stores in Malawi. We shall be going to one in the south, this afternoon. But first, you'd like a wash and a meal, I am sure?"

"Thank you. And a drink." Without asking, Alistair slid his window open as far as it would go and opened the vent in the dashboard to allow as much breeze as possible. The sweat cooled on his neck. There had been no point in introducing himself; the man would know exactly who he was.

They lunched at Ryall's Hotel, then afterwards Lee took them south on a metalled road that crossed the Shire River and wound through the mountains. He turned off on a track that led south-west between rocky ridges clad in green *M'sasa* woodland, through scattered

162

villages. Alistair's arm began to ache from waving back at the Africans that greeted, waving and grinning at the roadside. Neither Lee nor Smuts bothered. Smuts told him that thousands of villagers from Mozambique fled this way, escaping from the *Aldeamentos*. He explained what they were, that they were oppressive establishments, virtually concentration camps, where the Portuguese could control the local populace and enforce curfews. He did not mention that they were also for protection against wandering Frelimo bands that took what food and sex they wanted and coerced the men to join them. He also did not mention that there was allotted farmland for each family within easy walking distance of the pole and thatch dwellings.

It was well after four o'clock when they reached the store. It squatted on a low hill, an oblong bungalow with a full length veranda. It had once been white-washed but now it was a cracked and streaky yellow with a grime level up to human height. Shade was provided by a quadrangle of ancient bluegum trees. A thin young Indian man was serving at the battered wooden counter that ran the length of the store. Behind him, shelves containing tinned goods and rolls of gaudy material rose to the ceiling. Alistair followed the other two men into the gloom of the store, swaying to dodge the bicycle wheels and frames and dried fish that hung from the rafters. The customers were mostly women, some dressed in gay print cloth or blankets, often with infants on their backs. The air, thick with their odour, and that of fish and tobacco, was almost overpowering for the Englishman. The Chinese greeted the Indian briefly but did not introduce his companions. He was handed some keys. They followed him as he ducked under the counter and found themselves in a long dim corridor, the walls of which were lined to the roof with sacks of maize meal. Lee unlocked a door at the far end. He stepped into the darkness and opened some curtains, shutters, and windows onto the sunset. The yellow light revealed a small lounge with two doors leading off at either side. It was simply but tastefully furnished with local wood. In contrast with the rest of the store, it was clean and neat. A fridge and cabinet standing against one wall attracted Alistair's attention. Lee noticed him lick his lips.

"Scotch or a cold beer, Mr. Alistair?" He opened the fridge. Smuts opted for a beer, Alistair for Scotch. Lee poured himself a tall glass of iced water. After a second one, he got to his feet and held out his hand. "A pleasure to meet you, Mr. Alistair. I must be going. Mr. Smuts will look after you from here on. I hope that you see what you have come to see. Good luck and goodbye." He let himself out. Smuts locked the door behind him, and then lit three paraffin lamps. He opened one of the doors to show Alistair a small bedroom with a single bed, a shower and toilet. He passed him his suitcase and told him to make himself comfortable.

"We'll be off at four tomorrow morning, Alistair. Until then we stay in these quarters. There are sandwiches and a flask of soup for supper. Have another drink?" He cracked another beer for himself and began to talk about South African troops in Mozambique.

TWENTY-ONE

"*Vuka, inja*!" Wake up, dog! Piet Visagie practised his *Fanagalo* on Muller as he stuck a toe in Muller's ribs. The German groaned and sat up. The rest of them were stacking their mattresses in a corner to make way for their daily PT.

"Move your arse, Helmut!" Theunissen told him.

"Get stuffed. You aren't the boss anymore. We're all just rats in a cage. Pawns for their fuckin' game. Just you go and get stuffed!"

"Helmut. Do you really want to get taken apart?" Theo asked mildly.

"Fuck you." But he got to his feet anyhow, and began folding his blankets.

They had almost finished, when they heard the banging on the door. Reluctantly, they moved to the far wall so that they could be counted. Campos opened the door, counted, then beckoned to Nourse to come.

"You will fetch breakfast for all," he told him in Portuguese. Geoff translated and stepped out into the mid-morning sunlight. It was going to be another hot day. He walked ahead of Campos under threat of his G3, to a long low bungalow that the man indicated. There seemed to be no-one around, which was strange for a hunting camp as it normally would have been full of servants preparing for their guests. Then, two bungalows away, a door opened and a white man emerged. Geoff recognised him as the hunter and manager, named Reis, who ran the camp for Barros. He waved at him, but Reis gave no acknowledgement.

Geoff shrugged and started into the building as Campos prodded his back. The interior was panelled with beautiful *m'bila* wood and scattered about was locally-made partridge wood furniture. Sable and zebra skins covered the floors. A four metre stuffed crocodile surged across one wall. A set of enormous buffalo horns was mounted above the door, next to the long bar. Campos waved him through the door and down a long corridor that gave onto several guest rooms, beautifully got out in gleaming, varnished local wood and colourful Kenyan linen with African print. At the far end was a modern stainless steel kitchen where an ancient black man in an apron was about to take a coffee pot off the gas stove. Nourse said good morning and the old man grinned at him, almost toothlessly.

"From Rhodesia?" The old man enquired in English as he poured coffee into tin mugs. "Me, I know Rhodesia too much! Rusape, Marandellas, Salisbury, I know, too much!

"Good place, eh, *Madala*?" Nourse grinned back. The old one shook his grey head in recollection.

"Too good, that place!"

Campos told the old man to shut up and get on with the ham sandwiches that he'd started buttering. He was next to Nourse, then, and, before he could stop himself, Nourse gripped the G3 barrel with his right hand and smashed Campos in the face with his left fist. The thin Portuguese fell back against the steel-topped, hip-height counter, but he hung onto the rifle with surprising strength, snarling as he tried to twist away from Nourse's slamming left.

"Ribeiro!" called Campos. Nourse heard the kitchen door smash open and even as he twisted to meet the other man, Ribeiro smacked his rifle butt across his head.

When he came around a few minutes later, the old man had emptied his third bucket of water over him. Beside the awful throb in his skull, his side felt on fire and he guessed that Campos had got the boot in as he had lain there. Fortunately, the boots were the canvas and rubber type, not leather, or he could have broken some ribs. Despite his pain, he managed a twisted grin when he saw Campos's face. His lips were split and an eye would close soon.

"Bloody *macacos*," Geoff spat out at them. Bloody monkeys! The stainless steel world was spinning around him. Campos growled and advanced, but Ribeiro waved him back and told Nourse to take the tray

166

back to his companions before he got himself shot. Nourse managed to get to his feet, eventually, and staggered out with it, saying, "Stay well, old man," to the cook as he went. He felt nauseous and the bright sunlight made it seem as if his eyeballs would burst. He could hear an aircraft coming in to land and, without seeing it, recognised the sound of a Douglas DC3. That would be the Dakota with Manuela, da Silva and Sanderson aboard. He dared not look up for fear that he would fall over. He staggered to the store room that was their prison. Ribeiro banged on the door and counted the occupants once he had opened it. They gave a hearty guffaw when they saw Campos's face. The door was locked on them again. Soon afterwards, they heard a vehicle start up and guessed that it was heading for the Dak.

"You bloody fool, Geoff," McNeil said without much rancour, when he'd related what had happened.

"You mean bloody good try!" snarled Blair. "Only wish you had made it, then we might have had a chance of getting out of this mess! Christ, I wonder what the hell they are planning for us."

"Something dirty, anyhow," said Jan de Groot. "You say there was nobody else but this Reis guy and the cook. Maybe they are going to knock us off without any witnesses."

"You are forgetting the Dak," Dan broke in. "They have a Cessna to get here in. Why a Dak?"

An hour later, they were given a few more clues. Dan and Jan were driven in a jeep out to the Dakota where it stood on the grass landing strip of the hunting lodge. They unloaded nine Army parachutes and took them back to one of the long verandas. Manuela, in flying boots and white overalls, unsmiling and curt, supervised their packing, while Sanderson watched over them with a pistol.

The rest of the captives were returned to the Dak by da Silva, who was looking very pleased with himself, accompanied by the Dakota's pilot, a tall thin mulatto. They were guarded by Ribeiro, and Campos, whose eye was now entirely closed. They worked for the rest of the morning and part of the afternoon, painting out the CR registration and the blue and red stripes that were the Barros insignia. When Nourse overheard the pilot ask da Silva whether Mr. Barros was in his quarters, they deduced that Barros had also been on the plane. Reis, the camp manager, drove a fuel tanker out to the plane as they finished painting. He started refuelling, helped by the thin pilot. The puzzled prisoners were walked back to their prison.

"What's this lot for, Manuela?" McNeil asked as he started on his third parachute. She was sitting on the veranda's low wall, close enough to watch every detail of the packing, but out of reach in case one of the South Africans tried to jump her and use her as a shield against Sanderson's gun.

"You lot, so pack them well."

"But there are nine 'chutes and only eight of us."

"One spare, now shut up and get on with it!"

But Jan had seen Sanderson wince. "Hey, Dan, the ninth one's for that bastard." Dan looked at him, gauging him, but Sanderson refused to meet his gaze.

"You jumped, before ... er, Sanderson?" Bloody nearly called him van Rooyen, thought Dan.

The colonel only hesitated for a fraction of a second.

"Of course!" he snapped. Manuela's face twisted in anger. She screamed at them to get on with it.

"What's this all about, Manuela? Why are we making this jump? Aren't you scared that we will just run off into the bush when we hit the ground, or is this why this treacherous bastard is coming with us?"

McNeil was crouched on the floor, straightening the canopy in its folds and before he could raise his hands to protect himself, Manuela had sprung across the intervening distance and flashed the blade of her open hand across his neck. Dan collapsed on the rip-stop material. Jan hardly shifted from where he was taking the tension on the rigging lines before Sanderson's pistol was lined up on his body. For a long moment, nobody moved. Then McNeil groaned and rolled onto his side. Manuela stepped back to the wall, her look dripping with venom. Jan went to Dan's side and massaged his neck. Shudders racked his body. Eventually, he was able to sit up, his face pale. He crawled to the edge of the veranda and vomited. Jan turned to Manuela, cursing her in Afrikaans, but she just watched him impassively, only her neat bosom lifting and falling rapidly under her white overalls showed her tension.

"As for you, *jou fokken veraaier!*" Jan turned on Sanderson, "You fucking Judas, you're in this for the money. Selling out the country that nurtured you, for filthy money! Do you know how hard you fall in full kit? It takes months of training to survive the fall and you aren't fit. You're flabby! You'll break your fucking neck, you sod, and how we'll laugh!"

"I've jumped twice!" Sanderson blurted, his round face purple with anger, and, Jan hoped, with fear. He warped his mouth into an expression of scorn, but before he could speak, Manuela told him to shut up.

"If you speak at all, you speak English. What's he been saying?"

Van Rooyen, as Jan knew him, told her and it seemed to Jan that she probably felt the same contempt for the man that he did. He was almost asking her for reassurance about the coming jump. Jan later told Geoff that he guessed then that Manuela had been training the colonel for this one jump, probably here at the Mungari hunting camp. Probably from the Cessna. He wondered what the bastards had in store for them that this man, who had been his C.O. in Signals, was required to jump out of an aeroplane, which he seemed not at all keen to do. Jan knew that the colonel did not recognise him and knew it would not be a good idea to let him know that they knew who he was.

Dan wiped his mouth on the back of his hand and moved unsteadily back to the parachute. Jan changed places with him and they got on with the packing in silence.

—⁂—

As a pilot himself, Rafe Schulman wished he could get at the controls of the Dak. He told Geoff it was a few years since he had flown one, but he knew that he wouldn't have any trouble. God, if he could only get in there. He knew that all of them were keyed up with this comparative freedom after the routine of their prison. Perhaps they'd get a chance before they were forced to make this jump. He was sure that they would not survive it, but he could not say why he thought so. Why did they want them to jump? He thought he was the only one to have jumped under full kit, in combat conditions; he was the only true Parabat. Half of the others had probably forgotten how to roll, having been spoilt for so long under their luxury sports parachutes – their Papillons, Para-Commanders, Clouds and the like. Geoff agreed.

"You jumped before?" he asked Theo Theunissen who was painting on the other side of him. Theo started; his thoughts had been far away.

"Indo-China. About twenty jumps. A few more in Algeria. Hated it like the devil! Can't understand why you guys do it for fun." He saw da Silva looking at them as if to say, get on with it.

"Hey, da Silva." Rafe demanded, "You say we're going to jump out of this thing. Why? Where?"

"We know where the main Frelimo camp is and we'll drop you right into it." Da Silva seemed to be in a good mood.

"Why? It makes no sense. After the way you treated us, you still expect us to fight for you?"

"Yes," he laughed, "of course! You will be protecting yourselves and fighting for a free Mozambique. You have joined the cause, whether you like it or not."

Geoff was feeling a bit better now, recovering from his beating. He looked at Rafe. Rafe swallowed his anger but his puzzlement was obvious.

"But if we're armed, why would we not just take over the Dak and fly it home?"

"Who said anything about arming you?" da Silva positively shook with mirth.

"You bastards!" roared Rafe, "You are throwing us to them like scraps to the dogs!" He almost threw himself at da Silva, but the latter stepped back smartly and levelled the G3 at them.

"So, if they don't shoot you, you have a chance of living. You should be happy, no?" da Silva chuckled again.

That didn't make sense, especially when, after they returned to their prison, McNeil told them that Sanderson would be making the jump with them. He told them what had happened at the packing.

The following morning, they were woken at three o'clock and issued used South African Army camouflaged Para kit and webbing. They were each given an R3, the folding-stock version of the FN used by South African paratroopers, to be clipped into their kit.

Manuela, again in white overalls, lined them up in the lights in front of the veranda where the parachutes had been packed and she assured them that, although the weapons appeared to be loaded, the ammunition was dummy.

"Whether you are shot by Frelimo after you jump, or us before you do, does not matter in the slightest, so you had better behave. At least you have a chance of survival after you have exited, so we'd prefer no trouble before then."

"Bitch!" thought Nourse, his guts in a knot. Surely this was not the same woman standing here before them, condemning them to death, as the warm, soft girl he had made love to?

They were herded to the Dak, the engines of which were being warmed by the thin pilot. Manuela took her place in the right-hand seat and pulled on her headgear. Sanderson covered them from the cockpit end and Ribeiro from the gaping hole where the cabin door had been, while Campos handcuffed them to the naked ribbing of the plane's wall and they squatted on the bare floorboards. Da Silva, wearing a hip length sheepskin coat, climbed aboard. Ribeiro and Campos got out to join Reis, the camp manager.

"Watch the old man, Reis," da Silva told him, "and Rosa! Don't let them do anything stupid!" Above the roar of the big radials, they didn't hear the reply. Nourse translated into McNeil's ear. The deduction was shocking. Rosa was being held here to keep her father under control. Manuela's own sister, da Silva's wife! It seemed that her father was a virtual prisoner here, too.

Safari vehicles along the runway had their lights on, to form a flight path. The old plane began to move down it, bumping gently. It lifted at the second last vehicle and swooped over the last. Climbing, it curved north and west into the dark sky that was just beginning to show a faint glimmer of light over the faraway sea. It was four-thirty.

TWENTY-TWO

The short-wheelbase Landrover wound along what was no more than a game trail. It was a little after six in the morning. The air was fresh and cool, the sun had only just risen, a red orb, as yet without power, but still promising a hot day to come. Alistair clutched the dashboard to stop being bashed against Smuts, who was driving, and the lean black man in the left-hand seat who smelt as if he had not bathed for days. He was dressed in a ragged pair of camouflage overalls and cracked rubber and canvas combat boots revealed sockless feet. He held an Avtomat Kalashnikov 47, butt down, between his knees.

They had set out in the dark and it was evident that Smuts had been this way before. At a place that seemed to have no discernable landmarks, Smuts stopped and flashed his headlights. Three men materialised out of the dark, all armed. The one who introduced himself as Lieutenant Mtiwa in passable English, got in front, replacing the other man who joined the other two in the open back.

"Any action lately, Lieutenant?" Smuts asked when they were on their way again. Mtiwa hawked and spat out of the window, then grinned, showing large even teeth.

"Too much, every day. All over. We put mines, shoot cotton trucks. Last week we mortar Chamba; kill plenty Portuguese soldier there. Portuguese too much scare." He laughed uproariously.

"Seen anything of the South Africans, Lieutenant?" Smuts eased his way between two large boulders then twisted up a low hill to avoid a gully that had appeared. Mtiwa looked blank. His grin disappeared and he scratched his head.

"When last did you see any South African soldiers?" prompted Smuts, just a tiny touch sharply. Mtiwa's face suddenly lit up.

"Ah, yes. *Maburu*! Yes, they give us too much trouble. Plenty trouble. My men say they see some two days ago to the west. Near Rhodesia border. Last month, they kill eight of my men at their camp." His voice had taken on a flat tone, as he squinted at the top of the windscreen to get it just right. "Some wounded, too. Those Sul Africanos, they give too much trouble!"

"Don't the Portuguese soldiers give you much trouble, Lieutenant?" Alistair offered his cigarettes around, also out the open window to the soldiers in the back. They thanked him in Portuguese. Mtiwa grinned again as he bent his head to the light in Alistair's cupped hand.

"No problem, the Portuguese. They are afraid, too much. Only the *Fleches*, the Commandos, they are son of a bitch. They cut off ears of dead men and put in the pickle. Too much son of bitch! They fight pretty good! We go round the *Fleches* when we find them." He was lost for awhile in recollections of the terrible Commandos.

"Why are we stopping?" asked Alistair as Smuts pulled up in a shallow ravine. The soldiers clambered off the back and disappeared over the nearest ridge. Smuts told him in a low voice that they had gone to ask their fellows if there were troops patrolling the Tete-Beira railway line that was nearby. The woodland was quietly raucous with the sound of birds and insects, which Alistair found very pleasant and he could almost forget why he had come. After half an hour, the men came back to report in Sena to Mtiwa and he laughed.

"Okay, we go." Mtiwa said. Smuts started the Landrover and pulled out of the ravine, heading south again, over a ridge. The lines lay before them, winding through the hills, as incongruous as the vehicle in this wild country. With a couple of lurches, they were across the tracks and into the bush on the other side.

"Stop here," Mtiwa instructed, getting out to stretch his legs. He cleared his nose with a deft movement of thumb and forefinger then leaned against the vehicle and signed for Smuts to switch the engine off. They stood fifty metres from the railway lines that they had crossed. All was quiet. Presently they could hear the train as it approached from the west, from Tete. The ground shook with ever increasing violence, and then the train rushed by, visible in flashes through the trees, the beefy Portuguese driver leaning from his caboose, squinting down the track, the smoke pouring back thickly along the way and the shuffer-shuffer of the engine a noise that Alistair had not heard since he was in India three years ago.

"He Gomes," Mtiwa grinned, delightedly. "Only three drivers not too much afraid to ride this line! We blow his brother-in-law up near his store at Chuéze!" He chortled. Smuts frowned, thinking that it was hardly the thing to mention to an English journalist that they were attacking civilians. He was reaching for the starter button when it happened.

There was a boom, like a close vicious thunderclap. As was usual, the engine had three flat wagons loaded with sandbags ahead of it. The mine layers had allowed for these in the detonating mechanism and it was the engine itself that took the blast. Gomes was thrown clear as the engine rose like a rearing horse under him, but the fireman was less fortunate. He was flung against the steel cab and as the firebox door opened, a river of ruby coals was hurled over his legs. The engine left the rails and ploughed down a steep ravine, dragging its tender and five coaches with it, gouging the earth and snapping tree trunks and branches like gunfire. Only the guard's van remained on the track as it came to a halt in a cloud of dust. After a long moment's silence, a single burst of gunfire came from the guards van. The Frelimo men on the side of the tracks returned this with gusto but without much luck as several more guns spoke back from the smashed coaches, survivors popping up like moles from the skyward windows and raking the bush.

Mtiwa had run to the tracks to watch the battle happening three hundred metres away from the place that they had crossed. Alistair prepared to follow but Smuts restrained him.

"Don't be a bloody fool! What do you think would happen if Europeans were seen with Frelimo? They'll think you are a Russian instructor or something and other countries will take that as an excuse to step in."

174

Alistair lit a cigarette with shaking hands as the rattle of machine guns joined the snap of pistols, the crack of hunting rifles and the blast of shotguns, the civilians who were able adding their contribution to the firepower of the troops. Mtiwa returned, still grinning.

"Too good!" he said as he stepped in, "Now, we go!"

They headed westward, now, almost parallel to the railway lines, but slowly moving further away. The country became flatter and dryer, dense *mopane* woodland with shallow depressions of black clay that were obviously pig and buffalo wallows in the wet season. Here and there were ridges of rounded, water-worn stones that Smuts skirted.

The day wore on; it became a furnace. Sweat dribbled down their bodies. The engine boiled and they were forced to stop for half an hour to let it cool. They refilled the radiator from a jerrycan. A big river loomed up ahead, heralded by the line of huge riparian trees. Still without being guided by Mtiwa, Smuts headed through the trees to the bank. There was no track that Alistair could see. He mopped his face for the umpteenth time and held on tight as Smuts changed down, taking the little vehicle over the bank and into the river. It was dry, a ribbon of sand and rounded stones. A band of wild pig awoke from siesta in the shade of some deadfall and dashed down the bed, squealing. Smuts pushed the low-ratio knob and the sturdy vehicle struggled gamely through the sand after the pigs. From time to time, they skirted a muddy pool, the edges of which were churned with game tracks. Once, they rounded a bend and almost ran into four buffalo that were crossing the river. Smuts braked hard and the Landrover sank into the sand. The buffalo lumbered up the bank with the soldiers following them in their sights without firing. They could still hear the crashing of their passage when Mtiwa ordered them to start digging at the wheels. It was twenty minutes before they were moving again, but the strain made the engine boil once more. Smuts stopped on a harder patch and waited for it to cool.

Shortly after they got going again, their river was joined by another one from the right, also dry, but mostly a bed of jagged rock and little sand. Smuts gunned the engine over some flat rocks and the little truck tore up the further bank. They had crossed the Rio Minjova and now the going really got rough. There were knife-edged ridges of lava, everywhere, but at least there were signs of some attempt to clear a track through the scrubby *mopane*. They crested a rise and before them lay another river but the trees that lined it were less vigorous than those of previous rivers, due to the rocky terrain. At the rivers edge were a string of huts, almost hidden amongst the vegetation. Smuts hooted a signal and several men appeared from amongst the boulders, all armed and in camouflage kit. Grins split their faces. They waved. Mtiwa shouted something at them and the Landrover ground down to the huts.

"As far as we can go by car," Smuts said tiredly and switched off. They got out and stretched. Smuts handed Alistair the water bottle that hung from the front wing mirror of the vehicle and the journalist drank greedily. He was hardly able to take more than two bites from the ham roll he was given from the food box in the rear; the heat had taken away his appetite. The sun was at its zenith. Smuts drank more water then unrolled a sleeping bag and placed it in the shade.

"We'll have a bit of a siesta and go on when it is cooler," he told Alistair, "We are heading for that mountain over there. Mount Muambe. It's about five kilos to the camp, but we'll take it easy." He looked with some scorn at the journalist's plump figure. He lay down on the bag and seemed to fall asleep immediately. Alistair likewise got out a sleeping bag and lay on it. The villainous-looking Frelimo retired to their huts and silence fell on the small camp. The huts were simple: *mopane* branch frames covered with grass. Alistair did not try to sleep, knowing that he would feel awful when he awoke, if he did so. He lay looking at the mountain. It rose above the surrounding bush by no great amount. It seemed to have a flattish top with a dent a third of the way along on the left. The rocky sides had only the barest suggestion of vegetative covering here and there, as in the dent.

At three o'clock, Smuts sat up and looked at his watch. He shouted, "Lieutenant!" and rolled up his sleeping bag. Mtiwa stumbled from a hut, yawning. He, in turn, shouted to his men. These emerged and shouldered the kit from the Landrover. Mtiwa, six of his soldiers, Smuts and Alistair in single file took a path leading through the steep-sided river and up the far bank, heading for the mountain. The trail was well worn; the camps had obviously been here for several months.

"Don't the Portuguese army bother you here, Lieutenant?" panted Alistair. The stringy man grinned back at him.

"Nothing bother," he replied. "They know we in the area, but they cannot see us. Sometime they fly over with plane but we hide away. Near Tete, we shoot down one helicop' last year when they look, now they afraid for look."

Alistair saved his breath for the walk and only grunted a reply. The path followed a steep ridge that rose windingly to the mountain. For him the mountain seemed to get no nearer. The ridge led to a point just to the right of the dent. Here the path mounted boulders as giant steps and curved left towards the dent itself. Smuts called a halt to give Alistair a breather. He needed it. Sweat ran into his eyes and his chest heaved, raspingly. The rocky world swam around him. As he slumped on to a boulder, he nearly fell off it. His thighs ached. He felt them begin to tighten with cramp when he'd been sitting for only a few minutes and had to massage them.

At length, they set off again and the going was better as the path levelled off a bit in the floor of the steep-sided valley that was the dent. It was more like a split in the mountain than a valley. The ground began to dip down and turn to the right. Alistair had been stumbling down the steepening path for some while before he became aware that he was in the crater of an extinct volcano and the mountain through which he had passed circled around on either side to meet, four thousand metres ahead of him at a similar dent. The floor of the valley was covered with boulders and twisted trees. The inner walls of the crater seemed to be riddled with holes, probably formed by bubbles in the solidifying lava. The party was met by two armed soldiers who regarded the two whites with interest at first, but soon they were joking with their comrades. Alistair caught the word *Inglesi* several times. He ignored them, only too glad to be walking downhill. Then they reached the camp.

It was simply a series of caves at the foot of a cliff. Troops sat around on the ground or on boulders, some playing cards or a game like checkers with beer-bottle tops on a 'board' made by a drawing of lines on the ground. A bald, paunchy man came out to meet them. He roared at the men, who scrambled to their feet in some semblance of standing to attention. He peeled a smart salute off at the visitors and beamed. He gabbled something in rapid Portuguese for a minute or two, then he gestured at Smuts. The South African translated, as more men emerged from the caves.

"He is General Mucongáve and he bids you welcome and hopes you will be comfortable. He says that he personally will take you to the place where his men are engaging the South African insurgents, the day after tomorrow, when you have rested. He wishes to introduce you to ..." the general indicated two of the men behind him, "Colonel Wanga ...", a tall, intelligent-looking individual with spectacles perched on an unusually aquiline nose – a touch of Arab? "and Captain Chitamba," a squat, immensely powerful man with a flat, cruel looking face. Wanga smiled and offered his hand, which Alistair took. Chitamba scowled, and then followed suit. "The general thanks us for bringing him some beer and suggests that we drink to the speedy liberation of Mozambique."

The general growled at the men who had carried in the provisions from the Landrover and they produced three cases of 2M beer. Mtiwa gave instructions for Alistair's and Smuts's stretchers, sleeping bags, and holdalls to be taken to a cave near the officer's quarters.

Men brought low stools for the officers and visitors. Beers were opened, lukewarm. The general gabbled on. Alistair found that, after the second half-litre, he was quite relaxed and the tight knot of fear in the pit of his stomach had eased, somewhat. He found that Colonel Wanga spoke passable French and they were able to communicate quite well without any help from Mtiwa or Smuts. Wanga told him that he was destined to become the Minister of Education when Mozambique won her independence.

The sun slowly slipped behind the further lip of the encircling mountain. Smoke arose from a hole high on the cliffs, a natural chimney for the cookhouse cave, some fifty metres below it. Stew arrived, with potatoes that Smuts had brought with them. The two whites ate with utensils, the Mozambicans with their fingers. They all drank more beer. Alistair passed his cigarettes around, hoping that there would not be many takers as he was getting low. He saw men carrying food down the path that followed the cave-infested cliffs. The men went into a cave about eighty metres away, almost too far for him to see in the gathering gloom. The last light of day reflected off a metal strip that wound up the cliff above that cave.

"Odd place for a lightning conductor," thought Alistair, his usually acute sense of curiosity dulled by the vast quantities of beer that he had consumed. He gave it no further thought but relaxed, his back against a boulder, only half listening to what Wanga was saying. Mucongáve was chatting to Smuts; Captain Chitamba spoke in low tones to Mtiwa. From the tone of the captain's voice, Alistair decided that, whatever he was saying, it was not very nice.

They turned in at nine o'clock. The cave in which the white men found themselves was low of ceiling, but there were several holes in its walls, smaller tunnels, that gave it ventilation; although the through-draft carried with it the smell of unwashed bodies, it was not unbearable. With a short pondering on what the following days would have to offer, he fell asleep.

It was still dark when he felt someone shaking him. Where, in God's name, was he? After a moment's panic, he remembered. He heard Smuts's voice and felt something hot touching his hand.

"Have some tea. Hope you don't mind some condensed milk."

He sat up and sipped the sweet liquid gratefully. He heard a match scrape as Smuts lit a candle. He saw that Smuts was already dressed. How long had the man had been up? His watch showed five past five. Smuts paced the floor, impatiently. Alistair wondered what was bothering the man. His mouth tasted awful and his head felt woolly, but he had no headache, thank goodness. He lit a cigarette.

"Why are you up so early? I thought we were going to rest today?"

"Oh, go back to sleep, if you want to!" Smuts snapped. Then, in a gentler voice as if to take the edge off his tone, "No need for you to get up yet." Abruptly, he turned and went out. Once he'd left, Alistair felt very much alone. He sensed that the neighbouring caves were now empty of the men who had slept there during the night. Perhaps they had gone off on a raid, to lay mines or set an ambush or whatever they did. When he found that he couldn't stand the silence any longer, he sat up again and swung his legs off the stretcher. They ached from yesterday's march. He dressed slowly, wondering where he could get water to shave and wash. Like a genie, a soldier appeared with a tin basin of warm water. Alistair shaved by the flickering light of the candle using a hand mirror from his holdall. He put his towel away and went outside. Oddly, it seemed that Smuts was waiting for him.

A troop of men were gathered around Captain Chitamba who was checking their equipment in the pre-dawn light. For the most part, they were ragged and gaunt, but their weapons were clean and, oddly, there was a look of anticipation to their faces. Then Chitamba stopped and cupped his hand to his ear.

"*Um aeroplano! Depressa!*" he yelled. His troop scattered down the valley over a distance of two hundred metres and melted into cover with their rifles. Smuts grabbed Alistair's arm and led him into a cluster of big boulders where the general and Colonel Wanga were already crouching. The captain had gone with his men. Alistair remembered that he had not seen Mtiwa yet that day and wondered where he was. It was only then that he heard the drone of an aircraft that had seemed to have triggered all this activity.

"Why don't we hide in the caves?" Alistair thought he was asking the obvious.

"Shut up!" Smuts snapped, his eyes glued to the far off dent in the crater's lip. Alistair, too, looked that way. There it was, a silhouette against the lightening sky, a twin-engined aircraft that he recognised: a Douglas DC3 at a height of about four hundred metres, heading straight for them.

TWENTY-THREE

The cold morning air blasted in at the doorless hole, causing them to huddle in their thin battle-dress. In the cabin, the only man dressed for the occasion was da Silva in his sheepskin coat. He had strapped himself in opposite the door at the rear, facing forward so that he could cover the prisoners. There was a safe gap between him and the man next to him on his, the starboard, wall. This was Rafe Schulman who crouched, wondering how to get his hands on the Portuguese, but they were all shackled and would not be released until just before the drop. Next to him was Jan de Groot, depressed but not defeated. There just had to be a way out of this mess. He glanced at big Piet Visagie next to him. Piet was pale in the weak cabin light, nerves drum tight.

"Our only hope," he spoke to Jan in an undertone in Afrikaans, "is to hook up and go as soon as they free us. Drop as far from the target as possible – "

"Shut up! No speaking!" da Silva shouted over the drone of the engines.

Blair, nearest the door on the opposite side, suddenly yelled, "Fuck off, you bitch-balled son of a syphilitic whore!" and burst into bawdy song at the top of his voice: *Bang away at Lulu, bang her good and strong!* The rest of them joined in, yelling in desperate abandon. Da Silva went purple with rage and tried to get up, but his straps held him back. He shook the G3 at them and screamed for them to stop it but their voices only rose in volume as the delight at his frustration gave them courage and shook off the mantle of despair that had settled over them. McNeil, three metres from Sanderson, who covered them from where he sat at the cockpit bulkhead, yelled the same idea that Piet had told Jan into Nourse's ear. Geoff passed it to John Blair. It was their only chance and it wasn't much, but, if they acted simultaneously, they might not get in each other's way. They would have to chance being shot right here on the plane but McNeil was counting on the fact that both Sanderson and da Silva would be reluctant to spray the cabin with bullets in case they hit each other or the pilots. Sitting opposite McNeil, Geoff saw that Muller seemed also to have some sort of plan. Maybe he was thinking the same thing, because he leaned against Theunissen to whisper something in his ear. Theo was looking so strained that Muller appeared to notice with a shock that the man seemed to be near breaking point. Geoff was also surprised that he was not even singing with the others but, with clenched jaws, was staring at the space between McNeil and Sanderson, blankly. He must have heard because he shook his head and muttered something that left Muller with a baffled expression.

"Snap out of it, Theo! We can do it!" Muller shouted. Even Geoff heard that.

Theunissen only shook his head again. Muller gritted his teeth in anger and joined the raucous singing. Geoff saw him kick Dan's ankle and, when Muller had caught Dan's eye, he flicked a glance at Sanderson and, baring his teeth, made a snapping bite. McNeil nodded, almost imperceptibly.

They kept up the shouted songs for a while, ranging from *The Good Ship Venus* to *Eskimo Nell*, until da Silva no longer reacted.

Geoff was thinking about Sanderson and wondering how badly the South African government wanted him. He tried to recall what Brand had said and there seemed to be no doubt that it was a dead-or-alive situation. He was certain that Brand was in no position to do anything about Sanderson at the moment, although he must know where they were if the pens were still working. Of course, the range could be a problem. He could only pray that the batteries, or whatever they worked on, still had the power to cross the ever-widening distance. There seemed to be only one solution. He or Dan must kill Sanderson, themselves. He shuddered. He remembered what Dan had told him …

McNeil had killed, no, perhaps executed was a better word, another man besides the deserter. McNeil had been in charge of a small garrison of mercenaries in a little village in the northern Congo, near Aba on the Sudanese border. His opposite number in the Congolese army had been a cruel individual who was using his position to operate a protection racket on the locals. McNeil believed that he had also been in contact with the rebels, but was unable to prove it. Often, too, Dan had found that he had countermanded his orders. One evening, he had invited him to walk to the river with him to see if they could catch a canoe-load of arms that McNeil said was being smuggled in from across the border. Dan told him what a sonof-a-bitch he was and shot him in the face. He pitched the body into the river for the crocodiles and emptied his pistol into the surrounding bush before running back to the village to tell of a rebel attack and his narrow escape.

But this was different. Sanderson, or van Rooyen, was a fellow countryman. Still, he doubted that the man would hesitate to kill him or McNeil if the shoe was on the other foot. Sanderson was also jumping, willingly, so he was not expecting to be shot by Frelimo. How would they know the difference? Would he wear something that would make him stand out from the rest? Manuela must be in contact with the enemy by radio, but where was the sense in delivering some South African paratroopers – as the uniforms that they wore testified – into the hands of Frelimo? Not for ransom; they could have done that without the jump, so the jump must be a spectacle for someone. They would be seen, as members of the South African armed forces, to be interfering in the internal affairs of another country, something denied repeatedly by the South African government to the world. It would be to prove the South Africans liars. And they, the soldiers, would be too dead to deny the fact. Nourse grimaced. Sanderson would be the only one 'captured', perhaps, and would admit that they were acting on orders from the S.A.D.F. High Command. Geoff wondered if he was on the right track and who the show was being put on for. He glanced at Theo to see if he could elicit some support from the tough old mercenary, but Theunissen seemed to have withdrawn into himself of late and was not communicating. Geoff could not believe that a man of Theo's calibre had given up, but it was beginning to look that way. He hoped that Dan and Muller, if he had interpreted their signals correctly, would try to tackle Sanderson on their own. First, there was his pistol, then, Geoff was sure, the R3 in his kit which would be loaded with live rounds, unlike their own weapons. He watched Sanderson sitting sweating in his corner and knew he was afraid of the coming jump. McNeil must have read his mind.

"You are going to break your fucking neck, Sanderson," Dan yelled above the din, of the songs and the engines. "Throw in with us and we'll get you out of this mess you've got yourself into! No amount of money is worth it if you don't live to spend it! And, if the drop doesn't kill you, your bosses will when you've done what they want!"

"Shut up!" The eyes were large behind the spectacles. The mouth trembled. "Just shut the fuck up!"

"They'll shoot you when they've finished with you. Save themselves a pile of money. Who are they, Sanderson? Can't be Frelimo, must be someone behind them. The Chinese? Is it the Chinese, Sanderson? The Chinks will snuff you out like a candle! Join us, man, it's your only chance!"

"Damn you, McNeil! Shut your fucking mouth or I'll … I'll …" Sanderson half rose as if to hit Dan with the pistol but he didn't follow through. He just crouched, trembling. Dan grinned at him wolfishly, but his stomach was balled up tight and the cuffs cut into his wrists. It was now light enough to see the silver ribbon that was the mighty Zambezi below them. The Dakota started to lose height. Manuela appeared in the cockpit doorway.

"Be quiet! Or this man dies!" Heads turned and the noise died as they saw that her pistol was steady, pointed at McNeil's head. Destiny was on top of them and they all stiffened in fear and anticipation.

"You, Theunissen! Unlock the cuffs. Don't be foolish, there is more at stake than your miserable lives!" Manuela handed the pale Theo a key. He unsnapped his own cuffs, awkwardly, and massaged his wrists. He unsteadily stood up and turned to Muller. Each man whispered some desperate, hurried plan to him as he unlocked them,

184

but to each Theunissen shook his head. Their jumping drill was followed; as each man was freed, he took the snap link from the man ahead, ready to snap it onto the wire that ran overhead along the roof of the cabin.

It all happened as the last pair of cuffs clicked open. Da Silva had released his strap and moved to the corner by the open door, lining the G3 up on them and shouting; "Stay seated! Don't move until you are told!"

Nourse was yelling to Blair, "Don't be a bloody fool!" as he gripped Blair's snap hook tight with the static line wrapped around his wrist. John Blair threw himself forward, ignoring the G3 in his stomach and ploughed into da Silva. The G3 burped briefly as Blair wrenched himself and the Portuguese through the open door. It was the first move in a wave of pandemonium. McNeil turned his attention away from Blair's action to see Sanderson rap Manuela's wrist with his pistol and ram the girl backwards into the cockpit, slamming the door. Shaken by his decision and action, he stood gaping. Behind him, Dan was aware of the rest of them leaving the aircraft. – Go! Go! Go! – as he stepped towards Sanderson and tore the pistol from the trembling hand. He snatched the snap hook from Sanderson's pack and hit the overhead line with it.

"Go!" he yelled and shoved the frightened man towards the tail. He fired three shots through the cockpit door. There was a muffled scream but no-one appeared and the plane began to bank. Dan backed off to Sanderson, hooking himself to the wire as he did so. Except for Sanderson cowering against the rear bulkhead, the cabin was empty.

"I can't," Sanderson said. His face was ashen. McNeil took Sanderson's spare ammunition for the R3, wasting a couple of seconds and praying that they were not also blanks. He dived out the doorway, even as the Dak almost stood on its wingtip, pulling Sanderson after him. He knew how dangerous the double exit was, that they could entangle their opening 'chutes, but they were lucky. Their 'chutes jerked open, kissing edges. McNeil spilled air to move away, concentrating on the ground. One look was enough to spell it out. A few seconds later and he would have dropped into range of the rifles of the ant-like figures that swarmed towards him across the rock-strewn floor of what seemed to be an ancient extinct volcano. Splashes of rag showed him where his comrades had landed, stretching from the lip of the volcano towards himself and Sanderson. Then he was on the ground with a bone-rattling thump, doing a nearly forgotten parachutist's roll, narrowly missing a jagged boulder.

Sanderson was rolling in agony a few metres away. Dan slipped his own harness, rescued his R3, and dashed to him. He ripped open Sanderson's clips and left him to stagger to his feet, yelling, "Run, you bastard! Here they come!"

If Manuela had had her way, we would have landed smack in the middle of them, unarmed, thought McNeil. Even now, they had little chance of making it. He heard the burp of AK fire behind them, but it was far off as yet. He glanced back at Sanderson, saw him limping along as fast as he could, clutching his R3. Ahead, he saw his own men running as best they could for the cleft in the mountain. They had discarded their useless weapons with their packs, having no choice but to run for it. The exception was Theo, who, for some reason, had also retained his weapon. He saw Nourse and Schulman bending over a man on the ground. Muller, further along, was yelling back at them. "Leave him, he's had it!"

It was John Blair, the Englishman, with at least two of da Silva's bullets in his stomach. McNeil reached them. Blair was conscious, but in great pain. Blood ran through his fingers as they clutched his middle. He grimaced a greeting to Dan.

"Get the hell out of here, you two!" McNeil's voice was a snarl. He bent over Blair. "You haven't a snowball's, Johnny, you plucky bastard. See what you can do with this. It's loaded but not full."

"Thanks for nothing, you *Japie* cunt." Blair gasped. "So... so long, Dan..."

Then McNeil was away, leaving Sanderson's pistol on Blair's chest above his hands. Blair screamed with the pain as he dragged himself into the lee of a boulder and cradled the pistol over his oozing gut. That was Geoff's last sight of him as he glanced back one last time. He could later only speculate as to Blair's fate.

He fights the waves of nausea as he turns to watch his friends' progress. The furthest are climbing the lower slopes of the mountain, seeking no cover as yet as the AKs are still out of range except for a wild chance hit. Blair thinks he can just make out Jan de Groot in the lead, then Piet Visagie and Muller, Theunissen and Nourse, then McNeil and lastly Sanderson. He is confused about Sanderson; he cannot understand why the renegade is running, too. He had understood that the man had set them up for a massacre by the Frelimo, but now something has changed ...

"Ooh, Christ my guts hurt! What would me old mum say if she saw her Johnny, now!" He begins to weep, helpless, hopeless tears, as he watches the Japies running, ever slower, as the slope increases. The leaders are using their hands, scrabbling, now, sometimes out of sight amongst the boulders, almost up to the cliffs and curving towards their only hope of escape, the nick in the mountain over which they had flown, not so many minutes before.

"Ah, God ... ah God!" Blair feels the anger wash over him, anger at the waste, anger at the futility of it all, anger at the men shooting at his friends. They are near now, he can hear them shouting, excited, like hounds on the scent, then the clatter of their boots, the hacking of their breath. He lies still inside his pain and waits, almost impatiently, for them to come. They, too, are making no use of the cover; they have no need of it against unarmed men. They come in a ragged line, behind each other, a little to one side of Johnny Blair, their eyes up, fixed on the fleeing prey. All they have to do is get within range and pick them off as they appear on the face of the mountain, as they scramble towards their only hope, the fault in the rock. Even that will take some climbing to reach, for it cuts off only a fifth of the height of the cliffs. However, the slopes below it are not as sheer as the cliffs, and they are rough enough from erosion and rock slides to give a climber purchase, if not much cover.

Still, the Frelimo men are not giving up the opportunity of pausing now and then to send a burp of bullets up at them. Some of the bursts are getting uncomfortably close, forcing the fleeing men to move with more caution and slowing them down.

Two men in dirty camouflage stop to fire up the mountain. John Blair shoots the rearmost man in the back, holding the pistol in both hands. He shifts his aim to the foremost, who has not heard the single shot against the din of his own weapon. As he lowers it, Blair's bullet tears through his shoulder blade and lung and he falls to his knees. Blair huddles, waiting for the bullets of those following to tear him apart. A burp and splinters shatter off his rock; cries of Sul Africano! Blair fires at a face that appears but the bullet is wasted.

The grenade bounces and rolls to within a metre of him. He wants to reach for it, to toss it back, as they do in the movies, but he freezes, staring at it in fascination for the two seconds before it goes off...

Dan thought Sanderson had twisted his ankle, but it seemed to hold his weight, even though it was visibly painful. His breath tore at his chest and his eyes filled with sweat as he tried to keep up with McNeil.

It seemed to Dan that Sanderson must have realised that Dan was right. They would have forced him to detonate the bloody bombs and then they would have killed him and what use his money then? But they still had to get out of this mess ...

Sanderson must have believed they had a chance because the thought stopped him from turning and raising his hands and walking back down the slope. The other voice in his head would be saying: *they won't kill you, they need you. You can trick them into letting you go, later, before the bombs, after the bombs, what does it matter? This way, you will die, anyway.*

Although the sun had not yet cleared the eastern rim of the mountain, sweat dribbled down Sanderson's face, into his eyes again, and was wiped away with his palm. He pulled a blue cloth from his pocket and tried to fix it to his arm as he ran. A spray of bullets kicked up dust and gravel just ahead but he ploughed on after McNeil, using his hands now, too.

Geoff Nourse could only guess what they were thinking as he waited behind a boulder for them to catch up. As Dan reached him, they heard the grenade go off.

"John got two of them, anyhow, and now they aren't sure if there are any more of us down there." Nourse said.

McNeil looked back. "Poor sod, but a brave fucker, all the way!" he panted.

They were amongst a large cluster of rocks, the best cover there was to be had anywhere on that part of the mountain. It was the tail end of a landslide that had come from the fault above them. The others were slipping from boulder to boulder, but, climbing as they did so, they were exposed for too long between one piece of cover and the next. Frelimo's fire was increasing and they were now within range. Even Jan de Groot, in the lead, was obscured in a lash of bullet-raised dust, but McNeil saw him hug the rock and crawl away out of sight. De Groot was still a good way from the top.

"Look at that!" Nourse grabbed his arm. McNeil swung around to see the Frelimo men setting up a mortar. There seemed to be a man overseeing the operation, an officer of sorts. Another eight men started to climb after them, still assuming them to be unarmed except for Sanderson.

McNeil grinned, mirthlessly. "Sanderson must be worrying them! They didn't expect him to join us."

Sanderson, or van Rooyen, made his way into the shelter of the rocks and sank to his knees, white foam around his gaping, gasping mouth. His shaking hands put down the R3 and reached for a handkerchief to wipe his spectacles and mop his brow. McNeil noted the blue armband. The mortar was almost ready and nobody would make the top if they fired it. Even with the worst marksmen possible, they could start a landslide that would bury them.

"Sorry, Sanderson, but we need this!" Dan scooped up the R3 and handed it to Nourse, together with one of the spare magazines.

"No!" The protest burst from him, but he only half-heartedly grabbed at the weapon as Nourse took it. McNeil was kneeling, his own R3 on single. He fired, even as the bomb dropped down the muzzle of the tube. The officer was knocked sideways, but he was erect again in a few seconds, clutching his arm. A loud crump came as the round exploded somewhere beyond McNeil's party and the last of the climbers, but neither Nourse nor McNeil turned to look at it. They fired selected shots, knowing full well what the consequences would be if the weapon continued its barrage. Geoff dropped a man that lifted a second bomb. Dan badly scared the man that moved to take it over. Nourse hit the mortar tube without apparently damaging it. McNeil thought he hit another man as they began to drag the mortar away to another site, under better cover. Abruptly they dropped it and scattered. It fell in plain sight, much to McNeil's relief. Then the three South Africans were hugging the rocks as a hail of shots tore about them from a handful of Frelimo who were trying to outflank them.

McNeil's fingers dug into Sanderson's fleshy shoulder.

"Get up there and tell the others to wait for us over the top. We may be pinned down till nightfall, so nobody must move until dawn. If we aren't there by then, you must ..." he turned to Nourse to ask where they should head for but Nourse anticipated his question by continuing.

"Head downhill till you reach the Zambezi; it's not far. Go downstream, don't try to cross. It's all Frelimo territory. You'll reach a store at Bandar, there's an Indian there, if Frelimo have left him alone. Otherwise, continue downstream, there's another store at Fortuna, and beyond that there's the track to Lake Lifumba. There should be fishermen there, maybe a tractor to pull nets in. Further downstream are more stores, about thirty kilos apart."

"I'll tell you when to go, just keep your head down!" McNeil didn't try to keep the scorn out of his voice, but Sanderson took no notice. He was no coward – it took nerve to do what he had done, sell out his country to the Chinese – but he was a communications expert, he had never been under fire before.

Nourse quartered the area where the mortar had fallen while McNeil picked off two men in the flanking movement. Cover was scarce for the Frelimo men, but they found what they could and went to ground.

"Get going!" McNeil commanded, and astounded himself by adding, "good luck!"

Sanderson sucked in his breath and shambled off up the slope, heading for the next clump of boulders. The other two did not watch him go; their eyes were glued to the crater floor. The far end was still in purple shadow, the sun now well above the rim. The sky was cloudless; it probably would not rain again until November.

On the lower slope, a man began to crawl to fresh cover. Dan sighted on all he could see of him, his spine and head. Dan's finger whitened on the trigger, his shoulders shook with the recoil. The head dropped down, but whether with fright or death, Dan could not tell. For a while, only a carbine poked out with hardly a hand or an eye showing to guide it, and rattled off some wild shots.

Someone, it must be de Groot, Dan thought, had almost reached the top. Now and then, when he could risk a glance behind him, he would catch a glimpse of one or the other of the rest as they snaked from rock to bush to boulder. Then his attention was snapped forward again as a man made a short dash before Dan could fire. He waited patiently, watching the spot. The man, emboldened by his first success, left cover again. He fell on his face after two paces as McNeil's shot echoed against the cliffs.

Frelimo made only one attempt to rescue the mortar and gave up when the alert Nourse drilled a man through the leg and kicked up flinty dust at another man's heels. But then, they didn't really need it: another mortar suddenly gave its throaty cough from across the crater. Both men involuntarily ducked, but the bomb was meant for the escapees on the rim. For a range finder, it was not bad and the second one proved that the man in charge knew his business.

Jan was standing on the top, Geoff could see, safely out of range of AK fire. He knew his uniform would be wet with sweat, his knees shaking with fatigue, but he could only imagine the relief that would be rippling through him in waves so that he would feel nothing of the physical effects of what was now behind him.

Then, as Theunissen began to move up, the first mortar struck, thirty metres below and to one side of him. He lost his hold and slid back down into the cover of several boulders he had just left. That probably saved his life. The second bomb hit the lip of the notch right next to Jan who stood frozen in shock. His body was ripped apart like a chicken at a picnic. Chunks of rock erupted off the edge and rained down on Theunissen. Dan and Geoff could only guess if he had survived; he was out of sight.

The third bomb crashed and again splinters and lava debris flew, but it was a trifle over the edge of the summit and, it seemed, did them no damage. Again the mortar crumped, the mortar-man dropping his range by a hair. The slope shook and erupted chunks of rock, between where they thought Theunissen lay and the spot where they could see Piet Visagie and Helmut Muller huddling in inadequate cover. The rock slope started to slide.

The seemingly solid rock beneath the two desperate men trembled. It split and started to move, but when the dust cleared, Geoff had a glimpse of the two men disappearing into the trees on the crown. Several minutes later, another was visible for a minute, but when he snatched another glance from his vigil, the man was gone. Briefly, they later caught sight of the plump figure of the last man to make it over the crest, and for some reason there were no more mortars.

TWENTY-FOUR

Their ledge dropped away even as their desperate fingers found holds in the face in front of them. Visagie's hold was sure, he would later relate, though the fear cramped his throat and knotted his guts. Ahead of him, he saw Muller's fingers slip so that all his weight was on one hand and his heavy boots fought futilely for purchase, seemingly with a life of their own. A scream started from Muller's mouth.

Then one of the flailing boots found a bubble pocket in the broken lava and took the drag off the remaining sweating, slipping hand. Muller began to sob. Visagie tensed his powerful shoulders and lunged for another hold. He got it and his exploring feet found another. Suddenly he was on a higher ledge. He was dully aware of the sound of rumbling decreasing as the slide died away to a trickle of gravel and the mortar did not fire again. He was able to edge over to give Muller a hand. They curled up for a while in good cover to catch their breath. After five minutes, they started up again, hardly bothered by the occasional rattle of shots that splattered near them. They reached the top, stumbled back into the safety of the trees, and sank onto the rock slabs to rest.

Theo crawled over the edge and headed towards them. Piet managed to get to his feet to give him a hand. One of Theo's fingers was squashed; ripped open. He tore a strip off his shirt to bandage it. Shortly afterwards, Rafe Schulman arrived to join them, unscathed except for an abrasion on his head where a sizeable rock must have struck him. He still seemed to be dazed, sitting quietly, not joining in the conversation.

"Think they can circle around us here?" Piet asked, lighting a cigarette. They were in good, shaded cover and their position commanded a reasonable view of all approaches. Theo shook his head.

"Not for a while. They were expecting us to be dropped at their feet and that we would be totally unarmed. They wouldn't want to miss the fun, so I expect that every *Ter* in the area was there in the crater to watch. Even when things went wrong, they didn't expect us to get away. I never saw anyone moving out, but I may be wrong."

"I wonder what happened on the plane," Muller licked his bleeding finger tips, but his tongue was dry and the blood reminded him how thirsty he was. "The last thing I saw was Sanderson slamming that Porto bitch into the cockpit; then I was gone. I saw the bugger down there with Geoff and Dan. He must have chickened out of whatever he was up to, *hein*?"

"Well, man, if it wasn't for him, she would have shot at least a couple of us. Hell, if it wasn't for Dan and Geoff, none of us would have made it." Pieter gestured at the R3 at Theo's side, "Pity that thing isn't loaded; we could at least give them some covering fire from up here…"

"They don't stand a chance!" Theo said flatly. His eyes were cold. "They must be nearly out of ammo by now and Frelimo will be able to pick them off at will. It's ourselves that we must think of."

Rafe was staring away at the sky; he seemed not to have heard. Muller said nothing, he just nodded. Piet gaped at them, looking from one to the other in amazement. It was not in him to abandon his mates, even at risk to himself. Especially those two, for, even if he had been close to neither, they had made it possible for him to make his own escape.

"*Jong!* We can't do that. We could move along the mountain, cause a diversion, light a fire or something. Surely, something?" He thrust his thick fingers through his sweat-wet, wavy brown hair.

"Fire would do nothing, too much rock!" Theo scoffed. "You want to throw rocks at them? No, there's nothing that we can do except get the hell out of here and back down south."

But something, a shadow, moved in his cold eyes. Regret, pain, a memory? Theunissen had plenty of those, thought Pieter.

"What do you say, Rafe?" Pieter appealed to the silent Schulman, who blinked in surprise and looked at Piet as if he was from another planet.

"Watch out!" shouted Muller. Theo lunged for his weapon and Piet spun around. A shadow moved out of the trees. Then they relaxed, it was only Sanderson, limping, but otherwise unhurt. He stood, swaying with fatigue, but he watched the others warily, not sure of them. Piet knew he thought of them as men that he had almost sacrificed for his own gains and he was not sure that Sanderson might not do so again if the cards fell that way.

"What now, Mr. Colonel?" Muller demanded. "You lost your nerve, didn't you?"

"You'd be dead, if it wasn't for me," Sanderson said coldly, but Piet saw a strange look pass between him and Theunissen. The two men went off together far enough to have a private conversation. Piet had no idea what it could be about, but when they returned, Theo said that they would have to watch each other's backs and they would make it out alive. The colonel had guaranteed them all a bonus if they helped him get to Rhodesia safely.

"So, you're with us, then? What made you change sides?" asked Muller, roughly. "And what were you doing with those bastards in the first place?"

Sanderson eyed them from behind his dusty spectacles, "Money, man, same as you lot."

He seemed on the point of saying something more, but hesitated. His pale eyes darted from man to man.

"Give me some time to think it over, and maybe I can make us all a fortune. I could use some tough men," he said, "Or, were you thinking of getting the hell back to South Africa, where you'll be safe?"

You're bloody right, man! Thought Piet Visagie, but he said nothing. He was worried about Schulman, who seemed to be concussed. He could sense the interest rise in the other two mercenaries.

"Do your thinking," Theo Theunissen said, "and maybe we will listen. In the meantime, let's get out of here." Another look passed between the two men that went unnoticed by Muller, but Piet picked it up. He wondered what plot they had hatched.

"McNeil asked us to wait for dawn," Sanderson said in a for-the-record voice, "to give them a chance of getting out under cover of dark. If they don't make it, we are to go on without them," he added Nourse's instructions. "I don't see them moving from there; they are completely pinned down..." He had no intention of waiting five minutes, never mind twenty hours.

Theo shouldered his weapon. "Okay, then, Bandar, here we come."

Only Piet Visagie looked back at the crest over which they had come with an expression of doubt on his craggy face. He kept close to Rafe. They headed down the steep, rocky slopes from one clump of thorn to the next, then into the mopane belt. After two hours they stopped to gaze at the ribbon of water and sandbars that could be made out below them. They licked dry lips and walked on. Behind them, over the mountain, the vultures gathered for the feast. Frelimo men, John Blair, José da Silva, Jan de Groot. And there would be more.

TWENTY-FIVE

The crater became a brass bowl and sweat dribbled down the faces of the two men crouched behind the rocks, soaked their shirts and stuck them to their backs, until it seemed that they had no more moisture to give. Their mouths were slimy, their lips cracked. Even so they were thankful that it was well past mid-summer. It was after ten o'clock, now, quiet but for the small birds and the sharp yelp of lappet-faced vultures at their feast. They couldn't see the body, but they guessed that it must be da Silva who had fallen without a parachute. The mass of ugly birds were only thirty metres from them: huge, dark, untidy; tearing and delving. Around them, darting in when they could, were a few smaller hooded vultures, mindful of the huge beaks of their brethren.

His lean face lined from squinting into the glare, Geoff Nourse scanned the slope around where the mortar lay. It was no comfort to know that he was six shots into his last magazine. He said, abruptly, "How're you off for ammo, Dan?"

McNeil quartered the slope over the vultures; besides the birds, nothing moved. But he knew what lay behind the flat rocks beyond, effectively cutting off any attempt they might make of climbing the cliffs at their backs in daylight. Frelimo had not fired a shot in many minutes, but they didn't need to; all they had to do was wait for the South Africans to try their luck. McNeil grimaced. This was it, then. They were to die here in the wilds of Mozambique; by a quick bullet, if they were lucky, by dismemberment, if they were taken alive. Then, there was the thirst that was already squeezing them dry. They were losing moisture that they could not replace. But, they were unlikely to be alive long enough for thirst to make a big difference …

"Ten or twelve, no more. I wonder why that other mortar stopped? Must be out of shells, except for those with that bitch down there." He nodded at the nearer tube. "They should have grenade launchers and rockets, but they have thrown nothing else at us. I s'pose everything is out in the field to use on the Portuguese."

"Does seem strange," Geoff sucked at his dry mouth to loosen his tongue, "but your theory must be right. Now, you clever bugger, how do we get out of this one?"

Dan grinned, suddenly; his feeling of hopelessness lifting. Geoff hadn't given up and he was trusting Dan's experience to get them out of this pickle. He wished that he'd had Nourse with him in the Congo. Okay, analyse. They had twenty shots between them, or two short bursts each. They couldn't go up; they'd be cut to pieces. The same result if they went down. Except for small boulders, they were exposed all round. All they might survive would be a short dash with the other giving covering fire with the last of their ammo…

"It's quite simple, my china," he said, the idea suddenly leaping into his mind. A chance, a slim tenuous, odds-against chance. "Give it an hour. Let them sweat and get cramp and get thirsty. Let them think that we are never going to try it. Then, we try it."

"Up the kranz? You're mad, bloody bonkers. Captain, this is your crew speaking; we hereby mutiny."

"Shut up, crew, and listen. It may be a poor chance, but at least it's a chance. No, not up the cliffs. We go downhill. You…"

"Now I know you really have a screw loose. What preference do you have for being shot at close quarters instead of being shot at…?"

"Oh, Jesus, Geoff, shut up a minute. You take my ammo and put your rifle on rapid. You cover me. As we know, they're in two main pockets and by now could be pretty spread out. You have to cover the lot in very short bursts. I'm going to try for the AKs on the bodies down there near the mortar. I think the mortar is out of sight of the johnnies out here on my side so I'll have only those under cover near the mortar to contend with."

"Only," muttered Nourse, "that's all. Nothing to it. And if you don't make it, what the hell do I do then?"

"Then you can be Captain."

McNeil fired as a head and weapon snapped into view beyond the vultures. The birds rose, flapping, ungainly. The shot echoed back from the cliffs for nearly a minute before silence fell again. Nothing else happened.

"Think we'll have any ammo left by then?" Geoff asked, sardonically, as the birds settled again. "What; when our hero has taken the position? I suppose, then, I also have to run like hell?"

"Faster than that, but I'll have a cold beer waiting for you."

Geoff wished he hadn't said that; he could see the golden glass with the condensation trickling down. His furry tongue rasped over his dry lips.

The sun climbed and turned up the heat. Now and then they saw it wink on binoculars across the crater and they wondered who it was over there, waiting for this little pocket of resistance to be wiped out. They had guessed, by now, that the whole charade had been arranged as a spectacle for someone. The South African uniforms, the weapons. Nourse thought of the stupid little transmitter pen in his pocket and asked Dan where in the hell Brand and Cecile were, smothered in their cloaks and tripping over their daggers. Fat lot of help they'd been.

"And I had the man they were after in my hands and I told him to walk away up the mountain. Even wished the fucker luck! Still, he's changed sides, hasn't he?" Dan laughed without humour.

They both hoped that it hadn't been the worst mistake of their lives, but it was too late to do anything about it now. They would be vulture food in a little while. They reckoned that they had as much chance of making it out as they had of finding that cold beer Dan had promised Geoff.

You're as good as dead, their little voices said, *so just take as many of them with you as you can.*

The silence and the heat and the minutes dragged on. Across the crater, three or four men could be seen making their way from the bottom of the cliffs up to the bottom of the dent and through it. As McNeil pointed, they knew they were looking at the normal route in and out of the circular valley. Only properly equipped climbers could scale the cliffs anywhere else except for the route the escapees had taken that morning. It was McNeil's guess that the Frelimo just leaving were either being sent to circle around the rim to fire down on them from above, or to bring more mortar shells or an RPG2 rocket. Either way, Geoff thought with a bilious feeling in his stomach, they wouldn't finish whatever it was before he and Dan made their move. His watch said half an hour left. For what? To live? He glanced at Dan, but he gave nothing away; he merely grinned. Surely he, too, was quaking inside? Nourse returned the grin.

Suddenly Nourse fired and a man fell on top of the mortar. Another grabbed desperately at the weapon under the body of his companion, but hardly moved it before Nourse's second round took him in the hip. A third man picked up two bombs and started back. McNeil took his attention off his own sector to watch in agony as Nourse's next shot completely missed the bomb carrier. Again Nourse's weapon crashed, but his own sector was alive with attacking men and he was feverishly firing, seriously distracted by rising vultures. Something slapped his shoulder, and then it was over.

The bomb carrier was down, twitching, ten metres from the cover he had sought – now it only needed a man to risk a short dash to retrieve it for the other mortar. More men had made the protection of the rocks beyond the remains of da Silva's body which now had the company of two Frelimo who had not made the dash. Another had found a depression just beyond the others, but Dan said he could just see the edge of his shoulder as he flattened himself for dear life into the rock.

Geoff watched with concern as McNeil fingered the lava fragment that was embedded just under his collar bone. He said that the whole area still felt numb after the initial shock of impact. Slowly, the feeling returned in waves of pain while blood began to trickle down his chest and soak his shirt – just another blotch on the camouflage. The time to move was now – before this shoulder stiffened and the enemy had time to lick their own wounds – and before they had to use any more of their fast diminishing supply of cartridges.

More specks appeared in the clear sky. More food in the larder, so more guests for dinner, Geoff thought, as his pulse gradually returned to normal. He risked a glance at Dan to see the ever widening crimson blotch on his shoulder. There was a muffled click as McNeil's magazine came free. He handed it to Nourse and Geoff realised that Dan had decided to go. Now. His gut knotted. The last drop of saliva in his mouth dried up. He saw McNeil clip in another magazine from the pouch on his leg and realised that these were the blanks with which they were issued. McNeil caught the glance and smiled tightly.

"Some muzzle blast to fry their eyebrows. I do have one live one up the spout. Have you now got half a mag?"

"More than half, eleven, I make it." Geoff deftly thumbed those cartridges from Dan's magazine into his own and clipped it home into his weapon. "So, you're off then? Send a postcard."

"You're alright, Geoff Nourse. Just one thing. The one who'll move first will be the one that's the most uncomfortable. And there he is. That one over there who thinks he's a chameleon. Drop him first, then lift your burst to keep the bugger behind him down, then slam that nest of sods around the mortar. And watch you don't tickle my arse. Okay? That's it, up yours, I'm off!"

There were a few metres of good cover in the tangle of boulders, then they became more scattered and the surface was steep rock and gravel. McNeil was in full stride by the time he burst into view, making a minimum of noise as he ran on his toes, hurtling down the slope, incapable of stopping even if he'd wanted to.

He'd been right about the chameleon. Geoff's first two bullets hit the man in the chest even as he came to his knees. One man further back also half rose but dropped as the burst lashed gravel into his face. Then Geoff swung the muzzle; the splatter of rock chips hit the chest of the man near the mortar who had risen to meet McNeil's wild dash. The onslaught threw him backwards and his weapon spewed into the sky. Another man who had been crawling after the mortar rolled onto his back and lifted his AK, but McNeil's single live round went through his throat, then the R3 jammed on the blanks with not enough gas to eject. Even as Dan dropped the useless weapon, he was at the mortar and its complement of dead bodies. With a shower of flying gravel, he allowed his knees to buckle and he collapsed onto the nearest corpse, his hand reaching desperately for the AK at its side, his mind screaming: *I've made it! I've made it!* – while hardly daring to believe it.

He pulled the corpse around so that it afforded some scrap of protection and uncovered the spare ammunition pouches. He put short bursts into the rocks round about him. The weapon clicked empty and he tugged feverishly at the pouches for another, knowing that he was right out in the open. His shoulder was now a sea of pain and his head spun. It sagged onto the chest of the Frelimo corpse as he blacked out.

His heels were dragging on the rocky ground when he came around. He started to struggle, so Nourse put him down.

"So, walk, then, you lazy bastard," Nourse grunted. They were almost at some rocks that McNeil eventually recognised as those behind which these men who had attempted to recover the mortar had lain. From the distance came the rattle of another AK; it licked the dust some twenty metres off and crept towards them as the user corrected, then ran out of ammunition. Then Nourse was back with the mortar.

"Set this up, will you, Dan, while I go and get something to fire through it. Hey, Dan?"

"For Christ's sake, what's happening?" McNeil groaned, rolled to his knees and turned to watch Nourse trot with no effort at concealment across to the half dozen mortar bombs lying where the weapon itself had once lain. Besides themselves, the only things that moved were the vultures. Except across the valley…

"Hey! They're pulling out!" McNeil caught sight of some little figures snaking up the route to the notch.

"Seems like it, Dan," Nourse laid his load down near the base plate. "Now, give me a hand to try and stop them, will you?"

With McNeil aiming and Nourse loading, they sent three bombs off to the base of the notch. Slowly, the dust cleared. They could see nothing moving. The crater was quiet again and the noon sun beat down, uncaring, impartial.

"Help me with this shoulder, will you, and for Christ's sake, tell me what…"

"What happened?" Nourse found the strength to grin, wryly. Reaction was now starting to set in and he felt weak at the knees. "Very little, actually. When you set out on your dash, the opposition had all but had it, already. There are probably a couple of Frelimo out in the rocks who wish that Mozambique was also on the National Health, but they seem to be lying doggo until we get the hell out of here, I guess. The rest seemed to be trying to run for it before we – hold on, I can see it! It looks like a piece of rock." He shifted the lips of the wound so that he could see into it. The edge of the collarbone showed briefly white in it before the blood flowed again. Nourse managed to work the sliver of stone loose and out of the wound while McNeil called him all the filthy names he could think of.

"Yo mama din brung yo up proper, mon!" Nourse said, keeping a weather-eye on their surroundings for any sign of active enemy survivors. The tension still made his skin crawl. All he could think of was to get out of the crater and back into the relative safety of the surrounding bush. He armed them with AKs and five full magazines apiece. He nudged the mortar with his boot.

"How do we blow this thing up?" he asked Dan who told him to place the bombs, noses together facing towards the base plate and the barrel on top.

"Hit the base plate with a burst when we are safe in cover. Now, let's get the hell out of here, for Christ's sake!" Dan was feeling better now that the piece of stone was removed, but the whole shoulder was stiffening and ached abominably. It was now bandaged with strips from the legs of Nourse's trousers, which he had turned into shorts. He swayed drunkenly to his feet and took the AK that Geoff, with a look of concern, handed him. He waited for his head to clear, grateful that it was his left shoulder, not his right, then set off after Nourse, across the floor of the crater. From a safe distance, the latter detonated the mortars with a carefully aimed burst against the base plate.

The ground still sloped down for a while, but cover from the enemy, such as there might be, increased with gnarled fig trees, acacias, shrubs and bigger boulders. In one such cluster of rocks there was a small marshy patch that denoted a spring. Here a path led to another, larger spring where they drank, deeply, gratefully. Although the vegetation was denser, too, by climbing on higher rocks, Nourse could see enough to be relatively sure that there was nobody lying in wait. As they approached the cliffs after half an hour's careful advance, McNeil became aware of the caves. He called to Geoff in the lead.

"Hey, come back here a minute, will you?" He sat and lit a smoke, Nourse squatting beside him, cradling his AK, his eyes peeled. "Do you remember what da Silva said? You told me that he told you, when you were painting the Dak, that they were going to drop us into the Frelimo main camp?"

"*Ja*, so what?" Nourse looked at the pitted, towering cliffs and frowned. "So, the birds have flown, if they survived the mortars."

"How many did you see, running up that path or whatever it is, before we blotted them out? Five, six? Could you make them out? Weren't they all black guys, in camo?" Dan's voice rose in excitement as he became sure of his logic.

"Weren't we expecting some special spectators, so that our little exhibition had someone to impress? What happened to them, Geoff? I think the buggers are still here, in those caves, waiting to shoot the shit out of us if we go nosing around in there."

"Oh, shit," muttered Geoff, feeling suddenly quite sick. It made sense. He slid down behind a boulder, sweat starting out afresh on his brow. "Then, I'm not curious about what's in there. I mean, of course there are a hundred cases of cold lager in there, but who wants one, anyhow? Surely we can go around that far side and meet their path halfway up. We could be out of sight of the caves most of the time. Hopefully. Thank God they seem to have no more mortars – or rockets!"

Still pondering the enemy's lack of a larger armoury, but assuming the rockets and mortars such as they had encountered in the fights of Serra Chimbala and at the Pompue were in the field, or that supplies had run out, they made for the opposite cliffs. While keeping away from the threatening caves, they hoped that their route would also seem natural to any possible observer. An hour later, they reached the path leading up towards the dent and warily began to trudge upwards. They were half expecting to meet the group that had escaped up it recently.

They found some body parts at one of the mortar craters and knew that they had taken out at least one man.

The worst ordeal was climbing out of the dent to reach the main ridge, which, although jagged, actually had some sort of path worn on it, and was obviously a patrol route. They slowly circled the crater to arrive at the further niche in the ridge where their surviving fellow mercenaries had made good their escape that morning. It was sundown when they reached the spot where Theunissen, Muller, Visagie, Schulman and Sanderson has waited for less than half an hour. Nourse ferreted around morosely in the fading light.

"The bastards didn't wait long, then."

McNeil nodded. He knew that Nourse was adept at reading signs and didn't doubt what he said.

"I just do not understand why Theo moved out without some sort of farewell gesture. Not even a message. Perhaps he gave us no chance of survival and decided that waiting was a waste of time." Dan said, not without a little bitterness.

Geoff smiled wryly; he had given themselves no chance, either! Perhaps some Frelimo had forced them to move? Still, Theo had been acting pretty strange, of late. Maybe he was getting too old for this caper.

They set off on the trail of the others in the remaining light only stopping when they started to trip over things. They had nothing to eat and nothing to drink. McNeil's shoulder was a block of throbbing pain. Nourse gathered some grass and dried *mopane* leaves into a hollow in the ground in the shelter of some huge rocks. They felt a little cold, now, but dared not risk a fire this close to the mountain.

"I'm going to have a smoke, Dan. I don't care if there are fifty Ters out there waiting for me to light up. God, I'm buggered. I could sleep for a week." Nourse lit two cigarettes and passed one to McNeil. There were five left in his packet. After five minutes, they stubbed them out and crawled into their nest, not bothering to keep watch.

TWENTY-SIX

The silence was broken by a curse from General Mucongáve. Smuts said something to him in the Sena tongue in a sharp tone and it sounded as if the general told him to shut his white trash mouth. John Alistair huddled a little further back into the cave. He shivered in fear. He wondered who would shoot him first, Smuts or the general or the two South Africans who were outside.

Somehow or other, things had gone wrong. It was not difficult to realise that the whole thing had been set up for his benefit. When the Dakota first began to disgorge the paratroopers, Colonel Wanga, to whom he had just been speaking in French, had muttered in that language, "The fools! They're much too far away." Then, of the first two, one had plummeted straight into the ground. The rest has poured out in a bunch, then, after a pause, two had come out in a most unmilitary fashion. No sooner had they hit the ground than, instead of attacking, they had shed their kit and most of their rifles and headed in the opposite direction! Alistair's look of bafflement had been seen by Smuts who had tried to explain.

"Must be a recce party. Ha-ha, I bet they didn't expect to jump right into the enemy's lap! Look, they got such a fright, some of them have thrown their rifles away! They know they haven't got a chance against us."

"Yes," Alistair had said, feeling sick in the pit of his stomach. "Is this the first attack by air? I see the plane had no markings. Where do you suppose it operated from?"

Smuts eyes had narrowed, briefly, but all he had said was, "Probably from over the Rhodesian border."

The crater had echoed with gunfire and General Mucongáve cursed again as it had been apparent that there was still some considerable distance between his men and the fleeing South Africans, if indeed, that's who they were. Captain Chitamba returned briefly for a mortar and bombs, about which he and Colonel Wanga had an argument. Eventually, Chitamba had left with eight bombs or so and a murderous backwards glance.

"We are very short of ammunition here at the moment," the thin colonel had explained to Alistair. "There is some on its way from the Zambian border and we expected it here last week, but –" he shrugged, as if to say that very little of what was expected actually happened. Alistair had noted that, so far, none of the whites that appeared to be armed had fired a shot. He had seen a Frelimo, shooting at the fleeing men, go down, then a second one. The lighter crack of a pistol had come to their ears. General Mucongáve had demanded to know what was happening. The roar of a grenade came just after that, the only one to be heard that day.

Alistair, straining his eyes, had seen the faraway ants that were men, strung out, moving slower as they began to climb, and the pursuers closing the gap. Chitamba was directing his mortar crew to set up their weapon at a spot where the ground was not yet too steep, and, Alistair had thought, this would be the end of them. Another victory against the imperialist racists. He would be taken to see the bodies, what was left of them, in their South African uniforms, so that his indignant words would bear witness and stir the world's indignation at the military intervention etc. etc.

Then he had seen that some sort of resistance had been set up by someone in a cluster of boulders at the foot of the face that the fleeing men were trying to climb. Chitamba's mortar had fired twice without effect and that set the general to cursing again. He had roared a command to Colonel Wanga who had taken three men and scurried off to the caves to fetch another mortar and four bombs. Even then, as they had seen, Chitamba's mortar had been abandoned as the riflemen in the rocks had harried the crew. Someone else – it must have been Lieutenant Mtiwa – had led a party of men in a flanking movement, but it had slowly petered out as their cover thinned and their numbers had diminished.

The ants had been nearly at the top of their climb when Wanga fired. Nasty, shuddered Alistair. Wanga was an excellent mortarman. The bombs crashed onto the face, spewing rock and splinters into the air. General Mucongáve had roared his approval as the topmost ant had been shredded and flung away. Crash, crash again, then silence. General Mucongáve had looked at Wanga.

"Finished, my General," he had reported, sadly. The general's lips had thinned in frustration.

"Get some from Chitamba!" he had ordered. A man hurried away. Twenty minutes later, there had been a rush on the mortar and its bombs, that lay in the open. They almost made it, but, after a furious battle, the attempt fizzled out. Alistair had found himself hoping that the South Africans would make a getaway, even though, if they did, it would jeopardise his own position seriously. Damn the Commies and Frelimo for their sneaky little tricks. Sweat had broken out on him in a fresh wave of gut-shrivelling fear. He had tried to maintain an expression of unconcern on his face, but he knew that Smuts was watching him; he prayed that he had not given himself away.

—m—

Whilst General Mucongáve had issued orders that Wanga take some men and circle the mountain top to try and winkle out the marksmen in the rocks, Smuts had watched helplessly as a figure had gained the safety of the rim of the dent and disappeared. He, too, had been sweating with fear; the whole affair was going sour and there was nothing he could do about it. He had read Alistair's face like a book and knew that he would have to arrange his death, but that was a mere detail. The publicity side of the plan was less important than Sanderson getting away. He had tried to retain some hope that Sanderson had felt that he had been in no position but to fake a surrender, that he hadn't gone back on the deal, that he would return when he could. Smuts had been sent an expert interrogator to make

Sanderson shed his secrets under pressure if the need arose, but it had not been necessary. There was the down payment, of course, but the expert could not guarantee that they could sift the complete complex firing procedure from Sanderson's mind with the degree of accuracy required. There had certainly been no intention of paying the balance or allowing Sanderson to live after they had gleaned whatever military secrets to which he, in his position, had been entrusted.

Through his binoculars, Smuts had picked out the stocky figure, crawling up the face. It was easy to distinguish the blue armband. He had begun to feel sick – the chestnuts were well and truly in the fire and he could think of no way to snatch them out. The price for failure would be his own life. There had to be a way of getting Sanderson back; there had to be.

The battle had quietened down to odd shots; each was a quelled attempt to rush the rocks. Suddenly, a white soldier dashed from cover for the mortar, whilst a fusillade of shots banged out, then all was silent. Smuts waited only long enough to be sure that the mortar had fallen into enemy hands then he grasped the general's shoulder.

"Comrade General, we must get into the shelter of the caves before they can use the mortar!" General Mucongáve had stiffened at Smuts's touch, but he had seen the sense of what he said. He had looked at his remaining men, shrewdly, his eyes slitted. He snapped an order at a sergeant to take five men up the trail and hold the top in case the South Africans went up. They set off at the double. They were in fact a decoy while the general, Smuts, Alistair and two other men crawled into the caves. The general and Smuts had a hurried conference that they made certain Alistair couldn't make out; then Smuts slipped out again, crawling. The general and two men set up a machine gun back from the mouth of the cave.

Smuts was in one of the further caves with the Chinese soldiers when the mortar started. They gripped their AKs and huddled in the dark, waiting.

"No, Captain!" Smuts had whispered in Chinese, "You must not show yourselves. I think we can get them as they come this way, as they surely will, but they must not see you in case either one gets away. No, of course they won't, but there is also the English journalist. We will take him back to Malawi and arrange an accident there, otherwise someone may come looking for him. We cannot risk that."

He pretended not to see the Chinese captain smile in the semi-dark. It was a smile of contempt. The man knew that Smuts was not obliged to discuss these matters with him, a mere Captain of Communications in the Chinese Peoples' Army. He could smell fear on Smuts, and he knew that things had gone radically wrong. It would be Smuts who suffered the consequences. It was the captain's job to command the four radio operators with him and make sure that their equipment was functional. Well, for now. Smuts thought that the captain probably had other capabilities if he was called upon to use them. He saw the bastard smile again, and suppressed a shudder.

Smuts knew the captain didn't like him and would find it a pleasure to liquidate him if he got the order to do so.

They were safe in the dark of the cave, but Smuts positioned himself so that he could now make out the two South Africans at the foot of the crater. They had stopped. There was a burp of AK fire and a booming explosion; he realised that they had destroyed the mortar. The two men made towards the caves. They stopped once more. and the watchers tensed.

In his cave, General Mucongáve would be cursing. The bastards were skirting around them, and, although they were within range for a long shot, they were rarely in sight. An hour passed before Smuts deemed it safe to come out.

"Is there nothing we can do?" gritted Mucongáve, "I must warn all my men to look for them. They must be heading for the Zambezi."

Smuts nodded, unhappily. "What is more important, General, is the man Sanderson. It would be a pity if your men shot him, but he must be stopped. He must be brought back here alive.

The general grinned without humour. "It seems your plans have come unstuck, Comrade." There was a sardonic inflection on the last word. "When Wanga returns, he will personally see to it. All the whites that have survived will head for the big river; they will go downstream towards Mutarara, where there is a garrison of Portuguese soldiers.

There are some trading posts on the way, but they mostly co-operate with us. They are too afraid not to. We have informers in all the *aldeamentos* along the way. Few will help them. We will get them all. Will you be going with Colonel Wanga?" The yellow eyes watched his. Smuts knew that he would have to go. Getting Sanderson back was his responsibility. He nodded. It was Frelimo country. There was a good chance that the whites would not get away. His own life depended on it...

"Keep the journalist here, Comrade General. Please guard him well. I must take him back to Malawi and arrange an accident there. He is of no further use to us."

The general shrugged. It was no concern of his. Smuts guessed that he would be thinking that these foreigners were too clever for their own good. It had been a bad day, he had lost many men, Chitamba and Mtiwa among them, it seemed. The general sent a man down across the crater to look for wounded men and recover such arms and ammunition as he could. It would come, he knew, a free Mozambique, but he wished that it could be without the help of the Chinese or the Russians. They would extract their pound of flesh, he knew, and the price would be dear. Smuts saw him go to his radio with his operator and heard him as he called up four of his bands and gave them their instructions. They would all head for the Mutarara – Bandar road by the shortest route, putting out the word as they went. General Mucongáve obviously thought it a nuisance, but it was certain that they would get all the South Africans in a day or two. Most of them were unarmed. These last two that had caused the most damage were the biggest problem, but he warned his men to be careful. He had told them that they were *Sul Africanos* and that they were to leave them where they fell and not to touch their uniforms.

Smuts went to see Alistair. He found him in the shade near the cave mouth, smoking, fairly composed. They kept up the charade for the time being.

"Well, there you are, Mr. Alistair. They've never sent paratroopers before, so it looks as if the South Africans are hotting things up for us. For the true Mozambicans, I mean."

"Yes," Alistair said. "You will have to move camp now that they know where your headquarters are."

Smuts sighed, "I suppose so."

Not if we stop the South Africans in the bush, he thought savagely, kicking his foot abruptly against a rock with sudden temper. He noticed Alistair shiver. He realised that the man knew that his chances of survival were not much more than nil.

TWENTY-SEVEN

The mid-morning sun threw a vicious glare off the planes, the roofs, and the shining tarmac itself, so that the majority of onlookers in the concourse of Manga Airport, Beira, including Morné Brand, wore sunglasses. A Deta Airways Boeing 727 from Lourenço Marques touched down with minimal bounce and little white puffs of smoke exploded from the wheels. In less than seven minutes of its coming to a standstill in front of the terminal, the first passenger was squinting into the glare from the top of the stairs.

Both Bates and Duvenage had been on the flight and, although they knew each other well, neither spoke to nor acknowledged the existence of the other. Once through the official formalities that plagued even the internal flights in Mozambique, Bates made for the lounge and, catching sight of Brand, joined him. They swiftly went to the car park where they got into a grey Landrover and followed the taxi that Duvenage took into town to the railway station. In his wing mirror, de Souza, driving the Landrover, could still see the scooter that had been dogging them since he had picked up Brand and Cecile Cradock earlier that morning. Beira was just not crowded enough to lose it. Eventually, Brand told him to stop trying. It was too late for mere observation to hinder them. It was too bad that de Souza's cover was blown, but they were committed to action, now, in a desperate bid to find van Rooyen. The scooter stopped at the kerb as they pulled into the station car park. The mulatto on the scooter tucked his chin into his jacket to make use of the radio he had there.

They watched as Duvenage pulled his soft leather suitcase up under his arm and stepped back a few paces to admire the façade of the old building to give the taxi time to disappear across the bridge over the Rio Chiveve where it entered the docks. There were some twenty vehicles in the forecourt where he stood. Several were Landrovers – it was 4x4 country – but he put his money on a new grey station wagon with curtains in the windows abaft the front seats, that had just come in.

He was an athletic man with an easy, springy stride, an even six foot tall with a wiry frame, dark, straight hair, brown eyes, lean face and a quirky mouth. He disappeared into the brightly muralled concourse.

"All a bit pointless," said Brand, "but I suppose they ought not to know exactly when we leave Beira and in what direction and how many of us there are. Take this guy out before he can use his radio again."

Bates slipped out of the back seat. He was two inches under six foot, with a barrel-chested, powerful frame. He had blue eyes, very curly blond hair and a broad face with a wide mouth. He set off smartly towards the road to the front of the scooter. Cecile set off into the station to find Duvenage. De Souza was a Latin, short, wiry; wavy black hair. He opened his door, took the long route along the road to the entrance to the station and walked out behind the scooter. The mulatto turned and watched him approach, puzzled, but beginning to look nervous.

"*Desculpe, o Senhor, mas tenho horas?*" de Souza asked him for the time. Bates hit him hard from behind and caught him as he fell. They eased him to the sidewalk, took his radio and propped him against the rear bumper of a parked vehicle. Bates bent the mudguard into the wheel and put the scooter on its stand. They sauntered back across the car park to the grey Landrover. Cecile reappeared with Duvenage and the vehicle paused to pick them up as they left. There was no reaction from the few people around. The vehicle circled the traffic island, pausing under the windmill of the little Moulin Rouge for a minute, and then drifted casually past it. The street they were in was flanked by warehouses and workshops, where trucks were being unhurriedly loaded and vehicles unhurriedly repaired. Vehicles were parked half on the pavement and half in the street. The grey station wagon squeezed through and headed out of town.

Duvenage looked around him. Beside him sat the good-looking blond girl whom, until now, he had never met. She turned a freckled face towards him and smiled in greeting as Brand introduced them to each other. Up front sat Morné Brand, wearing a Stetson with a leopard skin band. He also wore wrap-around dark glasses. De Souza, whom he had met before, hooted at a trio of ragged street urchins who were rolling bicycle rims down the street. They scuttled away, grinning.

Brand explained the situation. He was almost sure that van Rooyen was not in Beira any more. The instructions to McNeil and Nourse had been to use the tracking transmitters to follow van Rooyen, but since they themselves had been taken prisoner, it stood to reason that they were not following him but only making it possible to indicate to Brand that they themselves were alive and to give their position. This location had been static for several days, indicating their incarceration and showing that things were coming to a head. With de Souza's help, and watching the movement of supplies and people, they had to deduce that the Barros hunting camp on the Mungari was the only possible place to have a look for van Rooyen. It was reasonable to deduce that all players in the know would make sure that they were out of range when van Rooyen detonated his box of tricks, and the camp was such a place. There were no military or police installations within fifty kilometres.

Then, early that morning, both transmitters had rapidly moved west.

"Both Barros's DC3 and the Cessna logged flight paths for the Mungari camp yesterday. Today, the speed and line indicated that they were aboard a plane," Brand said. "Then the transmitters stopped abruptly in the middle of nowhere, where no known landing strips exist. That ruled out the Dak landing, but the Cessna could conceivably land on a road. However, when I kept in mind that most of the mercenaries were parachutists, it kept the Dak in the equation and suggested a jump. Still, where is van Rooyen?"

The grey station wagon swung left into the Avenida Massano de Amorim. The road was peppered with pedestrians and unhurried cyclists and bumbling motorists that swerved to avoid potholes in the badly tarred surface without any warning, but Brand told de Souza to put his foot down.

Using the horn frequently and his voice more often, de Souza had them out of Beira without any signs of pursuit. As de Souza pointed out, the opposition would have no difficulty working out where they would head for and would radio a warning to the camp on the Mungari. They would know that it was a five hour drive and have plenty of time to prepare for them. So, there was only one thing they could do to catch them by surprise and that was to arrive much earlier than expected.

In half an hour, they were through the little town of Dondo and passing the new army barracks recently built on the site where, two years ago, two Rhodesian Special Air Services men had buried two canisters. They turned off the tar at the peeling signboard which said "Inhaminga – Vila Fontes". In a further twenty minutes they arrived at a railway siding used for timber extraction where the rail ran parallel with the sand road. In the clearing of the forest next to the siding, was a large shed left over from the sawmill that the siding had served. Behind the shed stood a little five-seater red and yellow Bell turbine helicopter around which the present occupants of the shed stood gawping. The pilot sat behind the controls. As he saw them swing in, he fired up the turbine. De Souza stopped well clear of the machine and switched off. Duvenage and Cecile unpacked the rear of the Landrover, while Brand, de Souza and Bates went to meet the pilot. He slipped out of his seat; he was skinny, very handsome, with long black hair. He seemed a trifle uneasy, but he flashed them a beautiful smile.

"You are the pilot, yes?" he asked Bates who was looking over the Bell in much too professional a way. "How many hours you got?"

"More than two thousand hours," said Bates and passed him a folder with a licence and a logbook. The Portuguese pilot's eyebrows shot up.

He took a key, opened the luggage bay under the rear seats for them, then handed the keys to Bates. De Souza, in turn, gave him an envelope, which the pilot checked, and the Landrover keys. The pilot then gave de Souza a Salisbury number where he could be contacted if they needed him earlier than the arranged three days. Duvenage packed the five steel jerrycans of jet paraffin into the compartment along with a carton of food and their personal effects. He and Cecile and de Souza climbed into the rear seats, and took a long canister onto their laps. Bates locked up and got behind the controls with Brand beside him. The other pilot waved briefly as the Bell lifted and Cecile thought she saw a look of approval on his face at Bates's handling. Then, with a harsh chukka-chukka of the rotors, it was turning and the road, rail and Landrover were lost to view. Within minutes, she could see the sea away to her right beyond the green carpet of woodland and they were heading north. Brand noticed that she shivered a little, probably in anticipation of what might lie ahead. It was a bit of the deep-end for the girl, but he was pleased with her, thus far.

Brand had gone over the situation with her, admitting that they might not find van Rooyen before it was too late. He had considered leaving her behind in Beira in case van Rooyen turned up there, but in the end decided that should they keep their forces together, to her obvious relief. Brand had fretted at the delay in waiting for his two men to arrive. She had met neither of them before but Brand said enough to reassure her that they were extremely competent agents. He had picked up enough from her seemingly professional questions to realise that she was especially interested and concerned about the possible fate of one Dan McNeil. So she would be thinking of the man, afraid that something had happened to him, and trying to push these thoughts away so as not to impair her professionalism. Brand thought she had better be kept busy. He issued orders.

Duvenage opened a heavy fibreglass case and Cecile helped to assemble the three 7.62 calibre R3 paratrooper rifles with fold-up stocks. Brand detected a flicker of nervousness in her, which was to be expected. Just pre-combat nerves. He thought about de Souza. Perhaps the agent had softened with his foreign living, he reflected, but he had a good record and Brand knew he could be completely ruthless. His mother was Afrikaans; his father was a successful market gardener near Pretoria, an immigrant from Portugal in the thirties. All in all, he had the best team he could expect, but not the resources he would have liked.

As they began to cross open grasslands, they could see huge black smudges on the horizon that turned out, as they got closer, to be vast herds of buffalo grazing on the floodplain, untroubled by the noise of their passing. Brand opened the receiver and a map on his lap.

With quick calculations he ascertained the direction of the transmitters. He said nothing, but half an hour later, he triangulated with another direction and pinpointed them. His finger jabbed the map.

"They're here, on this mountain, Serra da Muambe. What do you know about it, de Souza? It looks like a ring – like a volcano."

De Souza shook his head. "Never heard of it." He peered over Brand's shoulder. "That area is very wild. There are some stores along the Zambezi that still trade with the locals, I understand, but some have been burned and others bribe Frelimo to leave them alone. It is very dangerous. The tracks are mined; the army won't go there."

Brand nodded, frowning. He touched Bates on the shoulder, signalling him to lose height. Bates took the Bell down to tree-top level and turned to follow the river, moving inland. The banks of the river were heavily wooded, but away from it there were large tracts of floodplain grassland, flecked with *borassus* palms. Soon there were patches of dense forest on higher-lying ground, which increased in frequency until there was mostly forest with occasional pans of depressed grassland, with waterholes at their centres. Here, more buffalo, herds of sable antelope and waterbuck threw up their heads to watch them pass. Then, on a pan at the river's edge, they saw the Barros hunting camp. There were eight separate bungalows in an L with three on the short leg and the rest on the long. The nearest, as they swooped in to land, was the longest; it had no verandas and seemed to be a series of store rooms, workshops and garages. The rest were obviously the safari accommodation in the prime spots, overlooking the river, with the manager and staff quarters further back.

Bates put the craft down neatly just behind the garages to offer some protection should there be any gunfire. He kept the turbine going and stayed at the controls, while Duvenage and de Souza also stayed near the machine at the corner of the building, their weapons ready but out of sight. They had orders to cover Brand and Cecile as they walked to the larger of the safari buildings. Both the Dakota and the Cessna were standing on the airstrip that stretched across the pan. An elderly black man leant on his broom on the veranda, watching them.

"Where's the Boss, *Madala*?" Brand tried asking in Zulu, hoping the man had worked on the mines at one stage of his life. To his surprise, he replied in English.

"He inside. Boss *Senhor* Barros, inside." There was fear and apprehension in the old one's face. Then Manuela Barros walked through the doorway, her hands in the pockets of her suede jacket. She smiled at them brightly but gave no sign that she recognised Cecile. She walked past the old man and turned in the centre of the veranda.

"I'm Manuela Barros. You would like to see my father? He is inside, busy with some books. Won't you come in?"

Cecile's nerves were tighter than a drawn bowstring, but she smiled back and left the talking to Brand; who introduced them as Professor Hanekom and secretary and said that he would indeed like to see Mr Barros. Together, they went up the steps towards her. They passed out of sight of the men at the corner of the garage.

"Don't move, Brand!" There was an automatic in her hand and ice in her eyes. They froze, too far from her to jump her, knowing that she would not hesitate to shoot.

"Now, see here –" began Brand, relieved that coming here had brought matters out into the open.

"Shut up! Signal your men to come over, to shut down the turbine. Do it now!"

Brand moved to where he could see Duvenage and made a throat-cutting motion, then beckoned. Duvenage disappeared from view. They heard the turbine die then da Souza and Duvenage were walking towards them. Manuela could not see the Bell and would not have known how many of them there were, he hoped. As he turned back to face Manuela, it happened.

The *madala* hit Manuela over the head with his broom. She

sensed it coming, but turned too late and it caught her squarely above the ear. In three strides, Brand took her pistol from her limp hand as she folded. The old man had his hand over his own mouth in surprise at what he had made himself do, his eyes wide.

"Get back!" yelled Brand to his two men out in the open. They turned and fled as a rifle started firing at them. Brand ran along the veranda. The man behind the palm tree and Brand saw each other at the same time but before the man could turn, he got a double tap in the chest and fell against the palm.

"How many men here, *Madala*?" Brand asked urgently. The old man was crouching against the wall next to him.

"Five with *Senhor* Barros, Sah, and two daughter, this one and Miss Rosa. They lock *Senhor* Barros and Miss Rosa in a room. Is too much bad!"

Manuela was sitting up, nursing a split ear that coursed blood through her fingers. Cecile stood watch over her with a Beretta, from a safe distance. Manuela began to curse the old man in Portuguese, then Cecile in English. Cecile said nothing, but eyed her warily, guessing how dangerous she was.

Duvenage and de Souza, now with their R3s, came at a weaving run, bending low, while Bates covered both them and the chopper from the corner of the workshop. Brand took a deep shaky breath and stepped through the doorway. It was empty for a second, then a man stepped into it, carrying a light bag in one hand and a pistol in the other. Brand had a brief impression that he was thin, tall and dark-complexioned as he simultaneously saw the pistol in his hand whip upwards. Brand snapped off two shots at him before he could fire.

The man was thrown backwards, the travel bag skidding across the floor. He slid down the panelled wall and tried to lift the weapon again. Brand's finger tightened on the trigger, but he knew the man's strength and life were running out. The pistol sagged, the man sighed as it slipped from his lifeless fingers. Brand swallowed, his heart hammering painfully. This was the price of being back in the field again.

"Who's there?" A quavering woman's voice, English with a

Portuguese accent.

"Miss Barros? Where are you?" Brand thought that the voice came from a room at the end of the passage. "We have come to set you free, we are friends." Maybe. There was the sound of a lock being disengaged then the door half opened and a pale face with big brown eyes and black hair turned towards him.

"Who's that?" Brand pointed at the man sitting in the passage. She looked and gulped.

"My father's pilot. Is he ... dead?"

Brand looked into the beautiful big eyes and nodded.

"Who is in there with you?" He could see two men behind her; a heavy, paunchy man with a beard streaked with grey, and an older man, slim, tired-looking, in a cream safari suit and a maroon paisley cravat. He recognised Barros from photographs that he had studied.

"*Senhor* Barros," the paunchy man grabbed the other by the arm. "Tell this man that they forced me to help them! What could I do with those pigs, Ribeiro and Campos, watching me all the time? Before God, I –"

Barros looked disdainfully down on the hand that gripped his arm until the other removed it, and then ignored him.

"My name is Barros." He met Brand's gaze squarely. "Who are you?"

"Hanekom, South African Bureau of State Security. Normally, I would apologise for my intrusion, but I think that in these circumstances you won't object to our coming uninvited. I am hoping that you'll give me such information as I require, but firstly, I must be sure that nobody is going to shoot us whilst we're talking. Will you come with me to identify a body and tell us who else is around that'll give us trouble." He stood aside for Barros. As he shut the door on the paunchy man and Rosa, he told them to remain there for the time being. Duvenage came in a side door and reported that the place seemed to be deserted, not even servants.

"There's only the old man who cooks for us and does some light housekeeping," said Barros. "My daughter, Manuela, sent the rest of them away. My mechanic thought something was wrong and refused to go. Da Silva shot him … that's my son-in-law … everything seems to have gone … There were two men around, always armed, they should be about." He obviously did not know what to explain.

On the veranda, he stopped in front of his daughter. Manuela was now sitting at a low drinks table, her hand over her ear, staring across the pan.

"Are you alright, Manuela? Have they hurt you?" he asked, gently, in their own tongue. She ignored him, only her mouth tightened a little, thinning the normally full lips. Her father watched her for a moment, hurt and still unable to reconcile himself to this ruthless woman he thought he had known. Then he followed Brand to look at the body against the palm tree.

"Ribeiro," Barros turned away. "It leaves only that rat, Campos, to account for." he beckoned the old man, told him gently to bring beer and glasses. The *madala* nodded nervously and slipped away.

Brand instructed Duvenage to take over the guarding of Manuela then he, Cecile and Barros went into the lounge. De Souza arrived to report that he had seen nobody. Brand warned him about the missing Campos, told him to keep his eyes peeled, and to tell Bates to stay where he was.

"Where are the South Africans, where is this da Silva, where is that Sanderson man?" Brand asked Barros.

"Da Silva was Rosa's husband, very charming, but I never liked him. But let me start at the beginning." The old servant arrived with a tray of beer bottles, glasses, and an opener. Barros waved him away and poured for them himself. "I was born in Beira, I grew up here. I am surely the wealthiest man in Mozambique. I have plantations – tea, sugar, coconuts, cashews; a chain of general dealers, sawmills which export timber; I have interests in shipping and a lot more besides. All this is in Mozambique, very little outside.

"I am Mozambican first, Portuguese second. I would give my life for this country if I thought it would keep it in safe, responsible hands for future generations of Mozambicans. Two years ago, I started to recruit men who would help to smash Frelimo. The army was sinking into apathy, when what the country needed was a concerted effort at this crucial time. Some of the men that I recruited were army men and they were able to step up the pressure a little, but there were too many that would do nothing, given the choice. Defend only, not attack. Eventually, I tried to start my own army and bribed the regulars to leave them alone. Then Manuela persuaded me to recruit some South Africans, some of whom were ex-Congo mercenaries. This I did. But Manuela had her own plans for them. I had no idea that Manuela and Rosa's husband were Communists ..." His throat moved, constricting with emotion. He took a swallow of beer. Brand and Cecile sipped theirs, but said nothing. He had told them nothing new, as yet.

"In fact, the South Africans did very well and I was hopeful that we could swing the tide with them, if I could also get support from the local population. This was the difficulty because, although several chiefs supplied me with information on Frelimo's movements, I could not rely on them when Frelimo threatened their people. Then, about two weeks ago, one of the South Africans came to see me in my apartment in my hotel, the *Zambeze,* when they were back for a break. He was their leader, an excellent man to have. O'Donnell was his name. He told me that they could not go on, unless they had some sort of air support and they did not have to dodge our army, as well. I said that I could not guarantee non-interference from the army, but I would arrange to have a plane on call and perhaps a helicopter for medi-vac purposes. Then da Silva came in, told him to get out, and said he needed to speak to me urgently, alone." His mouth twisted with remembered humour.

"O'Donnell threatened to knock his block off, but I asked him to leave. Manuela came and the two of them told me I must not interfere with the South Africans, that they had plans for them that did not concern me. I was to keep my mouth shut and stay in the hotel or they would cut Rosa's throat! Of course, I could not believe ... Her own sister! To convince me, Manuela brought Rosa in and beat her up. Karate! Slammed her about until she lay bleeding on the floor while da Silva kept a gun on me!" Barros downed his beer in a couple of swallows and poured another. When he continued, his voice was calm again.

"An hour later, O'Donnell fell from the balcony to his death. He

223

must have been pushed, but one of his men saw it happen and insists it was an accident. I can't believe that! The rest of the South Africans were locked away until they brought them here a couple of days ago. Another South African, Sanderson, his name was, was here with Manuela and da Silva –"

"Sanderson! Where is he now?" demanded Brand, his voice hard.

"An associate of Manuela's, I was led to believe. I met him a couple of months ago. He was helping her to recruit mercenaries, she said. I didn't like him, he was very arrogant. I didn't try to find out more about him. I trusted Manuela … I should have looked into it, it might have given me a clue what Manuela and her Communist friends were up to. I understand he had something to sell to the Communists, I don't know what. Manuela trained him to jump from an aircraft, here. He and the others left this morning to jump somewhere. Manuela said the less I knew the better, when I asked. But, when the Dakota came back, Manuela said that everything had gone wrong and that da Silva had fallen out of the Dakota to his death. Sometimes I wish it had been Manuela that fell without a parachute! Mother of Christ, that I could have spawned such a devil! She is utterly without soul or conscience…" Barros was close to breakdown, but in an uncomfortable minute or two, he pulled himself together. Cecile felt overwhelming pity for the man and surreptitiously wiped the corner of her eye.

"The pilot," Brand asked, gently. "Was he one of them?"

"I think so. It was Manuela who persuaded me to take Pereira on about a year ago. He was a good pilot and gave me no trouble. Reis, the man you met, was the camp manager. He is really a good man, but he has no balls – excuse me, *Senhora*", he said to Cecile, who was still wearing her fake wedding ring. "No backbone. He accepted a bribe to help keep Rosa and me here as prisoners."

"Were the South Africans wearing uniforms?" asked Brand, shrewdly.

"I didn't see them, but Reis told me they were dressed as South African paratroopers, armed, but their ammunition was, how do you say, false?"

"Dummy," supplied Brand. "Blanks. You have no idea where they were going to drop? Their target? I have information that the place is a mountain, marked on my map as Serra Muambe. Do you know it? Would it be suitable as a Frelimo camp?"

"In my youth, I hunted there," Barros said, thoughtfully. "It is an extinct volcano, there is water there ... It would make an excellent place to hide. I don't know why I never thought of it before..."

Brand offered him a lit match for the cigarette that he was going to light and in turn lit his own foul pipe. Barros did not seem to notice. He leaned forward, pleading.

"Now, you will question my daughter. I beg you not to harm her. Whatever she has done, she believes in. But she is my flesh and blood ..."

"That is up to her, Mr. Barros. My primary concern is the man who calls himself Sanderson and the threat he constitutes to my country. If I can, I shall help the other South Africans, but they brought this on themselves when they joined you as mercenaries. Beyond that –"

"But our common enemy is Communism, Mr. Hanekom! Can you not get at the men behind my daughter? Get them to release their hold on her? I will undertake to see that she has nothing more to do with them!"

"If, as you say, she believes in what she has done, then it is a doctrine, not men, that has a hold on her." Brand spoke with sympathy, but not with hope. "Do you have a radio here?"

"In both planes, of course, and one in the room next door. Why do you ask?"

"It is conceivable that your daughter has been in touch with this Frelimo camp, if there is one there, and may know what happened after the drop and what happened to Sanderson and the others. It is time I talked to her." Brand got to his feet as de Souza came back.

"I've been through the whole camp. No sign of anybody. Perhaps this Campos has taken to the bush?" de Souza said. Brand asked Barros what sort of man he was.

"Yes, he is the sort of man that would run when things, how do you say, get hot?" Barros permitted himself a wan smile. "Yes, he would take to the bush."

"Okay, Mr. Barros, thanks for your help. I'm going to ask that

Duvenage watch to see that you don't do anything foolish while we talk to your daughter. Would you show him the radio? Perhaps one of your army contacts could use the information about the possible Frelimo camp on Serra Muambe? Wait until we give the go-ahead before you talk to them. Please prepare us some food, if you would be so kind, and we shall need to spend the night here. It is too late to try and find Sanderson today, but we must be away at first light tomorrow."

Barros nodded. "Just be as gentle as you can with the girl, that's all I ask. If you are not, I shall find a way of making you pay for it." Their eyes locked for a moment and Brand knew this was no idle threat. It would not help to antagonise the man without cause, or he would have to spend the rest of his life watching his back.

Brand told Cecile to be watchful and to let Reis and Rosa out of their room, but they were not to leave the building. On the veranda, the tableau had not changed. De Souza joined them. Duvenage went with Barros. Brand went to Manuela.

"Miss Barros, we need to ask you some questions. You will please come with us."

Before he could duck, there was warm spittle running down his cheek. He held his temper and wiped it off. "Take her to the workshop, de Souza. She knows karate, I understand, so be cautious. I'll take your rifle." He took the R3 from De Souza, who moved in on the girl. De Souza let his guard down just enough to tempt her and she flashed a stiff-fingered blow at his throat. She didn't see him move but the blow missed and her arm was suddenly behind her back, pinioned, her shoulder muscles in agony. She sucked at breath with a hiss. Brand realised, when he saw de Souza move, that he was far from soft. De Souza led Manuela away to the workshop, near where the Bell waited with Bates in attendance. Brand brought him up to date, warned him about Campos, and told him to refuel the helicopter. Then he returned to the workshop.

There he saw two Toyota Landcruisers fitted with wooden benches on the back for game viewing, and a swamp tractor with enormous balloon tyres that reached above Brand's head. There were two short-wheelbase Landrovers, bare to the chassis in front, their engines lying on a greasy piece of tarpaulin. Along the walls were racks of spares, nuts, and bolts, and rusty hardware. In one corner stood a portable welding plant and a forge. Near the latter was a huge blacksmith's vice set in a concrete block. De Souza was holding Manuela near the vice.

"We'd better gag her," he said, conversationally, "We wouldn't like to upset her father with her screams. Bring me some of that rag from the bench, would you? And some flex to tie her arms and legs. She is such a beautiful girl; it is going to be a pity to spoil her face. You know, I thought that if she doesn't talk with a bit of pressure in the right places, then we could take off her nose in the vice. What do you think?"

"No difference to me, George," Brand said indifferently, "It's not my nose. What about some acid? Some in those old batteries, over there." He fetched some flex from the racks and the oily rag. De Sousa applied a little pressure on her arm as Manuela struggled. Her back arched in excruciating spasms and she offered no resistance as Brand first tied her wrists together behind her back, then her ankles to the concrete block of the vice. Her dark eyes blazed her hatred and she clenched her jaw as Brand approached with the filthy rag. De Sousa's square fingers moved to her neck. Suddenly she screamed, but Brand choked it off with the rag. He held the rag in place while De Souza tied it in with some electrical tape. She struggled a while as the men stood back to admire their handiwork, then tears oozed out of her eyes and her shoulders began to shake with sobs.

"Do you think she wants to say something to the capitalistic pigs, Mr. Hanekom?" De Sousa lit a cigarette. Brand shook his head and reached for his pipe.

"How can she? She hasn't been asked any questions, yet. Perhaps I'd better ask them now so that she can nod her head when she's ready to answer them."

"She's going to have difficulty nodding with her nose in the vice."

"Ja, true. But she's a resourceful girl; I dare say she'll make a plan. Here are the questions, Miss Barros. Why were the South African mercenaries of your father's in the Dakota and why did they jump over

Serra Muambe? Why did Sanderson jump with them? What do you intend doing with the information that Sanderson is selling you? Is there a Frelimo camp at Muambe? How many radios do they have at this camp and who operates them? Were you in contact with this camp this morning, either during your flight or after the drop? What went wrong with the drop? Where is Sanderson now? Where are the other South Africans? Who is your contact at Muambe? What is your chain of command, your superior, their superior? Of course, I shall probably think of more questions as we go along, but these will do to start with."

"She is going to have difficulty breathing with her nose in the vice," de Sousa observed.

"True. The gag in her mouth. Ah, well, a little nod will allow her to breathe again." Brand looked speculatively at his prisoner. Manuela was struggling with every fibre in her body. Brand cranked open the jaws of the huge vice. "Do you think she understands my English, George? Perhaps you should translate it all into Portuguese. I'm sure she's not nodding."

"You're right," said de Sousa, applying his thumbs to the sallow column of her neck. Pain shot into her head and she tried to pull away, but down, down went her nose towards the vice until her face was between the gaping steel jaws. Brand sank to his knees to look at the no-longer beautiful eyes that were bulging in terror as Brand began to wind the handle. Manuela's head jerked up and down so that she bruised her cheek on the rusted steel. She was nodding.

TWENTY-EIGHT

Once or twice, while the others were resting in the shade at the side of the dry stream bed, Piet Visagie said later, Theo Theunissen had climbed to high ground to see if he could see the Zambezi, but all he saw was never-ending, leafless *mopane* trees. They had tried walking through it, but, although the *mopane* itself was not dense, every minute watercourse was lined with thickets of *salvadora* and sour plum, so, in the end, they stuck to the stream bed, ploughing through the loose sand and scrambling over the boulders. They saw several zebra, sable, impala and warthog. Once, a magnificent nyala bull plunged out of the *mopane* and through the bed ahead of them.

"God, there must be water, somewhere!" Piet mumbled through cracked lips. He had taken station near the still-concussed Rafe Schulman who plodded along in the rear.

But there was no water. Around every corner, they hoped to find a muddy puddle in the frequent depressions, but there was nothing. The shadows grew longer until the sun was just above the trees, then Theo heard it. He hissed for the others to stop. They listened.

There was a rhythmic thumping, and, very faintly, someone singing. Theo silently motioned them to wait, and that Pieter should go with him. With infinite caution, they walked down the river bed.

A black woman was kneeling on a flat rock with a tall wooden mortar between her knees. Her heavy breasts bounced on her belly with every strike of the pole that she used as a pestle. She sang to the beat of her work as she ground the millet in the mortar. At the foot of the rock on which she knelt was a pool of muddy water from which a well-worn path led up into the *mopane* to a pair of huts on the ridge.

She seemed to sense them, and rose, beginning a keening wail of fright. The mortar rolled down the rock, spilling the millet until it came to rest in the mud. She fled around the pool and up the path. Theunissen caught up to her just as she reached the huts. Two small children appeared, wide-eyed in terror, as well as an old woman whose naked dugs hung like barber's strops to below her navel. The younger woman flung herself to the ground and made no attempt to rise until Theo motioned her to do so with his rifle.

The huts were old and sagging, *mopane* poles and grass, but the inhabitants had planted a good patch of millet and cassava to one side. A pair of curs began to yap, but they kept well out of the way. An impala skin lay drying on the roof of one of the huts. Between the buildings, a fire smouldered under a three-legged pot. Strips of meat, probably from the impala, were hanging in a *grewia* shrub nearby. Flies covered the strips until it seemed they had a life of their own.

"*Oopi lo madoda ka wena?*" Theo tried Fanagalo. Where is your man? There was obviously a man around, the dead impala testified to that. The woman gabbled, but Piet caught the word Bandar. That was a store that Nourse had mentioned, according to Sanderson. Theo said he was worried about these isolated huts. Out here, there was no control by the Portuguese, so it stood to reason that the occupants were in contact with Frelimo. In the Congo, he said, he had shot women, even children, who were in a position to endanger him or his men. In this case, however, Frelimo knew they were in the area, so nothing would be gained and the bodies would tell the same story as easily as the tongues of these women. Piet agreed with relief.

"Take that gourd, Piet, and bring me water. Call the others."

Theunissen waited until they were all assembled before he went into the huts. There was nobody else there. They all had their fill of the brown water. Muller armed himself with an axe he found.

"Take us to Bandar," Theo told the woman, meaning both of them should come along. He indicated that the children must stay behind, to which the old woman protested shrilly. They were a boy of not much more than two years old and a girl of about four or so. Theunissen prodded her sharply in the belly with his rifle barrel.

"For God's sake, Theo," protested Piet, angrily, "Let her stay with the kids!" Theo swung around and eyed him, coldly.

"I am not allowing her to trot off to the nearest Frelimo so that they can ambush us, so belt up or you can stay and look after the little black bastards. Clear?"

Visagie looked away after a short, defiant glare. Sanderson seemed to be quite content to leave these decisions with Theunissen and even to take orders. He brought up the rear as they filed across the ravine, led by the two women. The crying of the two children left barred up in the hut did not seem to bother Sanderson; he was obviously more worried about the gloom of the coming night.

Theo had the two women gagged and roped together and gave their control to Muller so that he, himself, was free to move as he saw fit. It wasn't long before a moon rose to give them just enough light to discern the way. After an hour, they approached more huts which they skirted around with caution. Once they heard voices. Theo led them off into hiding, his rifle pressed against the younger woman's head, until two men had passed. After another stumbling two hours, they approached several more huts in a cluster. Dogs smelt them and started a cacophony of howls, snarls and yaps. Theo took off the younger woman's gag.

"Bandar," she confirmed. They had reached the bank of the mighty Zambezi. Beyond the huts, they could make out the square bulk of the trading store, from which came a glimmer of light from a paraffin lamp. They could hear a gramophone scratchily thumping out an African pop tune. As they approached, they could see figures dancing on the veranda to the beat. Several people sat on the wide steps; there was the glint of bottles. Theo's group kept going, bunched up. Someone shouted; the dancing stopped: those sitting came to their feet. But, so far, they detected no threatening moves.

"Who are you?" someone shouted above the beat.

The younger woman gabbled a reply and the atmosphere became electric. As they approached, they could see that the doors of the store were wide open and faces were peering back at them from within. The group moved up the steps onto the veranda and into the store, nerves drum tight and their guts in knots. A murmur arose around them from the villagers, menacing now. Here and there was a demanding shout.

The Petromax pressure lamp on the counter threw long grotesque shadows on the grimy walls and the sparsely stocked shelves. Shadows of dried fish, of bunches of scarves, bicycle wheels and dresses hanging from the ceiling, danced as the men brushed against them. In one corner, next to stacked sacks of maize meal, were two ancient treadle sewing machines. Three men slid off the counter where they had been sitting drinking beer. One of them was in a black uniform; there was an old 8mm rifle in the corner next to him, at which he briefly glanced, but the sight of Theunissen's weapon discouraged him from reaching for it. Several beer bottles littered the counter. Behind it, a young Indian licked his lips and tried to smile.

"*Boa noite, os Senhores!*" He croaked, nervously, "What can I do for you?"

Theo guessed at what he said. "Good evening. Do you speak English, French?" He spoke politely, but he motioned the man in black and the Indian to stay where they were and for the other two to get out. They did so quickly when he waved the R3 at them.

"A little, I speak," he licked his lips again. "I no hearing car, Sir. You having car?"

"Broken. You have a car?"

"*Sim*, gotting Landrover! Very old, very old, but going!" His proud smile began to fade as he realised that they might want it. "But not gotting any petrol ..." He surveyed the dirty, unshaven men in their crumpled uniforms and shrank before Theo's cold gaze.

"Who is this?" Theo indicated the man in the black uniform as he took the old rifle and passed it to Sanderson, who checked the magazine. "Mind it doesn't blow up in your face."

"He is Administrator *guarda* for village, Bandar, here."

"Does the Administrator come here often?"

"Not more. Not six month, now. Too much Frelimo here."

"*Viva Frelimo!*" came a voice through the window. A shutter covered it, but the shutter was broken at the bottom and they could see faces peering in at them. The murmuring increased and Theo's group stirred, nervously.

"*Viva Frelimo!*" Theo replied. "Muller, bar the back door, make sure there is nobody else in the building. Sanderson, get those women untied, then push them into the corner with that guard bloke. We may need some hostages. Also find and load some torches from this guy's shelves. Schulman and Visagie, get us all some food and civvies from the shelves, khakis will do fine." He kept his gaze on the store keeper who was watching in dismay as they ransacked his shelves for food and clothing. Theo shut the main door on the muttering, angry faces with another "*Viva Frelimo!*" and dropped the bar in its slot.

"You are paying for these clothes and foods and things, yes?"

The unfortunate Indian's voice quavered fearfully.

"No, my friend, you are. Open that drawer!" Theunissen was behind the counter with him. Under it was a drawer that served as a till. "You don't own this shop. Who does?"

The lad reluctantly fished out a bunch of keys. "There is not many money here. It is *Senhor* Hassim from Mutarara, he owns. He must pay Frelimo for not burn down shop, for not to putting *bomba* on road. Please, you not taking money from Hassim, he killing me!" He brightened, then, as a thought struck him. "You go to Mutarara, you paying *Senhor* Hassim for what you take?"

Theo allowed himself a grim smile. "Of course. Don't worry about old Hassim. How far to Mutarara?" He pulled out the drawer and counted the money before pocketing it. There was less than a thousand escudos.

"About a hundred and sixty kilometre, Sir."

"When did you see Hassim last?" Theo queried. The lad misunderstood and said he would be coming next week with a big lorry to replenish supplies and take the money. Theo repeated, annoyed, and the frightened man admitted that Hassim had not been there for over a month. He flinched, as if he expected the next question. He was not wrong.

"Then there is more money, this is not all you take in a month. Where is it?"

"No, no! Is all; peoples here not having much money, are poor peoples!"

Theunissen backhanded him hard, so that he bounced back against his shelves and his lip burst against his teeth. He fell over some cartons on the floor and then sat on them. He began to sob.

"Is more, Sir. Sorry, Sir, I show you …" He got to his feet. The others in the room watched in silence, some, like Visagie and the hostages, in sympathy, Sanderson with indifference, and Rafe unaware of the incident at all – he was fast asleep with his face buried in a khaki shirt on the counter.

"Come with me, Piet," Theo said, "Sanderson, watch the bastards. I'm going with the curry-muncher to look for the dough." He pushed the Indian lad ahead of him into the rear of the building. It consisted of a short, dim passage with a doorway on either side, one without a door. In the passage stood three two-hundred litre drums and a stack of full grain bags. In the room with no door, lit by a candle, was a table with, on it, a primus stove, a bucket of filthy water, some unwashed dishes and a toothbrush. On a shelf were more candles, some spanners, pots, a sable antelope horn and some magazines from India. In one corner, amidst crates of empty beer bottles and a few full ones, stood an ancient paraffin refrigerator with its door open. Muller, almost guiltily, handed them each an open 2M and pulled out another one for himself, trying to look as if he had not already thrown one down his throat.

Theo lifted it to his mouth and warned, "Just watch out on an empty stomach, Muller. Frelimo could be –"

The Indian ducked under his elbow, knocked the R3 aside and leaped for the opposite door. He was through it and had slammed it shut before Theo, cursing, regained his balance and swung his weapon around. The two shots through the door were deafening in the confined space. So, it really was loaded, thought Pieter, though not pursuing the possible significance before Theunissen kicked the door open and leaped inside. The youth was on his knees beside his bed, his hands tugging the shotgun clear as Theo's next shots threw him against the wall, screaming: three holes in his arm and chest. His scream started to bubble blood and changed to a gurgle as bloody froth ran down his chin.

"Stupid bastard!" panted Theo. "What the fuck did he think he was doing, Piet? Search this room; there is money, somewhere, and we need it to get to Beira. Muller, come, we'll check the front, and then I'll be back."

Piet, shocked and sickened at the ruthlessness of the man, did as he was told like a robot. He found the money in a box under the plank bed along with a box of shotgun cartridges. He brought it all to the front before Theunissen had a chance to return. Rafe was awake again, opening tins of food. Theo gave Sanderson the twelve-gauge and Muller took the old Mauser; which left only Rafe and Piet unarmed. When Muller came back with more beer for everyone, he contemptuously reported that the Indian was dead.

The exhaustion that they had felt had dropped away with the first bottle of beer. They ate and drank, feeling new strength seeping back.

All was quiet, outside; the gathering had melted away with the first shots. Even the dogs had ceased their yapping. The hostages huddled in their corner, staring wide-eyed at their captors. Visagie dropped three cans of bullybeef at their feet. Theo shrugged and Muller bit back his scornful comment. Rafe Schulman's eyes had lost some of their glazed look with food in his belly.

"Feeling better?" Piet asked him as he changed into his new clothes. The biggest trousers there were still too small, so he and Muller, who had the same problem, kept their uniform trousers on. With the killing of the Indian, Piet was an accessory to murder, now, and he tried not to think of that fact.

"Much, but bloody tired and my head hurts. What happened to the rest of us? Dan and Geoff? Jan? How did we get here?"

"You don't remember?" Piet recapped as far as he knew. "I am sure none of them made it, just us. We're trying to get to Beira, as far as I know." They were some distance from the others, but he lowered his voice to a murmur. "Sanderson is up to something, a plan to make some big bucks, and the others seem to be going for it. I don't know how. All I want to do is get back down south. What about you?"

"I want to get back too," Rafe said without hesitation, "but let's keep our mouths shut until we see how things are shaping. I don't trust that bastard …"

"Something else is worrying me, too, Rafe. How come Theo's got live ammo –"

"Come on, you two!" Theunissen barked at them. "Get our supplies near the door, get those drums of paraffin from the back and soak the place. Sanderson, Muller, watch those black bastards. Pieter, bring that petrol that Muller found and let's go look at this Landy. When I say the word, you chuck the supplies in and get yourselves aboard." He turned to follow Piet. "We'll leave the back door open, Sanderson, so stand where you can keep an eye on it."

They found the Landrover parked behind the store. After a careful check that there was nobody about, they went out to it. It was an ancient short-wheelbase vehicle without a roof. Piet found that the tank had lost its filler cap and a rag had been stuffed into the pipe. He emptied the jerrycans into it; about thirty litres, he reckoned. There was a good moon and no need for a torch. Nothing moved that they could see. They were on the bank of the river. Just below them was a fuel-drum and *mopane*-pole jetty with several dugout canoes tied to it. The water was a sheet of silver in the moonlight. Far off, a jackal howled, answered by another close by.

"The key won't turn the starter!" Pieter hissed desperately.

"There should be a knob under the dash on the fire wall, man."

A few seconds later Theo heard the starter turn, feebly, once. Pieter swore. The battery was flat. Theo told him that there should be a crank, somewhere; probably behind the seats. He found it and went around to the front of the vehicle while Theo got behind the wheel. He gave it half choke and waited impatiently for Visagie to find the starting dog and engage the crank. Visagie put his weight to the handle; the engine started with a roar. Clutching the handle, he jumped in and Theo took the little vehicle around the store, while the village dogs started to howl again.

Muller opened the front door; he and Schulman threw the supplies on board. Sanderson came out, backwards: his shotgun still trained on the prisoners. Theo told Piet to take the wheel. He gestured for the prisoners to go, indicating the back door. They scampered for it as he lit a piece of newspaper and dropped it, flaming, to the wet floor. In three seconds, he was aboard and Visagie was accelerating away. By the light of the flames, they could see people hiding in their hut doorways as they roared along the track down the river. A single shot fired ineffectively at them from a hut sounded like nothing they had heard before. It was from an 1856 Tower musket; one of a few dozen used for poaching, left over from thousands used as trade goods in the last century.

The track took them through a shallow ravine lined with tall trees and dense thicket. Ahead was grassland that only became visible when they crested the further slope. In the light of the only headlamp, Pieter saw a dozen figures diving into the scrub at the edge of the thicket. He huddled low over the wheel and tried to push the pedal through the floor.

"Get down! Ambush!" Theo roared. Bullets stitched the side of the bodywork. Theo fired back, short bursts. The shotgun in Sanderson's hands boomed twice, the recoil nearly throwing him off the back. There wasn't time for the fear that he'd felt in the Dakota and on the mountain to take its numbing hold of him. They picked up speed and got out of range. A grenade exploded with a shattering blast behind them; if anything, only helping their impetus.

Everyone seemed to be muttering curses, but Piet knew this was in relief. He bent forward to try and see the next pothole before he hit it.

"Anyone hurt?" demanded Theo, as he clipped in another magazine. Except for a graze on the back of Muller's calf from a shot that came through the door, nobody was.

TWENTY-NINE

The moonlight threw the gaunt, leafless *combretums* into grotesque, sinister silhouettes. A lion roared, shattering the quiet night. That woke Geoff Nourse. It took him several seconds to remember where he was. He was lying in a pile of leaves with someone. Dan McNeil. It was Nourse tensing up with frightened awareness and the throbbing pain in his own shoulder that woke McNeil, who sat up with a groan and looked at his watch. It was just after midnight; they'd had five hours sleep. It was enough. There was plenty of light to continue by. The next roar was very close and McNeil started with fright.

"Lion, quite close," hissed Geoff. Dan told him the time and said they should be on their way. Neither moved, ears straining to filter the night sounds. "Fuck 'em, anyway," said Geoff and they each lit up a cigarette, knowing it was foolish as they were both thirsty. They hoped the smell would warn the animal that there were men nearby. After ten minutes of silence, they moved out. The moonlight was enough for them to see where they were going. They found the dry stream Theunissen had followed – by the light of a match their prints were visible in the sand – and set off down it. There were signs of moisture in hollows, but they could not spare the time to dig. They rested every hour for ten minutes, then ploughed on.

"Hey, Dan, what's that glow, do you think?" There was a tiny fan of light on the horizon, to their right. They climbed out of the bed of the stream to see better, but this did not help.

"A fire of some sort," muttered Dan through clenched teeth. He clutched his aching shoulder. Then they thought they heard some gunfire; it lasted about a minute.

"It must be at Bandar, or near there, according to my reckoning." Nourse frowned. "I wonder how Theo and them are faring? I wonder if they don't need help?"

"How in Christ's name would I know? Now shut up, and let's try to get there! Then we'll know." Dan started back into the stream bed with Nourse following, chastened. Poor bastard, that shoulder must be giving him hell.

Then, around a bend, they found a muddy pool at the edge of which lay a wooden grinding mortar with millet spilled from it. By the light of another match, Geoff was able to read the signs and looked up at the black silhouette of the huts, his AK covering them.

"Cover me, Dan; I'll have a look-see." As he approached the huts, the dogs came alive, snarling. Someone, in the one hut with the closed door, started crying. Nothing else moved but a rooster that drew himself up and crowed. Nourse kicked the door open and leapt aside. When nothing happened, he called out in Sena and in a minute, two little children appeared, wide-eyed. He spoke gently to the elder, a four-year old girl, who told him that some whites had taken her mother and grandmother to Bandar. She pointed out the path. She did not know where her father was; he had gone off the previous morning.

Nourse trotted back to Dan and reported. They drank their fill of muddy water with the same gourd used by the others, then took the path that they too had taken.

"Used the women as guides, then?" asked Geoff.

Dan nodded, "And hostages, if I know Theo." They felt better for the liquid inside them. Now they were heading straight for the fire, but its intensity was fading as the sky lightened with the approaching sunrise, a pale yellow-grey band to the east. After an hour, they came upon more huts, but these were devoid of life. They presumed that the occupants had gone to Bandar to see the fire. They strode on, alert and nervous. Geoff asked after Dan's shoulder but the latter told him to belt up or they would walk into someone without hearing them. They gave a wide berth to some more huts, where an old crone was starting the morning fire with the help of several small children. Then they saw movement ahead and heard voices. They melted into the undergrowth.

Coming up the slope were three adults: a man in ragged shorts and a dirty vest, a young woman, and an elderly one. They were hurrying and chattering as they came. They did not see the two whites until they stepped onto the path. The young woman squeaked in fright, the man clenched his knob-headed stick tightly and waited, trembling but expressionless.

"Where are you going, my friend?" Nourse asked in Portuguese; he thought it wiser to keep his knowledge of Sena a secret for the time being. The man shifted his weight nervously, but they were trapped by the threat of the rifles.

"To my home, *Senhor*. My children are alone there. They will be afraid and hungry."

"Where have you come from? What is that fire that we see?"

"These are other whites," muttered the old woman to the man in Sena. "Not the same." He ignored her.

"From the store at Bandar; it burns down. The Indian man who runs it has been shot dead last night."

"Who did this?"

"Some soldiers, *Senhor*."

"Portuguese soldiers?"

He hesitated and licked his lips. "No, *Senhor*, they were *Inglesi*."

"Are they still there?"

"No, *Senhor*, they left after they started the fire. They took the Landrover of the store, then they were –"

"Do not tell them what happened, my son, the Liberty Fighters will kill us. We must tell them about these two and they will kill them. Their clothes are the same as the ones that took us from our home." The old woman's voice was fast and fierce. Geoff understood her, but he asked what she had said.

"She says that we must hurry back to the children, *Senhor*." Geoff smiled at the lie.

"We have seen your children, if it is the home with the impala skin on the roof. They are lonely, but they are well." He turned and reported to McNeil; he told him that these were Theo's hostages. He angrily told him about the killing of the Indian storekeeper, the escape in the store vehicle and that the old woman was all for handing them over to Frelimo, although he used the word *Ters* instead, so that the locals would not guess that they had been understood.

"In the Congo, we'da cut the bastards' throats to keep them quiet. Try and find out what happened while I think about it."

"What happened when the soldiers left?" Nourse didn't want to believe that his friend was capable of the act he had stated, so he put it down to his pain. He gestured with his AK. "Were they attacked? You must tell me the truth, or we will have to kill you."

The man trembled. The old woman screamed, "Tell them nothing!" The man seemed to make up his mind.

"Frelimo attacked them, but they got away down the Mutarara road, *Senhor*. There are many Frelimo here. They will kill me for talking to you. We are afraid; the Portuguese used to punish us if we aided Frelimo and now they do not come here anymore, so they cannot protect us from Frelimo. We must feed them and they sleep with our women when they want. Please let us go, we will say nothing."

"Yes, they were attacked by Ters, Dan, but they got through. He says there are plenty in the area. I suggest that we give Bandar a wide berth and head for Lake Lifumba. If there are still fishermen there, we may get a lift to Mutarara. Or we can steal a vehicle. We could take these people with us part of the way, or simply tie them up."

"Sounds fine. Just get on with it, will you?"

Geoff turned back to their captives. "Where is the path to Lifumba, which does not go from Bandar?"

From his expression, the man was surprised that Nourse knew of the lake. The old woman's muttering was ignored. "There is a path from the huts that you just passed," he said. "It leads to the lake."

"Take us there, but go through the bush until you meet the path." They were not far from the huts, but cutting across the grain of the country was awkward, especially for McNeil. When they reached the path, Nourse led their prisoners back into the bush for a hundred metres, tied them to separate *mopane* trees, and gagged them with bits of their ragged clothing. He knew it would not be long before they managed to free themselves. He apologised to the man and woman in

Portuguese, then, as he tied the old woman, with McNeil covering them, he told the old woman in Sena that she must listen to the man of the house in future. The man laughed from behind his gag and thanked them for sparing their lives with nods of his head.

The sun was well above the horizon now and it bolstered their spirits with a kindly warmth as they set off down the Lifumba path. Geoff was thinking with unease about the killing of the storekeeper and telling himself that it must have been necessary, that the man must have been in league with Frelimo, but it was a bad thing, killing a civilian. It must have been Muller, he told himself. He remembered the battle on the flat-topped hill when he was sure that the German had taken a shot at O'Donnell, although Dan had said he must have imagined it. Something strange about O'Donnell's death, too, but it transpired that Muller had been with Jan and Piet at the time. Theo said he had slipped ... Still, imagination or not, he would not like Muller to be where he could not keep an eye on him.

God, but things had happened since they had come here! Six left, out of, what was it, eleven? Friends, dead. Just like that! Arnie Sharpe, the cocky Kiwi, full of fun; Clem White; the senseless death of O'Donnell; Johnny Blair at Muambe, a fighter to the last, gutsy Pommy sod; poor Jannie de Groot, just as he reached the top of the mountains, blown to smithereens. Was he the last to die? Nourse thought, please God, no more! A mood of depression blanketed his previous optimism brought on by the sun. He was thirsty again, and so hungry. The sun was by now more hot than pleasant and sweat trickled down his ribs. Through yet another ravine, over yet another ridge. Then he heard it: a faint staccato sound. He stopped.

"What is it, Geoff?" Dan whispered. He, too, listened intently, head on one side, forgetting for a moment the pain in his shoulder.

"Chopper!" They said simultaneously. They looked around; there was nowhere near them for a helicopter to land. The *mopane* was too dense and there were plenty of taller knob-thorn trees, as well. They looked for a more open patch and found a possible place that had been cleared a long time ago. They stood on a large, fallen tree trunk, the better to be seen. They reached out with their minds, willing the chopper to find them. Chukka-chukka-chukka. Then they caught a glimpse of it, low down, towards the Zambezi. It seemed to be following the Bandar track. It was not high, only about forty or fifty metres above the deck.

"Bloody fool! Frelimo will shoot him out of the sky!" McNeil watched the machine with growing apprehension. It was south of them, now, almost past them, maybe a kilometre away. They waved furiously, Dan one-handed. What relief when it tilted and swung towards them, the sound of the blades harsher with banking. It was close enough for them to see the pale faces of occupants when, without warning, it happened.

A streak of flame hit the tail, near the rotor. It tilted crazily and began to spin, dropping. Someone had scored a skilful or lucky hit with an RPG2 rocket. The two men were in full stride when they heard the crash as the machine disappeared into the trees. *Mopane* saplings whipped their faces as they ran, dodging the larger trees and jumping over the fallen timber and shrubs. Then they saw the stricken Bell on its belly, its main rotor grotesquely crumpled, the motor dead. They staggered on, managing to stay on their feet, torn but unaware of it, their breath sawing in their chests. Nourse, in the lead, could see movement as someone pulled somebody else from the wreck. It was Brand.

"Get under cover!" shouted McNeil. Geoff saw Dan's chopping finger, signalling him forward. He and Dan plunged past the wreck and threw themselves into defensive positions, spread out to protect a wider area. They were none too soon; there was a shout down slope in the direction of a thicket-choked ravine. Nourse kept his eyes moving, searching the bush, his hands trembling, his heart a trip-hammer under his heaving ribs, his tongue a thirsty, croaking toad sitting in the dry, open cave of his mouth. He risked a glance at the helicopter, thankful that it had not burst into flames. Brand disappeared with his burden for a moment, then scampered back to the machine and reached into it. Nourse tore his eyes back to the ravine just in time to see a shiny dark face emerge and, incredibly, a white face behind it. The surprise of the sight made him hesitate. It was only as the black man's AK reached his shoulder with its sights on Brand, that Geoff found himself firing. He saw both men go down and all hell broke loose.

Dan fired burst after burst at figures that rose from the grass and shrubs. Brand was on the ground near the machine with the R3 that he had retrieved, but there was no cover. He rose to a crouch and plunged into the scrub, screaming as a bullet knocked his feet out from under him. He rose to his knees, searching for a target.

Someone still inside the machine moved and a gun barrel appeared at the shattered rear window. It, too, began to fire. Then there was a crack, a roaring streak of flame and a rocket tore into the wreck. The ground shook to the explosion. McNeil's next shot took away part of the rocketeer's head. Then there was a short lull with only the sound of their own desperate breathing and an occasional shout from further away.

Nourse found himself looking into the eyes of a man up a *mopane* tree, thirty metres away. They lifted their AKs simultaneously and fired as one. The bark under his shoulder lifted away and nudged him as it went; the man fell out of the tree and bounced like a sack. He lay unmoving. Geoff nearly vomited with relief. Someone began to whimper. Still the Bell did not burn although it was smoking. It was totally quiet when the whimpering stopped. For nearly ten minutes, nobody moved.

"Colonel Wanga?" a reedy voice called. A pause, as all the living waited for a reaction.

"I think he is dead …" It was in Sena. Nourse listened intently.

"Our captain is dead, too. Where is the white?"

"Also, I think … I am hit in the leg…"

"We must go, my friend," another voice said. "There were more in the bush, maybe ten of them …" Here and there a rustle, a snapping of twigs, a groan. They were retreating. McNeil fired at some waving grass. Someone cursed. The rustling slowly died away.

A small yellow skink with a blue tail moved down the tree trunk near Nourse's face. He began to feel the discomforts of his position, now, the bark at his shoulder, the twig digging into his thigh, his shirt plastered to his back with sweat that was slowly drying. He smelled the dust on the dry autumn grass; the sun began to burn his neck.

"You there, McNeil?"

"Yes." Dan paused to see if there was any reaction from the enemy to his voice. Nothing. "That you, Brand? Are you alright?"

"Hit in the calf. Bates, he was the pilot, has some injuries and another man, de Sousa, was still in the chopper. That rocket got him … Where is van Rooyen?"

Oh, yes, Sanderson. "Not with us, Sir. Can we talk later? Foe may still be about. Will you see to your friend, Bates, was it? Nourse and I'll do a bit of a recce."

"Go ahead, then."

Geoff got slowly to his feet; the skink, scuttling away, was the only hostile reaction that he caused. He and McNeil carefully searched the bush. They found six bodies and one severely wounded. Amongst the dead, besides the unknown white man, was a man with spectacles and makeshift colonel's insignia, and likewise, a captain. It was unlikely for two high ranking officers to be together, so they concluded that not only had at least two bands combined, but that there had been a very high priority put on finding the South Africans. Maybe it was Sanderson that was so precious?

If one of the groups was from the cratered mountain, it must have been the second group that had had the rocket, Geoff reasoned, the one that had tried to stop Theo on the road outside Bandar. He had been lucky not to have been blown up by the fearsome weapon. They did, however, note that the captain had been wounded previously; his arm had been freshly bandaged. None of the bodies had any form of personal identification, as was normal. The wounded man was unconscious; they left him where he lay. They collected three AKs and a Tokarev pistol, believing that the survivors had taken the other arms, including the rocket launcher, as they withdrew.

When they returned to Brand, it was to find him deftly bandaging his own leg. A blond stranger was lying flat on his back beside him, cigarette in his bandaged hand and an R3 in the other. His broad chest was also bandaged, with a strip torn from a shirt.

"Name's Bates," he greeted them with a wan smile. "Nourse and McNeil, I believe?"

"I'm McNeil," Dan said. "Geoff, keep watch, will you? I need some of this man's expertise." He nodded at the first-aid kit from the helicopter that lay open at Brand's side. It was not equipped for a fullscale war, but there were still some antiseptic and pain killers. "I'll take him to see that white Ter when he's finished me. He may be interested."

"A white man?" The creases of pain on Brand's face changed to surprise and his shaggy eyebrows shot up. "I certainly am! I must also see if the radio is still working. Top priority is to get hold of Duvenage and tell him the set up. Now, McNeil, fill me in on what's happened. Where the hell is van Rooyen?"

THIRTY

Pieter Visagie thought that it had been a major shock to Sanderson and Theunissen to discover that the bridge over the Zambezi was not a road bridge but a rail bridge. For Pieter and Rafe Schulman, it was a relief, although they had tried not to show it. It was three in the morning when they got there. They woke a sleeping guard at the Dona Ana station. He spoke no English. Eventually, Theo got through to him in French. No bridge for the car here. Must wait for the train at ten o'clock and put car on the train. If they didn't want to wait, then they must drive to the Shiré ferry, cross the river, go to Murrembala, turn south for Mopeia, catch the ferry there to cross the Zambezi, then they would be on the way to Beira … No, there was nowhere they could get petrol at this time of night, or, indeed, at any time. There was petrol at Baué, about five kilometres away on the Malawi road. But the shop that sold it only opened at eight o'clock.

As they turned to go, in fury, the guard slyly told them that he had a twenty-litre can of petrol to sell them. He collected it from his home only fifty metres away and sold it to them for twice the normal price. It was as well that he didn't see the Landrover they were driving, or he might have recognised it and wondered …

They tore down the rutted road across the flood plain to the ferry. Here, their luck was in. The ferry over the Shiré River was on their side and it was the self-pull cable kind. They manned the winch before the ferry keeper could wake in his hut nearby and stop them. He would have to cross by dugout to retrieve the ferry. They drove off under the looming silhouette of Serra Murrembala. Another twenty kilometres on a very bumpy, eroded road took them to the town of Murrembala.

Although they tried to snatch some sleep in the Landrover, it was impossible. At a quarter to four, they roared into the sleeping town, in need of petrol for the hundred-kilometre trip to Mopeia.

Pieter parked at the pumps on the dark, tree-lined main street. Everyone got out to stretch their legs while Theo went to wake the shop owner at the house set back from the street attached to the store. Eventually, a short, dishevelled man appeared and Theo silenced his protests with a thousand escudos worth of grubby notes from his roll. Within ten minutes, they were on the road again. It was deeply rutted by the huge trucks that plied it and they made poor time. Once, despite 4x4, the Landrover got bogged down in the sand and it took their combined efforts to push it out. One of the two stores in Mopeia was open when they got there at six-thirty. Truck drivers were waking in the four enormous lorries that had spent the night there on their way to Beira from Quelimane. They hawked, spat, and farted as they made their way to the bar for a coffee and roll. The South Africans dearly wanted to follow suit, but Theo forbade the stop. They crossed rich, alluvial farmland as they headed for the ferry. Several large trucks, mostly MANs and Scandias, and a Landcruiser were already there waiting for the ferry. The engines started as they got there and a crewman waved them on with the Landcruiser to occupy a smaller space under the ferry's bridge. Two trucks rolled on, tilting the ferry crazily. The ramps were raised, the skipper yelled at a man on the shore to let go the manilas and then they were spinning away into the current. The diesels roared as they set off into the mist that lay on the river; the far bank was invisible. The bank they had left faded as well and they were in a noisy cocoon as the ferry chugged on. The further bank appeared. The diesels howled, hard astern; the helmsman swung the wheel and they were alongside. They paid the mulatto who brought the grubby book of tickets. The ramps dropped, the trucks left one at a time, the ferry tilting; then it was their turn. On this side too, a line of trucks waited. On the bank was a store serving coffee and rolls where Theo stopped to let them stock up and to ask the owner the way to Barros's hunting camp with a lot of sign language. Ten kilometres along the Morromeu road, they took a track to the right, into dense forest. After an hour, they began to skirt pans with watering holes. At one of these they saw three elephant and a small herd of buffalo. Arriving at a sawmill, they again asked for directions and, after half an hour, they turned onto the track beside Barros's airstrip.

Schulman managed to sleep only after they were on the sandy track in the forest; when Visagie nudged him awake, he looked more exhausted than ever. Piet saw, though, that he had recovered from the battering he had received climbing the cliffs of Serra da Muambe and knew that all he wanted was to get back to Johannesburg. They had tried to get Sanderson to tell them his plans for this get-rich scheme so that they could make their own plans to get away, but Sanderson had brushed them off with a wait-and-see. They overheard a word or two as the latter discussed details with Theunissen, but not enough to make sense of the plans. While stretching their legs and filling up with fuel, Pieter and Rafe, now allies of a sort, managed to share a few words. Pieter admitted to Rafe that he wanted out of it, whatever it was. Rafe told him that they would have to be ready for an opportunity, but not to let on that they were anything but loyal and keen.

The party kept their weapons out of sight as they stopped in front of the main bungalow, but saw nobody until Barros himself came to the door. He was tired and strained, surprised at the sight of the South Africans. He said something to someone behind him. Theo levelled his R3 at him.

"Get under cover!" he ordered his men. He demanded, "Those bastards, Campos and Ribeiro, where are they? Where is that Commie daughter of yours, Barros?"

"Locked up over there." He bitterly indicated the store where they had once been incarcerated. "Ribeiro is dead, Campos has run away. There is no need for guns, now, Mr. Theunissen. I am glad to see you got away. Come in." But he was confused at the sight of the man he knew as Sanderson, whom he now understood to be in league with the Chinese and to be the man Brand was looking for so desperately.

"He's lying, surround the place!"

Muller dodged around the side of the bungalow. Piet dropped down behind the palm tree, from where he could watch. There was the sound of breaking glass as Cecile aimed her Beretta at van Rooyen, who ducked behind the old Landrover. She cringed as Theo aimed his weapon at the window and roared.

"Come out, you!"

She appeared at the door, looking pale. She looked familiar, but he couldn't place her. He took her gun. She tried to tell him that they were on the same side, but she was now muddled. How to tell Theo who van Rooyen really was without the latter being aware?

"It's alright, now, there is no-one else who will harm you," she said nervously, still holding out her hand to get her weapon back. "Manuela is locked up and the manager won't give trouble –"

"Who the fuck are you?" Theo snapped, his wiry body taut with the imminence of action.

"Jean Hanekom, the Professor's wife." Cecile tried to smile, but the smile was twisted. "I must talk to you alone."

"Later. What happened here – Barros?"

"After the Dakota returned," Barros took his cue from Cecile; he was suspicious of Sanderson's presence, "the Professor and his wife arrived. It was all the diversion that we needed. My manager and I managed to, how do you say, turn the table? – on my daughter and her friends. Ribeiro and my pilot were killed, Campos ran away – "

"Just these two, Theo." Muller pushed Rosa and Reis onto the veranda. "They were locked up in a room at the end. There's nobody else here except that old kaffir …"

"Sanderson, take the shotgun and go get Manuela, if she's there. Muller, keep an eye on this shower while I talk to this woman."

Cecile walked ahead of Theo to the edge of the stoop, out of earshot of the others, but Pieter could hear her clearly. She turned and spoke to him, urgently. "That man you call Sanderson, he was in the South African Army. He has some classified information that he is trying to sell to the Chinese, to Manuela's friends. It is vital that we take him back to South Africa. Please, you don't know how important it is –"

"He changed his mind, Mrs. Hanekom. He's not selling it to the Chinese, anymore. Tell me, who are you? Security?" The cold eyes bored into hers. Cecile bit her lip. Now what? She nodded, reluctantly.

"We must still get him back to South Africa so that the Chinese do not get their hands on him. If he has double-crossed them, they will redouble their efforts to get hold of him, to force him to tell them what they want to know."

"Where's this professor? He also Security?"

Cecile guardedly told him what had happened, that the helicopter had been shot down while looking for Sanderson, but had found Nourse and McNeil, that they were looking for transport to try and link up with Duvenage in Mutarara.

"Please, help me. Don't let him get away! I don't know what story he's told you but he's a real threat to the safety of our country." The words were almost puerile, but her tone was that of a deeply-felt plea. Theunissen looked at her for a long minute and ever so slowly, his lip curled and finally, he snorted. There was no response to her appeal in those cold eyes, only hardening contempt. She had put all her money on the wrong horse.

"So, old Dan made it, hey?" He shook his head in wonder. "Right, Mrs Hanekom, you get back to the others and behave. You are what is commonly called an expendable hostage and if you give the slightest bit of trouble, you will be shot. Sit down with your back to the wall where I can see you."

Numbly, she did as she was told. Theo told Barros, Reis, and Rosa to join her. Rosa began to cry; she put her head down on her knees and sobbed, her father put his arm around her shoulders and patted her ineffectually. It was, for them, a never-ending nightmare. Barros, on whose shoulders the mantle of authority had rested for years, was again being ordered about and threatened; just when he had thought it was all over.

Manuela crossed the ground from the storeroom, her head held high, her body proud. Van Rooyen followed her with the shotgun, a honed-down man, the rounded sides of his former softness gone; angular, hard. Schulman and Visagie joined them, surprised as Theo waved them into the group in front of him with his R3. When they

251

were all assembled where he and Muller could watch them, in all their hearing, he told them what Cecile had said.

"Okay, Sanderson, spell it out." Theo finished.

For a moment, van Rooyen looked stunned, and then he looked at his watch. He cleared his throat.

"I have the means to destroy all police and military installations and barracks in this country." His face was tense, sweating, his breath taken in short gasps, his eyes blazed behind his spectacles. "I intend detonating those in and around Beira and obliterating them, so that I and my men can sack the city of its valuables ..."

God, he's incredible, thought Pieter. Only he noticed as Rafe, beside him, battled to keep the laughter from bubbling up inside him, almost making him choke. The stupid goddamned bastard, couldn't he see how funny he looked with this bloody Hitler act of his. Boo, boo! Get off the stage, you ridiculous turd! He saw Rafe finally get a grip as reality caught up with him and doused the laughter. His scorn withered away to be replaced by the acrid ooze of fear. He himself swallowed back the go-to-hell that perched in his throat, so living a bit longer.

"Now, Mr. Barros, we have need of your Dakota and facilities at Beira Airport; your hangar and transport. We need to refuel. You will lose everything you own when Portugal gives up Mozambique shortly, as it surely will, sooner rather than later. I give you this chance of at least getting something out of the country. Join us."

"*Caralho!*" The obscenity spat from Barros's lips. "You are mad, a lunatic! You will kill hundreds of my countrymen and you seek my help? You can rot in hell!" He tried to get to his feet, spittle flying from his mouth in his rage.

"No, Papa!" Rosa hung onto him, but it was more the threat of the R3 that halted him. He sank back, shaking.

"You don't need him. I can arrange whatever you need." Manuela spoke for the first time since she had been fetched. A protesting outburst, a shocked, horror-filled appeal lashed at her from her father, but she ignored him. Theo was not surprised; a grim smile tugged at one corner of his mouth. She said to van Rooyen: "For me,

Mozambique is finished. You will be doing what you have been paid to do by the Chinese, except they will not be prepared so as to take the best advantage, but the result will be the same. Whatever I can do to help, I will do willingly, if I get a share in the takings. What will you do with it? Where will you sell it?"

"The Dakota will be a so-called load of refugees, escaping the chaos. In fact, we shall return here and build the goods into the plane itself, then fly to Rhodesia. We shall only be a few of many fleeing the country." replied the man they knew as Sanderson.

One thing Pieter had overheard them say, in fact, was something about their deciding to head for the Comoros, so he realised that Sanderson was lying. With South African and Rhodesian intelligence on the look out for him, Rhodesia was the last place he would go. Manuela was no fool, either, Pieter thought, but she said nothing.

"What about fuel?" Sanderson asked her.

"We have some in drums, but it is not much. We can refuel at Manga Airport in Beira, and then it would be better to operate from the Chota, which is the skydivers' airstrip. It lies nearer to the City. It is very private. Manga will be out of action when these mines detonate, anyway, no?"

Van Rooyen nodded. "If I so choose," he said. He turned to Schulman and Visagie.

But before he could speak, Rafe snapped, "What's our percentage?"

"Typical Jew!" van Rooyen laughed, unable to keep a sneer out of his voice altogether. "Five percent per man. After expenses."

Piet was also quick on the uptake. "We are stealing everything we need! There are no expenses. Ten percent!" He was glad he had said 'We'. This added weight to his opting in, but he had no intention of allowing mass murder, not for any amount. He would take any opportunity to get out, when it arose. He only hoped that he and Rafe were convincing enough.

"You're more of a Jew than he is!" van Rooyen said. Theo watched both of them shrewdly, but said nothing. This farce was just wasting time. "Five percent. And you'll both be rich men." Assuming this financial bartering meant that they were pledges of "we're in", van Rooyen turned to the camp manager, Reis.

He was pale grey with fear. He stuttered, "I will do anything you say, just take me to Rhodesia. I cannot stay in Mozambique ..." He had a brief search around for sympathy, but there was only contempt. Muller was openly sneering.

"Do as we tell you, and we'll look after you." Van Rooyen eyed Reis coldly.

Barros's radios were loaded on the plane and the arms stowed. Van Rooyen gave Theo a note which, after a glance, Theo clamped between the double doors as bait before he set the traps on the doors, assisted by Manuela. He did not trust her and made sure she was kept in sight at all times.

Manuela caught sight of the old black man, shuffling as unobtrusively as he could, onto the veranda. She snatched up the old Mauser that Muller had discarded in favour of a G3 automatic rifle and leapt after him, cursing. Her ear still ached from the blow she had received from his broom. The old man backed against the low veranda wall, pleading. She feinted at his face with the butt and as he whimpered, raising his gnarled hands to protect himself, she smashed it into his scrawny ribcage. His breath exploded from him with a whoosh, his hands fell down and she whipped the butt across his yellow-toothed mouth. He fell backwards over the low wall.

Cecile was on top of Manuela before anyone could stop her, clawing at her throat and using her knee. Manuela battered short, one-handed blows to Cecile's midriff; the Mauser glanced off her nose. Theo tore them apart, pushing Cecile so hard that she fell backwards. Manuela tried to twist away to get at her again, but Theo held her with one hand and tore the Mauser out of her grip. Muller looked on with amusement. Rafe glanced at Piet and they both wondered if the brief diversion had not been a lost opportunity. Theo told Manuela to cool off; there was no time for petty shit. She glared at Cecile, remembering that it had been her friends who had nearly crushed her head in the vice. Van Rooyen told Muller to get the hostages aboard. Barros and Rosa got up. Cecile, struggling to her feet, tried to prevent her bleeding nose from dripping onto what she had scratched with her nail in the floor wax. She groaned with the pain of her bruised ribs. Tears of frustration and anger ran down her cheeks.

The Dakota lifted off at sixteen minutes past nine, with Rafe in the left-hand seat and Manuela beside him.

THIRTY-ONE

A ntonio Pires, lately of *Gondonga* Commando, turned his Landrover off the river track and up another that wound through the trees the short distance to Lake Lifumba. He hunched his thick body forward to let the breeze from the open window dry and cool the wet rag that was the shirt on his back.

He had had the roof of the vehicle modified to canvas, stretched onto a light tube frame; if he hit a mine, he had a better chance of survival with a roof that would give way as his body was hurled upwards. He'd been mined before, after he had found his store in ashes and his wife dead. This was not very far from where he was at the moment. He was going to fetch the fish from his brother-in-law's little netting business on the lake. The nets were laid by dugout and hauled in by tractor. But the fish were fewer and smaller than they had ever been. After the Kariba Dam in Rhodesia and now the Cabora Bassa Dam in Mozambique were built, the Zambezi no longer flooded the lake, bringing new stocks of fish. The natural reproduction that took place in the lake was not enough. At one time there had been as many as eight commercial fishing companies in operation there; but, they had dwindled until just the two remained. Frelimo in the area were a contributing factor, but thus far bribes and fish as food for the troops had kept them in business. However, this did not stop them from mining the roads from time to time to discourage the army. A tractor with a trailer-load of women and children had been blown up on the Bandar road back in '71. Now, Pires's brother-in-law was throwing in the towel. In Pires's opinion, he should have done so long ago. As he had told Geoff, there was better fishing to be done in the oxbow lakes of the Zambezi delta, although it still took a marsh buggy to get in there. Pires knew a man operating out of Morromeu who took his tractor by barge through the delta branch channels to an island in the higher-lying dune country near the sea. He was doing well, and there were only the worst mosquitoes in the world, but no Frelimo ...

He had returned to his Mutarara farm after the last battle, at the flat-topped hill, because of the wound in his arm, but it had almost healed by now. He got on well with the Sena people, he knew their ways, but, like most of the third and fourth generation settlers, he both doubted their ability to successfully run their own country and was frightened of being tossed out of the country and losing what possessions he had to take the chance of finding out. He ruled those who worked his cotton fields with an iron hand, though he was generous and fed them well. He had needed a foreman to run the place when he was away with his fingers in other pies and when Francisco Mwaga said he was free, he snapped him up. They had fought Frelimo together and the South African, Nourse, whom he had bumped into from time to time, had spoken highly of him. Sometimes, on short trips, Pires took the cheerful, squat, powerful black man with him. Francisco's wound, too, had almost healed.

Pires drove with one wheel on the verge, when the vegetation at the side of the track permitted, for any mines planted would be in the wheel ruts. Mwaga sat on the passenger side holding Pires's double-barrelled twelve-bore and the Brno .30-08 between his legs, sweating. He hated these trips to Lifumba. He thanked God that they were few and far between. He always got a cold feeling in his backside and could feel his testicles attempting to climb back inside his body. He knew that his employer did not care whether they hit a landmine or not. He also knew that, for all his kindness, it amused Pires to make him sweat a little.

"Francisco, my friend, if it is written in God's book that you will die today," he would say, "you can stay in bed at home, but He will still find a way to kill you!" It was alright for him, he had no more wife, no children, but what would little Alfonso do without a father? He thought of his own childhood. As he had told Boss Geoff, his father had disappeared, some said with another woman, from their home in Marandellas, Rhodesia. The struggle was too much for his mother without family help, so she returned to her parents in Mozambique with her ten-year old boy. In two years she was dead and it was natural that he blamed his father. When he grew up, Francisco had wished to return to Rhodesia, but no-one would help him get a permit. As things got worse in the country – floods, famine and Frelimo – he dreamed more and more of going back to Rhodesia, or to *Africa do Sul*, of which Boss Geoff had told him so much.

"What's this, now?" Pires's harsh cry ripped him back to the present. A ragged scarecrow in tattered uniform was waving them down. A white man! They had just reached the lake's edge by the huge fig trees. "Son of a whore! It is *Senhor* Nourse!"

"Boss Geoff!"

"Francisco! What the hell are you doing here?" Nourse panted, gasping for breath. "*Bom dia*, Antonio, *como estas?*" He leaned with relief against Pires's door. He had run a good part of the way after he and McNeil had helped the two crippled men into cover near the Bandar track. "Antonio, I need your help. I have three friends, wounded, on the Bandar road. I must get them to Mutarara. There are plenty Frelimo in the area, as you must know, so, if you'll lend me your Landrover ..."

"I len' you farken nutting!"Pires broke into his own brand of English. "I drive; you sit on farken back with gun, okay?" He waved to Mwaga and snapped in Sena, "Take the shotgun and look after us." Already he was turning the vehicle, fishing forgotten. Nourse vaulted in. What luck, meeting up with Pires! He had visualised having to borrow a tractor and trailer at gunpoint from one of the mulattos who ran the netting. They would not willingly drive on the Bandar road.

—⁂—

Sand spurted from Pires's tyres as he pulled away. He yelled questions at Nourse as they sped along back to the junction in the tracks and then swung west. Nourse answered as best he could without going into detail about Sanderson. He told of their forced drop on Frelimo headquarters and their escape. Then he was too concerned about possible attack to talk further as they sped along mostly open grasslands with stands of *Borassus* palm. Pires managed to drive parallel to the track, most of the time.

Brand had identified the white man who had been killed in the Frelimo attack. He had seen him in Beira and done a check with his department. He had supposedly been in the textile business with a Chinese in Lourenço Marques. He called himself Paul Smuts, but he had fled South Africa at the time of the Durban riots and his real name was Herman Bosch. The question was: why had he been here in the bush with a band of Frelimo? His Chinese connections, their link to van Rooyen, the arrival of both of them so close to the Frelimo base at Serra Muambe, now began to make a clearer picture. Bosch had taken to the bush in a desperate bid to either capture van Rooyen or to kill him.

"So, it's over, then," Bates had said from his *mopane* pole stretcher, "as long as we can keep van Rooyen out of the hands of the Chinese. They will still be after him, but, with Bosch dead, they will not be able to reorganise in time. He has no other market, now."

"I'm not so sure," Brand had said, worriedly. The whole operation had been chaotic. There had been no point at which he had felt in control. He had been three steps behind, the whole way. He had not, until now, told either Nourse or McNeil the real reason why they still had to find van Rooyen, the ex-communications expert. It was still top priority. He had decided that if he was to retain their help, he might have to give them a bit more detail, particularly now that Bates and he were wounded and de Sousa was dead.

The short trip was uneventful, Nourse thanked God. No Frelimo, no mines. Geoff guided Pires to where the South Africans were waiting. Bates was asleep on his stretcher with several broken ribs, suspected back injury, and a damaged hand from the crash. They loaded the stretcher gently onto the bed of the truck. Nourse, Mwaga and McNeil sat in the back with him and Brand joined Pires in the front. They turned and headed downriver, past Ancuaze, another trading post, towards Zamira, where Pires's brother-in-law had his own store. In a low voice, McNeil told Nourse what Brand had told him about Operation Insurance and why they still had to find van Rooyen. He said that Brand remained afraid that van Rooyen would still try to set off these mines. Who would gain by the effect of putting all military and police installations out of commission, besides Frelimo and the Communists?

"Looters, criminals!" Nourse could see the chaos in his mind. "Remember Muller talking about raiding museums, jewellers, and banks?"

McNeil nodded. They'd all chatted about the possibilities of such raids when they were cooped up in the hotel. It had helped to pass the time. He remembered, now, that it had been Muller who had set the discussion in motion.

"No," he said doubtfully, "I personally think that van Rooyen will simply want to get out of the country. I don't think the others, except Muller, would want to be involved in such a caper; they would want to go home."

At Zamira, Pires stopped at his brother-in-law's store. Here, the road joined that which linked up to the village of Doa on the Tete-Mutarara railway line. They wolfed down a hurried meal prepared by *Senhora* Alves, then McNeil and Nourse changed into civilian clothes from *Senhor* Alves's shelves. Yes, said Alves to Brand's question, through Geoff; they had heard a vehicle pass by during the night; it had not stopped. Francisco, saying a swift farewell, was left behind when they hit the road again. Nourse hugged his friend and promised to keep in touch.

Mutarara consisted of a series of installations and villages strung along the Zambezi. First, there was the aerodrome, a minor Air Force base, at that time with a contingent of Air Force personnel and at times, some small planes. These were mostly used for spotting and recce work. Beyond the aerodrome lay Mutatara Nova, the new town – a few houses, a *pension*, a restaurant, the railway station and goods yard, and the Railway Club. Then followed a two-kilometre gap where the road and line are pushed up against the river by a row of red conglomerate hills. One then entered Dona Ana, where the line to Tete is joined by the line to Malawi to cross the Zambezi on a two-kilometre steel arched bridge. Beyond Dona Ana, lay Mutarara Velho, the old town. Here was the administrative section, the hospital run by a single male nurse, and the army barracks.

Pires swung in at the aerodrome, pulling up at the guard post. He pointed at the Barros Cessna 182 on the strip and told the soldier that they were expected. The guard stuck his cigarette back in his mouth and waved them in. Pires headed straight onto the hardstanding and stopped by the four-seater. Duvenage trotted over from where he had been chatting to some air force men. Brand introduced the agent to Nourse and McNeil. It was just after one o'clock, siesta time. The tarmac threw up a vicious glare. It was the only piece of tarmac for hundreds of kilometres; all the roads were sand or metalled. The buildings were covered with dust; even the newly arrived Cessna already had a film on it.

Brand had a last word with Bates. It was he who must report the loss of the Bell, deal with the paperwork and police statements with a reasonable cover story that would satisfy but give nothing away. Pires was to take Bates to the hospital and he agreed to bring de Souza's body and any loose kit back to Mutarara as soon as he could. He would also have to make such relative supportive statements as the authorities required. Geoff shook hands with Pires and asked him on behalf of Brand, to say as little as possible about anything he had overheard. The grizzled Portuguese grinned.

"I say farken nutting, my friend. Hey, sometime you come stay my house, okay? We go hunt big farken boofalow, *Sim?*"

"Okay, Antonio, sure thing. Look after yourself!" Geoff grinned back as he gathered the bundles that were the R3s wrapped in their discarded uniforms and newspaper and clambered aboard. The plane lifted and circled the dusty little town. They could see Pires's Landrover heading a spear of dust as it drove towards the hospital. Below them lay the railway bridge, ending at the drab little village of Sena, one of the first inland settlements of Europeans in southern Africa. Soon it was lost to view as they followed the brown ribbon of the Zambezi.

They saw several dugouts on the river and, at its junction with the Shiré River – which flows south from Lake Malawi – a paddle steamer carrying a deck cargo of sacks of grain.

"My God!" Brand gaped at it, "Just what century is this?"

"I know, I couldn't believe it, myself, when I saw it on the way up," Duvenage said. Geoff told them that there were still a couple of paddle steamers that plied the Zambezi between Morromeu and Luabo and also up the Shiré.

Brand told the agent that Geoff had been working in the area for three years and knew it well. He asked Duvenage what the situation had been when he left. Geoff and Dan were slumped in their seats, trying to keep awake. McNeil's shoulder had greatly improved with treatment but still ached.

"Quiet. Cradock has everything under control." That made Dan pay attention. "Manuela Barros knows that you were shot down and she might have wanted to try something while I am away, so we locked her in a storeroom." Then a look of alarm crossed his face. "I wonder, you don't think something could happen if van Rooyen arrives there?"

"Like what? Why would they go there? They were escaping from there, weren't they?" Brand asked, but he was suddenly worried. McNeil opened his eyes.

"Loot Beira." He told them what he and Geoff had discussed.

"It's no more than a remote possibility," Brand said as he fumbled for his pipe, and Duvenage rolled his eyes at the thought of that awful cloud in the cabin. "Seems most unlikely. But let's look at it. Would the men who are with him go for it? Would you, if van Rooyen had suggested it? He would need all the armed men he could get his hands on and a plane to fly them out of the country with the loot."

"In the Congo," Dan said, "I admit I helped to blow a couple of safes and took whatever came my way. But this involves the deaths of hundreds, maybe thousands of people to start with. I would not take him seriously. We're not sure who is with him. We think that the only one who didn't make it away from the mountain besides Blair was Jan de Groot, but we can't be sure. Let's assume there's Theo Theunissen; I don't think he'd go for it, he's had all the excitement he needs for a lifetime and I've never heard him express a desire to be mega rich. He makes a good living with his gym. Helmut Muller, what do you think, Geoff? He might say yes to a thing like that; a pretty ruthless bastard, I'd guess. Now, Rafe Schulman, no, he wouldn't touch it. A tough nut, but no gangster. Same goes for Piet Visagie. He may talk about it, but he is a softy, he wouldn't go for the killing. Only a bunch of madmen or hardened criminals would try it."

Staring at Dan curiously, Brand thought that he could rule out this hypothesis. But the question remained; what would van Rooyen do? Where would he go? He could catch a plane in Beira, or a train to Rhodesia or hire a car and drive to Malawi or Zambia or go north to Tanzania. We've lost him, he thought. Let's hope the Chinese have as well.

Using the reverse of the route that he had used to get to Mutarara, Duvenage swung away from the Zambezi and in twenty minutes, he was coming down to the strip at the edge of the Mungari River. Nothing moved.

"Good God!" Duvenage exploded, "the Dakota's gone!"

Nourse, without being told, ripped open the bundle of firearms. They were all tense with premonition. The Cessna's wheels touched, a slight bounce, and then they were down, taxiing towards the bungalows. Still nothing moved. It was an ordinary hot day. A slight breeze stirred the dense forest; it seemed to galvanize them into action. Brand, with his wounded leg, stayed with the plane, his knuckles white as he gripped the R3 to cover them. Duvenage started a zigzag run towards the buildings, McNeil and Nourse backing him up on either side. At a glance they could see that the storeroom door where Manuela had been locked in was wide open. The main doors, on the veranda, were, on the other hand closed. Stuck to one was a note. What Duvenage could see of it was in Afrikaans. McNeil had gone to one side of the building, Nourse the other. Duvenage reached for the door handle to release the note.

There was a groan from the palm tree where Ribeiro had died. Duvenage whipped around, sweating.

"Boss …" It was still more of a groan than a call. The seamed, bloody, black head with the grizzled, grey peppercorn hair moved slightly, just above the veranda floor. "Boss ..." the toothless mouth formed again. Duvenage shouted for the other two, keeping his weapon trained on the old man and his eyes flickering about the other bungalows. Geoff came up behind the hurt man.

"*Madala!*" He knelt at his side to put his arm around the thin shoulders. The old one had been badly beaten up. His teeth, such as they had been, had been smashed out of his jaw, which appeared to be broken. One arm was twisted at an unnatural angle. Geoff ran his hands over the thin body – some ribs were concave where they should have bulged. The old man hacked and bloody foam appeared from his ruined mouth, pink on the purple-brown of the old caked blood. Geoff was angry, and now scared, too. This thing was not yet over.

"Ask him if there is anyone else still here." Duvenage was still watching for movement. The old man got that and minimally shook his head.

"Gone ...," he breathed, "Doors ... Boss ... not open ... doors ... all got *skelm* ... kill you ..."

"Something to do with the doors" Geoff tried Sena which was stupid as the old man was a Rhodesian and understood English better. He switched to Fanagalo. "What devil is in the doors?"

"... like iron ... apple ... bang ..."

"Doors must be booby-trapped." Nourse saw Duvenage shiver at how close he had been to opening that front door. "*Madala*, who did this to you?"

"Miss ... Manuela ... missus try ... stop ... she hit missus ... too much ..." His voice was a slushy croak. Geoff leaned closer; "Taking guns ... radio machines ... to aero ... plane ... all ... people ... fly ..." The last word was a long sigh. How to ask him who went as prisoners and who as captors? Who let Manuela free? Nourse shook him ever so gently.

"*Madala?*" There was no response. He felt for a pulse on the scrawny neck. Nothing. He was unaware of the tears running down his own cheeks. He got to his feet, unable to see anything, blinking. When he had recovered, he followed Duvenage, who had broken a window to get inside. Dan managed to join them without too much strain on his shoulder.

"Shit, I don't like that!" McNeil said, looking at the booby-trap from inside the bungalow. A grenade was fixed so that the man opening it would have been blown to kingdom come.

"Oh, really," said Duvenage, sarcastically, "Well, I'm sure I –"

"No, not that. It is who put it there, it is like a signature." McNeil looked grey under his tan. The other two men looked at him in puzzlement. "Theo Theunissen. Only one man I know sets a door booby like that. And that's Theo. Besides, who else knows how to set one at all?"

"Maybe Sanderson forced him to?" Nourse said, but his tone lacked conviction. He watched as Dan carefully dismantled the trap.

"You stay here or you'll blow yourself up. Duvenage and I'll look the place over." The note fluttered to the floor as he opened the door, from whence Duvenage retrieved it.

All I want to do now is escape. I have no intention of trying to sell or use the information that I have of Operation Insurance or any other classified information in my possession. I made a mistake trying to deal with the Communists. I now realise that I cannot betray my country. However, I must ask you to stay here for 48 hours to give me a chance to get away, or I will be forced to execute Cradock and other hostages. Keep away from me and they will live. Signed: P.A.vR.

Duvenage pocketed the note for his chief's perusal. Dan shuddered. Geoff guessed that Cecile had been in his thoughts most of the while, but from the time that the Cessna had landed until he had heard of Manuela beating up another "missus" he had staved off the fear. Now bilious dread spread through his guts. His fists were clenched and he spat out an expletive through gritted teeth. Geoff darted a look at him and winced in sympathy.

McNeil turned abruptly and followed Duvenage through the bungalow. Nourse stepped onto the smooth, green polished concrete surface of the stoop. Some of that poor old man's work, this polishing, he mused as his eyes searched the surroundings for any suspicious movement. There was a path of dusty footprints across the polish to the edge of the veranda where the old man's body lay in the palms. There was a trail to the steps in front, to the table and chairs on the other side of the stoop, then their own prints to the window where they had entered, but his attention was drawn to some scratch marks in the wax polish on the floor below the window. He stood with his back to the wall, looking down at them. They were near a smear and a few drops of dried blood. They were definitely letters, he saw, probably scratched with a fingernail. A footprint blotted the middle of the last word; there were two or three letters missing.

vR 2 DET OP INS IMM LOOT BEIRA FROM C—A

"Duvenage!"

"What's wrong?" The agent was there within seconds, McNeil at his heels.

"Take a look at this!" Geoff indicated. Duvenage studied it.

At length, he said, "I make it van Rooyen to detonate Operation Insurance immediately. He intends to loot Beira, from … what? Could this be a place? Beginning with C, ending with A and two, no three letters missing. Obliterated by our own bloody careless feet!" He got down on his knees. "Crofa? Chofa?" He raised his eyebrows at Nourse. "Ring any bells? In Beira, near Beira?"

Geoff racked his brains, then he was suddenly sure. "Yes! It must be Chota! It's a sand dune relic across the flats, between the airport and the city. Lined with palm trees, it's got a landing strip on it the skydivers use, and their drop zone! It's flooded part of the year but should be dry by now. It hasn't rained for awhile. They always call it the Chota; Cecile must have heard them talking about it. They can land the Dak there, if they inform Manga Airport beforehand …"

So, their idle speculation had been dead on the nail. Duvenage nodded slowly, then he turned to Dan. He pointed.

"Check out those buildings for any clue to confirm this or help us. Nourse, look over the workshops and storerooms. Quick. Come to the plane when you have done it. I'll talk to the Chief in the meanwhile."

THIRTY-TWO

Dan was sick with fear; it twisted his guts, it seeped through his system like a poison, its acid ate away at his nerves. Nourse watched his friend from the corner of his eye with sympathy. There was nothing he could say to help; his own nerves were on edge. What they were going to do was tantamount to suicide, but where Geoff's fear was for himself, he knew Dan's agony was for Cecile. McNeil had had a verbal fight with Brand when the latter had said that there was nothing for it but to go to Beira and tackle van Rooyen, Theunissen, and their mob head-on. They had to assume that the South Africans had, like it or not, thrown in their lot with the raid. Manuela, too, must be with them. It would be she who knew of the Chota. It would be Rafe Schulman who would, willingly or otherwise, be piloting the Dakota. It was Theo who had set the booby traps from supplies meant for Barros's army; he could easily have pretended to set them and not done so – van Rooyen would not have been the wiser. So Theo was in it up to the hilt. Theo Theunissen ... something was nagging at Geoff about that man.

It was Brand's idea to drop a box of primed grenades onto the Dakota from the Cessna, if they could get there on time, then land and attack. This roused Dan to fury.

"You're not risking that girl's life! You can't just bloody murder her to get at van Rooyen. What about Rosa and Barros? You fuckin' well can't –"

"My dear McNeil, consider what would happen if the mines go off! How many people would die then? Hundreds, maybe thousands? And you don't think they'll let any of the innocent live when they make their getaway? I hate to say this, but I'm surprised they've let them live this long. It's not as if they actually need hostages at this juncture. And when it gets out who did it? And who put the mines in place in the first instance? Cecile Cradock is a very competent agent and she'll get herself out of this mess if it is humanly possible."

Just miserable words, you bastard, thought Geoff; Brand can't even convince himself, never mind Dan. The poor bugger isn't only in love with the girl, he is injured and in pain. It was going to be very nasty indeed, but without himself and Dan, there was no chance of a rescue at all.

"I'll have to get Duvenage to ram the Dakota, if it's still there." Brand said, not very convincingly, it seemed to Geoff.

The Cessna droned on at fifteen hundred metres above the ground. The back seats and a door had been swiftly removed by Duvenage while the two skydivers had adjusted and donned two parachutes they had found at the camp; these had probably belonged to Rosa and Manuela. It had been Geoff Nourse's idea, when he saw them, that they use the parachutes. If the Dak was on the Chota, they could drop on it with more chance of surprise than if the Cessna landed immediately. Their discussion was mostly conjecture. Cecile had said "immediate". How soon could van Rooyen get organised on arrival? What would be the ideal time? What organising would be necessary? Surely they would land at Manga Airport first to refuel? Brand reckoned that, for an expert like van Rooyen, the radios taken from the Barros camp could be set up in sequence in half an hour. In the meantime, they would have to organise transport to take them from the Chota or the airport to Beira and back with their booty to load onto the Dak. The Barros organisation would be able to take care of all that as Barros himself was there to give the order. They had about four hours' start on Brand but perhaps they did not yet know that Brand was on to them. However, it was still possible that when the Cessna arrived, Beira would already be in flames...

Brand said he might get some help from the Portuguese, but that this was unlikely. Indeed, the man who was Brand's superior had been informed and would get onto his opposite number in Lourenço

Marques. It would be impossible to convince him to act in time as he could not be told the whole truth and had been notoriously unhelpful in the past.

It was going to be difficult enough getting out of the situation diplomatically, too, even if they were in time, when they had the police descending on them for attacking a Portuguese plane with automatic weapons and grenades in the middle of Beira. However, in the unlikely event of their success, they would have averted a tragedy. Otherwise, there would be no police, no Beira. Perhaps van Rooyen was going to go the whole hog and detonate the whole country?

Four pairs of anxious eyes scanned the horizon towards the south, praying not to see smoke.

—⚋—

Duvenage gave a false registration as he reported their approach to Manga. He said he would circle Beira for the view and gave his altitude. There was some confusion as to where he had taken off from, but no panic. There was no point in getting the radar operator excited and scrambling the air force because of an unidentified blip. It gave them hope that Manga replied as this meant that the airport still existed. There were no columns of smoke either.

The wind tugged at Geoff Nourse's cheek, bending his nose, as he thrust his head out of the doorway into the slipstream. He blinked the moisture from his eyes as the wind found its way under his goggles. Below was a miniature Beira: the sea was just under the Cessna's tail, to the left sprawled the central part of the city, straddling the Chiveve on whose muddy banks lay the golf course. Ahead lay the swampy grassland through which a couple of raised roads meandered to Manga Airport and the air force base. Across the swampy ground lay several remnant sand dunes, lined with coconut palms and shanties. This is higher ground and, where the dunes run in the right direction, roads use their length and the safety they offer from flooding. Such is the Chota, now lying directly ahead, nearly five thousand metres below, a tiny, mottled ribbon, with the grass landing strip discernable on the near side. Geoff could just make out the silver cross of the Dak half concealed by the palms.

"She's there!" he shouted in relief, his voice all but whipped away by the wind. Duvenage cut the power down slowly so that it would not attract the attention of those used to listening to the sound of aircraft engines. There was no wind; they would go out beyond the target without the benefit of a full throttle-back.

Geoff saw Dan trying to ease the pressure of the harness on his wound and saw him wince. His own stomach churned; he thought that his bowels might let go at any moment. He had a thousand jumps to his credit, but there had never been a jump as vital as this one. He gave Dan a sickly grin. Dan was pale and strained, but he mustered a smile in return. Geoff turned back to the hole where the door had been. McNeil saw him push one leg out into the wind, watched it wander as it sought the step. One hand stretched up the strut as he moved his body out of the doorway. Duvenhage trimmed to compensate for the drag. Dan drew his feet up underneath him, tensing, and followed Geoff half out, careful not to dislodge Geoff's hold.

"Remember, we'll land a minute before you to keep their attention off you," shouted Brand. "Get the radios out of commission before anything else! Good luck!" They had been over it all three times and they still had only a snowball's hope in hell.

With a last elaborate wink at McNeil, Nourse hurled himself into space. Dan was so close behind that Nourse's boots brushed his chest. The two bodies rocked a little until they picked up speed, then stabilized in the frog position. McNeil closed up tighter to accelerate enough to join Geoff's level and they flew side by side, snatching glances to keep station, but mostly, with their eyes pinned on the Dakota below; hearts hammering, adrenalin sodden. A quick look told them that the Cessna was rapidly losing height towards Manga Airport as if to land there.

The borrowed altimeter on Geoff's wrist dropped through seven hundred metres, its red line warning the skydiver to go for his ripcord, but he went on down. Both men often went without the instrument;

they had enough experience to use their own judgement. But this was no ordinary jump.

Six, five, four hundred; the survival organism was screaming, oh, Christ, we're creaming in! Geoff Nourse tore the handle from its pocket, not caring that they had agreed upon three hundred, blood thundering in his temples as he felt the ground-rush suck at him, panicking, screaming, too low, too late, we're dead, oh, sweet Jesus!

The twin explosions of their simultaneously opening chutes sounded like the crack of doomsday and felt like the welcoming gong at the gates of paradise. Geoff found that he hardly had time to snatch the pistol from his pocket and correct the veering of his canopy when his boots hit the aluminium of the fuselage. He sat down to keep his balance but began to slide before he could stop himself.

A group of urchins who had been gawping at the Dakota began to run to the nearest shanty amongst the palms. Dan landed twenty metres from the tail, dropped to a crouch, and slipped his capewells; he was fumbling for his pistol as a pair of legs appeared on the ladder from the rear door of the Dakota on the far side. Someone in the cockpit turned a face towards him. The Cessna was down, racing over the short grass towards them.

Geoff's lines bent over the aerial, his canopy settled on the far side of the fuselage, arresting his slide, suspending him between two windows of the cabin, just forward of the door.

A lorry came around the nearest shanty. The afternoon sun made a blaze on the windscreen; Dan McNeil could not see the occupants, but both doors were opening and there was a blur of weapons as he began his dash towards the plane. He ducked under its belly and kept the tail wheel between himself and the truck. People were shouting. Weapons opened fire.

THIRTY-THREE

Despite the apprehension of all in the Dakota as they landed at Manga Airport, Beira, with Manuela talking to the tower to people who knew her voice, there were no problems in refuelling. Rafe was ordered to stay at the controls while Manuela dealt with the ground staff and signed for the fuel. The Dakota then taxied over to the Barros hangar where Manuela commandeered a four-ton Bedford from her father's vehicle pool. Now, dressed in civvies, with Theunissen, Muller, Visagie and Reis on board the truck, the latter guided them to the Chota. It was so close to the main airport that they arrived just as Rafe touched the Dakota down rather bumpily on the grass strip.

Cecile, together with Barros and Rosa, was tied to the ring-bolts in the main cabin. Whenever they tried to talk to each other, they were told to shut up by Manuela. Van Rooyen sat at the radios and began to input the complicated series of firing codes that would detonate the explosives in the Beira area. Theunissen had a last-minute meeting with Manuela and van Rooyen to confirm their timing, then he returned to the truck and they set off back towards the main road to Beira to take up position near the museum and Beira's three main jewellery stores. Pieter Visagie knew that he had lost his last chance to make some sort of desperate plan with Rafe to escape their involvement with this murderously insane scheme. He realised that each in his own way must try to do whatever they could, but it seemed that Theunissen and Muller did not altogether trust either of them so presented no opportunities. Then, as they turned onto the tarred road to the city, the Barros Cessna dropped out of the sky just above their heads.

"Fuck!" exploded Helmut, "That's trouble!"

"Turn, Piet, turn! Get back to the Dak." Theunissen snatched one of the rifles from under the blanket on the cab floor and Muller followed suit. Pieter u-turned the truck across the path of a black-and-green taxi that went off the road in a cloud of dust to avoid him. He gunned the motor and they shot back down the Chota track.

In the cockpit of the Dakota, Manuela had immediately recognised her father's Cessna. She cursed, tugging Cecile's pistol from the pocket of her leather flying jacket and yelling to van Rooyen who was still working on his precious radios. Five minutes would have seen them ready, synchronised, with four different frequencies simultaneously ready to unlock, arm, and fire the radio detonators of four tons of high explosive. In about forty minutes Theo would have signaled that they were in position and the murderous signals would have been sent out. She screamed into the walkie-talkie in her hand to Theo in the truck to come back.

"Here's the Cessna, it must be that bitch's security friends!"

"Oh, God!" van Rooyen sprang to the port to look, snatching up his G3. There was a loud report like ripping material overhead.

"Parachutes!" Manuela recognised the sound, her eyes were wide; she dithered in indecision, then she screamed at van Rooyen, "Detonate the mines, now!"

Distracted, van Rooyen stared at her dumbly, shaking his head. "They're not ready –"

"I don't care!" Manuela yelled, spittle spraying from her mouth. "Blow them!" Cecile guessed that she had intended to force van Rooyen to detonate all the rest when he had set off the Beira section. Then her job would have been done. She had no interest in gold and jewels. She aimed the Beretta at his head. "Blow them, or I'll kill you!"

Van Rooyen slowly sat down. Cecile saw that he knew he was a fraction of a millimetre from death. He let the G3 drop to the floor and his hands reached reluctantly for the dials. He switched on; probably seeing in his mind's eye the teeming barracks, laughing squaddies; officers, saying goodnight to their secretaries; guards being changed at ammunition dumps – then the shattering roar, the heaving ground, the splintering walls, searing flames, screams, the blood …

In horror she watched as van Rooyen slowly smiled a wolfish smile, his tongue appearing briefly.

There was a thump on the fuselage; the Dakota rocked. Manuela ran down the aisle to the rear door and stepped onto the ladder. With relief, she saw that the truck had turned and was heading back. The Cessna was two hundred metres away, moving fast towards them. A man where the door had been was leaning out with a rifle in one hand. Next to her, something moved. She turned.

Two metres away from her, Geoff hung in his harness. His fingers were on the release capewells, but the pistol loaned by Duvenage hampered him. For a long second, they looked at each other from sweating, desperate faces – there was no time for memories. He knew it was too late to bring the 9mm to bear; even as he tried, her finger tightened on her trigger.

The barrel that he was looking down twisted suddenly and the shot slammed against his helmet, whacking his head back against the aluminium. Dazed, he saw her fall, her ankles sticking through the ladder. McNeil had grabbed them. Manuela's head and shoulders hit the ground, the pistol jarred from her hand. She kicked free and began to crawl after the weapon.

The truck slewed as Piet yanked the wheel hard over, but it skidded and did not tip as he had desperately hoped. The cab doors exploded open as Theunissen leaped out, firing.

McNeil threw himself around the ladder just as Theunissen opened fire on him, the full metal jackets tearing through the pressed metal. Something tugged at his hip. Muller opened up on the Cessna while Brand returned fire, half obscured by the tail wheel of the Dakota.

Piet Visagie was sobbing, his eyes wild. He shot Muller in the back at point blank range. Theo turned to look for his men, saw Muller jerk like a rag doll and sprawl on the grass, saw Piet's weapon swing towards him, heard the sobbing, and felt the bullets tear into his chest. He staggered backwards, a look of total disbelief on his craggy face.

Reis dropped his rifle on the bed of the truck, slipped out and began to run.

Cecile saw Rafe Schulman crouched in the cockpit, unarmed,

muttering between clenched teeth, searching for a weapon. There was nothing. At Cecile's side, where she lay handcuffed on the floor, van Rooyen crouched, his radios forgotten, the muzzle of the G3 grinding into her neck.

Her breath came in terrified whistling gasps as she strained against the cuffs. She whimpered, then gave a little cry of agony as the steel bit deeper. A bulky figure appeared in the rear doorway.

"Drop that! Or I'll kill her!" van Rooyen screamed.

McNeil wavered, desperate, uncertain. Van Rooyen snarled the command again. McNeil let the pistol drop. As it hit the floor, van Rooyen lifted the G3 and fired as it swung into line and McNeil was starting to throw himself sideways.

Only two shots had left the muzzle when Rafe's boot crashed into the back of van Rooyen's neck. McNeil was thrown against the bulkhead and slid to the floor. Van Rooyen lay sprawled in the aisle, the rifle under him. Wriggling, moaning, he tried to rid himself of Rafe on his back, Rafe's hands were under van Rooyen's chin, cursing, shouting, forcing his head back and up; up until van Rooyen's moan turned to a squeak. Then there was an audible click. Although the body was limp, now, Rafe went on cursing, foully, insanely. Rosa was screaming, her head buried in her father's shoulder, but he could not lift his handcuffed wrists to comfort her.

Manuela reached her pistol as Geoff released his capewells and dropped to the ground, off balance. She screamed at him and aimed.

Who would ever really know what the dying man thought as he lay there, the fire that had been his life spluttering to an intermittent spark. Maybe, lying there, Theo wondered where he had gone wrong. It was too late, of course, because he, who had killed so many, was dying. Theo, who had lately betrayed those who trusted him, had in turn been betrayed. Did he know that he had become a rabid dog? Pieter had had to put him down. Pieter, who didn't want to leave McNeil and Nourse on the mountain. It was too late to right his wrongs now, but it seemed that Theo decided to try…

It was he who shot Manuela.

275

THIRTY-FOUR

Nobody appeared as a result of the firing. The inhabitants of the Chota shanties had no telephones and those further away thought they had heard the sound of the army rifle range. Barros radioed his own police contacts and, after half an hour, two police Landrovers arrived.

Brand radioed his boss to make certain arrangements. Barros agreed to keep quiet about some rather embarrassing facts regarding Operation Insurance in exchange for a sum of money to be deposited into a South African bank. Barros agreed that the information in the wrong hands would do untold damage to Mozambique. The new truth was that a bunch of criminals had kidnapped him and tried to steal the Dakota to get out of the country. The bodies of Muller, Theunissen and van Rooyen were buried quietly, without ceremony, in Beira. De Souza's body was flown to South Africa for burial. Bates and McNeil were flown to Salisbury, Rhodesia, where they, in time, recovered from their wounds and injuries. Brand gave Cecile three weeks leave, not by coincidence, aware that he was shortly about to lose an agent. She and Nourse went to Salisbury together.

Pieter Visagie and Rafe Schulman, promising to keep in touch, returned to South Africa with Duvenage and Brand. Rafe told Geoff that he had decided to return to Israel. Pieter said he thought that he might go along, just for a look, and then see something of Europe...

"I think that Geoffrey is a bum name. Can't we call him Zachariah Cholmondeley McNeil?" Dan asked, straight-faced.

276

"Not on your McNelly." Cecile laughed. "Geoffrey Cradock McNeil he will be!"

"Yech! That's the greatest common multiple!" McNeil protested. He was just getting used to the idea of being a father, now that Cecile had discovered that she was pregnant. They were pretending that it would be a boy. "Geoff, old buddy, I'm in shock. Unleash me another tame Lion, will you? Well, for a while there, I thought that Cradock was an alias, you being a spook and all, but I must say I was relieved when it wasn't."

He gestured at the six-pack on the stainless steel bedside table. The hospital rules were against it, of course, but the nurses were a cheerful, down-to-earth lot and were turning a blind eye. Nourse grinned and did as he had been bidden. He intended to stay around long enough to see his friend well and wed, and then he planned to go off to Europe to check out the skydiving scene there. Dan was to be released the next day, then they would wend their way south.

"What are you getting married for, anyway, Dan? For someone that has been in the mire before, aren't you being a trifle dumb?"

"Just you belt up, Geoff Nourse. We've enough bastards like you and Dan about without making another one." Cecile shook a stern finger at him. They laughed, the bonds of a life-long friendship growing. They were quiet for a while remembering, grateful to be alive and thinking of those who had died.

"Can't understand Theo, though." Geoff shook his head in bewilderment. He would never forget that bloody, bubbling whisper from Theunissen's lips, as he knelt over the dying man, admitting that he had pushed Ryan O'Donnell over the balcony.

"Good God, Theo! Why?" He had recoiled from the torn body in horror, stunned with disbelief. Theo's reply came through quite strongly, although they were the last words he ever said.

"Sold to the highest bidder."

They found a blue armband in his pocket.

"Why didn't he do what he was supposed to do after the drop on Muambe? He could have cut us down then. He and van Rooyen would have been captured, given the right answers for the observers, finished."

"We were too spread out, and then it was too late. When we were armed there was nothing he could do in case one of us survived to shoot him. Christ! When I think about him pushing Ryan!" McNeil exploded bitterly.

Nourse cracked two more cans and handed one to Dan. He was still bewildered. "He and Ryan were pretty close. Went through hell together, you say. I can't believe it was for the money, Dan. What made him do it?"

"I've been thinking about that," McNeil said slowly. His eyes saw nothing of the ward or his companions. "Twice, in the Congo, when things were rough, Theo asked me if I would join the other side if the money was better. I said that once I was bought, I stayed bought and my loyalty along with me. He laughed and said that I wasn't a true mercenary, then. I said that neither was he, in that case, but he laughed again and said it was because he didn't have the guts to fight against O'Donnell. Maybe there is a clue there and maybe there isn't, but Ryan was the better soldier and maybe Theo was afraid of him, envied him. Perhaps all the death that Theo saw had warped his mind, so that, to be what he called a true mercenary, became a sort of obsession. 'Sold to the highest bidder', was what he said, isn't it? But it wasn't for the money; he had plenty of that ..."

Cecile cleared her throat and squeezed Dan's hand, trying to shake off the mantle of depression that had settled over them.

"We think that the observer, or one of them, was an Englishman named Alistair, a journalist that Mr Brand and I met in Beira. We've found out that he flew to Malawi a couple of days before you made the drop. Herman Bosch, the man you killed in the bush, using the name of Paul Smuts, was on the same flight. Poor Alistair. I rather liked him and they would probably have liquidated him when their plan backfired."

Then there occurred one of those strange, inexplicable moments when they were, in their minds, meeting for the first time at the skydiving club. They were all comparing the then with the now and how what had happened had changed them. Enriched them. Strengthened them.

Simultaneously, they smiled.

THIRTY-FIVE

"The man who called himself Paul Smuts never intended getting himself mixed up in a firefight. He agreed to going with Wanga, sure, but for him it was the best possible way of retrieving that man, Sanderson, and he knew that it was his responsibility." General Mucongáve scratched his crotch and continued.

"Remember, I told you they had some scheme to blow up the army? Well, they met up with the captain from Bandar area that morning, less than an hour before the helicopter flew over, they told me. There was no hope of catching the escaping Sanderson on foot now that they had learned of the South Africans theft of transport from Bandar. Smuts's priority was to find himself some transport and the only hope of that was getting himself to Lake Lifumba, where the captain had told him that he might find something. My men tell me that he was shot in the neck, back there in the bush where he did not want to be. Smuts must have known it was too late, that all his plans were for nothing, that his life was about to end and maybe he was forming a protest as the bullet tore into his throat and ripped out bits of his vertebrae. What does a man feel in that last second? I think he felt nothing; but perhaps his eyes were recording a peaceful picture of leaves scattered across a blue sky like a movie camera left running, and his brain, as the batteries ran down, was regretting, regretting …"

The sun peeped over the hills; the black silhouettes of the *M'sasa* trees faded to grey, then dark green. There was a nip in the air which was not unpleasant. The sky lightened into a deep, cloudless blue.

Alistair's clothes hung baggily on him, ragged and filthy. Lack of cigarettes had forced him to give up smoking and he had not been so fit for years. He was resolved to keep it that way. He took a deep lungful of the pure air.

"I beg your pardon, General? You were saying?" He thought for a moment that the general was being poetic or something. Alistair spoke his own brand of Portuguese, adapted from a bit of French and Spanish, but he and the general understood each other well enough after a month together. His feet were once again on Malawian soil, the first leg of the journey home. He thought the general had been talking about Smuts.

"That way to Blantyre, that way to Chiroma. Take your choice." The short paunchy man laughed and pointed a stubby finger at the road, ten metres away. "It does not matter which way you go."

"Thank you, General. I shall remember your kindness."

They had moved out of the crater as soon as they heard of the deaths of Wanga and Smuts. The Chinese packed up their radios and set off for Malawi, en route for Tanzania, where they had an embassy. The general was firm in his refusal to let the Chinese take Alistair with them. He moved everything to the rim and waited. Two days later, two Portuguese Army helicopters landed, troops scouted around, found nothing, and left.

The general moved to another camp in the west, knowing that they could be back without warning. Alistair moved with them from one camp to another, hearing the battle reports as they came in. More mines and ammunition arrived. They blew up the rails five times, once derailing a train; they mined three vehicles, one a tractor and trailer on which three civilians were killed; they murdered a white storekeeper and burned the store after looting it. Once one of their men was killed; another time, some were wounded. They carried little in the way of medical supplies. They applied herb dressings which seldom did any good. Wounds usually turned gangrenous. If a man could not get to the hospital in Mutarara, he was as good as dead. With his knowledge of first aid, Alistair found himself acting as orderly, but he could do little. There was seldom enough food. Now and then they shot an antelope or appropriated maize or millet or cassava from the locals, but the general made sure that Alistair never went hungry. Guiltily, he insisted he was full, long before he was.

The general often spoke to Alistair about what they were doing. He was a pompous, often cruel, little man, but he was no fool and he was an effective commander. Alistair sometimes contemplated escape, but the general ensured that the opportunity never arose. Then three days ago, the general had announced that he was going to let him go.

"Believe me; I would kill you without hesitation, if I thought it would bring freedom to Mozambique. But it will not. You are a man who uses words and I believe that you came here with some sympathy for our cause. Perhaps what you have seen with me these last weeks has made you change your mind. Sometimes we have killed innocent people, our own people. But, perhaps they are not so innocent or they would be here in the bush, fighting with us. You know that you were tricked into coming here to see South Africans meddling in our affairs, see these men forced to jump over my camp at Muambe, that we were expecting them? Too clever, too complicated, a Chinese trick. We need the Chinese arms, the Russian arms, but they will take their payment later. They will try to take the place of the Portuguese and it will be worse. Worse! When we have our freedom, Mozambique will be socialist, but we will have to go on fighting, or we will drown. It is not South Africans I am afraid of, it is our friends and allies ... Go home, Mr. Alistair, and, with your pen, see if you can stop East and West playing football with Mozambique." Five minutes later, they heard the sound of a truck. The general moved back into the bush. Alistair stepped into the road and began to wave.

—m—

On 7th September, 1974, representatives of the Portuguese Government and Frelimo met in Lusaka, Zambia, to sign the *Acordo de Lusaka*. The transitional period to independence had begun. Portuguese troops were sent home in ever increasing numbers, exiles returned, political prisoners were released. The dream of the People's Republic of Mozambique became a reality on 25th June, 1975. It was the first socialist state in southern Africa. But, already, in May, a Russian delegation had visited to discuss the development of the port facilities of Lourenço Marques, soon to be Maputo.